I0818264

THE KEEPERS OF THE LIGHT

THE KEEPERS OF THE LIGHT

God Stones Book 2

OTTO SCHAFER

Sound Eye Press

All characters and events in this publication are fictitious and any resemblance to real persons, living or dead, is purely coincidental.

Published in 2020

ISBN: 978-1-7341154-0-6 (paper)
ISBN: 978-1-7341154-2-0 (hardcover)
ISBN: 978-1-7341154-1-3 (e-book)

Cover design by Damonza
Editing by The Blue Garret

Sound Eye Press
www.ottoschafer.com

For my wife, and the hours you sat patiently listening as I read aloud. And for the time I spent away, lost in the story. Mostly though, for always believing in me. Thank you, Boo.

Contents

1

Destroy the Instructions

Wednesday, April 6 – God Stones Day 1
Petersburg, Illinois

Garrett Turek had walked into Mr. B's taekwondo dojo in uptown Petersburg the same way he had walked in a thousand times before, with his best friend in the whole world, Lenny Wade. But this hadn't been like any other time, and today hadn't been like any other day in Garrett's life.

A couple hours ago he was convinced he and Lenny were there to test for their second-degree black belts. Since then, Garrett had had the crap kicked out of him by Mr. B – who he now knew could levitate, was over nine hundred years old, and was the leader of a secret society called the Keepers of the Light, which was created during the time of the Knights Templar.

Worst of all? Garrett learned *he* was the Light the Keepers existed to protect – the descendant of Turek, the firstborn male in a long bloodline and prophesized to battle an ancient wizard from another planet. According to Mr. B, his parents were Keepers of the Light too. Which if true, meant his whole life had been a lie. He wondered who else was in on it? Eugene, the nice accountant in the Victorian where they found the journal? Coach Dagrun? The way he was acting he must be a Keeper too. God only knew who else. Mr. Douglas, the dollar store owner? His boss out at New Salem? Jesus, for all he knew everyone in town might be part of this strange… prophecy?

Part of him, a big part, wanted to run away, to flee from the dojo and run home to his mom, to call bullshit on this whole ridiculous story, but there was too much he couldn't ignore. Mr. B floating several feet off the ground right in front of them, for one thing. Then there was what he himself had done. During Mr. B's test, Garrett found his focus and had somehow slowed stones falling through the air.

But the biggest reason for staying and listening to it all – the girl.

Breanne… Bre, the most gorgeous girl he had ever seen, and one who he'd thought, before the last couple hours, existed only in his dreams. Turned out she was real, and she said she needed his help to stop Apep or her father might die. He knew all this was just too crazy and he tried to tell the others as much, but then all his friends stood and pledged themselves to follow him. Lenny, Bre, David, Pete, Janis, and even Bre's older brother, Paul. One by one they pledged to be his sages and to join him in this insanity.

Outside, the low rumble of thunder pulled Garrett from his thoughts and he suddenly felt everyone staring at him expectantly. He turned to Mr. B and rubbed both palms down his face, drawing in a deep breath. "Okay, Mr. B. What happens now?"

Mr. B considered the seven new sages and allowed slip the briefest of smiles. "With the selections you have made, Garrett, the prophecy has been sealed. The future of the world rests with each of you."

Garrett wanted to ask the large man what the hell was so funny because they were probably all going to die, but Mr. B beat him to it.

"Do you know why I smile?"

No one spoke.

"I smile because I know the convincing is over. I smile now because you believe. Now there is hope." His smile waned. "Yet an urgency pulls at my patience, and it is telling me time is fleeting with the evening light. A great darkness is coming, and there is no more time for celebration… not even in the evanescent duration of a smile."

The air in the room went still as they held their breath, the gravity of Mr. B's words pressing in on all of them.

Garrett held Mr. B's gaze. He was committed to the cause, however insane. Yet the question hung in the air between them, electrified with the sheer excitement of whatever craziness he had just signed on for. *What happens now?*

"Mr. B?" Garrett asked, breaking the silence.

Mr. B's smile fell away, replaced with a tight line. "Yes, yes, of course." He drew in a breath. "Your test earlier was about focus. Focus is key in harnessing the energy of the God Stones. You will need to be able to tap into it at will."

Breanne shifted her weight to her other foot, bringing her close enough to Garrett that he felt the warmth of her arm against his.

"I thought you said casting spells required using the language of these old gods?" Breanne said.

"Yes," Mr. B admitted. "It is one thing to feel the magic of the God Stones coursing through you, to feel the energy even if your mind is fully open. It is, however, quite another to harness it through your third eye and truly control it. Deploying the full power of the God Stones requires knowledge of the gods' language, but unfortunately the gods' language is lost to us. And even knowing the language does not simply make one a master. Think of mastering the energy of the God Stones as reaching enlightenment. The Buddhist monk practices meditation his whole life to reach enlightenment, and yet he may never get there. The good news is you don't have to be a master spell caster to tap into the power of the God Stones, but you need to be able to channel it."

Breanne nodded slowly. "So somehow we need to open our third eye?"

"No, Breanne, not for you and not for you either, Paul. The fact you survived the exposure to the God Stones and your pineal gland didn't explode outright must mean your third eye has altered." Mr. B turned back to Garrett. "But both you and Lenny have been training to open your third eye for years."

"For years?" Garrett asked.

"Yes," Mr. B said, gesturing with his hand. "When you struck me, what were you thinking of?"

"Running," Garrett said with a shrug, knowing it sounded silly.

"And when you slowed the concrete blocks during their fall?"

"Trail running. It was like I was there on the trails, and then… then time slowed," Garrett said, shaking his head in confusion. "It's like I had all the time in the world."

To his surprise, Mr. B nodded. "Ah, it does not surprise me that you are at your most meditative state when you are running. But you didn't slow time itself, Garrett. You slowed the objects you were focused on. You slowed time in a specific radius. To Lenny and I, the objects were actually moving in slow motion, but time was passing normally. Think of it as an envelope. You slowed time in the envelope."

Garrett nodded slowly.

Lenny nodded. "It was crazy sick. I thought my eyes were playing tricks on me."

"What about Pete, Janis, and I?" David asked, thrusting a thumb into his chest.

"I suspect your pineal glands will open fully upon exposure but be patient, you haven't spent years training your focus as Lenny and Garrett have. Using the magic without focus could result in side effects or unintended consequences," Mr. B said.

"Or our brains could burst, and we could all die!" Janis exclaimed.

Mr. B held up a hand and paused for an uncomfortably long second as if contemplating. "Not likely. You are the prophesized seven. I am sure you will be fine."

Pete raised an eyebrow and shared a terrified look with Janis, then mouthed the words, "What the *f*!"

David smiled, rubbing his hands together. "Awesome!"

"As the energy from the stones saturates the world, all will change, and your powers will be greatly increased… that goes for all of you. But finding your focus is the key to harnessing it. To defeat Apep you will have to be able to do this. Apep won't stand around while you try and figure it out. He won't go easy on you like I did. Do you understand?"

Garrett caught Lenny's eye and raised his eyebrows in disbelief. *That was easy?*

"Okay, Mr. B, but it would be really helpful if you knew at least some of the language – some of the words or something. Didn't you learn any of these god words from Turek in all that time you spent with him?" Lenny asked.

"No. The stones were sealed, and spell casting was forbidden by Turek's order. He taught me many things, but never the language of the gods."

Garrett frowned. *What good would harnessing power be if he couldn't control it?*

"Wait, so you're telling us we all have to take up running?" David's mustache twitched disapprovingly. "The only running I do is when I'm being chased by something."

"No, not at all," Mr. B said. "It's different for each of you. You will each need to find your own way to inner focus."

"Mr. B, I just want to help my dad. Please just tell us what we need to do," Breanne said.

Mr. B looked to Peter. "You have Lincoln's journal and you have learned the location of the temple?"

"We know where the entrance is," Pete offered. "You know what's inside the temple?"

Mr. B nodded. "You must beat Apep to the temple and once there you must destroy what's inside. If Apep gets there before you he will learn how to assemble the God Stones into one complete stone called the Sound Eye. This is how he will open the portal. If he is successful in opening the portal, our planet likely will not survive it. This planet wasn't built for the God Stones, Garrett. You must stop him. Once you do, the stones must be sealed away forever for the earth to be set back to normal."

Garrett looked at his master with uncertainty. "What is it I have to destroy?"

Mr. B hesitated and Garrett could see he was holding back. "Mr. B, you have to tell me what I must do."

Mr. B pulled in a long breath. "Instructions. You must destroy the instructions. When you get inside and you see" – he paused – "do not hesitate. You will see it and you must destroy it before Apep finds you."

Garrett gave him a sideways look. What was it he wasn't telling him?

"Mr. B…" Pete gazed intently at the master. He looked like he was going to say more, but he pressed his lips into a tight line.

"Pete?" Garrett squinted at his friend.

"We've listened and have chosen to believe your entire impossible story. The least you can do is tell us all of it," Paul said, crossing his arms. "We need all the intel we can get if we're going to be successful in this mission. Tell us what we're up against here."

Mr. B sighed then nodded heavily. "You're right, of course. This is going to sound even crazier than what I have already told you, but I assure you every word is true, so brace yourselves. If Apep gets to the temple first, he will—"

The door rattled suddenly.

"Did you hear that?" Mr. B asked.

"Yeah… I did," Breanne said, looking at the door.

They all fell silent, following her gaze.

"Sorry, we're closed!" Mr. B shouted.

The door rattled again, then stopped.

Everyone froze, looking at the door.

"Do you feel them, children? The God Stones are here," Mr. B whispered.

Garrett's eyes went wide as a faint blue glow somehow permeated the door. The glow wasn't coming from under or even around it but through it, as if the door itself was emitting it.

"Children, go now! There is a door in the back."

All but Garrett and Lenny ran.

"What? Wait – no! We can't leave you," Garrett shouted.

The door rattled louder, and the blue hue grew brighter.

Running to the weapons wall, Mr. B yanked down a long staff of dark wood – one from the display section, not from the practice equipment. Turning to Lenny, he nodded. "Lenny, take this staff – it will serve you well. I used this when I trained with Turek."

The boys stood openmouthed as Mr. B grabbed a second weapon – a sword.

Slowly the door swelled inward, flexing like a balloon filling with air.

Mr. B motioned desperately at the children to run. "Garrett! I thought we would have more time. There's more you need to know! Go now and warn your mother and father of Apep's arrival," he said, glancing back to the door. "Garrett! You must go home first. Your father will have something for you. You must take it with you to the temple. Once you have it, go to the temple and destroy what's inside! Remember, you must destroy it before Apep can get to it! I will hold him here as long as I can! Now run!" he shouted.

The door creaked – an awful, ear-piercing sound – as the fibers strained to their max.

As the boys turned to run, a hand grabbed Lenny's arm. Mr. B pulled him close, but Garrett heard every word.

"Lenny, you have to protect him," Mr. B said. "Keep him safe – he can't do this without you. You're the head of the Keepers of the Light now." He turned away from Lenny, unsheathing his sword. The sword swished free of the leather scabbard as the old master idly tossed it to the mat.

They watched as Mr. B turned and marched fearlessly toward the door. Without looking back, he shouted, "Go! Go now!"

The others who had fled the mat at Mr. B's first command had already moved to the rear of the dojo. Shoes in hand, they made their way down the back hall past the locker rooms, pausing at the back door.

"Where's Garrett!?" Breanne shouted urgently.

"Garrett!?" Pete shouted back down the hall.

Garrett slid to a stop at the mouth of the hallway with Lenny on his heels. Pete frantically motioned for them to come, but Garrett couldn't pull himself away… not just yet. He needed to see who – or what –was at the door; he had to see it for himself. He grabbed Lenny's arm and pulled him down into a squat with one hand while simultaneously motioning for Pete to wait with the others at the end of the hallway.

The front door of the dojo exploded inward in a violent splintering of wooden shards. Along with the door, chunks of the door's frame and even a section of the wall burst forth like a too-ripe pumpkin getting stomped. Garrett gasped a sharp breath as a strange blue haze spilled in like a thick rolling fog, a prelude to the evil behind it.

Mr. B raised his sword, ready to strike, as a cloaked figure stepped through the broken door frame.

The figure walked casually across the entryway, hands clasped behind his back, not bothering to remove his boots as he stepped onto the mat with all the nonchalance of a curious tourist perusing an art exhibit.

"Hello, fat man. It's been a long time," the cloaked figure said.

"You're already too late, Apep," Mr. B said flatly.

"Oh, now, I don't think so. I would say I am right on time. I already have the God Stones and soon you will be dead, as will all these ridiculous children you've enlisted to fight the battle of a man long dead and forgotten."

Garrett peeked out from behind the wall just enough to catch a glimpse of Mr. B's lip curl as an ancient rage swelled inside him.

"You really think your Garrett and his little band of friends can defeat me?" Apep said, unclasping his hands. "Even when Turek could not? When all his men could not? When you yourself could not? Not only did you fail to stop me, you failed to save your master."

Mr. B's shoulders dropped slightly, causing his sword arm to droop. Garrett and Lenny exchanged looks.

"Oh, come now. Did you think I didn't know about Garrett? Really?"

"Yes. He *will* defeat you," Mr. B said, holding his sword high and ready, careful to keep his eyes fixed as he slowly circled. "He is the heir of Turek. The prophecy has already been foretold and your fate is sealed. He will destroy you, ridding the universe of your very existence once and for all."

"Pft! Prophecy," he huffed with a chuckle before pausing to study a sword hanging on the wall. "Your collection is very nice, very... authentic." He held out a gloved hand and splayed his fingers. The sword flew off the wall and into Apep's hand as if magnetically drawn right into his palm.

"I know this. You can't assemble the stones, Apep. You don't know how," Mr. B said.

"This is a minor problem soon to be rectified," Apep said, pointing one of the gloved fingers of his free hand at Mr. B. "You know, I've waited a very long time to end you. To finish what I left undone so, so long ago." He was matching Mr. B's circling motion step for step now as he began spinning the sword casually in his hand.

Hearing the stranger's voice, Garrett felt compelled to get a better look at the guy. Carefully he tried to ease himself ever so slightly past the edge of the wall and sneak a peek out from the hall. Apep was completely concealed under a long trench coat, his face shrouded in the shadow cast by an oversized hood.

"Careful, Garrett. Don't let him see you," Lenny warned, pulling at Garrett's dobok sleeve. "I think we need to go."

"Christ! They both have swords," Garrett whispered urgently.

Pete came belly-crawling up to them. "Maybe we should get the heck out of here like your teacher guy said," he advised.

"Hold on, Pete!" Garrett said, still trying to see what was happening. Apep was spinning the sword in front, then behind his back, then in front, back and forth in an advanced flowering technique Garrett had never seen. "Are you seeing this!?"

"I'll tell you what," Apep said, abruptly tossing the sword to the side. "Let's not bother with this. I'll let you see what you have been guarding all these years with your own eyes… before I remove them from your skull." Apep reached for the fastener of his duster with a gloved hand and unclasped it. Slowly he pulled one side open from his chest, and one by one the God Stones levitated out from an inside pocket of his coat. Inside each stone, a strange force danced with energy. As they rose upward, they spaced themselves apart evenly before forming a perfect circle. The circle of stones ascended above Apep and Mr. B, spinning slowly overhead.

Mr. B narrowed his eyes and stood fixed, his grip on the sword tightening despite his centuries of practice keeping it loose in his hand.

His whitening knuckles did not go unnoticed by Apep, eliciting a knowing smile and wag of his finger. "Tsk, tsk, Master Brockridge – control your fear."

Still peeking around the corner, Garrett was the first of the three in the hall to see the stones. Something inside his head went strangely and suddenly wrong – like someone had grabbed the funny bone of his mind and begun to squeeze. The pain went from dull to sharp in the matter of a few heartbeats and was quickly followed by the immediate impulse to vomit.

From the look on Lenny and Pete's faces, they felt it too. Both covered their ears and pressed their eyes closed, fighting the growing agony.

Garrett forced himself to look through squinted eyes, but the pain was so intense and getting worse by the second. Beside him he heard Lenny moan.

Apep held his hands out, palms up. "Alright, Grand Master Brockridge," he said, giving a sarcastic emphasis to the formal title. "I have a proposition for you. It's quite simple really – if you can beat me, the God Stones are yours. You can do with them as you please, bury them again, hide them in the dirt to satisfy your petty fear. Waste all their potential. Waste them and their power. But if you fail, oh my! I kill you and everyone on this wretched planet. I build my army and this world – this world burns, and I open the gate to my kingdom and leave this one behind in so much forgotten ash."

Bolting forward, Mr. B struck down with the blade at Apep's face with a vicious overhead chop.

Apep stood motionless with his hands to his side until the last possible second before sidestepping. The blade swooshed by, missing his shoulder by millimeters.

Above them, the God Stones spun.

2

Perfect Circle

Wednesday, April 6 – God Stones Day 1
Rural Chiapas State, Mexico

"Gabi!" a voice echoed from down the gorge.

A man with a wide-brimmed hat poked his head inside the tent. "Gabi, they're calling for you!"

Gabi's eyes sprung open wide with excitement. She sat the small animal bone and brush down on the tray and burst from the tent, rushing past Juan and into the hot Mexican jungle. The sky was a cloudless blue, as deep as the ocean and as still as a cenote. And there, high above, in the middle of it all, hung the burning sun, poised proudly against the royal blue backdrop, unmoving, as if nailed to the sky itself.

"Slow down, Gabi! The site is thousands of years old – it will still be there when you get there," Juan called after her, laughing.

A giant smile stretched across her face as she hurried down the well-worn trail. Gabi was fast, fast as the wind. Faster than any boy her age, that was for sure. The trail wove down deep into the gorge, zigging and zagging between shoulder-high piles of rubble extracted from the collapse that had nearly killed the Moores over a year ago. As she drew close to the crevice, she saw María waiting, a hand extending a helmet toward her as the other beckoned her forward.

"Is it time?!" Gabi exclaimed, gasping for breath as she pulled the helmet over her silky, black hair.

"Sarah asked me to find you. She wants you to join her inside," María said, her headlamp still on, though barely noticeable in the early afternoon sun.

"Down below?! Is it open?! Is she asking for me to come down to the lower chamber?!" The excitement spilled from her, overflowing like a fountain.

María smiled and laughed. "Yes, she is asking for you down below. Now come, let's not keep her waiting." María helped her with her chin strap as Gabi pulled her long pigtails above the helmet's backstrap. "¡Perfecta! Now in you go," she said, ushering her into the crevice.

In the process of clearing the collapse, the team had needed to widen the opening. As she walked easily through the crevice, she could only imagine the terror the Moores must have felt as this whole place came down around them. Gabi's hands began to sweat, but not because she was nervous about being deep underground. No, it was quite the opposite. She had been waiting for this moment for months.

Sarah said she had a strange feeling this site was old, really old. How old, she couldn't say. No one could – not yet. But it wouldn't surprise Gabi to find out this site stretched back three thousand years or more! What if it were the oldest site in all of Mexico! And given its south-central location, it almost had to be an ancient Maya site. Of course, they would need carbon dating to prove it, Sarah said, but with the bone and pottery shards they had sent to the lab, they would have confirmation soon enough.

The prospect of this site being the oldest Maya site in all of Mexico excited Gabi. Why shouldn't it? If it were true, this site was her heritage – her people. After all, her mother, Itzel, was modern-day Maya.

Most of today's Maya lived in southern Mexico and Central America and most worked in agriculture. But her mother had wanted something else. Itzel got into archeology because she wanted to protect her heritage, yes, but she also longed for adventure. Gabi felt that same longing too.

Her mother and father had met at university, where they bonded over their love for ancient Maya culture. Her father Andrés was born in Villahermosa, and though he wasn't Maya, he loved everything about history, culture, and archaeology. He always told Gabi the greatest mysteries of the universe were hidden just beneath her feet.

Gabi wanted to follow in her parents' footsteps studying ancient cultures like the Olmec, the Aztec, and most of all the history of her own culture, the Maya. But she was only thirteen and, even though she was the luckiest kid on the planet, a very real fear lurked at the back of her mind. A fear that they could hit a dead end, or run out of funding, or be driven out of the area by warring factions of the cartel, or any other of a hundred reasons they could be shut down and forced off the site. But the truth was, even if this site shut down, they probably could find work and they *would* be okay even if times got tough. But the real reason she worried had little to do with losing the dig site and much more to do with losing the woman leading it – Sarah.

Most lead archaeologists wouldn't allow Gabi, at only thirteen, onto the dig site. *No kids,* they said. *She will get in the way,* they said. *She will get hurt,* they said. *She will hurt something,* they said. Instead she had to stay at the base camp and complete her homeschool work and maybe, if she was lucky, she would be allowed to help catalog the less valuable items, such as broken pottery shards or items such as animal bones pulled from refuge pits. But Sarah was different. Even though Gabi had only been twelve when she arrived at the site, Sarah insisted she be part of the team. Not only part of the team, but right in the mix learning everything she could, either working with her parents or right at Sarah's side. Sarah said she reminded her of Dr. Moore's daughter, an American girl named Bre. It was Bre who had discovered the crevice. Sarah said Bre was going to be a great archaeologist someday, even better than Sarah herself. Best of all, Sarah said Gabi could be too, if she worked hard and applied herself.

Working hard was not a problem for a Maya, and she proved it every day, working until she was forced to stop. It didn't seem like work at all for her. Working with Sarah every day was an adventure!

For over a year now they had studied every inch of the mountain while another team worked to clear the collapsed cave. In all those months, they had been unable to find the alternate entry even after a careful search of the entire mountain, grid by painstaking grid. She got to learn about ground-penetrating radar and how to read the GPR graphs. What they confirmed was fascinating. The site was not a simple cave that led to a cenote under a mountain. It was a very cleverly, purposely concealed pyramid. One that had not been swallowed by time but swallowed by intention. It wasn't uncommon for new pyramids to be discovered that had long ago been devoured by jungle, but it was rare – no, not rare, unheard of – for a pyramid to be intentionally buried, especially one this big. If Sarah was right, this pyramid could be nearly double the height of the Great Pyramid of Giza! That would make it not only the oldest but perhaps also the largest in history.

To uncover the pyramid and find the opening might have taken decades, but thanks to Bre stumbling upon the eroded crevice at the bottom of the deep gorge, they didn't need to wait. All they had needed to do was clear the collapse.

It had been hard work. But after more than a year of painstaking effort, they could finally explore the innermost bowels and see for themselves what this chamber of the Moores was all about. Only today the team had removed the last of the blockage in front of the spiraling staircase. Finally, they would get some answers.

"Gabi," María said in a quiet voice from behind her as they crossed the first chamber. "What Sarah speculated was right. The trap the Moores sprung had been ingeniously designed to leave the lower chamber whole, but completely inaccessible. The entire lower chamber is unharmed."

Gabi gasped. "That's wonderful!"

Behind her the sound of grunts, sledgehammers striking stone, and stone striking hollowly against the basin of a wheelbarrow reverberated through the upper chamber. The laborers still worked to clear the chamber in the other direction. Perhaps soon they would be able to explore the pyramid above.

Here we go, Gabi thought, making her way past the single piece of pristine pottery. It was the only piece not crushed by the collapsing ceiling that nearly killed the Moores. Her mother, Itzel, stood next to the lintel archway leading to the lower chamber. "I can go down?" Gabi asked.

"Yes." She nodded. "Sarah and Fredy just went down a moment ago. We don't even have lighting set up yet. Your father is working on that now, but they said it is safe for you to join." Itzel cupped Gabi's face in her hands. "Just be careful, noconetzin," she said, leaning in to kiss her daughter's nose.

Gabi nodded, her focus fixed on the opening. She was so excited she wanted to run through the opening, but she knew better. "Aren't you coming?"

"I will be along as soon as your father gets back with the lighting. He's going to need María and I to help carry it all down," she said with a smile.

For the first time ever, Gabi passed cautiously beneath the large lintel and found herself descending a wide, curving set of stone stairs. As she stepped down and then down again, her mother's voice called after her, "And don't touch anything, Gabriela!"

She knew her mother meant business when she called her by her real name.

She stepped down a few more stairs, her eyes darting from left to right, trying to take in everything she could cast her headlamp on. *How long must it have taken to carve these spiraling stairs into the stone?* As tempted as she was to run down them, she slowed, inspecting the work. Along the edge of the steps ran a seam. She looked at the other side and found a seam there too. *What?* She turned back to face up the stairs and confirmed a seam ran all the way across the back of the step. Directing her light at the wall, she searched but saw nothing, only perfectly smooth stone.

Stepping down again she leaned in closer, and there she found a seam running down the wall in a crisp, straight line tight enough she would not have been able to fit a sheet of paper between the two… two what? Maybe it was limestone, but she wasn't sure. Limestone wasn't typically this dark. Surely it wasn't basalt? Either way, she only noticed the one vertical seam running from floor to ceiling.

There was no horizontal seam. The ceiling stretched upward several meters.

She descended four more stairs until she reached the next wall seam. *Couldn't be!* That would mean this one block, if it were a block, and it must be, or why else would there be a seam, must be two meters wide and four meters high. *How much would that weigh?* She couldn't know that without knowing how thick it was, but it had to weigh dozens of tons. On top of this revelation was the fact the whole section she was looking at was curved. Creating a curved block this big with such precision would take some serious mathematical skill. *This staircase wasn't carved into the cave. This whole spiraling stairwell was somehow… what? Placed here? Just the thought of it was crazy, but if it were true that would be crazy cool! But how would they have done it? How could they have gotten such big stones in here? Unless, unless this came before everything above?* She wondered if Sarah had noticed the seams.

She hurried down the remaining steps until she was suddenly standing on the bottom step, peering out into a pitch-dark chamber. Her eyes went wide as she caught her first glimpse of an impossibly tall statue. She could see someone's light a few meters away, coming from behind the giant, then suddenly another light filled her vision. She shielded her eyes as the silhouette of Fredy came into view. Gabi sucked in a short breath and held it before finally releasing it. "¿Neta?"

"Sí," the grey-whiskered man laughed. "It's for real, Gabi!"

Gabi thought of Fredy as the village elder, a wise man, always working close to Sarah as her trusted adviser. She wasn't sure how old he was, just that he was really old – fifty something, maybe even sixty.

Fredy handed her a notepad. "Prepare yourself, Gabi, it's remarkable!"

Gabi strained her neck to see past Fredy, her own headlamp pushing back the darkness of the chamber to illuminate giant stone legs. She followed the legs upward, tipping her head back to discover the giant wore an angry expression topped with a serpent headdress just like the one on the lintel at the top of the stairs. It must have been at least twelve meters tall, with the ceiling of the circular room stretching even further above.

"Breathe, Gabi." Fredy chuckled.

Gabi pulled in another short breath. "It's so big!" she exhaled.

"Come, Sarah is waiting for you." He leaned in close to her ear. "She said, and I quote, 'Get Gabi down here! I want her with us on this!'"

Gabi's blush was invisible in the darkness of the chamber, but her bright eyes and wide smile spread infectiously to Fredy, who gave a joyful burst of laughter. To work so hard for so long, unsure of what condition they would find the lower chamber in, only to find it completely intact – well, it was cause for high spirits.

"Come on you two, get over here!" Sarah's voice called in a mock order followed by her own giggles.

Despite the giant's extended hands and less-than-inviting expression that seemed to be saying, "Stop! Go back!" Gabi stepped slowly off the bottom step and onto the floor. She froze, unsure of what she thought might happen, but everything was still. The giant just continued to glare down at her menacingly.

"Gabi! You have to see this!" Sarah exclaimed from across the room. Sarah was a short, petite woman with almond skin and long curly brown hair. Even though Sarah kept it tucked under her hardhat, her long curls seemed to find their way out, dropping down along her cheek to frame her face.

As Gabi panned her light toward Sarah, it reflected across stacks of something bone-white. Not stacks – racks. Along the walls were racks and racks of skulls!

"Tzompantli!" Gabi breathed. "Sarah, these are Aztec?" Internally she wanted the site to be Maya, but she had prepared for this eventuality as well. Dr. Moore had said he had seen racks and racks of skulls. However, he and Breanne had only been in the dark lower chamber for a few brief moments before triggering the trap. This quick glance led Sarah's team to think he might have seen something else. Perhaps he had seen sacrifices with skulls haphazardly stacked along the wall. But there was no mistaking this. These were beyond a doubt ancient skull racks. The racks had vertical shafts with several rows of horizontal shafts spaced just far enough for the skulls to fit. The skulls were placed onto the rack by breaking out a hole on both sides of the cranium in the temporal and parietal areas then sliding them onto a wooden shaft one after another, forming rows. These racks stretched several feet up the wall taller than Gabi stood.

"I don't know, Gabi. For these racks to be here doesn't make sense. It didn't make sense when Charles told me about them over a year ago and honestly, they still don't. I think I convinced myself that whatever he had seen couldn't have been this, but here they are. The Aztecs used skull racks to warn their enemies they meant business. They were always displayed out in the open, near the top of a pyramid, near a ball court, or even at the city center, but not hidden at the bottom of a cave… or whatever this place is. I don't know which is the bigger question, Gabi – who or why? Come, let's have a closer look."

Gabi made her way over to Sarah, giving the giant stone statue a wide berth and choosing instead to stay close to the racks of skulls.

Meanwhile, Fredy made his way over to the circular hole in the floor between the giant's legs. "Fredy, careful – that's where Charles told me he stepped on the tile," Sarah said.

"Sí, compañera," Fredy replied, cautiously peering down the hole with his flashlight.

"Okay, Gabi," Sarah said, pulling her down next to her as she too squatted on the balls of her feet. Sarah smiled, readying herself to inspect the first skull rack. "I didn't want to start without you. Now, we just have to be careful not to touch them or bump them – I wouldn't want them to collapse."

"Sarah?" Gabi gave her arm a squeeze. "Thank you for bringing me down."

Sarah smiled. "No thanks necessary. You earned this, Gabi. You have worked just as hard as anyone on this team. I'm so glad you're here. In a couple weeks, Bre will be here too, and I think you two are going to be quite the team."

Gabi smiled and nodded. She couldn't wait to meet this girl she had heard so much about. She didn't have any brothers or sisters. Having another girl here was going to be like having a big sister.

"It's true, Gabi, what Charles said, all of it. I never thought I would see a whole tzompantli in my entire career. Now I am in a room full of them. But I still don't know why – why are they here? And I'm not convinced yet this is Aztec. We mustn't assume anything. We have to let the science guide us."

Gabi looked closely at one of the skulls, shining the beam of light right into the broken-out hole in the side of its head. The shaft of wood, perhaps oak or maybe mahogany, punched through one side of the skull and out the other. Gabi frowned, cocking her head to the side as she studied it. Something was amiss with this skull. She had seen many skulls on other digs, and once she even got to help a student clean a human mandible. She leaned in to get a better look.

"Sarah? Please, come have a look at this," Fredy said.

"Coming," she said, standing back up and shining her light in Fredy's direction. "Whatcha got?"

Gabi pulled her attention away from the strange skull and stood, following Sarah over toward the center of the room.

"This hole. It's very strange. It's too perfectly centered to be a natural phenomenon," Fredy said, as he panned his light back and forth across the chamber. "I bet if I measured the room, we'd find that this hole is precisely centered. This leads me to speculate either the room or the hole is not a natural occurrence." He removed a glow stick from a hip pouch and bent it in the middle, creating a bright greenish-yellow glow. With no flame, there was no risk of creating an explosion should methane gas be present inside the hole.

Fredy tossed the glow stick down the hole, and Gabi watched as it spiraled into the depths, lighting up the circular shaft walls as it fell, before finally settling to the bottom seconds later. The depth was hard to measure with the eye, but it was a good distance, dozens of feet, maybe even a hundred feet below.

"Did you see that?" Fredy asked.

"Yes, the shaft was perfectly circular all the way down!"

Fredy squatted and ran his hand around the edge of the hole. "Wait, what is this? Feel this!"

Sarah knelt and ran her hand around the edge.

"Gabi, feel this! Fredy, hold on to her just to be safe."

Gabi knelt next to Sarah as Fredy got a firm grip on her arm. This was why Sarah was the coolest adult on earth. She treated her like a grown-up, which made sense because she was already thirteen. Gabi felt around the edge of the hole until her fingers slipped into a notch. She walked her fingers down the wall, following a strange groove as far down as she could reach. Next, she concentrated her headlamp on the groove and followed it down as far as she could see – the groove continued out of sight. "What is this, Sarah?"

"I've no idea."

"Look here," Fredy said, pointing at the opposite side of the circular hole. "Another groove identical to the one across from it."

Gabi cocked her head to one side and allowed her eyes to split the difference between the two grooves and sure enough, there was another groove, and across from that groove was another. Four grooves in total. Each rounded groove was no more than a few centimeters wide by a few deep.

Sarah saw them too. "Fredy, these grooves aren't random – they are spaced into four equal distances around the hole. But why?"

"I have no idea, compañera, but they must serve some purpose," he said.

Sarah shook her head. "This hole, it would make sense that it was an opening to the underworld. I would have guessed it was a place to make offerings to the rain god Chaahk if we were dealing with Maya or, given the skull racks, it could be the Aztec god of rain, Tlaloc." Sarah threw up her hands. "But now… I just don't know."

Gabi paused to rack her brain, trying to somehow put it together in her mind. She spoke slowly as she puzzled it out loud. "The giant statue could be a representation of the Olmec feathered serpent deity Quetzalcoatl. Its feathered winged features sometimes make it look more like a dragon. Couldn't this explain the dragon headdress and images on the lintel and pottery?"

"Well, the Olmec are certainly mysterious. There is so much we still don't know, but the skull racks point more toward Aztec, and I have never heard of the Olmec coming this far inland from the gulf."

Gabi nodded, so maybe not Olmec but her gut told her something was off.

"What do you think this means?" Fredy asked.

The three of them peered back over the edge of the pit, where the glow-stick was still radiating like a distant beacon in the darkest of night, guiding them to something – but what?

Sarah shook her head. "I don't know, Fredy, but I have a hunch. The only way to be sure is to rappel to the bottom of this pit. Please head back up and bring the team, lighting, harness, and ropes. I need to get down there."

Fredy nodded.

With Fredy bringing the team and gear, Gabi and Sarah were left alone in the curious chamber. "Sarah, can we have another look at the skulls?"

"Good idea!" They stood and moved carefully back to the racks of skulls.

On one skull, a detached mandible dangled strangely askew, giving the skull a deformed look of open-mouthed surprise. The dangling jawbone caught Gabi's light and with it her attention. She leaned in closer to the jaw and froze, her heart leaping into her throat. "Sarah, look at this!" she croaked, blinking in disbelief as if it might make what she was seeing somehow go away.

Sarah turned, aiming her own headlamp at the jawbone. "Gabi! How could I have missed this before? Oh dear god, no. No, no, no. Wait. This can't be real. It isn't possible!"

3

Fracturing

Wednesday, April 6 – God Stones Day 1
Petersburg, Illinois

In the back of the dojo, Breanne quickly shoved open the back door and pushed Janis and a swaying David out into the alley. They wobbled down the stairs on unsure legs and gathered near the neighboring restaurant's waste container. David hunched over at the waist and vomited whatever school gruel he had eaten for lunch before collapsing to the ground, his back resting against the cool metal of the dumpster.

Janis threw herself down next to him, sick but keeping it in. "What the hell is happening?"

"What about the others?" David asked, looking peaked as he gasped for breath.

"It's the God Stones. Paul, you have to go get them," Breanne said. "They may have passed out like we did the first time!"

"I'm on it," he said, running back up the steps. But as he reached the top step, the door burst open again, and Pete staggered drunkenly onto the stairs, nearly colliding with Paul.

Paul grabbed him by his shoulders, attempting to keep him upright. "Where's your friends?"

"Ah! Let go! I… got… to get away… before I pass out," Pete said, pushing past Paul and down the steps. He squinted painfully toward Janis and threw himself to the ground next to her.

"Pete? Where are they!" Breanne begged.

"Apep and Mr. B are fighting! The God Stone things are… ugh, my head is killing me."

Breanne shot Paul a pleading look.

Paul nodded and disappeared through the back door of the dojo.

Mr. B moved faster than even Garrett thought possible, backing Apep across the dojo and into one of the wall mirrors, smashing it.

Apep recovered, kicking Mr. B in the chest. The sword Apep had cast aside earlier now flew back to his hand as he charged forward, releasing a furious cry. "Riaaaaahhh!" The sword sliced through the air faster than the eye could follow. "I'll enjoy watching your flesh burn!" Apep shouted in the guttural cry of a man gone insane. Then in a low, throaty voice, Apep began speaking a language unspoken for thousands of years. The blade of Apep's sword began to glow as if charged with lightning and suddenly ignited into a brilliant blue fire.

Garrett saw it then. The unnatural light illuminated the lower half of Apep's face. His twisted grin was distorted by rage, yet somehow it seemed familiar.

Mr. B planted his front foot in a determined defensive stance.

Apep launched forward in a rush, unleashing a series of explosive strikes. With expertly timed feints, accompanied by precision flicks and lunges, the evil wizard drove relentlessly forward, quickly closing the distance. Every clash of metal produced a brilliant burst of blue sparks.

Apep's flaming sword hummed strangely as the superheated blade cut through the cool air like some kind of sick lightsaber. Then the flame began to change. Stretching out, it snaked from the end of the sword. Now even when Mr. B successfully blocked a strike, the flames lashed out like a flaming bullwhip from the end of Apep's sword, burning through his dobok and into his flesh with each strike. The long, whip-like flames didn't stop with Mr. B; they ignited whatever was in their way, including the walls, ceiling, and floor. Within seconds, the mirrors lining the walls began to melt and pool onto the mats as they too turned to liquid and caught fire.

Garrett watched in horror as the dojo burned and their master fought for his life. Still ill in his gut, he swallowed back the bile and uncovered his ears. "My god, Lenny! We have to help him!"

Face drawn into a grimace, Lenny shook his head no. "I'm sorry, Garrett, but we can't. We've stayed too long already. We have to go!"

"What are you talking about? We can't leave him like this!"

"You don't get it!" Lenny said, his eyes glistening. "If we don't go now his sacrifice will be a waste. He is doing this for us. To give us time to get to the temple. If we don't go and get there first, everyone is screwed. We have to go, now!"

Looking back at Mr. B, Garrett's heart found its way to his throat and his vision blurred. But he knew Lenny was right – they had to go.

Footsteps bounded toward them from behind. Both boys looked back to see Paul approaching in a dead run from the hallway.

"You two okay? We thought you might have passed out. We need to—"

A loud, incomprehensible shout cut him off, drawing all their attention back toward the burning dojo. Their eyes widened as the blood-covered Mr. B raised his head and howled before launching himself fearlessly into the smoke and flames to strike out at Apep in a determined final assault.

Smoke began to choke the hallway and with it their view of Mr. B. The only evidence the fight went on were the flashes of blue light through the smoke and the sound of clashing swords ringing out from the burning chaos.

Wasting no more time, they turned and ran down the hall, leaping out the door and into the alley.

Once outside, they drew in deep breaths of night air and coughed to clear their smoke-filled lungs.

"I have to go home and warn my parents about Apep," Garrett said.

"Wait, maybe we should just go to the temple and destroy whatever this thing is so Apep can't get it," David suggested.

Pete nodded his agreement with David. "But I still need to tell you about the journal, Garrett. You're not going to believe this!"

Garrett held out his hands. "Really?"

"Okay well maybe you will but—"

From inside the dojo, a window exploded, followed by the sound of air drawing in like breath from a giant. Everyone froze in confusion. An instant later a loud *whoomph* preceded a fireball of flame that stretched across the alley. Garrett, Lenny, and Paul dove out of the way as everyone else instinctively dropped to the ground, covering their heads.

"Holy mother!" David shouted, standing and brushing himself off. "That was way too close!"

"You okay, Bre?" Garrett asked pulling her to her feet.

"I'm okay."

"Maybe we better get away from here," Paul said as the group moved down the alley.

"Okay, listen," Garrett said. "Everyone, go to the library. Lenny and I will head to my house and warn my parents. Then we'll meet you guys at the library and head to the drainage tunnel."

Bre's eyes pleaded with him not to go.

Garrett forced a smile. "Don't worry, it's only a short walk from the library to the tunnel." He scanned his friends' faces. It was plain none of them wanted him to go.

"Maybe we should stick together? I mean shouldn't we get to this temple?" David asked.

"We'll go with you," Janis said.

"Guys, I have to go home. Mr. B said my stepdad has something I will need. We'll be quick." His plan was given as directions, not intended to be questioned or debated. He swallowed the knot forming in his throat. He had to go get this thing Mr. B said he would need to destroy the instructions for assembling the God Stones. But it was even more than that. He needed answers. Whether this was the time or not, he had to hear it from his mom. He had to look her in the eyes and ask if she knew about Apep, the keepers, Turek… all of it. He couldn't believe she had been keeping something like this from him. Without another word he turned away from them.

He glanced over to Lenny, who nodded. He nodded back and they ran.

~

Paul put his hand on his sister's shoulder and gave her a comforting squeeze. "He'll be okay." Then glancing to the others, he arched his eyebrows and drew in a breath. "Well, guys, I guess we're going to this library of yours."

"Follow me, I'll show you guys the way," Pete said, giving Breanne a consoling smile. "Don't worry, Breanne, they'll be fine – besides, we could never have kept pace with Garrett and Lenny anyway. We would have either slowed them down or been dropped in the first block." Pete started to jog. "Come on – I think you will find my pace much more to your liking."

Moments later, the gang burst through the door to the Petersburg public library. From behind the counter, a prim woman with greying hair looked up from her paperback and peered quizzically over a pair of wire-rimmed glasses. "Well, hello, Peter. I see you have brought company. Who are your friends?"

"Um," Pete said, pausing only long enough to look from Paul to Breanne then back to the curious librarian, "just friends helping with a project, Ms. Cleary." He gave a discreet wave of his hand, signaling them all to the left toward a doorway with a sign above it that read, *Thousands of treasures below.*

Breanne followed single file, feeling the librarian's eyes on her and knowing the questions that would come – the ones she couldn't answer. Still, when she stepped in front of the counter, she couldn't help herself. "Excuse me, ma'am, may I use your phone? I need to call my dad and… check in."

"Sorry, dear, the phone lines are down. I suppose it's this crazy storm."

Breanne's shoulders slumped. She wanted to call the hospital to check on her dad or at least talk to Ed. She needed to know they were okay. Paul had done his best to set Ed's busted leg, but he had passed out from the pain and her dad was… God, she hated to even think it. He had never woken after he was exposed to the God Stones. He was in a coma.

"Oh dear, worrying won't do you well," the librarian said with a frown. "Now, I'm sure you children have much to focus on with your project. I will come get you if the phone comes back up." The librarian turned her attention back to the paperback.

Breanne turned away, following the others down the stairs into the lower level of the library.

"Welcome to my office," Pete announced proudly, as he led everyone over to the big, round table at the far end of the long basement room.

Once huddled around the table, Breanne and Paul exchanged detailed accounts of the days leading up to today. Everything from finding the God Stones during the dig on Oak Island to the strange dreams of fire that led her to Petersburg and to Garrett. She told them about the bones in the swamp, the Templar cross, the altar, and the worst part – when Apep showed up and killed their friend Jerry. Pete and the others had heard some of it at the dojo, but the full story was frighteningly unbelievable.

Pete focused on bringing Breanne and Paul up to speed on the rest of it, carefully recounting the finding of the journal in the basement of Eugene's old Victorian, President Lincoln's involvement, discovering the initialed bricks inside the culvert, and the run-in with Jack.

"The journal had just been there behind the wall of the basement for all those years? What are the odds? It almost doesn't seem possible, right?" Breanne said in astonishment.

Pete stared at her in amazement. "Breanne, you've got to be kidding. Your story about what happened on Oak Island is way crazier than what we've had going on." Pete waggled a finger in the air. "But now that you mention it, I guess none of this really seems possible, right?"

"No, I guess not, and you can call me Bre. That's what my friends call me."

"You know," David said, twisting the corner of his mustache. "Mr. B did seem to believe in this prophecy angle. Now that you mention it, it's kind of weird. Like, what are the odds all this would happen the way it happened and when it happened? You think there could really be something to it?"

Paul rolled his knuckles across the table and shrugged. "I don't know. But I know I had a dream about that Templar guy and Bre had a couple. She even dreamt about Garrett. Seems like that should say something."

As the conversation wound down, worry consumed Bre's mind. Every minute that passed seemed to take longer than the one before it. Soon all conversation ceased, and nervous silence fell upon them.

In the quiet moments that followed, the lights in the basement flickered, flickered again, and went out. Absolute darkness folded in around the new friends as they sat waiting in the basement of the public library, just as it did for the entire town of Petersburg.

4

Settling Old Scores

Wednesday, April 6 – God Stones Day 1
Petersburg, Illinois

The inferno spread strangely across the walls of the dojo. Mr. B caught the erratic movement of the flames in his peripheral vision as they multiplied all around him, little miniature fire beings taking humanoid form as they danced and skipped across the walls, pausing as if sizing up the distance, then jumping from wall to ceiling. On the ceiling they summersaulted, crawled, and rolled back and forth, as if trying to put themselves out, defying gravity as everything they touched turned to flame and the ceiling became an inferno. The God Stones were at work, affecting everything just as Turek said they would. *Keep them sealed in lead and never open the chest.*

Mr. B slashed again and again, slashing and stabbing with the sword but finding nothing but air. The raw power of the God Stones permeated the room, enhancing his focus, and with the energy surging through him, he stepped right foot over left and spun, using his momentum to lash out at Apep with a spinning sword strike of such speed it seemed to defy the laws of physics.

Apep, with all his power, could not dodge the blade strike. So, instead of dodging, he somehow *willed* the blade to slow, forcing it to stop an inch from his face.

Mr. B's eyes widened as the sword stuck fast, motionless, hanging in the air as if wedged in an invisible tree. He didn't allow his shock to last long though. Reflexively, he let go of the sword completely and stepped in close to Apep, launching a vicious jab square into what must have been, judging from the sound of breaking teeth on knuckles, the mouth of the shadowed man.

The sword dropped free of its invisible hold as a stunned Apep staggered backward off balance.

Extending his foot beneath the sword's hilt, Mr. B caught the blade just before it hit the ground, kicked it back up, and snatched it by the hilt.

From beneath Apep's hood came a cry of agony.

A confident smile formed on Mr. B's face. "I've spent my days preparing for the time when you would show yourself again. Honestly, I'm disappointed. I find you lacking."

Apep spat a mouthful of blood dotted with broken bits of teeth onto the mat, his body shifted, and it was apparent he no longer found this amusing.

Mr. B set his feet.

Apep swept his flaming sword in a wide upward arc.

Mr. B leapt backward. The blade missed, but the whip of electric-blue fire extending several feet beyond the sword tip bit deep into his shoulder. He turned his face just in time to avoid losing his left eye but not his ear. He screamed and cursed under his breath as his ear fell to the mat.

Apep grinned through his broken teeth.

Mr. B wasted no time stepping inside Apep's guard before he could draw back his sword for another strike. Feinting with his sword hand as if preparing to swing, Mr. B thrust out with his right leg and front-kicked Apep in the ribcage, feeling bones break against the ball of his foot.

Apep grunted, instinctively placing his hand over his ribs.

Mr. B sidestepped a piece of falling ceiling tile, set his jaw, and lunged forward, thrusting his sword toward Apep's throat.

Tiny sprites screamed with excitement as they rode the falling tile to the mat.

Apep slapped the blade away with the palm of his hand and stomped down with his booted foot.

The bones in Mr. B's bare foot crunched audibly as white-hot pain blotted out his vision. He wanted to scream out in agony but refused to give Apep the satisfaction. Instead he shut his mouth and clenched his teeth so tightly they threated to crack under the pressure.

As the ceiling burned overhead, the little flaming figures yanked and pulled at the ceiling tiles, breaking them loose in chunks that rained down all around Mr. B. Giggles and laughter came from everywhere. His vision quickly cleared when he wiped a sleeve across his face, but the pain remained.

He dared to take his eyes off Apep just long enough to glance into the flames. A fire sprite grinned wickedly, its long red hair shooting up off its head in spikes of flames that waved back and forth like a tree in the wind. But there was no wind, only a stifling hell. The tiny fire sprite punched its little fist into the ceiling, grunting, yanking, and laughing. The sprites jumped from the fallen tile to the mat and began to spread, three becoming six and six becoming twelve – each tenacious in their desire to consume anything combustible. Some of the sprites chewed at the mat, others pulled and ripped, while some gleefully danced about, spreading tiny little footprints of fire that quickly grew into new sprites.

Apep leapt over the flames toward Mr. B, smashing the pommel of his sword against the bridge of Mr. B's nose before spinning and striking with a downward arc.

Mr. B felt the sword coming and tried to spin away, but both the blade and the fiery whip slashed and burned across his shoulder and back, opening a long gash that bit deep into bone. Mr. B felt warmth spill down his back as a stream of bright red gushed from his crushed nose. The blood pooled on the vinyl mat beneath him, slippery under his feet. He took two painful steps to the right to find new purchase beneath him.

A brief pause, a moment nine hundred years pregnant, as the two men stared down a hate for one another that stretched nearly a millennium.

Mr. B switched his sword to his left hand. All around him flames closed in, nearly impossible to dodge and even harder to breathe through. Suddenly a fire sprite leapt from the burning mat to the lower leg of his dobok. He slapped at the sprite. The sprite put its hand over its mouth in mock disbelief then split into two, then four, then six, quickly consuming his whole pant leg. Mr. B swatted back the sprites with an open palm. Each time he struck a sprite it exploded in a rain of sparking embers. The sprites fought back, grasping with their tiny hands around his fingers and biting at his knuckles. The flames blistered his hands, but despite the pain he was finally able to slap the fire out. Desperate to put distance between himself and the sprites, he shuffled sideways away from the nearest floor fire.

In his frantic efforts to put out his burning dobok he'd completely lost track of Apep. He jerked his head up, quickly scanning the dojo. Smoke and flame filled his vision, but no Apep. Then he heard something strangely and horribly wrong. It came from inside him, this wrong breaking sound.

Mr. B dropped to his knees.

The blue fire whip drew back through his chest and lungs as Apep pulled the sword from Mr. B's spine.

Mr. B fell backward onto the mat, his sword bouncing out of his hand. He tried to reach for it, but his hand wouldn't move.

"Didn't Turek teach you?" Apep said, squatting down next to the old master. "Never lose your focus."

Mr. B lay on his back, sucking in short gasps of breath. Something else was wrong – something below him. He tried to look down toward his feet, but it was a futile effort. He couldn't lift his head. He wondered why and his face furrowed as he tried to understand. He was pretty sure at least one of his legs was on fire. Only pretty sure though, because it wasn't the pain telling him he was burning. Mr. B could no longer feel pain, nor could he feel his feet, or even his legs for that matter. However, his sense of smell was still intact, and he was quite certain that the foul stench assaulting his nostrils was his own hair, skin, and flesh as it burned. In the background he could hear the sprites' giggles and laughter.

Apep spat blood and held his side, oblivious to the pain of his broken ribs. "Bah! I told you, so weak and pathetic! I *told* you! I would watch your flesh burn. Oh, yes, indeed! And I'm in no hurry. I think I'll stay a while, watch the flames crawl up your body until they find the parts that still feel. Then I'll savor your screams as you beg me to finish you. And do you know why? Do you know why?!" Apep shouted. "I'll tell you why. Because you wronged me just as your master wronged me. You got in my way. You took part in delaying my destiny! A destiny you know nothing of!" He paused only long enough to suck in a deep breath. "I will watch the light go out in you with the satisfaction of knowing you can do nothing to stop what is to come."

Mr. B had no more interest in Apep; he managed to get his head to turn away. He stared toward the back of the dojo and he smiled. "Go, my sages. Go and finish this," he whispered.

Apep's face twitched as he followed Mr. B's eyes down the hall. He bent closer to him, trying to hear. "What are you babbling about? They were just here, weren't they? And what did you tell them? Where did you send them?" Apep asked, a slight hint of concern betraying his voice.

Mr. B managed a gargled chuckle. "I… told you… you're too… late."

"Well, I best be on my way then. Give my best to Turek." He stooped over the dying master and thrust the flaming sword into Mr. B's chest.

Searing pain beyond the world consumed him as the steel scorched flesh and fractured bone. The last thing Mr. B felt was his heart combusting into flame.

No. No, I am not too late. In fact, everything is going perfectly to plan. Still, a sense of urgency pulled at him. Apep didn't know why, but now he felt he must hurry. It was irritating really – he so wanted to relish this moment. He straightened and held open his coat as one by one the God Stones returned single file to the pocket of his duster. Despite his newfound sense of urgency, he gave the now-burning Grandmaster Brockridge one final appraisal, allowing himself only a brief moment to bask in his victory. Finally, his eyes came to rest on the erect sword protruding from the burning man's chest. Its hilt rocked ever so slightly back and forth, slowing a little more with each sway, until it stopped completely. Satisfied, Apep ripped the sword from Mr. B's chest and spat in his face. The blue flaming whip retracted as the blue fire faded away.

The entire dojo was a fulminating inferno, and yet Apep walked unharmed through the flames. The tiny fire sprites parted, providing an unobstructed path as he made his way toward the back door of the building. *The boy will try to warn his parents of my presence, then he'll lead me to the temple. Perfect. It seems tonight is a night of unsettled scores.*

5

When the Time Is Right

Wednesday, April 6, a few moments earlier –
God Stones Day 1
Petersburg, Illinois

Jack squinted as he blinked back tears of pain. He had been hit in the head plenty, but he had never felt pain like this. Heavy smoke poured from the hole in the wall of the karate place. Wiping his eyes on his flannel sleeve, he got to his feet. He had no idea how long he had been unconscious, but weird flames had already consumed the opening, and he couldn't see a way to get inside.

If Garrett and everyone else were still in there, they would have to escape out the back – and soon. He ran as fast as he could along the chain of storefronts until he reached the intersection and circled around to the alley. Jogging back toward the karate place, he heard it – someone heaving. Carefully, Jack crept close, staying in the shadowed edge of the alley until he reached the backside of the dumpster behind the pizza place. He knelt down and listened. He could hear people just on the opposite side talking.

The first voice he heard was Garrett's. "I have to go home and warn my parents about Apep."

Then David saying something about a temple before that little weasel Pete piped up. "But I still need to tell you about the journal, Garrett. You're not going to believe this!"

He knew it! Pete had translated the whole thing.

Suddenly, there was a loud sound of breaking glass followed by an explosion of fire across the alley. Jack pressed himself up against the dumpster, instinctually slapping his hands over his ears.

"Holy mother!" someone shouted.

Jack shuffled to his feet, peeking out from behind the dumpster in time to see the group moving away from the karate place. Flames poured freely out the back now, but they didn't look like any flames he had ever seen before. These looked strange – almost… alive. Quietly, he maneuvered to the other end of the dumpster as he watched the group begin to move down the alley.

The last voice Jack could make out was Garrett directing the rest of the group to the library and then the drainage tunnel. A moment later they were gone. Jack stepped out from behind the dumpster. He knew it. There was way more to that old journal than they let on. Something major was going on. He looked back toward the flames pouring from the building. He couldn't see past the back doorway, but he could hear shouts and the sound of metal striking metal. *Sword fighting?*

Garrett had said the drainage tunnel was a short walk from the library. There was only one drainage tunnel he knew of close to the library, and he was willing to put money on it being the same tunnel he had followed Lenny and Pete to the other day. *Okay, Garrett. I'll see you and your friends at the tunnel and then you'll have to face me.* First things first. He was going to need some help.

A shadow appeared in the flames. It was the cloaked man from earlier. He walked through the fire. No, not through it. It moved for him. Jack froze, still as a cobra, too late to try and hide now. The man paused in the doorway holding his side. He said something Jack couldn't understand. Blue-grey, smoke-like stuff came from his fingers in streams, snaking into the man's side and into his face. After a moment, the grey-blue smoke disappeared. The cloaked man let go of his side and stood up straight.

The man stepped down from the doorway into the alley and fixed his eyes on Jack. "You were in the street earlier, were you not?"

Jack nodded.

"I felt you there, Jack."

Jack's eyes went wide at the sound of his name.

"I feel something else too. Hate. So much of it. Enough to fill an ocean."

Jack swallowed hard.

"You know what else?" The man didn't wait for an answer. "Power, Jack. In time you can harness your endless pool of hate into power, and I can help you."

Jack recognized something in that moment – call it a feeling or an instinct, or maybe it was just plain desperation. Whatever it was, he felt it – the weight of it. The weight of the moment. Something important. Jack couldn't articulate it if he tried, but he could feel it sure as heat from a flame. Now and then the sun shines on even a dog's ass, and today the sun was finally shining on his. Jack cleared his throat, finally finding words. "I know where Garrett is going. I know what he has and… and where he is going. He has this journal and—"

"Ah, good," the man interrupted, stepping closer to Jack. "But I already know these things, Jack. Go, follow your path. Follow your plan and when the time is right, seek me out."

"But how will I find you? How will I know when the time is… right?"

"My name, Jack. All you will need is my name. You will know when to speak it," the man said, turning away from him.

"Your… your name?"

The man paused but he didn't turn back. "My name is Apep."

Jack watched the cloaked man as he moved steadily down the alley through the slowly falling ash and embers. The sky cracked with lightning that came too close for comfort. He blinked reflexively, taking his eyes off the man only for a second, but when the oddly colored lightning finished its dance through the clouds – the man was gone.

6

Overlooked

Wednesday, April 6 – God Stones Day 1
Rural Chiapas State, Mexico

Gabi and Sarah stood there for a long moment, swallowed by silence broken only by their own increasing heartbeats and heavy breathing. The focus of their attention was a large jawbone with a double row of teeth, which looked different, sharper than human teeth, almost like… canine teeth. But that wasn't all. It now became clear to Gabi what had bothered her when she only had a chance to glance over them earlier. These skulls were larger than they should be.

"Sarah? Do these skulls seem too… big to you?" Gabi asked quietly.

Sarah didn't answer – not right away. She cocked her head to one side then the other and said in the same soft tone, "I was so taken aback by the racks, and with only our headlamps I guess I hadn't noticed." Sarah swallowed dryly. "Let's see, the circumference of the average adult skull should measure between fifty-four and fifty-seven centimeters max," she said, continuing to speak quietly as if the two were sharing some great secret they didn't want anyone else to hear. Sarah unclipped a cloth measuring tape from her side and very carefully checked the circumference of the skull. "Seventy-eight centimeters. This just isn't possible, unless… unless this person had a deformity. Yes, of course, that must be it. This individual must have suffered from gigantism. But the teeth? Perhaps a deformity caused by the gigantism? I… I just don't see how…"

As Sarah carefully began to measure the next skull over, Gabi stood silently in the dark and, not for the first time since descending into this place, she held her breath. Even without the tape, the next skull looked too big and so did the next and the next. Somehow, she knew – this wasn't gigantism or deformities, this was something else.

"Seventy-five centimeters. What the… Two people with the same condition?" Frantic now, Sarah checked the next, nearly knocking the rack over. "Seventy-three centimeters," she gasped. The double row of teeth was visible on this skull as well since the lower jaw appeared to be missing. She checked the next, and the next, and the next, and found all were too large, the largest being eighty-one centimeters in circumference.

Gabi stayed quiet as Sarah continued to talk to herself out loud now, scrambling in near panic to find reason in what she was seeing.

"A whole race of people with gigantism and double-rowed teeth? No. No way… it couldn't be. Come on, Sarah, be rational. Wait! Could these be *Gigantopithecus*?"

Gabi's eyebrows creased. "What's that, Sarah?"

"They were a genus of giant ape that lived over a hundred thousand years ago in China. They were giant, to be sure. Some even reached nine feet tall, but these skulls don't belong to apes. Their features are too human and not only are there no records of them here in Mexico, but they didn't have double rows of teeth." Sarah wiped her face with one hand as if she were pulling off cobwebs. "Plus, the timing is all wrong! How could a prehistoric ape skull be present on an Aztec skull rack?"

"Sarah, I don't think these are apes, but whatever they are I don't think they are Aztec."

Sarah froze. "No, Gabi, I don't think they are either. It's just so impossible! My god, how big would these people have been? Here, hand me your notepad."

Gabi passed her the pad of paper, and Sarah began calculating. "No, this can't be right – I did something wrong with the math. Can't be right – can't be!" She did the math again and after a moment she looked up from the pad, able to answer her own question. "Oh, my dear lord! Charles, what have you stumbled on to? Gabi, these people would have been between ten and twelve feet tall!" she said, jutting her shaking finger repeatedly into the pad. "We're looking at an undiscovered race… a race of people far above average size… a race of—"

Gabi's eyes exploded wide as the word burst from her lips, "Giants!"

7

Home

Wednesday, April 6 – God Stones Day 1
Petersburg, Illinois

The cold evening air stung Garrett's lungs as he plunged forward, Lenny on his heels. They burst from the alley, crossing the highway where a row of parked cars lined the street, bumper to bumper. Without a single moment of hesitation or course adjustment, Garrett leapt over the hood of a brown station wagon, just barely clearing the vehicle. With all the grace of an acrobat, Lenny jumped up only enough to allow his butt to land on the hood of a maroon sedan. Momentum carried the boy effortlessly across the smooth surface and he too landed on the sidewalk, never missing a beat. Bounding down the sidewalk, the boys cut right, crossing the parking lot of the pizza place. They were only a few blocks away from home.

As they ran, the boys could hear the fire trucks behind them in the distance. Garrett glanced over his shoulder, instantly regretting the decision – his heart sank. The sight of smoke and flames billowing from the dojo constricted his chest as he fought back the tears. The fire appeared huge now, too big to be just the dojo. It must have spread by now, engulfing the restaurant next door, the antique store on the opposite side, and maybe even Double D's Dollar Store. By the looks of it, the entire north side of the town square was engulfed.

Garrett swallowed hard. Mr. B was dead, wasn't he? He knew it, felt it in his heart. *Would they all die before this was over?* He didn't know what to think or what to feel. He knew what he must do, but he didn't know how. The path had been laid out for him, and he had to complete what Mr. B died for. *Go now and warn your mother of Apep's arrival. Then get to the temple and destroy what's inside! You must destroy it before Apep can get to it!*

Garrett pushed harder, reaching deep inside himself.

Lenny began to fall behind. "Slow down, Garrett! I can't… hold… your pace," he said in short grunts.

"We have to get home! He's coming," Garrett said, his jaw clenched tight as he sucked air through his teeth and nose.

Heavy clouds stacked one atop another pressed down low in the sky, blotting out the setting sun. It wasn't supposed to be dark for almost another hour, but it was dark and getting darker by the second. It was not until they turned onto Fourth Street that Garrett noticed the streetlights. First, they flickered on like they normally would, taking a few minutes to warm up. But then they continued to flicker, creating a strobe effect all the way down his street. With two blocks to go, the lights flickered off completely and the entire neighborhood went dark. No streetlights; no light at all, not even from the porches or windows.

Garrett was forced to slow in the sudden darkness.

Lenny caught up to him then, and once he slowed, he began hacking. "You think… the power outage has… something to do with what's going on?" Lenny asked between gasps.

"It's more than that, Lenny. It's too early to be this dark. Even with a thunderstorm building, have you ever seen it this dark?" Garrett spun in a circle, trying to see lights up on the bluffs, but all he could see was darkness. The only light came from the distant glow of the burning buildings uptown. From his left, Garrett heard a screen door slam.

"Goddammit! Why is it always during my favorite show the power has to go on the fritz? I think they plan this! I think it's a damn government conspiracy," came a voice from the direction of the slamming door.

Garrett recognized the voice of Mrs. Belford – one of his neighbors.

A light flicked on then, as Mrs. Belford flicked a flashlight beam up toward the power lines, looking for the source of the outage.

"What the hell are you doing, Maribeth? Are you going to climb the pole and fix the power? Get your ass back in the house and help me find some candles," came Mr. Belford's gruff voice.

"Shut up, Larry! I'm telling you it's the government!"

"Come on," Garrett whispered. "I don't like this." The streetlights had always been Garrett's nemesis, the clock he was always racing home to beat, but he missed them now like an old blanket. He wanted to go back. God, he wanted to back this day up. And he wanted the damn streetlights to come on. They hustled blindly down the street, Mrs. Belford's voice fading as she continued to rage about government conspiracies.

Moving cautiously in the dark, Garrett found his front porch and then the door. Quickly locating the handle, he gave the screen door a pull then pushed his way inside. "Mom!" he yelled into the darkness.

No answer.

Lenny hesitantly slipped in behind him. "This is freaky, bro."

Garrett shouted again. "Dad!" *There's no way Apep could have beat us here – is there?* But then Garrett wasn't sure how the guy traveled either. Did he drive? Did the God Stones give him the power to fly? Or could he just magic himself from one place to another? As he stood there in the entryway, he found himself suddenly hesitating. With all these thoughts racing through his mind he felt less and less confident he should be yelling at all. *What if he's here now?*

One thing was for sure – something was wrong. His parents should be in the kitchen. He should smell the fragrant aromas of his mom's cooking, and his dad should be sitting with his back to the wall in his favorite chair – the king's chair. His dickhead of a brother should…

Someone grabbed him.

He tried to cry out, but his feet went out from under him and he hit the floor hard on his back. Something pressed on his chest, and he couldn't move. He heard Lenny grunt, then a second later he was lying on the floor next him.

Instinctively Garrett rolled his fingers into a tight fist and punched at the object pressing down on his chest. Lying on his back, he couldn't chamber his fist properly, and the distance to the object was short. His strike had little effect.

"Knock it off and shut up! Both of you," came a commanding whisper from the darkness.

"James! What the hell!" Garrett demanded in an angry hiss.

"I said shut up. We don't have much time. Apep's coming – isn't he?" The comment was as much a proclamation as a question. James didn't wait for an answer. "Now both of you get to your feet and follow me," he said, removing his foot from Garrett's chest.

"How do you know about Apep?" Garrett asked, quietly getting to his feet.

James pulled Lenny up by the wrist, and when both boys were on their feet Garrett heard the distinctive flip top of James's Zippo lighter as he flicked it open and struck the flint wheel. The three boys were illuminated in the soft light from the flame. "Little brother, if you want to live, we need to move now."

Quickly they moved through the house, guided by only the flame from James's Zippo, and a strange flickering glow spilling through the kitchen window. The streetlights were blinking on and off as the city's power fluctuated, unlike anything Garrett had seen. But not the lights in Garrett's house – those stayed dark, which meant they must not be turned on. As they hurried past the kitchen window, he noticed that not only his parents were missing, but so was the king's chair. Suddenly the streetlight outside grew impossibly bright and burst with a loud pop.

Garrett tensed, missing a step as Lenny ran into his back.

"What the hell is going on, James, and why are the lights off?"

"I said be quiet."

They moved onto the back porch. *Are we going outside?* There was nothing in the backyard except rabbit cages. *Unless, maybe they were going to the garage?*

James crossed the back porch, walking past the washer and dryer before stopping in front of the basement door. "Come on," he urged, giving the door a tug.

"We're going down there?" Lenny asked skeptically. "I've never been in your basement. I didn't even know you had a basement."

"Well, it isn't much to see," Garrett said, having only been down there a few times himself. From the groans of the old wooden planks, he wasn't even sure the stairs would hold all three of them at the same time. He hesitated, unsure, then he turned and motioned Lenny to wait. Once James stepped off the last step, Garrett motioned back to Lenny as he descended the stairs. He stepped down, looking back apprehensively in the low light. Lenny's face scrunched as he hurried forward to catch up. The basement was damp, with a pungent mildew smell.

The set of rickety wood stairs landed on a poorly constructed patchwork of concrete. The piecemeal floor looked like an afterthought, or possibly a clever plan to conceal a body hidden long ago. Red brick walls, old and crumbling, stopped halfway up to reveal a dead space of sloping dirt. Pillars of crudely stacked stone placed precariously on top of the half walls were all that supported bowing floor joists darkened by time. Plumbing and wiring ran this way and that between and sometimes through the floor joists themselves.

James held his Zippo out in front of him like a torch as he led them across the small room and past a sump pump protruding from a dark hole in the floor, silent now but ready to evacuate water should the need arise. Further still, they went past a pair of hot water heaters, one a rusting antique long ago replaced but never removed. The other was rusty too, but it sat hissing, elevated atop a platform of cinderblocks, a pair of tarnished copper pipes extending from the top.

Lenny poked Garrett in the back. "What are we doing? Why is he taking us down here?"

"I don't know," was all he could manage. His mind spun with questions. Somehow his brother knew about Apep. As much as he didn't want to think it, he knew the question burning in Lenny's mind. Should they be trusting him?

Beyond the small first room there was a second. Garrett had only gone in this room once. Not because he was forbidden to go, although his father had made it clear there was no reason for him to be playing in the basement and he should keep his ass out of there, but because it was just a single boring room very similar to the first. It was dank, dark, and creepy. To the best of Garrett's memory, it held nothing other than the furnace. The one time he had gone in there was when his father asked him to go down and tell him if the furnace's pilot light had gone out. Though his father hadn't said it, Garrett knew it was hard for him to make the trip up and down the stairs with his bum hip.

James rapped on the door.

"James, who's in there?" Garrett asked, stepping backward into Lenny.

James ignored the question.

Lenny shot Garrett a look that he returned with a sideways nod toward the stairs. No words needed to be exchanged to know the plan: if this goes bad – make for the stairs. The sound of a bolt sliding open from the other side of the door broke the tense silence. Garrett didn't even know it locked from the other side. Why would it lock from the other side? Slowly, the door swung inward to the room beyond, and light spilled out, washing over them. James snapped his Zippo shut and stepped inside.

The first thing Garrett noticed was the king's chair. It sat empty by a folding card table. On top of the table sat three nearly empty glasses of sweet tea and a lantern. Leaning against the chair was his father's ivory-handled cane. As he made his way through the open door and looked to his left, he saw his mother. He pushed past James and ran into her arms.

She pulled him close, hugging him tightly. "Oh, thank god you're okay!" she said.

The embrace triggered a release of emotions, and Garrett sobbed freely in his mother's arms. He pulled back enough to look her in the face. "Mr. B is dead."

His mother's face fell as she glanced back over her shoulder. Following her gaze Garrett noticed his father standing along the far back wall with his back to them, a brick in his hand. The walls in this room were complete, stretching all the way to the ceiling. His father held a brick slack at his side. Garrett craned his neck to see around his mother. A whole pile of bricks were stacked near a large void in the wall. At the sound of Garrett's words, the brick tumbled from his father's hand, his shoulders slumped, and he sagged forward, leaning heavily against the wall.

The room fell quiet.

Finally, James broke the silence. "Father, let me do that."

James's tone was concerned, caring – not a tone Garrett recognized from his brother. He'd also never heard James refer to Phillip as *father.* It was always *dad.*

His father turned, allowing his dark eyes to find Elaine's.

Garrett noticed it then, a look shared between his mother and stepfather. A look of deep sadness in their eyes as though they had just been told a dear friend had died. Yet as far as Garrett was aware, his parents had barely known Mr. B. He squeezed his mother tight, never wanting to let go. As long as he could stay right here in this moment, he knew whatever in the hell was going on would somehow be okay. But then Elaine did something completely unexpected. She pushed him back out of her embrace.

"Enough. Stop crying. If you want to be sad, be sad later. Right now you have to act." Her voice was stern and commanding. Not her normal *I'm giving you the what for to save you serious trouble from your father* tone of voice. No, this was different – she was different. This woman meant business. The sudden shift left Garrett dumbstruck, but he found himself straightening up, nonetheless.

Lenny's face contorted in confusion.

James ran to the wall and continued pulling bricks, exposing an opening to something beyond the wall. "Lenny, give me a hand!" James said, waving him over.

Lenny quickly shook himself out of his shock and ran to the wall. He paused only briefly, then nodding to James he began yanking bricks out of the wall as quickly as he could. The bricks were mortared in, so after pulling the loose bricks James motioned Lenny to stand back as he swung a small five-pound sledge, giving the next couple rows a good whack to fracture the mortar around several more bricks.

With both hands on Garrett's shoulders, his mother looked him in the eyes. "I know you have a thousand questions about what's going on, and I'm not even sure how much John told you but—"

"John?" Garrett managed, bringing his emotions under control.

"Sorry," she said, her mouth a tight line. "John to us. Mr. B to you."

"You knew him then?" Garrett asked.

"Of course we knew him – we are all Keepers of the Light," she said, as if that were a given.

So, there it was, the confirmation he needed. *We are all Keepers of the Light.* "But I still don't—"

She cut him off. "Didn't he tell you all of this? He was supposed to tell you everything. That was the point of giving the signal. The point of announcing your closed test session. He was supposed to test your focus and then tell you everything." She smiled weakly. "But I guess none of us could have guessed Apep would get the God Stones and come so quickly. Well, there's no time for this now. Look, the wall is open," she said, pointing at the hole. "We must go."

Above them came a loud boom of splintering wood and shattering glass. Dust rained down from the ceiling as if a hundred people had jumped all at once.

"He's here!" James said, drawing two sai from his waistband, one in each hand.

Garrett pulled back, his eyes going wide.

His father limped over to the king's chair and threw himself down hard. "I have waited for this day for a very long time."

Slow footsteps clunked overhead.

"As have I," James said.

"No. We stick to the plan. You get them out." Phillip said, pointing toward the opening in the brick.

"And what about you? You expect us to just leave you here?" he asked, lowering his voice to an urgent whisper. "We'll be stronger together."

Phillip shook his head. "No, James. You knew the plan. You must go and keep them safe." He turned in his chair and faced Garrett. "Come here, son," he said, motioning him over with two fingers.

Garrett approached his father.

"We are out of time now," his father said. "But I need you to know a few things before you go." He placed a hand on the boy's shoulder. "Everything we have done has been for you and for this moment and the moments that will follow. All the training and all the rules. It's all been for this day – to prepare you for right now. You *will* fulfill the prophecy. The world doesn't know it now, but it's depending on you." He pressed his lips into a tight line. "I'm going to be honest with you, son. This situation isn't fair and it isn't right, but your whole world… no, *the* whole world is going to change."

Elaine, Lenny, and James crowded around as his father continued to speak. In the low light of the lantern, Garrett felt as if he were receiving some ancient wisdom from a man he had never met.

"In the coming hours and days, or maybe even longer, things are going to be difficult, but know this, my son – every single day of your life has been to prepare you for this. The martial arts, sword training, survival training, even the running at school. I know I was strict, Garrett, because that's what you needed – what you had to have. But you did it, Garrett. You did all the hard work – you are ready." Phillip turned to Lenny. "You too, Len. I know it must have been strange for you. But you have both done so well." He turned back to Garrett. "Now, did John tell you what you must do?"

Garrett hesitated, almost forgetting who John referred to. "Umm… yes. He said I must go to the temple and destroy what's inside before Apep gets there with the God Stones but—"

"No buts, Garrett. Do it. You must! James can't do it. Your mother can't do it. I can't do it. Only you. You take only the sages with you and you get it done," he said, pointing a thick finger at Garrett.

Muffled laughter filtered through the floorboards overhead. The laugh was high-pitched, then low and angry. The psychotic laughter sounded as if it were coming from separate people. "Do you think you can hide? Maybe you hope I will assume you fled away, off to the temple?" The voice above them degraded into a seething, hateful slur. "I can feel you, smell the stench of your fear, each and every miserable one of you! Cowering down there like rats in a barrel won't save you!"

"Go get it, James," Phillip said motioning to the void.

James nodded then slid his sai back into his waistband. He quickly crossed the room and stepped inside the newly opened void, disappearing into the darkness only to reappear seconds later with a long parcel, wrapped in an old-looking piece of canvas.

Phillip pushed aside the glasses of tea and lifted the lantern. "Here," he said, motioning to James.

James placed the bundle of canvas down on the card table.

The footsteps faded toward the back of the house.

Garrett watched silently as Phillip unrolled the canvas, revealing a sword sheathed in some sort of leather hide. The hilt gleamed white as bone or maybe ivory. There were carvings in the handle, but Garrett couldn't make them out in the low light.

"This is yours," Phillip said. "It was Turek's, but now it belongs to you." He picked it up and handed it to the boy. "This sword is exceptional, Garrett. Turek told me it was made especially for him long, long ago. The stories say he used it to slay a great beast." He lifted it from the table and cradled it in his hands like a newborn baby. "He wanted you to have it. When you get to the temple, use this sword to destroy the—"

"Give me the boy, Phillip!" came a shout through the door.

"Time's up, son. James, get them out of here," Phillip said, then he placed his hand under the card table and flipped it.

With a quickness Garrett could never have fathomed possible, his father leapt to his feet, snatching up his cane before the table even struck the far wall.

Elaine and Lenny disappeared into the void, but James stood fast, grappling with the decision to leave his father.

Phillip turned toward Garrett and James. "Garrett, I love you. I always have – like you were my very own son. Always know that."

Garrett paused, meeting his father's eyes. "I… I love you too, Dad."

For a brief moment, Phillip's eyes softened, and he managed a small smile. With a final nod to his son, he flicked the wrist of the hand holding the cane. The ivory handle flipped up, locking into place to run parallel with the body of the cane. But this was no old, warped cane. Phillip drew a gleaming, curved sword from the bamboo body.

His soft eyes turned hard once more, and the smile hardened into a grimace. "Now go!" he shouted.

The eye contact between his father having been broken, Garrett's eyes welled once more as he turned to go. But something compelled him to hesitate, to risk a final sidelong glance back at the man who had spent the last ten years as his father, and when he did, he froze in awe. Phillip faced the door with his back to them, assuming a strange sword-fighting stance. Familiar, yet different. Garrett's experience was limited to the sword instruction from Mr. B. This was something else, something… other. He stood paralyzed now, transfixed by his father's flawless technique. He had slid into the stance as if sliding into a pair of old slippers, as if he had spent years waking every morning before the sun to practice this very technique. After all, one does not simply learn the sword and hold that knowledge in one's back pocket for a rainy day. Even Garrett knew a skilled swordsman lives the way of the sword, breathes it, day in and day out.

Garrett gaped, transfixed by the technique. *Had he? Had Phillip woken every day and practiced the sword while we slept? Who was this man?* Without breaking his gaze, he nudged James. "James, how does he know how to do that?" Garrett asked.

James lifted his chin. "This is the chudan stance in Japanese kenjutsu."

Garrett blinked. "But how does—"

"You would be surprised what he knows, Garrett," James interrupted. He drew his sai and ran to their father's side. "No! You're supposed to come with us. We get out together. Then we set the trap!" he said in a forceful whisper.

Phillip shook his head and forced a reassuring smile. "I must stay. It's the only way."

James clenched his jaw. "Then I will stay and fight with you. You're not settling the score without me. Please, father. We had a plan!"

From the other side of the door, a slow mummering chant could be heard.

"Son, please," Phillip said. "This was always the plan. I just didn't tell you. Now, go… save our family." He wore a thin, pleading smile, like a tin badge false in its comfort. Suddenly the smile transformed into a hard line. "Go, set the trap – settle the score. Avenge Turek!"

"I love you, father," James said.

Phillip nodded then looked to the door, once more adjusting his grip on the hilt of his sword.

James's eyes pooled as he grabbed Garrett by the arm and pulled. "Let's go! What the hell are you waiting for?"

Garrett's trance broke with James's tug, and he rushed into the void just as the door to the room ripped outward from its hinges as if sucked into a tornado.

Once inside the void they made it about a dozen steps when James stopped and turned back.

"What is it? You heard Dad. You can't go back, James," Garrett said uneasily.

"I'm not going back," James said as he reached up and pulled a lever. The small tunnel they had entered was narrow, and they had to stay in a half squat to avoid hitting their heads. Once inside it opened much wider, but the ceiling stayed low. The wide area lasted only a short distance before they crossed back into a narrow tunnel.

What Garrett hadn't known – couldn't have known – was that they had crossed under his concrete porch and were now standing just on the other side, under Fourth Street.

The lever released whatever cleverly created system was in place to hold up that thick slab of concrete porch. In a thundering instant, the whole porch and probably the roof above came crashing down into the tunnel. The ground beneath Garrett's feet shook as the tunnel was sealed by the falling concrete slab.

"Jesus Christ, James, how is Dad going to get out?" Garrett asked.

"He isn't getting out, Garrett," James said.

"What? but he'll… Apep—"

"What he'll do is give us time – time we desperately need. Now move," he said, flicking his Zippo to life.

Up ahead, Lenny and Elaine waited where the narrow tunnel turned.

~

Apep stepped easily through the doorway to a waiting Phillip. Rather than acknowledging him and the sword he held out with ill intent, his attention fell beyond the man, to the hole in the wall. The hole now sealed with concrete.

"Hello, Phillip. I see you're trying to be clever," Apep said.

Phillip stood fixed, looking at Apep with a combination of disgust and hate.

"You know you're only delaying the inevitable, don't you? And because you force me to play this petty game – I will make you suffer. Just like I made your friend, Master Brockridge, suffer."

Phillip's mouth twitched.

It was a small thing, but Apep noticed and beneath his hood, he smiled. "Oh yes, he suffered horribly," Apep said, unclasping his duster. "This Master Brockridge of yours was a kwan jang nim, was he not? A supposed grand master, and yet, what I find amusing is that he died so easily. Just like you will. Please," Apep said in a mock plea as he pressed his gloved palms together in the gesture of a beggar. "Please understand, Phillip, I don't say this as a threat. It is but a simple truth." His hands separated, palms out, showing he had nothing to hide. He laughed softly and reached into the duster, drawing from it the blood-stained sword he had plunged through Mr. Brockridge.

Now Phillip's jaw clenched, his flexing cheek muscles the only sign of the rage he fought to contain. He began to slowly move, circling Apep with the tip of his sword pointing at the man's throat.

"You were Turek's best swordsman? Better even than your Mr. B. You were his number one," Apep said, pointing a bony finger. "I wonder though, were you a better swordsman than Turek himself? I only ask because I killed him so easily." Apep raised his own sword above his head.

Phillip leaned back, centering his weight perfectly in his abdomen, choosing the stance specifically to hide whether he intended to defend or attack. Then, summoning strength and flexibility that hadn't been his for years, Phillip launched his attack.

Humans were so predictable. Even ancient ones.

8

Meet the Neighbors

Wednesday, April 6 – God Stones Day 1
Petersburg, Illinois

They reached the end of the tunnel and faced another brick-and-mortar wall. "James, where are we? We can't have gone very far," Garrett asked, his heart still pounding violently, threatening to break out of his chest.

"We haven't, we're at Glen's."

"What? Glen's basement?"

"Yep."

Garrett and Lenny shared a confused look.

"Wait a minute, you're telling me even our neighbor is a Keeper of the Light?" Garrett asked in disbelief.

James frowned. "Glen? Not hardly. We wouldn't take a wife beater into the Keepers. He doesn't even know he's about to be invaded." He handed Garrett his Zippo. "Now, all of you stay behind me and let me go in first."

James stepped back. Then, stepping forward, he gave the brick wall a powerful kick. The mortar cracked, but the bricks held.

"Um, guys, have you ever been in Glen's basement? Because if not there's… um… something you should know before we go in there," Lenny said, stone-faced serious.

Garrett had not been in Glen's basement, but he already knew Lenny's big secret and nodded in agreement.

"It happened last summer," Lenny began. "Glen's son, Tyler, had been begging me to play catch with him. I kinda felt sorry for the little guy and figured what the heck, I've got a few minutes, so I'll play with the kid for a bit and get him off my back. The problem with Tyler is he's the kind of kid that never stops talking – to the point it's annoying. Anyway, we're playing catch and he's babbling on and on. I'm only half listening when suddenly he mentions his dad grows flowers in the basement." Lenny paused, looking nervously back down the dark tunnel.

James narrowed his eyes at the wall, repositioning his stance for another kick. He stepped forward and kicked again. The cracks in the mortar extended further, but still the wall held.

"I thought, flowers in the basement? That makes no sense. So, I start asking him more questions. He really wanted me to stay and play catch, so he had no problem telling me all about his dad's *flowers*. He says the flowers were growing in large metal tubs under some special lights. Tyler said they were all green and didn't have any flowers on top yet, but he was sure they would soon."

Elaine frowned.

"I know, right? I asked if I could see the *flowers*, but Tyler said he would get in big trouble if he got caught showing anyone. But once I agreed to play catch for a while longer Tyler agreed to sneak me into the basement. The basement was big and empty except for these big metal horse troughs. They were lined up in rows under fluorescent lighting. But I knew before reaching the bottom of the stairs, the flowers were definitely pot plants," Lenny said.

"Because people don't usually grow flowers in the basement?" James asked, rearing back to give the wall another kick before launching his foot with a loud *thwack*. This time a large section of the wall flexed outward.

"No, because they stunk so bad," Lenny said, twisting up his face. "The plants were huge and bushy, with large buds. I didn't stay but a second before I freaked out and ran back up the stairs – and straight into Glen. Literally – I ran right into him, practically knocking him off his feet. He started yelling, 'What the hell were you doing? Did you go down there!' I bolted out the back door and never looked back. It scared the crap out of me. For weeks I thought the guy was going to come kill me in my sleep!"

"Lenny, why didn't you tell someone?" Elaine asked.

"No way, I was too sca—"

Thwack! James's next kick cut Lenny off. A shaft of light from the other side of the wall funneled through as the first brick fell away, thudding across the floor. Garrett flipped James's Zippo shut and handed it back to his brother.

James reared back and gave the wall another kick and then another. Artificial lighting poured through the small opening, along with a faint smell of marijuana. Making no effort at stealth, James began rapidly kicking free brick after brick around the newly created hole. On the other side, bricks clattered noisily to the basement floor. A few moments later he was able to step through the hole into the bright basement light. "Wait here," he said, holding up a hand.

Garrett peered through the jagged hole to find the basement was just as Lenny described, but in place of large pot plants there were small ones, only a few inches tall. That would explain why the overpowering smell of weed he expected to encounter was only a faint odor now.

Being very still, James waited just inside, holding up a hand. From above came a hurried shuffle of footsteps, followed by a rummaging sound. A moment later the basement door burst open.

A voice shouted down the stairs. "Whoever's in my goddamned basement better believe I'm armed, and I will shoot you on sight!" The angry man's threat was followed by the sound of a pump-action shotgun racking a shell.

Garrett recognized the voice. It was Glen.

James reached toward his waistline, feeling for something that wasn't there. When he couldn't find it, he just paused, felt around for a second longer, then continued forward. By the time Glen made it to the last step, James was there blocking his path.

The lights flickered off, then back on.

"James?" Glen said in surprise. "What are you doing in my basement?" Glen craned to see around James. "Who's with you back there? What the..." he started then gasped. His forehead creased into deep lines, and his eyes widened at the sight of the hole in his basement wall. "You... you were trying to steal my crop! My god, you tunneled here from... from where? Your house? To steal my crop! You tunneled here from your house!"

"Just stay calm, Glen. We aren't here to steal anything. We are just passing through."

"You aren't passing through shit until you tell me what all this is about!" Glen shouted, leveling the shotgun at James's face.

"Please, Glen. You need to let us pass."

"I don't know what this is, but I know this – I never liked you Tureks. Seems to me that mother of yours can't mind her own business. If she ain't busy putting ideas in my Jennifer's head about leaving, she's calling the cops and trying to get my Jennifer to press charges. The last time they showed up I thought sure they were going to come with a warrant, and the last thing I need is cops snooping around here." He pushed the gun forward toward James's face. "And I ask you this, what man ain't got the god-given right to discipline his own wife when she gets out of line?"

"Well, Glen, when *your Jennifer* shows up on *our porch* with a bloody lip and a black eye, the cops are going to get called. Now please, do the smart thing here and let us pass. We won't tell anyone about your little grow operation." James tried; his hands were still held out, palms open.

Garrett watched wide-eyed from the cover of the tunnel. "Holy shit, he has a shotgun pointed right at James's face! What do we do?" he asked, looking to his mother for help.

"You shut up and wait, like your brother said!" she said in a lowered tone as she moved carefully forward to the mouth of the tunnel.

Garrett blinked in stunned disbelief. She had never told him to shut up. *Who were these people?* He glanced to Lenny, hoping to catch his eye, but Lenny's attention was on James and Glen, who was becoming more agitated. The barrel of the gun was practically pressed to James's nose. It was close – too close.

James held up his hands. "Last chance, Glen, I want you to calm —" He stopped short when Glen's eyes flicked to Elaine as she slowly eased through the hole in the wall behind James. James used the distraction to grab the barrel of the shotgun with his left hand, then Glen's trigger finger with his right.

Garrett gasped.

The power went out and the lights flicked off again.

When they came back on, James yanked back on Glen's trigger finger until it snapped.

Glen wailed in pain, instantly letting go of the gun.

James flipped the gun around and struck Glen on the bridge of the nose, eliciting an immediate spray of blood from the neighbor's nostrils.

Glen let out a high-pitched shriek as he dropped to his knees. His eyelids fluttered, but somehow he stayed conscious.

Upstairs they heard more shuffling, rummaging through drawers, then a woman's voice. "Glen! My god! What's going on, Glen!" she screamed.

The lights continued to flicker in and out, the power unsure whether to stay on or off. Garrett felt disoriented, like he was inside the Wacky Shack fun house at the Menard County Fair – only the smell of barf was replaced with the smell of weed and coppery blood.

The power issue didn't slow Glen's wife, Jennifer, as she came down the stairs with utter disregard for her own safety. Jennifer was a slight woman, but she was wiry and brandishing a butcher knife. When she stepped off the last step, her eyes darted to Glen.

Glen was on the floor on his hands and knees, bleeding profusely from his nose. Despite his condition, he was making a good effort to get to his feet.

Jennifer's eyes flicked from Glen to James, and her face screwed up in a fleeting moment of confusion that quickly turned to rage. "What have you done!" Jennifer screamed, lunging at James with the knife.

He sidestepped, dodging the thrust. The woman didn't slow and began flailing wildly, slashing at James again and again.

Glen was back on his feet and pissed. "You broke my nose! You son of a bitch! You broke my nose!" He turned, staggering away from James back toward the wall near the stairs.

Jennifer continued frantically brandishing the knife back and forth through the air.

James backpedaled, dodging the wild swings of the blade, occasionally using the shotgun to block a strike he couldn't avoid. "Jennifer, please? Don't!"

From the shadows behind the artificial lighting, Elaine emerged. "Jennifer!"

Jennifer turned, her face twisted in a combination of surprise and fury, the butcher knife held high. "Elaine!"

"Jennifer, it's okay," Elaine said calmly.

"They're trying to rob us!" Glen shouted over his shoulder.

Jennifer's head shook side to side in sheer panic. Her eyes darted from Elaine to the hole in her basement wall.

"No, hon, we're not."

"Don't you dare listen to her! He broke my nose!" Glen said, lifting a long-handled garden shovel from its hanger.

Fear clouded Jennifer's face, but it wasn't fear of Elaine… it was of Glen. She swung the knife at Elaine's face.

Elaine moved with sudden speed, grabbing the wrist of Jennifer's knife hand, twisting until the knife fell free.

Jennifer screamed.

The knife clanked to the floor as Elaine pulled the woman in close and whispered something in her ear, but Garrett couldn't hear what it was. Next, Elaine yanked Jennifer's wrist across her body, forcing the smaller woman into a spin until Elaine was suddenly behind her. Elaine wrapped her arm around the woman's neck from behind then braced it with the other hand, leaned back, and squeezed. "I'm so sorry, Jennifer, but we have to move," Elaine said, as the woman's eyes rolled up in her head.

Jennifer struggled briefly, her bare feet dangling uselessly inches above the floor before she went limp as a noodle.

Garrett and Lenny's eyes went wide in disbelief as Elaine eased the woman gently to the concrete floor and rolled her onto her side.

"Bro, did your mom just put your neighbor in a rear naked choke!?" Lenny said.

But Garrett's attention was back on his brother. "Look!" he said, pointing.

Glen squared up on James, his garden shovel drawn back over his right shoulder like a batter ready at the plate. "You made a big mistake, you son of a bitch!" Glen said, bloody spittle spraying from his mouth.

James stared unflinching, the shotgun in his right hand, but the way he held the gun told Garrett his brother had no intention of shooting the man. Then, slowly, he switched the shotgun to his left hand and waited.

The basement lights continued to dance strangely. Garrett knew it was somehow the work of the God Stones. He could feel them.

Glen sucked in a breath, tensed, and cocked the shovel back a few more inches.

It was the tell James was waiting for. Rather than react to the coming swing with a block or try to dodge it, he did what Glen didn't expect. James stepped forward, closing the gap completely as he drove a wicked right elbow into the man's face before the shovel even left his shoulder. Glen dropped to all fours as the shovel slid harmlessly across the basement floor. James wasted no time and stepped forward again, this time booting Glen in the gut.

Glen rolled onto his back, choking and coughing.

James struck him in the head again, this time with the butt of the shotgun. Glen didn't move, but that didn't stop James from striking him a third time just to be sure.

Elaine nodded at James approvingly, then swiveled her face back toward Garrett and Lenny. "Let's move!"

9

Giants

Wednesday, April 6 – God Stones, Day 1
Rural Chiapas State, Mexico

"Sarah, Are you okay?" Gabi asked.

Sarah held out a hand as she tried to pull in several slow breaths.

"I think you are hyperventilating. Maybe you should sit down?"

"No!" she managed, waving Gabi off. "I just… need to… to breathe. God, Gabi! This is life-changing… history-changing!"

Without warning, she grabbed the young girl with the raven hair and pulled her close, squeezing her in a tight embrace. Too tight. "Sa… rah," Gabi groaned, laughing. "I can't… breathe."

Sarah loosened her grip and laughed too.

Footsteps echoed off the stone steps as Gabi's mother and father, with the rest of the team, made their way down the spiraling staircase.

Sarah pushed Gabi back and held her at arm's length, her headlamp beam washing over Gabi's face. "We got to get it together, girl. Don't let the team see you freaking out!" Sarah said, as much to herself as to Gabi.

Gabi nodded, suppressing another laugh.

Sarah let go of Gabi's shoulders and rubbed her sweaty palms down her pant legs. They nodded to each other and turned to the stairs as Fredy, along with María, Manuel, Andrés, and Itzel, the core of her archaeology team, entered the chamber. Each team member was loaded down, carrying coils of rope, harnesses, plastic tubs, camera gear, and tripod lighting equipment. Up above, the local laborers led by Juan, the foreman, would continue their efforts to clear debris in the other direction of the cave.

"Team, we have something major here," Sarah said carefully.

The team froze in place, looking at her expectantly.

Sarah looked at Gabi, pressed her lips into a tight smile, and turned back to the team. "The skull racks appear to be holding the heads of a… of a… of a race of giant people with double-rowed teeth."

Fredy blinked, then very slowly he sat a lighting tripod down on the floor with a soft clack.

No one else moved.

"See for yourselves," she said.

Still, no one moved. They stood transfixed, perhaps in shock at Sarah's spectacular claim. It was as if they had just stared into Medusa's eyes and turned to stone.

Fredy was the first to break the stone-like trance, approaching the nearest rack, where one of the horizontal wooden shafts had rotted over time, causing several skulls to slide off onto the floor of the chamber. It only took Fredy a brief moment of close inspection. "Dios mío!" Fredy gasped. "Sarah's right – they're too large, and the teeth… I've never seen anything like it!"

The chamber exploded with excited energy, everyone talking at once. Andrés and Itzel began assembling the lighting and soon the circular chamber was bathed in artificial light. Fredy, Manuel, and María went to work measuring, photographing, and cataloging all the data the chamber had to offer.

"Gabi! Itzel, can you believe this?" Andrés said, taking his wife's and daughter's hands in his. "In my wildest dreams, I never thought we would discover anything like this place."

Itzel shook her head. "No. Never. It's truly amazing. This changes everything we thought we knew about the past. The implications are… my god, they're…"

Andrés kissed her hard on the mouth then, pulling back, he smiled. "I know, my love! I know." He grabbed Gabi, lifting her as he spun in a circle.

"¡Papá!" Gabi screeched as she twirled.

"Andrés! Please be careful! We can't have you falling down in here."

Andrés spun away, still grinning with excitement.

Sarah laughed to herself as she watched them. Then her laughter faded as her thoughts went somewhere else.

Gabi closed the distance between them. "Are you okay, Sarah?" she asked.

"Yes," she breathed, "better than okay. I just wish Charles and Bre were here for this. Look there," she said, pointing at Itzel. "It's your mom I'm worried about."

Gabi watched as Itzel's smile changed to concern when she suddenly realized she was still wearing her wedding ring. Her mother always removed her ring before each day's dig. Now she stood chewing her lower lip, apparently deciding whether to stuff the ring into her pocket or risk leaving it on her finger as she worked. "¿Mamá?"

"It's fine," she said with a forced smile, finally deciding to drop the ring into her front pocket rather than risk damaging it or knocking the small diamond loose.

Sarah approached her mother, pulling a long gold chain from beneath her shirt. Unclasping it, she pulled the chain through the eyelet of a small charm. "This charm was a gift from Breanne. This gold chain was a gift from someone else." Next, she removed a thin bracelet from her wrist, attached the charm, then placed the bracelet back around her wrist, double-checking the clasp.

"Itzel?" Sarah said, approaching the woman. "Can I see your wedding ring?"

Surprised, Itzel smiled. "Of course." Carefully she removed it from her pocket and passed it to Sarah.

Sarah slid the ring onto her gold chain and smiled in return. "Now turn around."

"Oh, Sarah – I can't take this."

"Yes, you can," Sarah said reassuringly as she pointed at the ring. "Now please, I insist – take this before you lose your ring."

"But, Sarah..."

Sarah gestured to her to turn around. "Maybe someday I will have a ring to hang from it and you can give it back to me," she said, with a small smile.

The pain in Sarah's eyes did not go unnoticed. Itzel started to turn but then suddenly threw her arms around the woman. "Thank you! I promise I will keep it safe for you until you need it." She turned around, pulling her long hair to the side.

Sarah clasped the necklace around the woman's neck. "There you go. Now then, let's go make history!"

Itzel spun back toward her, tucking the necklace into her shirt. "Yes! History!"

"Gabi, if it's okay with Itzel, let's take another look at that hole."

Itzel nodded. "Just be careful, Gabi. I am itching to get photos and measurements of these skulls, and did you see the murals? We should photograph those right away. Just in case the air or all of us breathing in here causes a reaction with the pigments."

Gabi knelt down, reexamining the rim of the hole under the new wash of artificial light. She could see no tooling marks in the four equally placed notches, nor could she see tooling marks around the walls of the perfectly circular hole. Finally, she said, "Sarah, I don't think this place is real."

Sarah nodded. "I think I know what you mean, Gabi. How closely did you look at the stairs when you came down?"

"The seams on the stairs? And the ones on the walls of the staircase?" she asked. "You noticed them too?"

"I did, but I don't think the others have, and I don't have an explanation for it... not yet. Do you?"

"You're asking me?" Gabi asked in surprise.

"Of course," Sarah said, matter-of-factly. Lowering her voice, she continued, "Listen, Gabi, sometimes you have to use your intuition." She pointed at her gut. "I believe in it as sure as I believe the sun shines. So, I ask you, Gabi, what is yours telling you about this place?"

Gabi gazed aimlessly at the top of the chamber, considering Sarah's words as she tried to consciously access her gut, to feel something inside her, to listen for it to tell her how she felt. But that wasn't how it worked, was it? No. She knew that. Instinctively she knew that just like she knew this place wasn't natural. "Sarah? I think this place was constructed. Just like the pyramid above isn't really a mountain, this place isn't really a cave. The whole thing – the stairs, this whole room, and this hole too – I don't think it leads to a cenote," she said, gesturing with a nod.

Sarah nodded too, looking around the room as if for the first time. Then she looked back at the rim of the hole and ran her hand along the surface. "Smooth as glass. Maybe you are onto something, Gabi. Fredy, come here, please," Sarah said, scanning the chamber.

Gabi's face stretched into a wide grin.

Fredy came to her side, his eyes dancing all around the newly lit room. "Sarah, this place is incredible. The skulls… they're, they're… Sarah, this is a whole new race of people right in the heart of Mesoamerica! And unknown until now! Have you looked at the walls? The murals! María and Itzel are brushing them now, and the colors they are revealing are as vibrant as the day they were painted! Sarah, they may tell the whole story of this place! Just think of it! Until this very moment! A race completely forgotten by history! I… I just… just…" But the words wouldn't come.

Gabi giggled. It was funny to watch Fredy struggle with the initial shock of what she and Sarah had already experienced.

"Alright, Fredy," Sarah said, chuckling. "You're going to be world famous, but first let's figure this out. This place is just starting to show us its secrets." She pointed down the shaft. "I need to get to the bottom of this shaft. Help me gear up. I'm going in."

Gabi looked at Fredy as concern washed over his face like a dark shadow.

Suddenly Fredy found his voice. "Sarah, please, wait. I recommend you send Andrés first. We don't know what this is or what problems you may encounter." His scowl deepened as he pressed his lips into a tight line.

Gabi looked back to Sarah.

"I'll be fine," Sarah said firmly, her own face hardening with determination.

Now back to Fredy.

Fredy's jaw tightened as he seemed to realize he was in for an argument he couldn't win. But he made one more effort. "Andrés is a professional climber. Let him go first and at least make sure it is safe."

Before Fredy could finish, Sarah had her harness on and was connecting the figure-eight device to a length of cord like she had done this a thousand times. Gabi thought she probably *had* done this a thousand times in a thousand places all over the world.

"I know, Fredy – that's why he is going to come double-check my gear and make sure my tie-off is secure."

As Gabi listened to the back and forth, she realized that if Sarah was getting this much trouble out of Fredy, there was no scenario that was going to have Gabi rappelling down the shaft next to Sarah.

Fredy knelt beside Sarah, placing a hand gently on her upper arm. "Please, Sarah, reconsider. It may be booby-trapped like the tile was. Let us not forget that whoever built this place put in a false ceiling in the upper chamber. We still don't understand how they were able to get all those stones in place. I beg you, Sarah. Who knows what they were capable of!"

"Which is why I can't let Andrés go first." She smiled then, placing her hand on Fredy's. "Fredy, I will be fine."

Fredy could only nod as he handed her a two-way radio. "Andrés," Fredy called out, "Sarah needs you to check her gear. She is going to descend into the shaft."

"Me estás tomando el pelo," Andrés answered in disbelief.

"No. No, I'm not kidding."

Andrés crossed the chamber, making his way around the foot of the giant statue. "Sarah, let me go. This could be very dangerous. There could be traps… or gas… or—"

Sarah held up a hand and rolled her eyes.

Gabi never tired of watching Sarah grab the lead and take control. Sarah was a strong woman – and a fierce leader, just as Gabi planned to be when she was running her own digs.

Andrés looked at Gabi. "What? What did I say?"

Gabi shrugged. "If you don't know, Papá, I'm sure not going to tell you," she said with a smirk.

Andrés's eyebrows went up.

"You didn't say anything, compadre. Sarah is just muy obstinada." Fredy frowned.

"Ah… I can see that," Andrés said, giving Sarah's figure-eight knot a firm tug before nodding his approval.

"What's that, Fredy? What did you say?" Sarah asked, pulling on her leather gloves.

Fredy smiled as he clipped the gas sensor to Sarah's waist. "I was just saying you are very determined."

"You know, Fredy," she started to say as she backed to the edge of the shaft. "I speak Spanish… enough to be dangerous anyway. And I would not have gotten this far if I *weren't* stubborn."

Now Fredy rolled his eyes.

Andrés held up his hands. "¡Culpa mía! ¡Lo siento!"

"You should be sorry," Sarah said, an ornery smile spreading across her face. She reached up and clicked on her helmet-mounted headlamp, then leaned back over the opening until the rope pulled taut. Sarah met Gabi's eyes, grinned, and winked. "Keep them in line until I get back, Gabi!"

Gabi's face lit up as she returned the smile.

With not an ounce of hesitation, Sarah jumped backward, dropping into the shaft.

This was the woman Gabi wanted to be. The woman she *would* be: strong, fearless, and unapologetic.

But as Gabi watched Sarah disappear over the side, a strange sensation panged in her stomach. If this was intuition, she didn't like it.

10

The Samurai

Wednesday, April 6 – God Stones, Day 1
Petersburg, Illinois

The tip of Phillip's sword nicked Apep's neck on the first lunge. Without missing a beat in his rhythm, he spun and struck at Apep's side.

Apep easily deflected the strike and retreated as Phillip advanced.

When Phillip made the plan, he knew the basement ceiling was low and the back room too small for a proper sword fight. He also knew that he needed to force Apep to stay within striking range. Give him too much space or time, and he would use the God Stones. Phillip had no intention of giving Apep either and responded with a flurry of lunges, backing Apep across the small room until the heel of his foot struck the wall. He had him against the ropes. Once cornered, Phillip began an assault of precision strikes, gracefully flicking his wrist back and forth.

Apep struggled to match Phillip's speed and technique.

It was time to end this. Phillip stepped in close to Apep, grabbing him by the throat with his free hand. Flexing his jaw in determination, he squeezed with all he had in hopes of crushing the bastard's throat.

He looked Apep dead in his soulless eyes as he raised his sword horizontal to Apep's face.

As soon as Phillip's hand wrapped around Apep's throat, Apep reached out with his empty hand. He flexed his fingers, drawing in the power of the God Stones.

Phillip felt the God Stones' power electrify the air. It was familiar – even though he hadn't felt it since the days of Turek, he knew that power. But not like this, not free of the arc; never free of the arc. His mind screamed in agony as he took aim at Apep's right eye, thrusting the business end of the sword toward Apep's face.

Raw power surged into Apep's hand. With the tip of the blade only millimeters from his eye, Apep grabbed Phillip's sword with his bare hand, wrapping his fingers around it as if gripping a stick and not a razor-sharp blade. With an easy twist of the wrist, he snapped the ancient blade with a metallic crack.

The sound from the fracturing blade was wrong. A sound that should not be possible from a blade impossible to break. Phillip's eyes stretched wide, first in horror then in rage. He renewed his grip on Apep's neck, feeling his fingers sink into the soft tissue. He would rip the throat from his neck with his bare hands if that's what it took.

Apep began to laugh. Then he drove the broken piece of sword into Phillip's chest.

Phillip twisted, trying desperately to slip the strike. The awkward maneuver locked up his bad hip and shot white-hot pain down his leg and into his toes. While he managed to protect his heart from the strike, the blade still hit home, biting sharply as it slipped between the rib bone just below his left shoulder. The cold steel had missed his heart but not his lung.

Apep gave Phillip a push and stepped forward, away from the wall. His hood fell back, revealing a familiar face, wreathed with an unfamiliar psychotic smile.

"You!" Phillip said, raising his broken sword.

"Surprised? I've been here in this tiny town for some time now, Phillip. Did you really think I was unaware of what you have been up to? Did you think I did not know the Keepers' plans?" Apep said, stepping forward again.

Phillip retreated now, backing slowly toward the collapsed tunnel.

"You're all fools to believe Garrett is your savior. You tried to hide him from me, changing his name, then changing it back. Ridiculous. I've known who he is for years. I've inserted myself into his life, gained his trust. Turek always thought if he put enough sand and dirt on top of what he didn't like, somehow that would make everything go away. He could never do the hard bit, could he? Never just kill what he didn't like – and that is why humans will always be inferior. You see, Keeper? Turek tried to hide me under the ground, but I didn't go away!" Apep spat. "No amount of dirt could keep me buried."

Phillip coughed bloody spittle into his fist. His lung was filling with blood. He wasn't sure if it was the coppery taste of blood or Apep's foul voice that was causing the bile that stung the back of his throat.

Apep spun the sword in a figure eight as he stepped forward again.

"You have made this too easy. I think even Turek would be disappointed in you. You have unwisely instructed the boy to lead me to the temple. To the very thing you don't want me to find. How could you be so stupid? Before you speak, I know, I know – you're human. But even that should be no excuse for a faux pas like this."

Apep stepped forward again. Phillip had no more room. One more step and Apep would be in range to strike. He needed to think of something.

"Now look at what your stupidity has gotten you. Once I align the stones back into the Sound Eye, I'll soon have my army and this wretched world will be nothing more than a distant, burning memory."

"It wasn't… stupidity… Apep. It was… careful planning."

"Yes, of course – your little prophecy. To believe in such foolishness is worse than if you had just erred. How will your people ever forgive what their blind faith is about to cost them?"

Phillip grunted as he leaned forward, scooping up the lantern from the floor.

"You sure you want to do that, Phillip? The whole fire thing didn't work out so well last time. Too bad about that hip – damn thing seems to be on its last leg." Apep chuckled at his own pun. Suddenly he advanced on Phillip, his face twisted anew as he bit down on his lower lip and raised his sword.

Phillip's hip screamed again as the pain tried to rival that caused by the steel blade lodged in his chest. He shuffled sideways past the collapsed tunnel to the furthest point from the basement entrance.

Apep charged forward.

Phillip threw the lantern just as his feet tangled, and he fell back hard to the rough floor. The lantern sailed past Apep, smashing into the threshold of the basement doorway.

Reflexively Apep ducked as the inferno exploded to life, flames blocking the only exit.

With Apep distracted, Phillip reached for something else.

Apep turned back to him with his sword at the ready. Then towering over him, he pressed his blade to Phillip's throat as his face contorted. "You missed."

Phillip had known all along this was a one-way ticket. Raising his eyes to meets Apep's, he stared obstinately into the man's soul then choked out a mouthful of blood onto Apep's feet. "I wasn't… aiming at… you," he said quietly.

Stepping forward with his left leg, Apep bent closer to hear the dying man's words.

"I was distracting you!" Phillip shouted, swinging his right hand from behind his back with all the force he could muster. He saw the revelation in Apep's eyes as the long prong sank into his left thigh with a sharp sting of metal.

Phillip let go, made a fist, and then hammered it down onto the handle of James's sai, sinking the weapon through Apep's leg and out the other side. The two shorter curved prongs didn't stop until they reached bone.

Apep cried out, scrambling backward away from Phillip.

Phillip sagged back and let his butt rest on his heels. *Now, son – do it now!* he thought.

Apep screamed again but this time his voice wasn't full of pain… it was full of rage! He rushed forward, dragging his left leg behind him, the sai fixed deep into flesh and bone, with the long center spike protruding from the back side of his blood-soaked thigh.

Phillip could see Apep drawing his sword back like a lumberjack preparing to fell a tree. He lifted himself off his heels and raised his head proudly. As the swing came, Phillip found Apep's eyes again and steeled his own. He shouted as loud as he could, making sure the message was clear as a raging Apep struck out with the blade. "You will never defeat us! Turek forev—"

Phillip's head toppled to the floor.

Flying up the basement stairs two at a time, James scrambled to break free of the neighbor's house. He shouldered through the back door, not even bothering to unlock it, then nearly fell down a short set of steps leading to the backyard.

In the background, a young boy's panicked voice shouted, "Mom! Dad! What's going on?"

"James, wait for us!" Garrett yelled into the yard. Then James did wait. He stopped cold, freezing in place, looking at the side of their house from across the fence.

Garrett caught up, followed closely by Elaine and Lenny.

"What is it?" Garrett asked, noticing that even in the darkness of the neighbor's backyard James had paled, his face white as the moon.

James's shoulders slumped as his eyes glazed over, wet with emotion.

"James?" Elaine asked.

He looked at her.

"Phillip?" Her voice cracked.

James looked down at his feet and let out a shuddering breath.

"Oh no, Phillip. No. God no!" she said.

"What is it?" Garrett said, looking back and forth between them. "Tell me! What!"

"Finish it, James – finish it now!" Elaine said.

James nodded, swallowing hard. "Lenny take Elaine across the street into the cornfield. We'll meet you there. Garrett, come with me," he said, turning away from them. He ran toward the chain-link fence that separated Glen's yard from their own.

Garrett followed, hopping the fence with ease. "James, are you going to shoot him?" he whispered.

"What? Oh… no," he said, tossing the shotgun to the ground.

Garrett looked at his brother like he had just lost his mind and bent to pick up the gun.

"Leave it and come on," James ordered.

They made their way to a small wooden shed where his father kept the rabbit feed and gardening tools.

"I don't understand. Why don't you just shoot this guy? What is he – bulletproof? Is that what the God Stones do – make you bulletproof?" Garrett asked.

"Maybe, but we're not going to find out."

"Goddammit, James – I need some answers! What the hell is going on? I'm running around with a sword and Lenny has a stick, and we just tossed a perfectly good shotgun to the ground!"

"I thought you knew what's going on," James said, pulling open the door to the shed and stepping inside. "That's what Brother Brockridge was supposed to do, tell you what was going on."

Garrett followed him into the shed. *Brother Brockridge?* "Yeah, well, psycho showed up and I'm pretty sure…" Garrett struggled with the words. "Killed him. So, I think I missed some key parts."

James knelt, sliding his hands along the bottom of the wall until he found whatever it was he was feeling for. Garrett heard a *click*, and James stood and walked to the other side of the shed. He quickly moved the push mower and knelt again, this time pulling up floorboards. "Listen, we don't have time for this now, but I will do the best I can to answer your questions."

"I need to know what's going on! I can't be expected—"

James cut him off. "Look, we can't risk going back in there to try and shoot him."

"But our dad's in there fighting him!"

James looked up, eyes sharp. "Our dad is… he's dead, Garrett. It's up to us to finish this!" He turned back, reaching beneath the floor.

For a moment, Garrett just stared at his back as he dug around. *How could he say that? How could he even say their father was dead like that?* Then finally he shouted, "You don't know that!"

"Yes. Yes, I do, Garrett," James said, retrieving something from the hidden compartment.

Garrett caught a whiff of something. Smoke. It was smoke. He leaned out the door and noticed it. His house was on fire. Smoke was coming from the back porch on the other side of the house. He couldn't see flame, but the smoke was rolling across the yard. "Jesus Christ, James, our house is on fire!"

"It's about to get a whole lot worse than fire," he said, uncoiling something as he backed toward the doorway.

Garrett didn't understand what he was looking at. It looked similar to a small coil of thin rope. "James. Who are you?"

Ignoring the question, he pushed past Garrett and out the shed door. "Come on! Let's go!"

Garrett followed him out of the shed, the cool evening wind nipping at his cheeks. He was too busy puzzling over his brother's strange behavior to even notice the cold.

When James was a few feet away from the shed, he knelt down and removed his Zippo from his jeans pocket. Flipping the lid open, he struck the flint. A small flame materialized from the lighter, illuminating his face and eyes in the soft glow.

Garrett could see it then, something beneath the scars on his cheeks. Something beyond the fiery reflection in his eyes. Something.

He lit the end of the rope and it burst to life like a sparkler. "You burned me once, you son of a bitch. Now feel *your* flesh burn!"

Garrett's eyes stretched wide at the realization. His brother had just lit a fuse.

James flipped his Zippo shut and leapt to his feet. "We should run – fast!"

It took them less than thirty seconds to run around the side of the house, past the collapsed porch, and across the street.

They jumped the ditch and ran into a barren field, recently plowed and ready for this year's planting. Elaine and Lenny waited about twenty yards in, watching the flames as they began to flicker up from the back of the house.

"Back! Back! Everybody back!" James shouted, running toward them.

Elaine and Lenny turned to run. Elaine's foot caught on a dirt clod and she fell to the ground. Lenny reached down and quickly pulled her to her feet.

"Please work, please work!" James said to no one as he ran. Then, turning to Garrett, he said, "I isolated everything to protect the fuse from the energy of the God Stones, but obviously I had no way to test it."

Garrett looked at James as though he were speaking Portuguese. "What are you talking about?"

James stopped abruptly and turned to the group. "This should be far enough," he said.

"You okay, Mrs. Turek?" Lenny asked, looking down toward Elaine's ankle.

Elaine nodded to Lenny and forced a smile.

Garrett watched James as he stared intently back toward the house. James's scarred face was barely visible in the barren field, but his eyes – they reflected lifetimes of pain. In that very moment something clicked, and Garrett knew who James was. A veil was pulled back, revealing the truth. The scars on James's face, arms, and torso weren't the result of a child playing with fire. Even more, he knew who his father was. His artificial hip wasn't from a car accident. The last several hours had been so tangled up it was like watching two spiders wrestle, but those few words James had spoken when lighting the fuse provided Garrett with critical comprehension. He heard the words from Mr. B echoing in his mind:

There was a fire – it burned all around us. I could see Turek through the flames, but I couldn't get to him without abandoning them. Two other Templars made it to him and stood with him, battling Apep, but neither were powerful enough to stop him.

After freeing his wife and child from the flames, I arrived only in time to pull the two Templars out before they were killed. One of the Templars had been nearly burned to death and the other was partially crushed by a collapsing beam while trying to save Turek.

He gazed at James through new eyes. No longer did he see his brother, but rather an ancient man – a Templar Knight!

Suddenly several deep flashes emitted from below Garrett's house, momentarily pulling him from his revelation. The flashes were followed in rapid succession by just as many concussive blasts. Chunks of foundation exploded outward as the house collapsed in upon itself.

Through the dust Garrett could see his house was now nothing but burning rubble. The roof was sitting at nearly ground level, consumed in flame. Everything Garrett owned was gone. His home, his clothes, everything – all lost. But what dropped him to his knees was the loss he could never replace. He knew now that what James said was true. If his stepfather hadn't already been killed… he was dead now.

11

Sentheye

Wednesday, April 6, moments earlier – God Stones Day 1
Petersburg, Illinois

Apep stared down into Phillip's hollow eyes.

He placed his boot on top of Phillip's head and rolled it back and forth with his foot before giving it a booted kick into the hungry flames.

He looked down at his own leg. The blade had not only left three puncture wounds in his outer thigh, but it had come out the other side just below his ass. For the first time, Apep felt a hint of real panic pulse through him, radiating like a cold shiver on a chilly night. He reached down and grabbed hold of the sai's hilt, clenched his jaw, and pulled. He felt every inch of the metal prongs as they slid through his flesh and across his bone. He retched in agony as the blade tugged free. Blood pulsed out in spurts with the rhythm of his heart. For the first time since waking up under the sand, he found it difficult to hold the human form. Normally he didn't even need to think about it. It was as simple as breathing. But now he felt the façade slipping away. His skin began to change color. His hair turned silky black and began to lengthen as his body lengthened too, easily stretching another foot in height.

Apep closed his eyes and chanted the word *Sentheye.* A word of immense power. A word spoken by the seven gods. Focusing on the Sentheye of the God Stones, Apep let his mind relax. He wasn't ready to return to his true form – not yet. He needed to stop this bleeding. He had to focus.

Since reclaiming the stones, he'd found drawing on the Sentheye was easy, even after so much time separated from it. It was like having amputated legs given back to him strong and fully functional years after they had been lost. He didn't need to learn how to use them – they were just part of him once again. The ancient Sentheye was again his to command. He could feel it rushing forth in him like water from a powerful stream.

As the Sentheye drew into him, the center of his mind pulsed, then throbbed, filling like a balloon on the verge of bursting. Mumbling the ancient word, he placed each hand over the wounds on either side of his leg and focused on the power of the seven God Stones. The Sentheye took the form of dense, blue-grey shadows. The shadows obeyed, snaking from his palm and fingers – like smoke, but alive, moving with purpose and direction. The shadows slithered into the punctures, and seconds later his bleeding stopped. Apep continued to concentrate, and the shadow smoke wormed its way inside mending the tissue in the deepest parts of his wound. With a little more focus he was easily able to pull himself back into human form. For the second time that night, he had healed himself with the power of the Sentheye.

As the Sentheye repaired Apep's injuries, it also elevated his senses. Abruptly he stopped and the shadows dissipated. *Something is wrong. Something is very wrong,* he thought. The panic he had felt before returned, but this time it came back tenfold. He looked around. The basement was filling with smoke very quickly and the flames were out of control. *No, something else. A trap!*

He turned to the tunnel, but it was sealed with concrete. Then back to the door consumed in flame. He moved toward the flaming doorway.

Then he heard it – a strange sizzling sound.

Every precariously stacked brick column in the small basement exploded, virtually simultaneously. Hundreds of bricks became projectiles, launching in every direction. The instant disintegration of the columns and foundation left nothing to support the house and it dropped like a rock.

Apep screamed.

12

The Grooves Are the Key

Wednesday, April 6 – God Stones Day 1
Rural Chiapas State, Mexico

Fredy ran forward, shouting after Sarah, "Be careful, compañera!"

"I'm good, Fredy!" Sarah shouted back. "There's just not much room in here to rappel. I'll have to go really slow."

Gabi peered over the edge, shining her headlamp down at a dangling Sarah.

"Careful, Gabi," Fredy said.

"Why in the hell wouldn't she go slow?" Andrés asked, as he assessed the rigging of Sarah's anchor point to ensure it was holding secure. They had decided the giant statue's ankle would make as solid an anchor point as anything they could create. As expected, it was holding fine.

"I have worked with Sarah for a long time, compadre – you don't know her like I do. The woman is fearless and maybe even a little loco," Fredy said, twirling his finger next to his head.

Gabi stared down, unblinking. Her own heart pounded against her chest as Sarah jumped back a few inches off the wall and dropped away. Again and again, she jumped back and dropped down, the light from her headlamp retreating a little each time she repeated the technique, slowly making her way down the shaft. A moment later the swaying light stopped.

Fredy depressed the button on the radio. “Everything okay, Sarah? Over.”

As Fredy released the button, the radio crackled to life. “Yep, I’m good. Just taking a pause to investigate and check for gases. Gauges are good. I don’t know, Fredy, part of me thought maybe it would just be the top, but it’s still perfectly circular and I can’t find one tool mark. They couldn’t have just bored a hole through solid stone.” The radio went silent for a long second. “I think this must have been a natural hole. The shaft started out smaller, then its creators must have widened it into this perfect circle. I suppose it’s possible they rubbed away any tooling marks with harder stone using an abrasion technique. Everything else must have been formed around it. The chamber, the stairwell, all of it. The question is why? Why would they go to the trouble? Maybe they widened it out to allow sacrifices to pass through to the underworld. I can buy that. But to create this perfect shaft and hide the marks… I don’t get it. I have never seen anything like this.”

Fredy shared a confused look with Andrés then with Gabi. “We agree, Sarah. This makes no sense.”

Gabi watched on, eyes fixed as Sarah’s light began to sway hypnotically. Her mind reeled as she tried to puzzle out the mystery, but it simply made no sense. When the light finally stopped its metronome cadence, it was a faraway glow, a fading light at the end of a long vertical tunnel.

“I’m down,” Sarah announced.

Fredy pressed the button. “What do you see, Sarah?”

María and Itzel stopped their work and joined the others, everyone gathering around Fredy and the radio. Gabi continued to peer over the edge, watching the light below.

“I must be around one hundred feet below you. The floor feels soft and uneven but stable. Wait! There are smooth curved structures protruding from the material making up the floor of the shaft. Jesus! Stand by.”

“Sarah!” Fredy shouted.

"It's okay. They're bones, Fredy. Bones upon bones – god, there's no telling how deep these go."

"Or how long this shaft was used for sacrifices?" Andrés muttered. "Tell her to check her gauges."

"Check your gauges, Sarah. Are they still clear?" Fredy asked through the radio.

"Shit, I forgot! Stand by."

"Come on, Sarah." Fredy sighed but he didn't depress the button on the two-way. "She knows better. All those bones. They could be releasing poisonous gases as they decay!"

"She is just excited, Fredy. She will be fine," Itzel reassured him.

"Just excited! She could be breathing lethal doses of methane—"

The radio chirped and Sarah's voice rang out, "I'm good! The gauges are flat, but my god, Fredy, there're bones everywhere!"

"What's your next move, Sarah?"

Sarah's voice came back. "It would be easy for me to spend the next several days, maybe even weeks, sorting through the material under my feet. But I am telling you there is something more to this than a hole created to toss sacrifices down."

Her intuition, Gabi thought. And she felt it too. There was so much more.

"First off, this chamber and shaft required way too much work to simply be used for sacrifice," Sarah continued. "Second, most places specific for sacrifices would lead to the underworld – well, at least to underground caverns or cenotes. Almost always something full of water. But there is no cavern here – no water either. Maybe it dried up, but I don't think so. So, what then, Fredy? We're supposed to believe this is just a shaft deep in the ground leading to nothing? I'm not buying it."

Gabi reached out over the rim and ran her hand along until she found one of the grooves. *The grooves are the key,* she thought.

From across the chamber Itzel called out, "Gabi, come join me, we can work on the wall together."

Gabi traced her finger up the groove. *I know it's the grooves, Sarah – I feel it.* "Coming, Mamá!"

One hundred feet below, Sarah ran her hand along the wall until she found one of the grooves. *It's the grooves, isn't it? The grooves are the key.* She pressed the button on the radio. "It's the grooves. They must be the key. Stand by, team."

Sarah knelt down, following one of the grooves until it disappeared into the floor of bones. The stale air was cold, and she felt a shiver as she carefully began removing material, following the groove down the wall. A few inches down, the groove disappeared behind a skull that was held fast by a dark amber substance, like a giant bug stuck in tree sap. Very carefully she pulled it from its centuries'-old hold. She placed it on the growing mound of material behind her and continued removing bones.

She had followed the groove nearly a foot beneath the layer of decayed remains and still she couldn't find the bottom, when Fredy's voice crackled from her two-way, causing her to jump.

"Sarah! Status report."

"Christ!" she said before depressing the button on the two-way. "I'm fine, Fredy, but I'm going to be a few more minutes. I have a hunch and I need to see it through."

"Fine, just keep us posted – we're all getting anxious up here," Fredy said, his voice laced with worry.

"Okay. Sorry." Sarah checked her watch and then said, "I'll check back in ten minutes."

"Okay," Fredy said.

Sarah continued to work further into the strata, peeling it back like an onion until she created a deep pocket next to the wall. After another check-in with Fredy, ten minutes turned into twenty as she wondered, *How deep could this be?* Maybe at one time this shaft did lead to an underground cenote, but the bodies filled it up. If that were the case, forget weeks – they could spend years excavating this shaft. She began to feel like her hopes of finding bottom were unrealistic. She would have to give up for today. The team would need to set up a system for removing the material bit by bit.

She shook her head. *What the hell am I doing*? She had been a fool to try and follow the groove down the wall like this. How much damage to the remains had she already done? Dammit, she knew better than this. Better than to let the excitement of her theory put the material she was digging through at risk. Still, even as she thought it, she shifted her body from a squat to all fours, reached down well past her elbow, and pulled loose yet another bone from the bottom of the hole. She reached in again, and this time she felt a smooth surface.

Sarah's heart began to pound so hard she could feel it in her ears. Frantically, she scooped and brushed clear dirt and bits of bone from the smooth surface along the bottom of the hole. Finding where the groove met the smooth bottom, she worked to clear the area. Pulling her arm back out she shifted to shine her headlamp down the hole. It was about a foot and a half deep. *Did the groove stop at the floor?* She couldn't tell. She reached in again and poked her finger into the groove, trying to see if she could shove her finger below the flat surface she had cleared. Suddenly, the dirt filling the groove gave, and her finger dropped down the hollow, below the floor, all the way to her knuckle. She knew it!

She pressed the button on her two-way. "I know what the grooves are for, Fredy! I know what they're for! It's a lid of some kind! A lid!" Sarah shouted through the radio. "The notches are how they lowered it down. Once in place they must have dropped the ropes through the holes so that it could never be pulled back up!"

"Dios mío! Are you sure, Sarah?" Fredy asked, his voice crackling back through the radio.

"It has to be. There's something under here Fredy – I can feel it!" Sarah said excitedly. *Something important,* she thought.

"Sarah, are you ready to come up?"

Sarah hesitated. The shaft was only a few feet across. If they were to just clear the bones it wouldn't take that long. "Fredy, I don't want to wait. Send down a basket – I'm going to clear the bones so we can figure out how we're going to remove this lid."

"Sí, compañera," Fredy said. "Come up and I'll send Andrés back down to clear the bones."

Sarah smiled. "Fredy, you worry too much. I'm good. I want to stay and work this. If I get tired, I'll tag out."

"Sí, compañera." Fredy sighed.

13

In the Distance

Wednesday, April 6 – God Stones Day 1
Petersburg, Illinois

The library basement was swallowed in darkness so absolute it almost felt crushing to Breanne. Crushing like the tunnel in Mexico. Crushing like the vine room on Oak Island. Crushing like her mother's car right before Christmas. She felt her heart rate rise and a real fear she might lose it.

Then she heard her brother whisper, "It's okay, Bre, just breathe."

She took a deep breath. She wasn't being crushed. She wasn't in a cave or an upside-down car in the middle of winter. She was just in the dark.

Everyone froze in place.

"Guys, what the hell just happened?" Pete asked.

"I can't see my hand in front of my face," David said.

"Everybody, stay calm. The power just went out," Paul said.

Next to her, Janis gasped.

"Janis? Are you okay?" Breanne asked, rifling through her backpack for a light.

"Um, yeah, I guess. But um… I can see just fine."

"What do you mean, you can see just fine?" Pete asked.

"I *mean*, I can see just fine. Like the lights aren't even off."

"Whoa! Night vision. You got freaking night vision? That's awesome. I'm happy for you, Janis," David said.

In the pitch black of the basement, Breanne didn't need to see the disappointment on David's face to sense it. Something in his voice, beyond the excitement and happiness, betrayed his own desire for a special power. "It will happen, David. I think it's just different for everyone," she said encouragingly.

David sighed. "I don't know. Mr. B said most people may not even be affected."

"I think there is a reason you are here, David, just like there's a reason we're all here. Just give it time…"

"Thanks, Breanne. I've dreamed of having a superpower my whole life. I know this might sound stupid, but you have no idea how much time I've spent contemplating which superpower I would want. I have seen every superhero movie and played every game that has to do with magic or superpowers. You know what I always end up deciding on?" David asked.

Breanne shook her head, answering absently as something invaded her vision. "No, David, what?"

"Invisibility. I mean you could do so much with it," David said excitedly.

"You realize you're a douche canoe, right?" Pete asked.

"Yeah, and you're a real dick," David shot back.

"You know what, David…"

The voices were growing distant, fading into the background as Breanne was suddenly somewhere else. Or at least her mind was somewhere else, while her body seemed to stay in place in the library. What was she seeing? A basement?

And what was happening? Something unspeakable.

She watched a man die. Then she saw a wounded Apep standing over him, a bloody sword in his hand. She stared into the dead man's hollow eyes. She didn't recognize him but somehow knew who he was. "Oh no!" she gasped.

"What is it?" Paul asked, clicking on a headlamp he retrieved from his pack.

"Dude? Why are your sister's eyes clouded over?!" Pete asked.

"Oh, shit! They're completely white!" David said, pointing.

"Be quiet – she's seeing something!" Paul said, reaching for her and finding her hand.

A few seconds later her eyes cleared. "I just saw something… I think it was Garrett's dad. Apep… oh dear god! He… he killed him!" she cried.

"What!?" Pete asked frantically. "How can you know that?"

"It's her power, bro!" David said. "Are you sure it was Garrett's dad? Is Garrett okay? What about his mother? Lenny?"

"I… I don't know. I only saw Apep and this other man."

"What do you mean 'saw'?" Pete asked.

"They were fighting with swords. There was fire and then… Apep… he… he cut off the man's head!" she cried, burying her face into her hands. But before anyone could say anything else another flash lit up her mind. She threw her head back involuntarily, her eyes opening wider than should have been possible.

"Look! She's doing it again!" David shouted.

She was back in the basement but now something sizzled like frying bacon, then everything exploded inward. Bricks and fire smashed into Apep's body as he screamed in a combination of pain and rage.

When the vision was over, the voices around her turned up like the dial on a radio.

"You mean she gets visions of what's going to happen right before it happens?" Pete was asking.

"Yeah, something like that," Paul said.

Breanne blinked as the cloudiness cleared from her vision. "Guys, I just saw Apep screaming and then everything around him blew up."

"What? Are you sure!" Janis asked.

"So far every flash I've had happens right after I see it," Breanne said.

"I say we go up and wait out back. Maybe we can see something," Janis said, reaching for Pete's hand. "I'll lead you out."

"Or…" Pete said, rustling around in his backpack for a flashlight. He retrieved it, illuminating Janis with a soft click of the switch.

"Oh, okay," Janis said, starting to pull her hand away.

Pete squeezed it as she tried to let go. "Or we could do the hand-holding thing, either way…"

"Are you okay, Janis?" Breanne asked, noticing her complexion had paled in the low light.

Janis nodded with a weak smile and left her hand in Pete's. "Come on, let's go."

They went upstairs single file. Mrs. Cleary sat in her same chair behind the counter, reading her paperback illuminated by the golden glow of an antique oil lantern. "Ah, glad you made your way up, and I see you have lights with you. Good. The storm is coming, and I fear it's going to be a bad one."

"Yeah, looks like it is," Pete said, leading the group to the front door. "Well, good night, Mrs. Cleary."

"Peter? Shouldn't you wait for Garrett and Lennard?" Mrs. Cleary asked.

Pete froze, hand on the door handle.

Breanne looked back at the librarian, who sat unmoving, peering at Pete over the top of her glasses.

"Mrs. Cleary, how do you know we are waiting on Garrett and Lenny? I didn't say anything about them."

Mrs. Cleary held their gaze for a long moment as silence filled the room.

Breanne looked at Paul, who returned the look. A look that said something was wrong.

"Peter," the librarian finally said, "don't go out the front. Not tonight. Tonight, go out the back."

Pete let go of the door handle and turned to face the suddenly mysterious woman behind the counter. "Mrs. Cleary?" Pete said, swallowing hard. "Who are you?"

Ms. Cleary smiled. "I'm a friend, Peter. And tonight, you should go out the back and wait for your friends behind the library. Stay out of sight, and when they get here get on with it. Tonight isn't a night for lingering. Now follow me. The back is this way." She pulled her spectacles from her face, folded them gently, and placed her paperback along with her readers on the counter. She didn't wait for anyone to speak as she lifted the lantern and moved toward the back of the library.

They all shared uneasy looks, but they followed single file.

Mrs. Cleary opened the back door and motioned them out. "I wish you the best. All of you."

As they poured out the back of the library, Breanne watched Pete turn as if he wanted to say something but didn't know what to say. Finally, he just said, "Thanks, Mrs. Cleary."

Mrs. Cleary nodded and as the door swung slowly shut, she said, "We're counting on you."

"What the hell was that about?!" David asked.

"That was weird," Janis said.

"Incredibly weird!" Breanne agreed.

"No, don't you guys get it? She is a Keeper," Pete said.

"What!" David said, looking back toward the closed door with a newfound awe. "You think so?"

"I know so. It's the only explanation. It makes total sense. All this time she has been here observing us. Observing me. She knew all of our comings and goings. Remember what Mr. B said? There are so many." Pete shook his head. "All this time. A Keeper was right here."

"Do you guys hear that? Sounds like sirens," Paul said.

The group walked to the north edge of the building, carefully peeking around the corner toward the town square.

"Holy shit! The whole side of the town square is on fire!" David said, pointing.

Sirens could be heard as firetrucks, ambulances, and squad cars poured onto the square in an effort to stifle the flames.

The burning square held no interest for Breanne as she focused all her attention toward Garrett's home. She prayed he was okay. She needed him to be okay. "Is this the direction Garrett lives in?" she asked, pointing. Her brow crinkled as she squinted into the shadowed evening.

"Yep, that's right," Pete said, following her finger with his gaze. Squinting himself, he removed his glasses to clean them on his sleeve.

With his glasses off he glanced back up toward Garrett's place. "Holy hell!" he shouted.

"What? What do you see?" Janis asked.

"There in the distance, don't you see it? It looks like Garrett's house is on fire!"

Everyone was looking in the direction Pete was pointing now.

"I don't see anything?" David said, standing on his tiptoes.

"No, me either. It's too dark," Paul said.

"Right there!" Pete said, pointing between the buildings toward Jackson Street, then holding out his hands pleadingly. "Come on, none of you see it?"

"Whatever you see, Pete, I don't see it either," Breanne said apologetically.

"The orange fiery glow rising up… the smoke in the distance. You guys really can't see it? It's right where Garrett's house would be."

"That's like eight city blocks, Pete. No one could see that through town and all the neighborhoods. Especially not in the dark," David said.

"I'm telling you…" Pete began.

"Um, follow me for a second," David said.

They jogged back around the stone library to the south parking lot with everyone in tow. "Okay, now look down the street to the DQ. Can you see the sign?"

"Of course."

Breanne could just make out the sign, about two blocks away.

"Okay, now can you read the sign?"

"Duh, it says DQ," Pete said with a scowl.

"Okay, you knew that. What about underneath the sign. The smaller sign. From here can you see what is says underneath?"

Everyone squinted into the distance. Breanne couldn't make out a word in the darkness.

"Dammit, David, don't be an ass. You know I have bad eyes as it is, and no one could read that from here. Not even if I had perfect twenty-twenty vision," Pete said, placing his glasses back on his face then pushing them onto the bridge of his nose.

"Just try, Pete," David said.

Pete squinted toward the DQ sign. "No, jackass, I can't see it. In fact, I can't even see the Dairy Queen that well – everything is blurry."

"Take off the glasses and try."

Pete made a show out of sighing in great annoyance then removing the glasses in an exaggerated gesture. He looked back out toward the Dairy Queen. Then he froze, studying something in the distance for a long moment. "New Summer Blizzard Menu." Then, squinting, he said, "Today's special was a cheeseburger basket for five bucks."

David raised a skeptical eyebrow. "Wait a minute, how do you know that? They don't put specials up on the sign."

"No, they don't. It's posted on the counter inside. I can see it through the glass door," Pete said, turning back to the group, a surprised smile spreading across his face.

"Ha!" David said. "That's crazy cool – you have super-vision!"

Everyone squinted in the direction of the DQ, trying to see if they could see inside through the door. No one could make anything out. Breanne couldn't even see this sign they were talking about.

"I can see in the dark like it is daytime, and I can't see that sign from here," Janis said.

Pete shrugged. "I don't know, it's weird. It's still dark. And when I glance back now, I can't see it." Then he paused, appraising the glass door in the distance again. "It's just that when I focus on the sign, it's like it magnifies. Pete started to put his glasses back on then stopped abruptly. Still smiling, he tucked the glasses into his pocket. He turned, looking back in the direction of Garrett's house, his smile falling away. "I'm telling you guys," he said, hitching his thumb toward his friend's house, "something is wrong at Garrett's."

That's when they heard a distant explosion. A second later they could feel a soft rumble traveling across the asphalt of the parking lot.

Janis turned to Breanne and began running back around the library. "Oh my god! That was it, wasn't it!? The explosions you saw!?"

Breanne nodded, trailing Janis. "Pete, what do you see?"

Pete slid to a stop, squinting in the direction of Garrett's house. "I don't have a clear line of sight, but judging from the mushroom cloud in the distance I don't think Garrett's house is there anymore, guys."

14

Just Cut Off Its Head

Wednesday, April 6 – God Stones Day 1
Petersburg, Illinois

Dark smoke plumed into the night sky to merge with thickening rain clouds. Hot wind washed over Garrett, and the acrid smoke from his burning home assaulted his nose. This he could ignore. But the loss of his home assailed his soul, and the loss of his father and Mr. B. attacked his heart. These wounds were impossible to brush off.

"What now?" Garrett asked thickly.

"We move. This will only buy time," James said, looking to Elaine's ankle. "Can you run, Elaine?"

"No. It may be broken… I… I rolled it pretty good," she said, grimacing.

James positioned himself so that Elaine could lean on him and take the weight off the bad ankle. As quickly as they could, they made their way around the block and into an alley.

"James, what do mean 'only buy time' – don't you think he's dead after that?" Garrett asked hopefully.

"I would love to think so, but he has the God Stones. Unfortunately, the prophecy doesn't end with him dying in our basement. You still have a mission." James looked back over his shoulder as if he expected Apep to come running toward him from around the corner. "You have to get to the temple, while we still have a chance."

Garrett looked to Elaine. "Mom, I have so many questions."

"I know you do," she said, wincing as she shifted position from one foot to try and put most of her weight on the other. "This isn't the way you were supposed to find out. All the Keepers knew the signal, knew that when Brother Brockridge called for the closed test it was time. What we didn't know was that Apep would obtain the stones before we were able to properly… enlighten you."

"I want to be so pissed off right now," Garrett said. "But I can't. I want to run away – but I can't. I want to just sit down and cry – but I can't even do that!" He lifted his head and met his mother's eyes. He searched them and found what he was looking for – love. He knew at least that much was true. If everything else was nothing more than a lie, at least that much he knew had to be true.

Elaine smiled and hugged him hard. Then she pushed him back and found his eyes again. "You're right, Garrett. You can't do any of those things. Not now anyway. The prophecy has been written and your path is waiting. Now you must go." She squeezed his shoulders reassuringly.

"And you?" Garrett asked.

"I must go too. James and I must warn the other Keepers and tell them of the loss of Brother Brockridge, of Phillip," she said, her voice cracking. "We must tell them it has begun and Apep is here. We will be safe. Find me after," she said, forcing an unconvincing tight-lipped smile.

"Find you? How will I find you?"

"Find your way back to the dojo."

"But the building burned."

His mother bent forward and kissed him on the cheek. Then she turned to Lenny. "Brother Brockridge put that staff in your hand for a reason, Lenny. Take care of my son. Keep him safe."

Lenny nodded.

"Okay, little brother. I must go with your mom."

"What? Wait, you obviously know what you're doing – come with me… help me," Garrett pleaded.

"Garrett, most everything in your life has been carefully orchestrated to prepare you for this moment. Sure, we had to improvise when your real father lost his shit. But we made it work. We gave you what you needed and taught you how to survive with less than most. We raised you poor so you would appreciate what you had when everything was taken away from you. We made sure you grew up strong because we knew you would need to be. I treated you like crap because you needed to learn to stand up on your own. Phillip treated you with tough love because the journey ahead will test all your morals – morals we have ensured you possess. Your mother loved you and made sure you knew love so that when the time came you would understand what was at stake." James stepped closer and laid a hand on his brother's shoulder. "This journey is yours. You will find all the help you need in your sages. The prophecy of Turek tells us no one can alter the course set forth. Find me when you destroy what's in the temple. Right now though, I need to get your mother to safety."

James turned to Elaine and, just as they started to walk away, Garrett blurted out, "Wait!"

James turned.

"At least answer one question first."

"Sure."

"What's in the temple that I have to destroy?"

"What!? Brother Brockridge didn't tell you?" James said, turning completely around and stepping back toward Garrett.

Garrett held out his hands. "No. Apep came and, well…"

"Did he at least tell you of the great battles and of the old ones who brought the God Stones to earth through the tear in space?"

"Yes, he told us about the battles and the seven sages who defeated the seven old ones and even that Turek and Apep were both part of that group."

Lenny nodded.

James reached up and scratched at a patch of whiskers. "Inside the temple lies one of the old ones, Garrett."

"What? You're telling me there's a space alien inside there?" Garrett asked.

"Yep. It is in a state of suspension."

Ever since they found the journal, Garrett and his crew had speculated about what they would find inside the temple. A secret treasure? An ancient worshipping place built by the Masons? In truth, he had no idea what he'd expected to be inside Lincoln's temple. But an ancient space alien? "I was hoping it would be some kind of God Stone instruction manual sitting atop an altar. But an alien? I thought all the old ones were destroyed by the sages?"

"Not destroyed, Garrett. Defeated. The place you're going isn't really a temple as much as it is a prison. One of seven prisons across the world. One on each continent and all connected by the same spell. It's a prison never meant to be found, with a being inside never meant to be awakened. Well, not until now. If Apep wakes it, the old one will show him how to assemble the God Stones into the Sound Eye. If that happens… God help us."

"And I have to go in there and kill it?" The words slipped from Garrett's mouth, taking all the moisture with them. He tried to swallow. He didn't need the answer – he just needed to say it aloud.

"Yes, that's where that sword strapped to your back comes in. All you need to do is get there first and use it to cut off the old one's head. You do that, and Apep won't be able to wake it up."

"Seriously?!" Lenny said.

"Serious as a heart attack, Lenny. Now both of you, go." And with that, James turned to Elaine and the two of them hobbled into the shadows of the alley in the opposite direction from Garrett's destiny.

For a moment, the two boys stood next to each other, silently watching the darkness of the alley that had just absorbed Garrett's mother and brother.

Garrett blinked, unable to speak as his mind reeled. *Cut off its head! That's all, Garrett, just cut off its head. You know… with a sword! No big deal, right!?* He couldn't let the gravity of it all weigh on him – not now. If he dared pause here, staring into the darkness too long, if he dared think beyond the next moment, he might just crumple right there in the alley unable to move. Finally, he turned to his friend. "What have we gotten into, Lenny?"

Lenny gazed back down the alley toward his own house. "Garrett?"

"Yeah?"

"I don't think we will ever be coming back here."

"Don't say that—"

Lightning cracked across the night sky, lighting up the neighborhood in an orange glow. It was beautiful, strange, and wrong all at the same time. With the crack of lightning, the power stopped fluctuating and Petersburg went completely dark. Two police cars sped past the mouth of the alley toward what was left of Garrett's burning house.

Orange flashes fractured the night sky again, followed by a boom of thunder. The night sky began to spit fat drops of rain.

Lenny felt the first drop hit his cheek and panic consumed him. "Come on! Garrett, we got to go now!" he said, breaking into an instant sprint toward the library.

"What's wrong?" Garrett asked, matching pace in an easy stride.

"The rain! The tunnel!"

As the boys exchanged horrified glances, understanding slapped Garrett as suddenly as the next drop of rain. The first rule of exploring Petersburg's drainage pipes was to never, *ever* do it in the rain. "Oh, this is just perfect! It's going to fill!"

Lenny shook his head back and forth. "What happens if we can't get in Garrett!?"

Elaine stopped in the shadows and turned to watch Garrett and Lenny as they ran away into the night – into their destiny.

"Are you okay, Elaine?" James asked.

"No, James. No, I am far from okay. We have already lost so much. Now I stand here watching my son go off to… to…" She shook her head and squeezed her eyes closed, trying desperately to hold it together. "It's like when a relative you love comes home and then has to leave after a long visit. You stand at the door watching them go, wondering when you will see them again and how much you will miss them. But the difference is" – a sob broke loose from her as if ripped from her soul, unable to be held any longer – "I know he is going to die!" she cried out, throwing her face into her hands.

James put an arm around her. "Elaine. I know this is hard, but you know he has to do this. It has already been written. Even the part where he dies."

15

Brushwork and Magic?

Wednesday, April 6 – God Stones Day 1
Rural Chiapas State, Mexico

Gabi crawled back from the pit opening and pushed herself up onto her feet. "Really, Mamá! I can actually help you with the wall mural?" Gabi asked hopefully.

"Sí, sure you can help. As long as you can answer this question."

Gabi's eyes narrowed. "What question?"

"There are a few methods we can deploy for the preliminary cleaning of wall paintings. What are they?"

"Easy!" Gabi held up three fingers, closing each as she ticked them off. "Mechanical cleaning of dry soil residue with brushes and a scalpel if needed, chemical cleaning of carbonates and other deposits, and extraction of salts."

"Good! What method will we be using?" her mother asked.

That was two questions, but she was pretty sure she knew the answer. "Mechanical?"

"That's right, just a light brushing for now. What we want is the least abrasive method that will yield the best results."

The scene on the wall began above the skulls, starting just to the left of the stairwell and wrapping around the entire room, but large portions were completely covered with a layer of dust and dirt.

Itzel pointed at the scene. "So far I can see these images here depict a great number of people battling with another group. See, here you can see these people are much larger."

"Those must be the giants!" Gabi said.

"Giants – such a strange word. Even in our own language. Gabi, who would have ever thought we would be referring to people as *gigantes*!"

"But they are, Mamá," Gabi said.

"Yes, María Purísima, I suppose so. I can't tell what happens after so let's start over here and work our way back," Itzel said, pointing at the far end of the battle scene where everything seemed to fade away. "Listen to me, Gabi, you are going to be next to me on a ladder. I will position the ladders for us, and you must be careful not to drop your brush onto the skull racks, or to bump into the skull racks, or to—"

"Mamá, I promise I will be so careful."

"I know you will. You're a woman, Gabi. You are nearly fourteen!"

Gabi and her mom went to work carefully brushing the wall. Slowly, so slowly, the layer of time drifted away to reveal a long-forgotten history.

"Look at this! It's the pyramid!" On the wall before them was a depiction of a massive pyramid, but part of the top was missing. "Look! Gabi! This must be a depiction of how the pyramid was made!" Itzel repositioned her ladder and climbed back up. She began brushing around the part of the pyramid that was missing stones.

Gabi climbed down and stepped back to take in the scene. The horsehair bristles of her mother's brush danced delicately, almost gracefully, side to side. A tiny cloud of dust lifted off the wall and floated away, as if by magic. Magically, too, the paintless brush revealed the secret of how the pyramid was built. The young girl's eyes grew wider and wider as a deep crinkle split her brow.

Her mother's own eyes matched those of her daughter as her hand suddenly froze. "¡Ay, María Purísima!" she gasped.

"Do you see this, Gabi?" Itzel said. "María, Come here. Please look at this!"

Gabi gaped at the wall, unblinking.

"Am I seeing things or do the pyramid stones look as though they are floating up and into place?" María asked.

"Yeah, and it looks as though that giant man is pointing at the stones as they float up," Itzel said.

"He is even bigger than the other giant ones battling the smaller ones," María said.

"Yes, twice as big, but that can't be," Itzel said. "That would be ridiculous – impossible. The scale must be off. We have seen this plenty of times on Egyptian hieroglyphs."

"Itzel, scale doesn't explain the floating blocks and the pointing."

Gabi tried not to blurt her revelation, but her excitement overpowered her mouth and forced it through. "Not pointing!" she announced.

Both women had been so deep in thought they turned to Gabi in surprise, as if she had not been standing between them all along.

"What do you mean?" María asked.

Gabi pointed at the giant then to the highest stone hovering there like a leaf that had caught the wind just right. "Not pointing," she repeated. "Guiding, he is guiding them up… with magic."

16

A Hard Rain

Wednesday, April 6 – God Stones, Day 1
Petersburg, Illinois

Again, Garrett found himself running across town, back through the pizza place parking lot, through the row of parked cars, and into the alley that would lead to the Petersburg Public Library. The rain fell harder every second. Quickly the roads and sidewalks went from being spotted with raindrops to being completely saturated as water began to form puddles in low-lying areas. Garrett's face screwed up with concern, forcing his brows to furrow. He pushed to the back of his mind the obvious questions, such as how his own family could have kept this from him his whole life, how some of this prophecy talk came across like he was somehow the center of a creepy religious cult, and how in the hell was he, a sixteen-year-old kid, expected to hack the head off some sleeping space alien before the evil non-sleeping space alien caught him, woke up the sleeping alien, and destroyed the world. No, he couldn't worry about all that. Instead, he had to focus on just how the hell they were supposed to get into a drainage tunnel that would soon become a powerful discharge of surging rainwater.

He couldn't think about others who might be in on this whole thing or why they couldn't help him. Like Coach Dagrun – he was a freaking war hero. He had been in combat. Was he a Keeper? If he was, why couldn't he help? Just to be able to talk to someone. To take a moment and get some goddamned advice. God, what he wouldn't give to be able to swing by Eugene's house and discuss next moves over a glass of lemonade. He trusted the accountant. If he had time, Eugene would be the perfect adult to provide council. But he didn't have time. He had to run.

They turned into an alley one block from the library just as a wood-framed screen door flung open with a groan. A bearded man reeking of alcohol and cigarette smoke staggered out. The man was moving too fast, his feet unable to keep pace with his body. He fell forward, sprawling onto his hands and knees in the gravel. Garrett and Lenny slid to a stop, nearly running into the man. He was too thin, almost sickly. He looked back in a panic, and it was instantly clear the booze wasn't the cause of his fall. Before the screen door could snap shut, it was intercepted with a larger man's foot. The door flung back open, smacking into the wall of the tavern, as a large potbellied man, followed by two other men, poured into the alley.

"That's right, you son of a bitch! You touched the wrong girl's ass!" yelled the large man.

"I didn't mean to, Terry," the bearded man begged.

"Beat his face in, Terry!" one of the other men shouted.

"Damn you, Joe – you think just on account the power goes out you can get all touchy-feely with my girl! My GIRL!" Terry staggered forward awkwardly and kicked Joe in the ribs.

Joe tipped off his hands and knees, falling into the fetal position.

"Those candles on the bar weren't put there for you to go romanticizing my girl." Terry reared back to kick Joe again but lost his balance, lurching to the side instead.

In any other moment before tonight this would have been the coolest thing in the world to stumble upon. He and Lenny would have been talking about it for days, probably weeks. But in this moment, Garrett just wanted to get past them.

"Terry, holy shit! Do you see that?" one of the other men said, noticing the orange glow from somewhere in the distance over the building's roof.

"Those are sirens!" said another.

The night sky crackled with the sound of thunder gone hoarse. A split second later it lit up in fractures of brilliant amber. The golden lines webbed across the sky as if it were made of cracked glass.

More people spilled out of the bar now, no doubt hoping to see a fight.

"Jes-sus! If that ain't the strangest lightning I ever saw," someone said, their head tipped back, mouth ajar.

"Yeah, the sky is all weird. Maybe we're about to get hit with a tornado?" someone said.

"Look over there! That glow, I'll be damned if that isn't a fire. Come on, let's go check it out," another said.

Terry frowned at the sky. "God help ya if I come back and you're still here, Joe. God help ya."

Garrett stepped to the side as the men rushed past, ignoring him completely.

"How in the hell does half the square catch fire and these guys just now notice?" Garrett asked, shaking his head.

"Too busy playing grab-ass by candlelight with Terry's girl, I guess," Lenny said.

"I guess. Come on. We need to go," Garrett said. But as the crowd continued to pour out, choking the alley, a dozen pairs of eyes fell on them.

A middle-aged man jutted a finger toward them and slurred, "Well whatdowe… have here?"

Another man stepped forward, sounding equally as impaired as the first. "You boys… look like you're… uptonogood."

Even in the rain Garrett could smell the strong odor of cigarette smoke and whiskey on the man's breath.

"Excuse us, please. We need to pass," Lenny said.

A woman with sunken eyes, wearing a short skirt, pushed past the men. "You two ain't going nowhere. It's obvious just looking at you you're probably the cause of whatever that fire is across the street. Trying to make your escape, I'm guessing."

Lenny rolled his eyes. "And here we go."

Garrett leaned in toward Lenny. "Lenny, we don't have time for this, let's just turn back and go around. These drunks could never catch us anyway."

"Is that it, boys? You two been out causing trouble?"

"Maybe lighting stuff on fire," came another voice.

More people were coming out of the bar now and moving in behind them, surrounding them.

Joe still hadn't managed to get up.

"Move out the way and let me through," boomed a deep voice from somewhere behind the forming mob. "I said, get out the way!"

The crowd parted as a stocky man with his sleeves rolled up to reveal dark, hairy arms appeared from the crowd.

Garrett didn't recognize the man. He looked over at Lenny, who shrugged.

"Garrett, it's okay," he said, placing a hand on Garrett's shoulder.

Garrett frowned at the man, then at the man's hand.

Lenny mouthed the words, *What the?*

"It's okay. You go on now, Garrett. You and Lenny have a big night ahead of you. These people won't bother you anymore." He turned to the crowd. "Get out their way. I won't have this mob crap in my establishment."

"We're not in your establishment, Ben, we're in the alley," a man said, holding a pool stick in one hand and slapping it in the other.

"Roger, by god, you talk one more ounce of shit, and I will close your tab. That goes for the rest of you too! Now make way! Or so help me I will blow those candles out, lock up, and the only thing you will be drinking is water from your own tap!"

There was no hesitation. The crowd parted without another word.

Garrett stared at the bartender, his forehead creased.

"It's alright, Garrett. Go on now," he said.

"Thanks," Lenny said.

The bartender pressed his mouth into a tight line and bowed slightly. "My pleasure, Lenny. Now go on, boys. Go."

They ran.

"Garrett, you think?"

"A Keeper? Yeah, I mean what else makes sense?" Garrett asked, shaking his head.

"How many could there be?"

"I don't know. Mr. B made it sound like there could be a lot."

"This is crazy, Garrett."

"You're just figuring that out?"

A minute later they were at the library.

"Garrett, look!" Lenny said, noticing the gang was walking toward them.

"Why aren't you guys inside?"

"The power is out, and it's pitch black in there, plus we were worried about you," Breanne said, her eyes searching Garrett for any sign of injury.

Garrett wasn't sure what prompted him – maybe it was the look of worry in her eyes, maybe it was the loss of his father, or maybe it was the connection he felt to her – but whatever it was, it compelled him. He ran to Breanne and pulled her into his arms, hugging her tightly. Amazingly, she hugged him back, her face buried in his neck like she belonged there. He took a breath, his senses filling with her. He took it all in, her smell, her warmth through damp clothes, her breath on his neck. He wanted to stay right there, in that moment, in the rain, with her, but he knew he couldn't.

"Are you okay?" she asked, still in his embrace.

"No, no I'm not, but I'm glad you're here," he said softly.

"Dude, is that a sword on your back?" Pete asked.

"Guys, as much as I love to see true love blossom, we have to move," Lenny said, tipping his head back to consider the night sky. "The rain. We need to get in the tunnel and find the opening now before it fills with water and we can't get in at all."

Fortunately, no one could see Garrett blush as he reluctantly released Bre. When she let go, he didn't think she wanted to, but he couldn't be sure if that was true or if he was telling himself that. Later, when the time was right and Lenny was least expecting it, he was going to slap him in the sack, good and hard.

"Crap, you're right," Pete said. "Lucky for you guys, I came prepared with a couple cheapy flashlights and some tools for removing the bricks." He patted his backpack with a smile. "Let's jet."

Lenny nodded down the alley. "This way, guys," he said, breaking into a slow jog.

Everyone started jogging behind Lenny.

Breanne stayed next to Garrett, and Pete next to Janis.

"Did you kill him, Garrett?" Janis asked.

"Kill him?" Garrett asked.

"Apep. Bre said she had a vision that he exploded. Then we heard the booms. Is it true? Did you kill him?"

"I… I don't know, but James doesn't think so," Garrett said. The talk of explosions reminded him Apep wasn't the only one in the basement. His father was there too.

Pete cocked his head. "James? James knows about this too?"

"James isn't who you think he is," Garrett answered distantly, his thoughts on Phillip.

"So, he's not a dick?" Pete asked with a smile.

"Hey! Pete. What the hell is going on with you?" Lenny asked suddenly, turning around and jogging backward to face him.

"Huh? Going on with me… what?"

"Your glasses, what the hell?"

Pete started mumbling in a soft whisper.

Rabbits in the garden
Rabbits in greens
Rabbits run from the farmer
Rabbits run free

Lenny held his hands out. "What the hell was that?"

Pete hesitated. "That was a nursery rhyme by A. O. Schafer. My mother taught it to me when I was little to help me with my *r*'s."

"Strange time to practice your speech, Pete," Lenny said.

"Look, while you and Garrett were gone, I developed some kind of super-vision."

"What!? Come on, seriously?" Lenny asked.

Janis shrugged. "And I can see in the dark like it's daytime."

"No way!" Lenny said, exchanging looks with Garrett.

"It's the God Stones," Paul said. "They change you. How do you guys feel now?" he asked, looking at Lenny.

Lenny shrugged. "I don't know – too freaked out to be sure of anything."

Garrett felt something. First, he felt it during his test before he ever laid eyes on the God Stones. But Apep had them at that point, and they were out in the world. Somehow through his focus he had found their power, using it to slow time around him. Since then he had been exposed. Even now in the distant part of his mind he could feel the ghost of a headache and his body tingled with this strange electricity or energy. He imagined it was like how someone felt right before they were struck with lightning.

"I don't think I feel anything," David said disappointedly, slowing to a walk. "And can we please stop with the running?"

"I thought you'd never ask," Pete said, stopping to lean on his knees.

"You boys call this running?" Paul laughed.

"Pete, I still don't understand, what's with the nursery rhyme?" Garrett asked.

"I was kind of hoping the God Stones would have fixed my speech too. I would gladly give up super-vision just to talk normal," Pete said softly.

Janis took his hand in hers. "Petey, I already miss the glasses, so don't be so quick to change the cutest thing that makes you who you are."

Pete blushed.

"I wouldn't change anything about you, Pete," Janis said.

"Me either, Petey," Lenny said, winking wryly as he prodded him with his elbow.

They made their way onto the railroad tracks and followed them down past the sub sandwich shop until they were behind the bank. The bizarre orange lightning continued to flash and crackle, sizzling across the sky, a spiderweb of brilliance inside rolling clouds as black as the space between stars. The steady rain was beginning to pick up momentum, becoming sheets of water falling in waves.

"This is the spot," Lenny announced.

David peered down the steep bank toward the dark, churning water below. “Oh, hell no!” David backed away from the embankment as if merely standing there might tempt the Sangamon River to lash out and yank him into its murky depths. “Hey, Lenny, how are we supposed to make this climb down in the dark? It’s going to be a mudslide. I can’t even see the tunnel from here and if we miss… if we land in that water, it’s over. You won’t be able to see which way is up and there is only like two blocks before the broken dam.” David’s voice rose in pitch as he finished, and he began to breathe hard.

“Calm down, David, we can do this,” Garrett said, placing a hand on his shoulder.

“We don’t have a choice and we don’t have any more time,” Lenny said, turning to Pete, who was babbling on about Abraham Lincoln to Breanne and Janis. “I’ll go first. Pete, give me a flashlight.”

Pete, not missing a beat in his Lincoln conversation, reached into his pack and fished out a light, tossing it to Lenny. “Since Mr. Offutt went out of business all suddenly, it left old Lincoln without a job, so with no income he decides to enlist in the Black Hawk War.”

Lenny, Paul, and Garrett peered over the edge of the embankment.

Lenny pointed the flashlight down the slope. “Even with the light I still can’t see exactly where the culvert is, but I think it should be right here. When I get down to the culvert, I’ll flash the light so you know where you need to slide down at. Guys, you need to slide onto the top of the culvert. If you start to lose control, grab a tree, a root, anything, but yeah… don’t fall in. The river is wicked through here and it don’t care how good a swimmer you are.”

Garrett turned to Paul and made a poor attempt to wipe the rain off his face with the wet sleeve of his dobok. “He’s not kidding, a lot of people have died in this river. I would rate this somewhere between stupid and crazy.”

Paul nodded and smiled.

Garrett raised an eyebrow at the unexpected reaction. He was suddenly reminded, he really had no idea who this man was. He turned back to Lenny and grabbed the flashlight out of his hand. “Let me do this, Lenny.”

Lenny frowned at Garrett and snatched the flashlight back away from his friend. "Are you nuts! Oh, that would be just great wouldn't it? Our leader, and the world's only hope, falls in the river trying to find the culvert. Then what? I got to destroy the alien? I don't think so."

"Um, did you just say destroy the alien?" Paul asked.

"Um, sure did, big guy. That's the plan – destroy the alien before magic psycho murderer wakes him up and they start swapping stories of the old days, including how to put that Sound Eye thingamabob together." Lenny leaned out over the edge and studied the embankment for a second then turned back to the group, hooking a thumb toward Garrett. "My boy here is going to use that sword to hack the alien's head off," Lenny said with a confident nod, then turned back to the embankment – and jumped over the side.

Garrett and Paul ran forward.

Garrett watched as Paul's headlamp illuminated Lenny just in time to see his feet go out from under him. He landed on his ass, continuing to slide, the leaves and muck offering him no purchase as he scrambled to find something, anything to slow his descent.

"Lenny!" Garrett shouted helplessly.

Halfway down, Lenny's body jolted as he flailed for a grip. His fingers wrapped around a small sapling as the momentum twisted him onto his stomach. Even with the new handhold, gravity continued to yank him toward the dark water. The young sapling flexed all the way over, straightening like a stiff rope. He didn't stop; couldn't stop. Instead, he continued down the embankment toward the river – toward his death. His hand slid down the sapling, ripping tiny budding branches from the thin trunk. As the end of the sapling neared, it became thinner and thinner.

"God, Lenny, don't let go!" Garrett shouted.

Lenny twisted his hand, looping the tiny sapling like a rope. Then finally – he stopped.

"You okay?" Paul shouted.

For a long moment, Lenny lay there facedown in the mud.

Finally, he turned himself over onto his side and, with his free hand, flicked the switch on the flashlight and peered toward the culvert. "I'm good. Almost on top of the culvert," he shouted back. He let go of the sapling, sending it catapulting upright as he slid down the few remaining feet, landing precariously on top of the protruding concrete tube.

Carefully Lenny turned, pointed his light, and yelled back up the embankment. "Alright, guys, aim for my light and, uh… try and grab some branches or roots on the way down – it's pretty slick."

"You think?" Garrett shouted back.

"Look, I will scooch all the way to the back edge of the culvert to give the next person room to land and try to keep them from going over."

"Well, that's reassuring," Garrett said.

"I'll go next," Paul said. Then with no further hesitation, he slipped over the embankment, rolled to his stomach, and slid toward Lenny's light like he had done this maneuver a hundred times before. Finding the top of the culvert with his feet, he landed into a perfectly balanced squat next to Lenny. "I'm down," he shouted.

"Okay, Paul, go ahead and swing down into the tunnel and wait there!" Garrett said.

Paul disappeared over the side.

"Paul's in," Lenny said. "Next."

"So, with the Black Hawk War over, Lincoln was discharged," Pete said, still explaining to the girls what he had learned in the journal. "He collected his pay for his service and headed back to Petersburg. According to history, he traveled with a companion. But history was wrong! I know, I know – hard to believe, right? Turns out, he and the other soldier he was traveling with actually parted ways in Havana, Illinois. He told everyone he made the last part of the trip, about twenty-three miles from Havana to New Salem, on his own. But here is where it gets interesting. According to his journal, he stumbled upon an injured Potawatomi boy. I'm not sure how young he was, but Lincoln referred to him as a boy. He could have killed him outright and probably been a hero for it, but seeing he was injured, young Abraham decides instead to help him! He makes a fire, treats the boy's wounds, and cares for him, providing him food and water."

"That's crazy!" Breanne said, huddling close to the tree they were sheltering under in a failing attempt to stay dry. "That would have put Lincoln at risk of being charged with treason."

"Yeah, for sure," Pete said. "It was a risk – if anyone stumbled upon them, they both would have likely been killed. Like you said, Lincoln for treason and the boy – well, just being Native American would have been enough, and not only that but he also had participated in the war." Pete pulled his shirt up, wiping his soaked face. "And it gets better! I don't know how long Lincoln stayed with him, but at some point, the young boy thought he was going to die and decides to confide a secret he is sworn to keep. He tells Lincoln of a cave leading to a temple close to New Salem. He explained that for hundreds of years it had been his people's responsibility to protect the secret and now he was the last one left who knew of the location. He told Lincoln that it could never be found and asked him to promise to ensure no one ever finds it. Then he tells Lincoln what's inside!"

"Pete, finish your story when we get inside," Garrett said, motioning with a wave of his hand. "You're up."

"Yeah, but Garrett you need to hear this too. When I deciphered the other half of Lincoln's journal, I found out what's inside the temple! I have been waiting all day to tell you," he said excitedly.

"Pete, I already know what's in there, and I know what I have to do. What I need you to do is get us past the traps. Can you do that?"

"Yeah, I think I can. But you know?! How?"

"Yeah, James told me."

Pete hesitated, staring at his friend expectantly, but when no further explanation came, he steeled himself for the descent over the embankment. Sitting on his ass with his feet extended out in front of him, he looked as if he were about to go down a playground slide. Then he frowned, reconsidering, and rolled onto his stomach. Right before he pushed off, he looked at Garrett. "And you really believe that's what we will find in the temple?"

"We're about to find out," Garrett said, smiling weakly.

Pete disappeared over the side.

"David, you go next and then I will send the girls down."

All the blood drained from David's face and he looked as though he might hurl. "Garrett, I'm not sure I can do this."

The light below flashed, signaling Pete was safely inside the tunnel.

"Piece of cake, man," Garrett said, slapping him on the back.

Water beaded on David's mustache, which did nothing to hide his terror. He sucked in a deep breath and eased himself off over the side. The path down was getting more and more slippery as each of them took their turn and the rain increased. Once in position, David could barely keep himself from sliding. "Garrett, I don't know. I got a bad feeling about this!" His eyes pleaded with Garrett like those of a death row inmate hoping for a stay of execution. But no reprieve came.

Garrett nodded. "Just let go, David."

David swallowed hard – and let go. He flew down the slope much faster than even Garrett expected. In a pure state of panic, David began flailing and grabbing for anything he could find, but it was no use – by the time he reached the culvert he was completely out of control.

"Lenny, he's coming too fast!" Garrett shouted, illuminating David with Pete's flashlight. Oh, dear god, there would be no way for Lenny to stop him from going over.

David *was* coming too fast. Lenny watched helplessly as David barreled toward him, screaming. It only took a split-second for Lenny to conclude there would be no stopping David's momentum. They would both be thrown from the culvert and into the waiting abyss below. But a second was all Lenny needed. From his squatting position, he jumped straight up into the air just as David reached him.

In the dim light of the flashlight beam, Lenny caught a glimpse of the terror on David's face as he scrambled helplessly, trying and failing to dig his fingers and heels into the soft earth, but no hold could be found. He sailed under Lenny and off the culvert – into the empty night.

"David! No!" Lenny shouted, landing safely back on top of the culvert only to turn and lunge forward in hopes of making a desperate grab for David's hand. But he didn't even come close, nearly losing his balance and almost sending himself into the currents below.

David vanished over the edge.

Lenny closed his eyes in a slow, disbelieving blink.

"Oh my god! David! Lenny, is he okay?" Garrett shouted down the slope.

Lenny leaned out over the edge of the culvert to search the water, his heart sinking. He knew it was unlikely, but maybe, just maybe, if David had fallen close enough to the bank, he could find something to grab before being washed down river and over the dam. *Jesus! Or sucked under by the undertow,* Lenny thought.

But nothing prepared him for what he saw when he peered over the edge. David was right there, suspended just outside the opening to the tunnel. At first, Lenny couldn't comprehend what he was seeing. David was somehow floating. Then he noticed the arm protruding from inside the tunnel. Lenny blinked. But it was still there, an outstretched arm and a black fist gripping David's collar.

"Damn, bro!" Lenny said.

"Ah… can you… pull me in… please?" David said, his feet dangling.

Paul had somehow reached out and snatched David in mid-fall – with one hand. Lenny gawked for a few more seconds, then David disappeared into the tunnel.

"Lenny! Do you see him?!" Garrett's voice rang out, frantic through the rain.

"Um, yeah, he's good."

"Good?" Garrett shouted back down.

"Yeah… good. He's in. But we need to do something different to get you three down here, Garrett!" Lenny said, yelling louder now just to be heard through the pouring rain and increasing thunder.

"Okay, don't worry, I have a plan!" Garrett responded.

"Well, if it includes me catching you, forget it!"

"We are going to make a human chain. Janis first, then Bre, then me."

"I don't see how this is going to work when we get to you…" Lenny started so say. But it was too late – Janis was already over the edge and Breanne was right behind her.

Janis didn't have far to slide once she let go of Breanne's hand. She still came quick, but Lenny managed to grab her and steady her before she lost her balance. Breanne, on the other hand, had an additional body length to go. She let go and slid fast down the embankment toward Lenny. He lunged for her but couldn't hold on. She slid over the culvert to her waist. Lenny lunged again, grabbing her wrist.

"Lenny! Don't let me go!" she said.

"You're okay. I have you. Just slide down the rest of the way, hang from your hands, and drop in." Slowly Lenny eased her hands to the top of the culvert, where she hung before disappearing inside the tunnel.

"Bre okay?" Garrett asked.

"She's good! But, bro, I mean it when I say I can't catch you, and you're going to be coming in way too fast for sure!"

"Go inside, Lenny! I don't want to hit you when I come down."

"This won't work! Maybe Paul could catch you?"

"Just go in! I don't want to risk knocking you into the river!" Garrett shouted.

"Fine! Stubborn ass!" he said, swinging easily into the mouth of the drainage tunnel where everyone waited.

Garrett lay facedown, firmly grasping a small tree. He knew when he let go, it was going to be on. Sucking in a deep breath, he released the tree.

Garrett flew down the embankment like a bobsled on ice. He had no idea when it would come, but he knew it wouldn't take long – only heartbeats. He would feel his body separate from the ground as he went airborne off the embankment and into the river. He reached back over his shoulder and drew the sword his father had given him. In the space of a gasp he realized he might be making the most epic of bonehead moves. *I really hope I don't break an ancient sword needed to prevent the end of the world.*

He spun the sword in his hand so that he could stab down, but the sword was too long and he couldn't get it to bite in – instead it just twisted as it raked down the embankment. He realized he needed to put some space between himself and the ground, so he pushed himself onto his knees. He reached above his head, both hands gripping the ancient sword as he slid backward. Mustering all his force, he thrust the sword down. The ground went out from under him as the sword sank deep into the earth, not stopping until it reached the hilt.

Garrett stopped sliding with an abrupt jolt that ripped his left hand from the hilt, leaving all his weight hanging from the other. Slowly his hand began to slip. He looked down but could not see the culvert, only dark churning water that was far too close. He looked left and saw nothing but the dirt embankment falling away to darkness. He looked right and there, above his right shoulder, was the culvert. He had missed it altogether and was now positioned below it and out of reach.

Lenny's head poked out from the culvert. "You missed, bro," he said evenly.

"Really? I hadn't noticed! Thank god you are here to point that out. How about a little help, Lenny?! I'm… slipping."

"Well, don't. That wouldn't be good," Lenny said, assessing the situation.

"Wow! Thank… you… captain obvious!" Garrett shouted. He was only a few feet away from the opening, but water was already spilling out, making standing close to the edge risky for those inside. If Lenny tried to lower himself, he would be washed out into the river.

"Paul, can you get him?"

Paul poked his head out, his headlamp illuminating Garrett's dire situation. "I'll try." Then without hesitation he lowered himself into the rushing outflow of water, and, hanging from one hand, he swung out to Garrett. Garrett reached, but his position was awkward, and he missed.

"You have to switch hands then reach for me!" Paul shouted as water poured over his body. It was as if he were holding himself suspended under a waterfall with one hand.

Garrett swallowed hard and thrust upward with his left hand, grabbing the hilt of the sword. He managed to take hold, but then the sword began to pull out from the soft ground slowly losing purchase. "Not… good!" he managed.

Paul swung again, reaching out with his left hand as Garrett let go with his right. Straining, he reached Paul and they locked hands to wrists just as the sword slipped free from the earth. As Paul swung back, Garrett sheathed the sword then reached up to the edge of the culvert. Instantly Garrett was greeted with the rush of water. The deluge blasted him relentlessly, threatening to push him into the river. Thankfully, Lenny and David were there pulling him up into the culvert. Once Garrett was safely inside, Paul pulled himself up with little effort.

Finally, they were all inside.

Garrett gasped heavily, his hands on his knees.

"See! I knew you'd be fine! Now, catch your breath later, man. We got to move. The water is rising fast," Lenny said.

"Yeah, I don't think we can stay in here long," Pete said.

From deep within the tunnel a flashlight clicked on. Then another, and still another.

Everyone squinted into the bright beams.

They weren't alone.

17

Rise

Wednesday, April 6 – God Stones Day 1
Petersburg, Illinois

Two police units arrived at what was left of Garrett's home to find the flames burning out of control. With the whole house collapsed, there was nothing they could do but watch it burn.

Glen wiped his eyes and staggered out the back door of his house next door.

"If there was anyone in there, heaven help them because we sure can't," Officer McMullan said, his thumbs tucked into his gun belt. "Radio it in, Dan. Tell dispatch not to bother sending fire and rescue – there's nothing here that can be saved, and the rain will put it out."

"Car three to dispatch, we're on the scene but there's no hope here. Leave fire and rescue in place up town. No use pulling any of the units off what they got going for this. It's a lost cause. Over."

"Dispatch to three. Copy that. Athens fire department is in route to assist up on the square, but even with their help we would be hard-pressed to free up an engine. I will keep you posted. Over."

Lightning fractured across the sky like thin ice under a heavy load.

Officer McMullan pulled the hood up on his rain jacket and looked to the sky. "What the hell do you make of that orange-colored lightning? That's damn strange."

"I don't know, but with the north side of the town square on fire and now the Turek place, we need all the rain we can get. This is turning into—"

"Help me! Police!" Glen shouted from his backyard.

Both officers turned to see a man in a bloody cotton shirt and a pair of boxers staggering toward them.

"Glen? That you?" Officer McMullan asked, clicking on his flashlight and directing it toward the bloody man's face.

Glen shielded his eyes. "My wife. She's in… um… well… shit. She's in the basement and she's unconscious," he said, realizing too late what he had done. Jennifer wasn't the only thing in his basement.

Officer Brown reached across his chest and depressed the button on the handheld clipped to his shoulder. "Dispatch, we're going to need an ambulance at two-seventeen North Fourth Street. Over."

"What the hell happened here, Glen?" Officer McMullan asked.

"James Turek did this to my face! And his mother – Elaine – she beat my Jennifer unconscious! They came through the basement wall! The goddamned basement wall!" Glen said, his arms flailing wildly.

"Elaine Turek came through your basement wall and assaulted your wife?" Officer Brown asked.

"Yes! And her boy broke my freaking nose!" he said, trying to keep his head tilted back.

"Mr. Patterson, have you been drinking or participating in the use of recreational drugs this evening?" Officer Brown asked, clicking on his own small flashlight and shining it into Glen's pupils.

Glen squeezed his eyes shut and flinched away. "No! I'm not on drugs and I'm not lying! What, are you guys blind? Just look at me! And get those damn lights out of my face!"

"Now just settle down, Glen," Officer McMullan said, keeping his flashlight trained on Glen's face. "You didn't have another altercation with your wife tonight, did you?"

"No! I already told you! The Tureks did this!"

"You're sure?" Officer Brown asked, raising his eyebrows.

"Yes, I'm sure! Come on, I'll show you!" he shouted in frustration as he turned back toward his house. Then he paused, considering once more the weed in his basement. He knew it didn't matter though; his Jennifer needed help and if that meant going to jail, well, that was just too bad.

"Hang on just a second, Glen," Officer Brown said. "Are James and Elaine still in the basement?"

"Well, no, not now… they escaped!"

Officer Brown leaned in close to Officer McMullan, his face pasted with skepticism. "I'll check out this basement – you want to stay here and monitor this?"

"Sounds good."

"Alright, Mr. Patterson, let's go see this basement," Officer Brown said.

Deep below the burning debris of Garrett's home something stirred. At first, Apep didn't understand where he was or what had happened, but slowly the memory came. *Bricks, an explosion, pain. How long was I out?*

He had felt something was wrong and reached for the power of the God Stones – the Sentheye. It came to him like a cold chill, liquid ice crawling into him. It was instant, and consuming, but so had been the explosion. He hadn't had time to fully protect himself in an envelope of the Sentheye, but it was enough to live. He picked his head up, peeling his face from the coagulated puddle of blood on the concrete floor. He felt something heavy across his back, and he could see burning rubble all around him.

He closed his eyes and focused his mind. He felt pain but focused past it. He felt wetness, *his leg, probably blood.* He focused past that too. Ribs were broken, maybe even his back, but he set all that aside and focused. He had to know where Garrett was – how far he had gotten while he had lain here unconscious on the floor. He reached out with the Sentheye, opening a line of communication through thought.

Where are you? he asked.

We are at the river in the tunnel, an answer came.

Good, he responded, then changed his focus. He let the horrible pain come back to him, and to it he sent the Sentheye, drawing it from the God Stones, only to release it into his damaged flesh and bone. In only seconds, his bones began to heal, and seconds after that his flesh began to mend. Healing one's self was the most difficult task for any mage, and Apep was no exception to this. This was the third time tonight he'd had to use the Sentheye on himself. He felt weak, drained, and was longing for sleep, but this was no place for rest and no time for sleep. He pulled again, extracting more shadow – more Sentheye. The God Stones responded, refreshing his body, pushing away his need to rest – for now. His fingers tingled and his head ached slightly. The constant use of so much power, he supposed.

The chunk of flooring lying across his back fractured as he spoke an ancient word of power and gestured in a specific way with his fingers. Apep rolled to his side, pushing the rest of the debris off his hip. He sat up and sighed. It was time to leave this place and claim what was his.

Glen and Officer Brown made their way down the stairs into Glen's weed-growing operation. Officer Brown led the way, his revolver thrust out in front of him in one hand and a flashlight in the other. He shot the beam around the room, the gun pointing wherever he aimed the light. Even with the power off, it only took a few seconds for realization to hit.

Officer Brown whistled.

Glen swallowed hard. "I know… I know, you got me, okay? I grow weed!" Glen said, holding his hands up submissively, then pointing across the room. "But look! Over there!"

"Boy, Glen, you're in deep shit for this," Officer Brown said, mistrust seeping into his voice as he eyeballed the bloody man. "This is way more than you can smoke yourself, and even growing that much is illegal."

"I know, listen, please forget the weed and just look at my Jennifer," Glen said. He watched as the officer panned his flashlight beam in the direction Glen was pointing, illuminating a large hole in the basement wall. As they made their way forward, Officer Brown finally noticed Jennifer on the floor. She was moaning but at least she seemed to be coming to. "There! You see! Elaine did this to her. And James broke my nose!"

The officer ran forward and squatted next to Jennifer. "Officer Brown to dispatch, we have something strange going on at two-fifteen North Fourth Street. Send backup! Over."

"Dan, did you mean two-seventeen? Over," came the dispatch operator's voice.

"No, I'm at the neighbors' now and someone has tunneled into Glen Patterson's basement and assaulted both Glen and his wife. There is a marijuana grow operation here – could have something to do with it. Over."

"Ten-four, Dan. We have more units on the way. You sit tight and stay out of that tunnel until backup arrives. Over."

"Roger that!"

Officer McMullan's voice cracked over the radio. "Dan, I'm on my way down there. Over."

From his seated position on the basement floor, Apep appraised the tunnel. "Very clever, Tureks – very clever indeed." Pushing a chunk of burning floor joist out of the way allowed him to finally stand and face the massive chunk of concrete porch blocking the way. In an easy motion, he stretched his arms out in front of himself and placed his palms together as if preparing to dive into a pool. Apep began chanting the ancient words, "Ray doeeshozmue, rah ak ff esh!" Then, with a deliberate motion, he pulled his hands apart, opening his arms wide. The concrete slab split into two pieces, pushing away to both his right and left until a void formed that was wide enough for him to walk through.

Apep had only taken a few steps when voices found him. Continuing forward he reached back, lifting his hood into place.

Apep peered out from the shadows to find Officer Brown kneeling next to Jennifer. "What was that?" Officer Brown asked, standing back up and drawing his Glock. He took aim at the tunnel.

"I don't know, but the last time someone came out of there, I got my face broke!" Glen said, too loud.

"Who's there?" Officer Brown demanded.

Apep stepped into Glen's basement. "Good evening, Officer Brown."

"Freeze right there! Don't move! Don't even breathe!" the officer demanded, training his weapon with a rail-mounted light on Apep's face. "I… I know you. You're—"

Apep cut him off. "I'm afraid we'll have to skip the formalities, Officer, and get right to it," he said, taking an aggressive step toward Officer Brown.

"I said, don't you move!"

Apep took another step, closing half the distance.

Officer Brown pulled the trigger. The hammer dropped onto the firing pin, and the round backfired. Simultaneously every round in the magazine detonated in the same instant. The gun exploded in Officer Brown's hand with the force of a hand grenade. Officer Brown fell dead to the floor, never realizing the impossibility of what had just happened.

Glen had stayed far back, his fear saving him from the shrapnel. He began to weep as he put his hands up in the air high above his head and groaned. "Plllleeeaaassseee don't hurt us."

Apep frowned and shook his head. "This world is so weak, it is no wonder humans were banished from Karelia long ago." He reached out with nothing more than a feeble amount of the Sentheye, twisting his hand slowly in the air. Glen's head twisted on his shoulders until finally it could twist no further. Glen turned off like water from a tap.

Jennifer, who had regained consciousness at the sound of the officer's exploding gun, managed a scream.

Apep looked at her with a sorrowful expression. "Would you like me to spare you?"

Jennifer nodded hysterically through the bloody tears.

"Of course you would."

"Stop!" Officer McMullan shouted, as he descended the last of the stairs. "You freeze right there! You so much as twitch and you die!"

Apep sighed. "Oh, good, I can watch you blow your face off too."

The officer frowned, quickly appraising his partner's hands and face. It must have been enough to put together that using his sidearm was a bad plan because he holstered his weapon and drew his nightstick. "Apep!"

"Ah, another Keeper! How delightful."

He rushed Apep, swinging at his face.

Apep caught the stick in his hand, broke it, and shoved the remaining piece through the eye socket of the officer, driving it deep into his skull.

As the officer collapsed, lifeless, to the floor, Apep turned in time see the woman scrambling frantically on her hands and knees across the concrete, trying desperately to get away. She made it to the opening in the wall and scrambled inside like a rat scurrying for cover. That's what all humans were, he thought – *rats*. He could call the Sentheye and pull her back to him. Instead, he just watched her go. It wasn't because he felt sorry for her, or a desire to be merciful. It was quite the contrary, but he felt a sense of urgency to go and she was insignificant – just like a rat.

He walked up the stairs to the landing, where he paused before exiting the Pattersons' home. A small child stood at the top of the short set of stairs leading into the house. He looked terrified. Apep looked up at the boy, met his eyes, and smiled. "I allowed your pathetic mother to live. Someday, if you somehow survive what's to come, find me… and thank me."

The only acknowledgement that the boy even understood was the movement of his eyes as they widened.

Once outside, Apep turned his attention to the two police cruisers and the ambulance that were screaming down Fourth Street with sirens blazing.

"No more wasting time. Rah ak ff esh oz eshmue eshoz eshflah!" he shouted, as he raised his hands and all three vehicles lifted off the street. Their fuel tanks exploded, engulfing them and their occupants in an instant inferno. The vehicles landed hard back onto the street, both cruisers veering into the ditch as the ambulance careened in the other direction, crashing into the burning rubble of Garrett's home.

"No more wasting time," Apep repeated to no one.

18

A Bad Idea

Wednesday, April 6 – God Stones Day 1
Rural Chiapas State, Mexico

Sarah wiped her sleeve across her forehead. For the past hour or more she had been awkwardly testing her yoga pose dexterity as she shifted her body to and fro, systematically clearing the bones and other strata from the bottom of the shaft. Exhausted as she was, her inner drive to know consumed her. *What was this strange lid? How did the giant skulls fit into the picture? And the strange structure itself – how was it created? If not carved in place, then how was it built?* The questions persisted, begging to be answered, but each clue only added to the enigma. She knew she wouldn't understand it until she found out what was underneath the lid. The answer to all the mysteries was right under her feet – it had to be.

She had already filled bucket after bucket, each one hoisted topside where the material inside was no doubt being methodically cataloged by Fredy and Andrés. These bones weren't those of giants, they were just bones of normal-sized humans. Sacrifices. Normally, Sarah would conclude sacrifices of this nature were offerings to the rain god Chaahk, but that didn't fit. For the love of it, she couldn't understand why whoever went to all this trouble would plug a hole meant to offer sacrifices to the underworld. And why at the bottom of the shaft? Why not cover it at the top? This place… it didn't fit – it didn't make sense. It just didn't feel like this hole was for Aztec or Maya water rituals. No, this was for something else.

She bent to pick up another bone. *If only you could talk to me. Tell me what you saw. Tell me how you ended up in this dark, cold place.* Whether it was the thought of the bone she held, alive and weighed down with flesh, or the cold clamminess of the shaft, a shiver grabbed hold of her and raised goosebumps on the skin of her forearms.

Suddenly, Fredy's voice crackled over the radio. "Sarah."

Sarah's heart jolted in her chest as if the dead themselves had shouted her name. She flinched upright, smacking her head on the bucket. "Christ! Dammit!" she said, then rubbing her head with one hand she pressed the button on the radio with the other. "My god, Fredy, you scared me half to death."

"Sorry, Sarah. Are you ready to come up? It is getting late and you must be very tired."

Sarah stood and stretched her back. Beneath her feet the bones shifted slightly, and the toe of her boot slid forward awkwardly. She grimaced, keenly aware of the damage she might be causing to the fragile bones. She tried to ease her foot back, but it was wedged in tight. *Dammit.* Fredy was right, she was tired. She could hear the concern in his voice. No matter how bad she wanted to see what was under this plug, she knew she wouldn't be able to get it cleared tonight, and even if she could, she wasn't sure how she was going to remove it. Would they even be able to retract it? How thick was it? If they couldn't remove it, could they bring in a jackhammer of some kind and break through it?

She could just imagine telling Charles, *So yeah, we jackhammered through a priceless, ancient stone lid. I mean, we had to see what was underneath, right?* She laughed to herself. *Charles… I can't wait to tell you about this!* she thought.

Sarah sighed. "Yeah, Fredy, let's call it a day. Give me a minute to tie back on, and I'll signal when I'm ready to start the climb."

"Standing by. Oh, Sarah? Andrés says be sure to triple-check your rigging."

There had been some argument when Sarah had decided to remove her rig while she worked. Fredy didn't like that Andrés wouldn't be there to check her rig when it was time to come back up. But in the end, and to no one's surprise, Fredy lost the argument.

"Jesus Christ, Fredy, I promise. I'll double-check, just hang on," Sarah said, her face splitting in a grin. She wasn't going anywhere until she figured out what the hell her foot was hanging up on.

Fredy sighed. "Alright, standing by then."

She moved her other foot methodically, careful of its placement. The floor, or suspected lid, wasn't completely cleared of strata, and she didn't want to do any more damage if she could help it. She tried to pull up and back on the wedged foot again. This time the bone her foot was caught under shifted up oddly, unnaturally, like it was attached to something at one end. It felt… wrong. Her foot was free now, so she slid it back under the object and moved her foot against it again, and it moved up then dropped back down. She searched for the cause of the anomaly, and with the help of her headlamp, found it protruding from the partially cleared material in the center of the lid. *What the hell?* She knelt and began clearing the area around what appeared to be some type of mechanism recessed into the stone floor. Sarah paused, giving the device a long, hard look. *Who in the hell were these people?*

"Sarah? Are you secure?" Fredy asked.

Sarah double-checked her knot and sucked in a deep breath. "Stand by, Fredy. I've got something here." She looked back down at the lever. *Girl, this is a bad idea.* She positioned herself over the lever and squatted down, taking hold of it with both hands.

19

Not Alone

Wednesday, April 6 – God Stones Day 1
Petersburg, Illinois

The feeling of safety from finally having everyone inside the tunnel turned out to be fleeting. Three separate beams of light shone from deep inside the culvert.

Garrett waded forward, maneuvering around everyone. The water was already over his feet and moving fast down the tunnel. "Who's there?"

"Who do you think? You lying coward!" Jack said, forced into a hunch as he sloshed forward.

Garrett's stomach tightened.

"When you didn't show up, I wasn't surprised. I always knew you were afraid to fight me, Garrett!" Jack said, stopping directly in front of him, his flashlight pointing at his face. "You didn't think I would figure it out, did you? The book led you here. I already know it's a map, and whatever it leads to is mine. Right after we settle up and I kick your ass!"

"So what, Jack, you had to bring your big brother and his thugs with you?" Garrett asked, squinting past Jack's light to find Danny holding his own flashlight in one hand and something else in the other. If anything, Danny was far more of a bully than Jack and probably twice his size. Garrett didn't know who the other two guys were, but they were older than Jack, so it was safe to assume they must be friends of Danny. All and all, this was about the worst possible time for Jack to show up. They needed to get past this tunnel before the water rose and before Apep caught up to them.

Garrett drew in a breath. But he knew something else. He couldn't run, and he was all out of excuses. This thing with Jack had to end, here and now. Garrett looked past Jack. "What's up, Danny? Figured you were still in jail. You come to fight your baby brother's battles?"

Jack's lip curled up. "They're here to make sure you fight me this time, chickenshit. So, let me tell you how this is going to go. First, I'm going to beat your ass," he said, punching his fist into his palm. "Then your loser friends are going to give me that book and tell me everything they know about it, including how to open the entrance, or we're" – he hooked a thumb over his shoulder – "going to give all them a beating too."

The water was rising fast, almost to Garrett's ankles now.

Paul stepped forward next to Garrett. "We need to move. If the water continues to rise at this rate we're going be swept out. You want me to handle this?"

Garrett shook his head. "Thanks, but this is mine to deal with."

Jack laughed. "You going to deal with me, are you?"

"Alright, Jack, let these guys through so they can get to work finding the entrance before the water rises so high no one finds it," Garrett said, pointing past Jack.

Jack held out his arms. "Whatever, man. Just don't try anything or I'll have these guys start working everybody over."

Paul rolled his eyes.

Everyone hugged the curved wall single file and made their way past Jack and his thugs, leaving only Garrett and Lenny in the mouth of the opening. Lenny leaned in close to Garrett, his brow wrinkled in concern. "I don't like this, man. I'm not leaving you."

"Lenny, you got to get down there and show them the bricks you found. They can't get inside without you."

"Garrett, listen, I love that you're going to face this, but they're not going to fight fair," Lenny whispered, nodding at Jack.

Garrett smiled weakly. "My kung fu is better than these losers' kung fu any day of the week."

The worried crease on Lenny's forehead only deepened. Even for Lenny, this was no time for jokes.

Garrett leaned in close and lowered his voice to a whisper, "I need to do this, Lenny. If I don't… I'll always be afraid. Just go, man, I will be right behind you."

Lenny nodded reluctantly, making his way down the tunnel.

When Lenny tried to get past Jack, Jack made sure to shoulder Lenny hard, checking him into the concrete wall of the culvert. "Good job, Lenny – way to know your place."

Lenny pushed himself off the wall. "I would kick your punk ass myself, but I don't want to deprive my boy here of the fun he's about to have with your face. God, I'm going to enjoy watching Garrett kick the crap out of you!"

Jack doubled up a fist and punched it into his hand. "Don't worry. This won't take long," he said, pointing a finger in Lenny's face. "Your turn next!"

"You just don't get it, do you, Jack? It's like the lights are on but it's just a big dimly lit space up there."

Jack frowned, clearly confused. He turned back toward Garrett, raising his fists.

Garrett didn't understand why, but he felt a strange sense of calm wash over him. Maybe it was because he had just accepted that this was inevitable and had inwardly come to terms with it, releasing him of his fear. Or, maybe after all he had witnessed and learned that evening, his emotions were just depleted. Whatever it was, he felt oddly relaxed in this looming moment.

Paul started forward with ill intentions toward Danny and his two thugs, but Lenny grabbed his arm. "No, Paul. Don't."

Every muscle in Paul's body flexed, but he stopped. "Why?" he asked incredulously.

"Let Garrett deal with him," Lenny said.

"Yeah, I agree, this has been a long time coming," Pete said.

"A long, long time." David nodded.

"They're not going to fight him one-on-one, Lenny," Breanne said pleadingly.

"I know," he said, maintaining his grip on Paul's arm.

"So, what then? We're just supposed to look for this secret passage, and what? Hope he doesn't get beaten to death?" Paul asked, through gritted teeth, clearly ready to throw down.

"Hell, no!" Lenny responded with a smile. "Rising water or not, I wouldn't miss this for the world. Besides, if these dicks decide to get froggy and jump… we jump." Lenny said, letting go of Paul's arm.

Paul nodded reluctantly, "Well, let's get close as we can then." The group worked their way closer and positioned themselves right behind Danny and his thugs, everyone vying for a space to see in the circular culvert.

Garrett's heart beat against his chest. No more running, no more standing by and letting it happen – letting *Jack* happen. Win or lose, this was going to end now. "Jack?" he said in a low voice, barely audible above the roar of water.

"You say something, chickenshit?"

"I truly hope you can swim these currents in the dark."

Jack turned to his brother and laughed.

Danny and his crew started laughing.

Those with flashlights shined them toward the two boys as they squared off. He really wished Bre and Lenny weren't watching, but it hardly mattered now. His back was to the river, and his only way forward was through Jack.

The corner of Jack's lip curled as he sloshed forward and threw his famous roundhouse punch.

Garrett watched the sweeping roundhouse coming at his jawline with a strange detachment. Almost like the punch was not coming at his face but at someone else's, and he was just an onlooker like everyone else. Then, suddenly his focus changed, and the trail appeared, blocking out his vision as an intense pressure began to slowly build from somewhere deep in his head. The world slowed around him as time passed at a different pace in his mind.

Just like with the three concrete blocks during his test. It was as if he had all the time in the world and a fist weren't on a bone-cracking collision course with his face. Garrett found himself in a slowed moment of time, contemplating the many ways he could counter the punch.

Everyone watching wouldn't understand why Jack was throwing a slow-motion punch, nor why Garrett was just standing there.

As the punch closed in, two things occurred to Garrett. The first was that he had somehow found the focus again and slowed time around him, at least slowed Jack.

The second thing that occurred to Garrett was that he didn't want to beat Jack with the magic stuff from the God Stones. He wanted to do this on his own, with his *own* abilities. He shook his head no and mouthed the words, "Not like this, Lenny."

Then he heard Breanne's voice, full of panic, but it was slowed too. Not as slow as Jack's fist but slower than normal. "What's he saying, Lenny?!"

"He's not going to use it! He's not going to use the focus!" Lenny answered.

"What? What do you mean?" she asked, but Lenny didn't answer – he just stared. They all just stared.

Garrett listened to the voices distort as they reached him, and he wondered why their voices were not slowing down as much as Jack's fist. Then he realized the speed of sound was obviously much faster than the speed of Jack. So, wouldn't it make sense if time slowed differently depending on how fast the thing being slowed was moving? *I should probably contemplate this later.*

"What is happening?" Danny shouted to Jack. "What's wrong with you?!" Having seen enough, Danny lunged forward toward Garrett.

Garrett felt a movement rush toward him from behind the beam of a flashlight but as Danny drew closer, he too began to slow, and when he was within three feet, he slowed to a near stop.

Garrett pressed his lips together in tight determination. He'd made his decision. Nodding reassuringly toward his friends, he let go of the focus.

Time for Jack and Danny returned to normal.

Garrett reached up and caught Jack's fist in his left hand.

Jack's eyes stretched open like a doe about to be struck by a car.

Garrett squeezed the boy's fist hard, pressing his middle finger deep into a pressure point in the back of Jack's hand, eliciting a surprised cry.

"Ahhh!"

Garrett kept the hand, pivoted his foot, and pulled the bully in close, placing Jack between himself and Danny. In the same motion, Garrett drew his head back then thrust it forward with a sudden jerk and headbutted Jack in the mouth, forcing Jack's bottom teeth through his lower lip.

Jack reeled backward, stumbling into Danny with a stunned cry. Involuntarily, Jack turned his wounded face away from Garrett, exposing his right ear, which Garrett graciously accepted as his next target.

Stepping forward with a short, right-hand punch, Garrett connected with Jack's exposed ear, generating another pained screech from Jack.

Jack seethed. "I'm going to hurt you! You hear me, Garrett? I'm going to make you pay!" Jack ran forward in a crouch, almost falling in the rising water. He swung another bar-room punch at Garrett's face.

Seriously, the same punch? Garrett thought as he easily ducked the encroaching fist. Confidence surged in him. Suddenly he knew, really knew, he could do this. Still in a squatted position from slipping the punch, he couldn't keep the grin off his face as he countered with a knuckle punch to Jack's nut sack.

A sharp squeak barely audible over the rushing water escaped from Jack as he folded forward. Somehow, he managed to stay standing as he bent over, holding his testicles, face distorted in pain.

"Yes!" Lenny shouted, releasing a hearty belly laugh that reverberated down the tunnel. Garrett started to stand when Danny rushed forward, grabbing Garrett from behind by the back of the collar, and yanked.

Paul shouted a war cry and ran forward but before he could reach Garrett, Lenny shouted, "Wait, man, just watch this."

"But—"

Garrett flew back, his feet coming out from under him with the force of Danny's pull. He landed hard on his back in the water. Danny grabbed fistfuls of Garrett's collar with both hands and tugged, intent on dragging him further into the tunnel where the two other thugs were waiting.

Rather than try and break free, Garrett allowed Danny to drag him as he reached back over his head with both hands and locked on to Danny's wrist with a tight grasp. Using Danny's wrist as leverage, he fired four hard kicks over his own head, and into Danny's face.

By the third kick, Danny was screeching in agony as teeth broke and something fractured in the older boy's face, probably his nose. It wasn't until the fourth kick that Danny was finally able to break free of Garrett's grasp.

Still lying on his back, Garrett spun himself around to face Danny. Water rushed over Garrett as he began to slide toward the mouth of the tunnel.

Danny threw both hands over his wrecked face and shouted in a tone that could only be produced by a unique combination of pain and rage, "Arrrgh!" Pulling his bloody hands away revealed a disfigured face that was distorted as much by pure anger as it was by the crooked nose and busted lips. Squinting through his watering eyes, Danny found the cause of all his anger and agony. Garrett was mere feet away, lying on his back as the rushing water swept him helplessly toward the opening. A determined expression fixed on Danny's face.

Garrett could almost read his thoughts. Danny wasn't going to let the river have him – not yet.

Danny seized the opportunity and rushed the defenseless boy. When he was within reach, he leapt, launching himself toward Garrett.

As Danny flew toward him, Garrett smiled. Danny had seen exactly what Garrett wanted him to see.

"Here we go!" Lenny shouted.

It was too late for Danny to change his mind when he noticed Garrett pulling his knee to his chest. Danny's eyes went wide in helpless anticipation as he landed on top of Garrett's cocked leg. With his foot centered perfectly on Danny's gut, he grabbed him by the collar with both hands and rolled backward, his own face disappearing briefly underwater. But Garrett didn't need to see as he kicked out his cocked leg with all his might.

Danny launched airborne backward over Garrett's head in a classic hapkido throw.

"Oh ho! Atta a boy!" Lenny cried out. "What did I tell you!" he said, punching Paul in the shoulder.

Danny landed too close to the edge of the culvert's opening to stop himself from falling over the side. As both members of his crew ran forward, stomping past Garrett in a desperate attempt try and grab him, it was gravity that won out. Danny let out a short cry that was stifled abruptly by a loud splash.

The two big brutes and now Jack, who had finally managed to stand upright, stood near the edge of the culvert, and it was Garrett who stood with his back to his friends. "I'm going to give you another chance Jack. You can turn around right now and follow your brother, or I can put you in a whole lot more pain and send you after him myself."

Jack winced, one hand still holding his testicles. "You bastard! That's my brother!" He waded forward again, but this time he slowed, realization dawning on his face as he apparently decided it wouldn't be wise to throw his signature punch for the third time. He paused, motioning at the other two. "Let's get him!"

Garrett noticed the one on his left was holding a bat while the guy on his right brandished a black bar of some kind. A crowbar maybe? It was hard to tell in the low light.

Jack smiled a bloody grin and pulled a knife.

The water was rushing midway up Garrett's shins now and just standing in the culvert was becoming dangerous in itself. They were running out of time.

"I'm helping him – this is ridiculous," Paul said, wading forward.

Lenny nodded. "Let's go!"

The guy with the bat wasted no time and swung at Garrett's face.

Garrett spun into the swing and grabbed the man's wrist with his left hand, then with a hard, right-hand chop he broke the man's forearm. The bat fell into the rushing water, vanishing over the edge of the culvert.

The man screamed in white-hot agony as Jack, ready to take advantage of an opportunity to get the drop on Garrett, rushed forward, thrusting his knife at the distracted boy's side.

"Garrett!" Breanne shouted over the rushing water.

Garrett yanked on the man's broken arm as he stepped back to avoid Jack's attack.

The man's scream pierced the night as he lurched awkwardly sideways, occupying the space between Garrett and Jack, perfectly positioned to receive the thrust from Jack's knife. Jack's blade sank deep into the screaming man's shoulder.

Jack let go of the knife as his mouth fell slack with the awfulness of what he had done.

Garrett gave the screaming man a final shove toward the opening.

The man staggered backward, his arm dangling, and fell out into the night. There was no more screaming, only a splash.

The big guy with the crowbar cautiously approached, his weapon cocked back for a swing. But before he could reach Garrett, Paul placed a hand on Garrett's shoulder, stepping around him.

The big guy paused in the glow of flashlights.

Paul smiled and advanced. "Come here, big fella."

The big guy shuffled backward through the water toward the opening. He looked back at Paul, then back at the opening. The chances of surviving the raging Sangamon – in a storm, in the dark, and above the broken dam – would be slim, but the big guy must have liked his chances better than facing Paul. He dropped the bar, turned, and jumped out the opening, vanishing over the edge.

Paul's face dropped in utter disappointment.

It was only Jack and Garrett now.

"Don't touch him. This has to be me and Jack. No one else!" Garrett closed the distance in three steps.

Jack dove forward, driving his shoulder into Garrett's stomach. Both boys fell back into the water. Jack managed to get both hands around Garrett's throat. "I'm going to kill you, Garrett!" He shoved Garrett's head underwater.

Garrett was blind under the freezing water. His head was pressed hard against the concrete of the culvert with all the weight of the boy on top of him, pinning him immovably below the rushing torrent, squeezing his throat with all he had. As Garrett lay there, a thought flashed through his mind. Lenny and Breanne were watching Jack kill him. In a moment, Lenny, or maybe Paul, would come to his rescue and save him. They would probably toss Jack out into the river and, just like that, the threat of Jack would be washed away. The shame of having to be rescued, however, would never be washed away. He would have to carry it with him forever, unable to look his friends in the eye. And worse, if they saved him now, he would never know if he could have won. *No.* He had to do something.

Before going under, Garrett had sucked in a ragged breath and tucked his chin tight to his chest. The maneuver was not keeping him from being choked completely but it was helping. Placing his hands over the back of Jack's, he wrapped his fingers around the boy's thumbs while pressing his own thumbs into the back of Jack's pinky knuckles. Then he twisted. Then he kept twisting.

Jack's wrist contorted unnaturally, and he let go of Garrett's throat with a sharp cry.

Thankfully for Jack, the slippery water allowed him to yank his hands away from Garrett before they twisted to the point of breaking.

Garrett bucked Jack and twisted to the side, tossing Jack into the water beside him.

Jack beat Garrett to his feet and quickly stomped down in an effort to keep Garrett from standing.

Garrett spun with the rush of moving water, avoiding Jack's foot, but he wasn't able to avoid being swept dangerously close to the opening.

Breanne gasped.

Garrett managed to get to his feet, but even standing in place was difficult.

The two boys squared off again.

"Let's finish this, Jack!"

"I'm going to finish you!" Jack seethed, charging forward.

This time, Garrett ducked low and flipped Jack over him, then pounced on top of him. He quickly tangled Jack's arm up behind his back, wrenched it up unnaturally, and shoved him face-down under the water.

"Let's see how you like it, Jack!" Garrett shouted from deep inside his guts, but what spilled forth was a crazed scream as all the calm slipped away, replaced by a suppressed rage no longer held in place by fear. Something inside him snapped, and he lost control.

Jack struggled below him, fighting for breath, but Garrett held him firmly under water.

"Garrett, stop!" Lenny shouted, running forward. "He isn't worth it!"

But Garrett didn't stop. "You will never hurt anyone else!" he shouted.

"Garrett! You're going to kill him!" Lenny begged, pulling at his dobok.

Garrett didn't hear his friend. There was nothing else; no one else. He would not stop until he felt the life leave Jack's body. He hadn't been sure he could kill another human being. Now he was sure he could, and he would. He would kill Jack here and now.

"Please! Garrett, stop!" Lenny begged.

The fight began to leave Jack as his body slowly succumbed.

Breanne rushed forward and bent down beside him. "Let him go, Garrett. You can't kill him. If you kill him, he wins! He becomes the victim. You're better than him." She reached under the water and found Garrett's hands and placed hers gently on top of his. "Look at me, Garrett."

Garrett found her eyes, and the anger slipped away like a fish from the hand. He shuddered and let go.

Jack lurched upright from the water, choking and coughing. He pushed himself away from them, close to the edge of the culvert, and puked. Gasping, he leaned out over the side and looked out toward the dark water, then down river into the night. He looked back at them with hate. Hate unlike anything any of them had ever seen.

Garrett was the first to feel it. A sickening in his stomach, a turning. Bile crept up the back of his throat and he started to gag. It hit Lenny next, and Garrett watched, helpless, as he went down to his knees vomiting. Then Bre, then Paul, then the rest of them – all sick, all gagging like they'd just eaten something rotten.

"My skin, something is wrong with my skin," Lenny managed.

Garrett frowned, feeling his tongue swell as his teeth began to ache. His head started to thump painfully with his pulse, and he became suddenly cold. The thumping in his head increased as his heart began to race. A dull twinge started to radiate down his left arm. His nostrils filled with the smell of death. It was bad, like the time he stumbled across a deer that had lain in the sun until it bloated and popped.

He heaved again, turning back to Jack, only able to squint through the pain. Jack was different. He was focused. Fixed in an expression of hate. His visage that of a madman. Suddenly Jack looked strong again, and there was no longer a hole below his lip where his teeth had come through. Garrett knew it then. Somehow… Jack was doing this.

In a final show of defiance, he looked at Garrett. "This isn't over, Garrett. This will never be over." His statement was that of a calm promise void of threat. He turned to the dark river and, without another word, tipped over the edge of the culvert. The only sound was that of a soft splash, barely audible over the ever-rising water.

Instantly, the pain in his head and arm disappeared and his stomach settled.

"What the hell was that?!" Lenny said, rubbing his hands across his arms.

"He must have gotten close to the God Stones somehow," Paul said, swallowing dryly.

Garrett threw his arms around Breanne, pulled her close, and hugged her. His whole body shivered as emotion racked his core. "Are you okay?"

"I'm okay," she reassured him.

"I would have killed him, Bre. If you hadn't stopped me, I would have killed him," he whispered.

"Hey, it's going to be okay," she said consolingly.

"Yeah," he said, unable to meet her eyes. "I'm just freezing, that's all. We better move."

20

Lincoln's Gauntlet

Wednesday, April 6 – God Stones Day 1
Petersburg, Illinois

"It's no good!" Lenny shouted over the rush of water. "The bricks I found are below the water! Dammit, it's too high!"

Pete bent beside him. "Lenny, look again – are you sure?"

"Yes, I'm sure!" Lenny said. "The water is up to our freaking asses! When I was here the other day it was only up to my mid-shin, and the bricks were only like two rows above the water line. We're so screwed."

When the gang moved out of the first section of round culvert and into the arched tunnel, they had to step down another foot deeper into the water. When it was Breanne's turn to step down, she gasped as she dipped even deeper into the cold water. This section of tunnel was the lowest section and thus the deepest.

"Paul, remember when you lifted the crane? Can you do the same thing but this time just smash in the wall?" Breanne asked through chattering teeth.

"You're joking, right?" Paul asked.

Anyone who could see her face would see she was in fact not joking. She knew they had to do something.

"Bre, that's like me asking you to just have a vision of what's going to happen next. I'm not in any more control of my strength than you are of your visions."

"Well, we have to do something!" Breanne said.

"I don't know, if I focus," he said with a shrug. "I might be able to punch through it if I don't break my fist. I mean I don't know if the water is too deep to get a good kick. The question is where do I punch?" he said, sizing up the wall.

Pete held up his hands, waving off the idea. "Wait… No. I got a feeling that may not end well. Unless you have superman invincibility to go along with your super-strength, you're definitely going to break your hand if you punch this wall. Besides, the whole place is rigged with traps. We got to do this right."

Garrett reached under the water, trying to feel for the initialed bricks. "Well, think of something, Pete. This isn't working. And my hands are freezing."

Janis touched Breanne's arm. "Hey, put your hands in the water."

Breanne looked at Janis quizzically.

"Just try. Can you feel it? Can you feel the water flowing around us? It's like a living thing – powerful and intelligent. I had this strange feeling earlier too when I realized I could see in the dark. It's the same energy. I can feel it now, right here, coming from all around me – from the water, from the earth, from the air."

"Um, okay, Janis," Breanne said, not feeling anything except the difficulty of keeping her balance in the strong current.

"Garrett, point to where the bricks are," Janis said.

Garrett looked down the wall toward the archway to orient himself again. "Right in this general area where I am standing," he said, pointing down at the water.

Breanne's mouth parted as she watched Janis move through the water toward the spot with an effortless ease. It was strange, as if the girl were speaking to the current, coaxing it to move in a different direction than where the natural flow of gravity was telling it to go.

The water changed course, flowing around Janis, Lenny, and Pete as if an invisible wall had been inserted into the water around them. Gradually, half the tunnel was choked off. Breanne, Garrett, Paul, and

David rushed forward into the dry pocket created by Janis's invisible wall.

Janis opened her eyes and smiled. "Can you find them now, Lenny?"

"Whoa! Janis? That's awesome!" Pete said.

The others all shot one another awed looks. But not David. He just smiled tightly. Breanne knew he was still waiting and hoping. She wished she could give him her visions. "Just be patient, David."

David looked down at the wet brick floor. "Didn't Garrett and Lenny's teacher guy say we would all feel something? Didn't he say we were all Garrett's chosen? Sages, right? Which is like mages. Which is the same thing as wizards. Well, I still don't feel anything and honestly it sucks. I want to help, Bre – I want to do something," David said quietly.

"Don't feel bad, bro – I don't feel anything either," Lenny said.

"Like you need it. You're a freaking martial arts expert and a circus acrobat all rolled into one. Plus, you got that badass staff the teacher guy gave you. I got squat."

Lenny shrugged. "Well, you have a manly mustache."

"Really, Lenny?" David said.

Lenny shrugged and turned away, pointing the flashlight toward where the rows started to curve from wall to ceiling, and began counting in a low, rapid mumble. When he reached row thirteen, he shouted it aloud. "Thirteen! Yep, right here! Okay, this one says J.C. on it. Give me the screwdriver and hammer, Pete!" Lenny held out his hand.

"Wait… Wait, wait, wait, just wait," Pete said, waving him off.

Lenny shot him a look. "Wait for what? We don't have time to wait, Pete, we need to move."

"I worked on this passage a little more and I'm pretty sure we have to do this right or something bad will happen."

"What do you mean something bad?" Breanne asked.

Pete pulled a folded-up piece of paper out of his backpack. "I copied the instruction parts down separately, so we would have them." He cleared his throat. "It says, *Once inside, look for the archway, which holds a* **xxx xxx xxx***. When you find* **xxx xxx** *remove* **xxx** *beloved* **xxx** *and, once removed, reach inside and pull the lever. This will allow the way to open, showing you the path.*"

Breanne scanned the brick wall with reverence. She couldn't believe Abraham Lincoln actually built this. "So what does it mean, Pete?"

"If we do this wrong, I think we'll trigger the first booby trap. Look, we have four bricks with initials. J.C., who we know is John Calhoun. B.G., who we know is Bowling Green. A.L.,, Abraham Lincoln, and then our mystery brick initialed A.R."

"Okay?" Garrett said.

"After close analysis of that sentence, I believe the key word here is 'beloved.' This leads me to believe we are looking for a woman's initials, which could only leave us with A.R. Why, you ask? Because—"

Garrett spun his finger. "Please, Pete!"

"Okay, I will get right to it, but only because I am cold, and we are probably going to die if I don't." Pete cleared his throat dramatically. "*When you find* **xxx xxx** *remove* **xxx** should read something like, *when you find her initials remove my beloved A.R.'s brick. And once removed, reach inside and pull the lever.*" "So here is my theory: A.R. was Abraham Lincolns first love – Ann Rutledge. His beloved Ann Rutledge."

"Nice, Pete," Breanne said.

Janis waved her hands back and forth in the water wall and giggled. "You're a genius, Petey."

"Alright, man," Lenny said, holding out an open hand. "I'll take your word for it. Now can I have the screwdriver and hammer?"

Pete smiled and gave Lenny the tools.

A moment later Lenny had freed the brick initialed A.R. He started to reach inside the hole, then stopped abruptly. "Pete. How sure are you that you're right about this?"

"Pretty damn sure. Like ninety-nine percent," Pete said.

"And if, on that one percent chance you're wrong, what will happen to my hand?" Lenny asked.

"I thought you were going take my word for it?"

Lenny paused, his fingers wiggling in front of the opening.

"Honestly, I don't know. But whatever it is, it won't be good," Pete said.

Lenny stood up. "I like my hand, bro."

Pete bent down and reached into the hole. "Ninety-nine percent is pretty good odds."

"Please be careful, Petey," Janis said.

"Guys, I feel the lever!" Pete grabbed it and pulled. Nothing happened. He grunted and pulled again as hard as he could.

Near the opposite end of the old brick portion of the arched tunnel, a single brick fell from where the wall met the curved ceiling, splashing into the current.

Everyone spun, aiming their lights toward where the brick had fallen just in time to see a huge chunk of wall and ceiling collapse. Bricks rained down, splashing into the current below.

"Holy crap!" Lenny said.

"Wow, guess that's our path," Breanne said.

Everyone followed her toward the newly collapsed section of brick. Janis moved too, which moved the dry pocket along with them.

"I'll go first," Garrett said. The opening was high enough that he was forced to jump up and pull himself over the wall. Lenny went next, and together he and Garrett helped pull everyone else over while Paul helped lift them from his side. Once Janis was pulled over the wall, the now raging drainage water resumed its natural flow, much deeper and fiercer than before.

David glanced over at Janis. "I sure hope you can do something with this water when we leave, or we won't be able to get back out."

"We'll figure something out," she said.

"Everyone, be still. Don't move until I get my bearings." Pete shone his light along the wall of the arched tunnel. They were now on the opposite side, behind the wall they had stood in front of only moments ago. "My god, this place is amazing," Pete said, motioning everyone to follow. Carefully he led them down some crudely cut steps along the narrow corridor.

"Look at that!" Breanne said, pointing at mechanisms on the back side of the brick wall. Metal-forged blades connected to pivoting bars on counterweights. Everything was covered in rust, but the blades still looked sharp.

Pete stooped to inspect one. "Lenny, Garrett – ho-ly, look at this!"

They eased forward, stopping next to Pete and Breanne.

"Whoa!" Lenny said.

"Yeah, if we had reached inside any of the other bricks and pulled those levers…" Pete swallowed.

"Yeah… it would've released the counterweight and no more hand!" Garrett said.

"Exactly."

Lenny looked up and studied some old wooden beams. "What do you make of that, Pete?"

"I think if we'd broke through the wall, the tunnel itself would have collapsed. See those?" Pete pointed at a few precariously positioned timber braces near the ceiling of the tunnel. "If we'd smashed the wall, those would've come down, and I think the tunnel would have come down with them – at least the entrance."

Lenny whistled.

Breanne felt a thudding in her chest as memories began to flood her. Memories of a collapse on a dig site in Mexico where she nearly got her family killed. Then a flash of a more recent memory on Oak Island, trapped in the treasure tunnel at the bottom of the Money Pit. Had it really happened that morning? It felt like a lifetime ago. She started to breathe really hard as the worst memory came. This one was a lifetime ago but felt like yesterday. The memory she feared most. The memory of her mother, shattered glass, and blood.

"Can you guys believe we are inside Lincoln's hidden freaking tunnel!" Pete said, trying to take it all in. "These beams were put here by Lincoln and Bowling Green! Those mechanisms… and look over here," he said, pointing to some old tools – shovels, a pickaxe, and an axe. "Can you imagine the value of this stuff? These are Lincoln's tools!"

Breanne wished she could give a shit, she really did, but the fact was she couldn't. She didn't figure anyone else really did either. She needed to find a way to wake her father, and they all had to stop Apep – stop the end of the world.

Maybe it was the melancholy look on Garrett's face or lack of enthusiasm on everyone else's, but Pete's excitement seemed to fade quickly as he flushed with embarrassment.

Garrett looked at Pete with an empty smile that said he knew his friend meant well.

Pete smiled back weakly with a look that said, *I'm sorry, man.*

In that moment, Breanne knew these were good kids – good friends. In a way she envied that. Her life had been organized around a sole purpose: become a great archeologist like her father. Her mission simply didn't lend itself to close relationships outside of her own family. She knew, too, whether she wanted to admit it or not, her isolation was self-imposed. She chose to shut everyone else out. As she watched the wordless interaction between Pete and Garrett, she knew she had missed out on something important.

Pete aimed his flashlight down the tunnel, but it revealed only a sharp bend some fifty yards ahead. "Okay, according to Lincoln, the next trap is a hidden pit. If we fall in, we die," Pete said.

"Um, yeah, that sounds awful, so uh, what's the plan for the pit, Pete?" David asked.

"Lincoln said once we turn the corner, the pit is twenty paces ahead."

They all started walking in single file downward at a steep pitch. Once they rounded the corner, the small man-made tunnel funneled down to a cave that was obviously natural. It widened only slightly, but the ceiling rose higher – maybe twenty or thirty feet.

The smell was rancid, and the taste of the air was even worse, like a mix of feces and ammonia. Breanne knew that smell. She stopped short and pointed her light upward.

The entire ceiling was covered in bats.

The Petersburg kids gasped. "Oh my god. Please tell me those things are going to stay put?!" David asked, practically pressing his face into Paul's back.

Paul shrugged him off and shot him a disapproving frown.

"It's okay, David. Just move slow and be quiet. They will likely stay put until time to feed," Breanne said.

"You're not afraid of them?"

"I've been in caves and underground places all over the world – this isn't the worst thing lurking in the dark," Breanne said matter-of-factly.

David spun to face Breanne, his eyes widening in horror. "What? Really? You had to say that!"

Breanne laughed. For the first time since she danced with her father at the bottom of the Money Pit, she actually laughed. It felt good, for a second, but then the guilt washed over her. She had no right to laugh – not until her father was safe.

"So, when do these things feed?" David asked, turning his eyes resolutely forward.

"Usually, well, right around now, I would guess. They're nocturnal, so—"

As if on cue, the cave erupted in shrill squeaks as the bats dropped from the ceiling, consuming the group in a cloud of flapping wings. David screamed at a pitch Breanne wouldn't have thought possible for a boy. Everyone dropped to their hands and knees, ducking their heads. Everyone except Janis. She smiled and watched as the bats flipped their wings all around her. Within seconds nearly all the bats had evacuated the tunnel into the wet night air with the exception of one.

Breanne watched in horror as one lowly bat landed on David's back.

David screeched and began flailing like a man on fire, blindly pushing past Paul, swatting frantically and screaming, "Get it off! Get it off me!"

"It's okay, David, just stand still," Breanne said, trying to calm him down.

"David, stop running! The pit, David! Stop!" Pete shouted, but it was no use. A second later, David dropped like a rock.

21

Red Rubies

Wednesday, April 6 – God Stones Day 1
Petersburg, Illinois

"David!" Pete shouted.

Everyone jumped to their feet and ran forward toward the pit.

The pit had been cleverly concealed with flat, thinly milled boards, then covered with dirt and, over time, a thick layer of bat guano. The old rotted boards collapsed easily under David's weight.

Pete was the first to get to the edge. "David! Oh man! Hold on!"

"Help me, Pete! Jesus, help me! I'm going to fall! Shit! I'm going to fall!" he shouted as he clung to the edge of the pit, trying desperately to hold on.

Pete dove forward and grabbed David's wrist just as his fingertips slipped off the edge. Pete couldn't hold him and now he was being dragged headfirst over the side.

"Christ, Pete, don't let me go, man. Please don't let me go!" David pleaded, his eyes filled with a genuine fear.

"I'm not going to… let you… go! Guys… little help… please!"

Garrett and Lenny dove in unison, sliding on their stomachs, arms outstretched and fingers splayed, until they were clutching Pete's ankles with both hands. For a long second, they hung there, not moving either up or down.

"Guys! I can't see the bottom! I don't think there is a bottom. Oh god! What if there isn't a bottom?" David shouted.

"Don't look… down… David," Garrett grunted.

"Now you tell me not to look down. Now you tell me!"

Breanne was almost there when Paul made it to Pete and threw himself onto his stomach. He reached down, taking hold of one of David's wrists, allowing Pete to secure David's other wrist with both his hands. "Alright, David, we got you. We're going to pull you up."

Breanne was at the edge now on her hands and knees. Maybe she could help calm him down. "It's okay, David, they have you – just relax."

"I don't want to be invisible anymore! I just want to be able to fly. Oh man, please let me get the power to fly," David begged, his eyes locked with Breanne's.

As Paul stretched out into the pit, his headlamp flashed over the side, panning across the bottom far below. It almost seemed as though she was looking down onto a twinkling city from a mountain top, but instead of white lights it was a city made of glittering red rubies. But the illusion shattered when she noticed the ruby lights were moving.

Breanne drew back involuntarily as her eyes widened and her breath hitched.

"What? What is it?!" David shouted, swiveling his head to look down.

"Don't! David, don't look. Look at me!" Breanne begged.

But it was too late.

David began kicking wildly at the wall. "Get me out! Get me out! Oh god, please get me out!"

"David, stop fighting us. You're going to fall!" Pete shouted, unable to hold David's wrist any longer. His hand slipped from Pete's grasp.

David flailed and twisted, his back now facing the wall of the pit.

"Dammit, kid!" Paul shouted, now holding all his weight by one twisting wrist.

Breanne watched in horror as below him a thousand rat eyes shone in her brother's headlamp.

David continued to flail.

"Guys, grab me and pull me back before we both go over!" Paul shouted.

Pete, Lenny, and Garrett jumped into action, grabbing Paul and together pulling a flailing David up and over the edge of the pit.

David lay there gasping.

"That's twice in the last hour I have saved your ass, kid – don't let there be a third!" Paul said.

Lenny was leaning out over the edge of the pit, shining his flashlight into its depths. "I've never seen river rats this big!"

Garrett joined him at the edge. "Yeah, well, I have once. Saw one dead in the road. Those things can get as big as a small dog. I've just never seen so many. You can't even see the ground."

Pete brushed himself off and peered over the side. "Well, look at it this way, David, I don't think the rats would have been an issue for you had you fallen." Pete pointed at the spikes sticking up from the floor of the pit. "You would have been shish-kebabbed by one of those spears long before the rats ate you."

Breanne watched David's eyes get big as the blood drained from his face.

"You think Lincoln dug this pit? It's got to be twenty-five feet deep," Garrett said.

Breanne eased over next to him and studied the pit. "No way. Even with his pal, that Bowling Green guy, it would have taken them years to dig this."

"Yeah, you're right. Lincoln only refurbished it. Tricked it out with spears. It was the Potawatomi who dug this pit long before Lincoln ever had anything to do with it," Pete said, nodding his head at Breanne.

"Really?" Breanne asked skeptically.

"Yeah, that's what I was telling you, this Native American kid told Lincoln all about this place and what was inside. He convinced him if it were ever discovered the world would end. He said his people fought to come back here to ensure the white man never found this place. The plan was already in place for Petersburg to be built practically right on top of the entrance, and the Sangamon River was becoming busier and busier with trade.

"Lincoln promised the boy he would find the entrance and conceal it. Of course, Lincoln didn't fully believe the sensational story until he found the entrance right where the boy said he would and saw for himself what was inside. If Lincoln was anything, he was a man of honor – a man of his word. And even though it practically destroyed him, he took the secret to his grave… Well, except for the journal."

Observing the distance across the pit, Lenny turned to the group. "Any ideas how in the hell we're going to get across this pit? It's way too wide to jump. Wait? Does anyone have superpower jumping abilities that I don't know about? Paul?"

The lines on Paul's face deepened into a frown. "What do you mean 'Paul'?"

"Well, you have super-strength, right? Can you just jump across, or flex across, or maybe He-Man yourself across, or something?"

"I don't know what He-Man myself across means, but sure, maybe I could jump across. However, I'm not planning to find out by trying to clear a – what? – thirty-some-foot jump over a rat-infested pit of death spikes. Besides, even if I could, that doesn't get the rest of you across."

Lenny held up his hands in surrender. "Fair point, bro."

Pulling the backpack off his shoulders, Paul sat it on the ground and peered inside. "But I have an idea," he said, pulling a coiled rope from the pack.

"Jesus, dude, is there anything you don't have in there?" Lenny asked. "And why didn't we use that to get down the embankment?"

Paul chuckled. "I served in the United States Army – we pride ourselves on being prepared. I knew we could get down the embankment without the rope and that we'd likely need it later. That's one thing I learned while working on difficult dig sites in remote locations with my father – don't leave your key gear at the top." He paused, his smile fading, his thoughts momentarily drifting somewhere else.

Breanne watched her brother's expression fall and a pang of pain shot through her heart.

Garrett forced a smile and gave Paul a slap on the shoulder. "Well, I'm glad you came prepared because other than a couple cheap flashlights, a screwdriver, and a hammer we're about as unprepared as it gets. I'm curious though, you aren't expecting that thin little rope to hold our weight, are you?"

"Of course it will hold us – this is military-grade climbing rope with a working load rate of eight hundred and twenty pounds." Paul scowled, then yanked the rope in each direction as if to show how strong it was. "It'll hold at least three or four of us at once, *easily.*"

David perked up. "I don't think I like where this is going."

Paul rummaged some hardware from his pack, quickly finding what he needed. "I'm going to scale the wall high enough to anchor in above your heads, then scale horizontally across the pit to the other side, cross to the other wall, and anchor off near the floor. You guys will then slide across on the rope," he said, making a swiping motion with his hand, starting at his head and finishing near his waist.

Garrett nodded slowly. "How will we *slide* across the rope?"

Paul smiled and pointed at Garrett's black belt. "That belt wraps around you twice, right?"

"Yeah…"

"Perfect – between you and Lenny we can cut enough lengths of belt for everyone to loop it over the rope and use it to slide across."

"Wait a minute, bro, you expect us to cut our black belts into pieces?!" Lenny said.

Paul smiled. "Yes, that's exactly what I expect."

Breanne watched as Paul did something strange. He placed a hand on Lenny's shoulder like a big brother might do – like Ed might have done when Paul was Lenny's age.

"It's just a belt, Lenny. Do you think I am less a soldier because I don't have a uniform on? The belt doesn't make you who you are. Take it away and you're still a black belt, right?"

Lenny sighed then nodded and began reluctantly untying his belt. "Yeah, you're right."

"Alright, guys, train your flashlights on the wall and give me as much light as possible." Paul climbed the wall a few feet, then skillfully anchored a cam into a small fissure and knotted the rope. "Everyone listen up," he said, jumping back to the ground. "I anchored this only high enough that you should all be able to easily climb to it."

They looked up at the rope.

"Lenny, cut that belt into approximately twenty-four-inch pieces," Paul said, passing Lenny a black-handled folding knife. "This is my baby, Lenny – take good care of it and get it back to me when we get to the other side."

Lenny unfolded the knife, flicking it into place with a soft click. "Did you get this when you were in the military?"

"No, they don't give you a knife like this one in the service. This one is special."

Lenny nodded sharply and went to work cutting his belt.

No one else noticed, but Breanne saw her brother's face sag just a little. Her brother Ed had given him that knife.

"Garrett, you too," he said.

Garrett quickly untied his belt.

Paul motioned for Lenny to hand him a piece of the belt. "Pay attention, people. You'll need to wrap one end around your hand, gripping it tightly like this," he said, holding it in his left hand as he wrapped the belt around it. "Then I want you to loop it over the rope and wrap it around the other hand the same way. You have to do this right. If you try just holding it in your fist, it will slip out no matter how hard you squeeze." He gazed sternly around at the group. "I repeat, if you don't wrap it around your hand, it *will* slip."

"Um, I was right. I don't like this," David said.

"Wait, we're actually going to zip-line over that pit?" Janis asked.

Without acknowledging Janis's question or checking for understanding, Paul started his horizontal scale of the wall. "You'll need to hold on like your life depends on it and don't let go until you hit the ground on the other side."

Lenny finished cutting his belt and handed the knife to Garrett.

Paul was already halfway across the pit, making the climb look effortless. "Oh, and you probably shouldn't look down either. Just shut your eyes and don't open them until you hit the other side!" He jumped to the ground, crossed the tunnel, wedged an anchor into a crack close to the floor, and tied off the rope. "Okay, let's do this!"

Lenny took the knife from Garrett, who was finished cutting up his belt, and tucked it firmly into the back pocket of his dobok before tying the staff onto his back. "Paul? Incoming!" Lenny shouted as he jumped up onto a jutting section of cavern wall and looped the segment of belt around over the rope, twisting to create the wrap Paul had shown them as if he had done it a thousand times.

Everyone watched anxiously.

"Careful, bro," Garrett said.

Because moving at the speed of natural gravity wasn't enough for Lenny, he kicked off the wall and whooped as he slid swiftly down the rope and across the pit, handing Paul his knife once he landed.

"Show-off!" Garrett shouted across the pit.

"Who's next?" Paul asked.

Pete went next and everyone else followed – no one as effortlessly as Lenny, but all made it without any issues.

Even David crossed without incident, though he made sure everyone knew he hated every second. Once in flight, he let out a whoop of his own, but rather than mimicking Lenny's shout of confident exhilaration, David's came out more a shout of terror. He slid down the rope, landing hard on his ass, but he followed Paul's instructions to the letter, keeping his eyes closed the entire time and not letting go. Once safely across, he still didn't open his eyes or let go of the rope. He sat there, not daring to breathe, his hands still fixed on the belt, knuckles white.

Breanne knelt beside him, placing a hand on his shoulder. "It's okay, David, you made it."

David opened one eye, looked around, then let out a long breath.

"Alright, Pete what's next?" Garrett asked.

"We walk. I'd say we still have a mile or so before we get to the temple entrance."

"What about traps?" Breanne asked.

"Yeah, one more section, but it should be obvious."

"How's that?" Lenny asked.

"We're going to get to a section that narrows. Lincoln lined the floor of the narrow section with fur traps."

"You're shitting me," Garrett said.

"What do you mean 'fur traps,' Pete?" Breanne asked.

Pete lowered his voice as deep as he could to summon the voice of Lincoln. "*In the narrow crevice, I placed several steel traps of varying size. I bound these traps by stake. As the years have passed, I no longer recall the number of traps I set forth. I know only that there were many.* Or some shit like that," he said, returning to his normal voice.

"Oh! You were doing Lincoln! I thought you were impersonating Darth Vader," Lenny said.

"Wrong! I was impersonating your mom, asshole!"

"Hey, so how narrow is narrow?" Garrett asked. "I mean since we crossed the pit it has gotten narrower – we're just a couple shoulder widths now."

"And what does he mean by 'varying sizes,' Pete?" Janis asked.

"And please don't answer in your Lincoln impersonation voice… ever again," Lenny said.

"You mean your mom's voice?" Pete said, punching Lenny in the shoulder.

"Alright, you guys!" Garrett said. "Pete, seriously? I don't want to go walking blindly into these things."

"Alright, alright, listen – you're fine," Pete said easily. "Lincoln said the tunnel narrows so that a man can barely fit through sideways." He turned to Janis. "The varying sizes must mean animal sizes. Trappers use different size traps depending on the size of the animal. For example, you wouldn't use a bear trap if you were trying to catch a rabbit, nor would you use a rabbit trap if you were trying to catch a bear."

"That actually makes good sense. You don't think there are big traps, do you?" Janis asked.

"Yeah, I do, but here's the thing. Lenny has that staff with him so he can just tap it out in front of us as we go making sure it's safe. I figure any small traps will likely have already been triggered by the ra—"

"Dumbass! This is an ancient weapon passed down from Turek himself. I'm not using it to test for traps!" Lenny said firmly.

Pete rolled his eyes. "Like I was saying before I was so *rudely* interrupted, it's likely small game like rats have already triggered all but the big ones. We'll just need to be careful."

Breanne followed behind Garrett, with David and the rest of the gang on her heels, as they hiked onward and noticeably downward for another twenty minutes. At least the smell seemed to get better the further they went – that or they were just getting used to it. Finally, they came to a section in the cave about twenty feet long that was covered in standing water. As they scanned their lights across the glassy stillness, they could see the floor rise up sharply out of the water into a single path that narrowed drastically. But that wasn't all they could see. On the opposite side, two pairs of red eyes flashed as the light passed across them.

Garrett pointed his flashlight directly at the eyes, illuminating two large rats who didn't seem to be at all bothered by the light and continued to drink from the stagnant water.

"This must be it!" Pete said.

"What about them?! And how deep you think that water is?" David asked apprehensively.

"David, stay calm," Breanne said. She could just see this kid freaking out and running blindly into the standing water. No telling how deep it was.

Paul stepped up next to Garrett. "Look, you been leading for a while, so I'll go first. I'm not worried about a few rats."

Garrett hesitated.

Paul smiled. "Garrett, a good leader understands that sometimes he has to delegate. Leading doesn't always mean you go first. Let me take this."

Garrett nodded reluctantly. "Okay, but listen, you can't go into that narrow area on the other side of the water without some way of checking for the traps."

"Yeah, you're right. We also don't know how deep the water is. For all we know, it could be a mile deep or a shallow puddle."

"For all we know, there could be sharpened spears hidden just beneath the surface," David offered.

Garrett looked at Lenny, who stood with his weight shifted on the staff.

"What?"

Now everyone looked at Lenny.

"It's invaluable! It's the last thing Mr. B gave me!"

"Lenny, he would want you to use it to keep us safe," Garrett said.

Time ticked away as an obstinate Lenny stared back defiantly.

Finally, under the penetrating glare of the group, Lenny folded. "Fine! But I swear, man, if you trash my staff I'm going to be pissed!"

"Look, Lenny, I know your teacher gave this to you and it means a lot. I promise I'll do my best not to trash it, but here" – Paul held out his special knife – "I know it isn't an ancient staff, but it has been with me for a very long time. Why don't you hang onto it for me until I get you your staff back?"

"I'll take good care of it," Lenny said in a thick voice as he reached out to take the knife. Then, offering his staff in return, he nodded to Paul.

Using the staff to test the depth and sweep the bottom as he stepped, Paul crossed to the other side and motioned the others across.

As Breanne stepped into the water, one of her father's favorite sayings came to her. *Baby girl, sometimes a cigar is just a cigar.* The stagnant pool, as it turned out, was just a cigar, nothing more than a low spot where water had collected.

As they crossed, Paul shone his headlamp into the mouth of the narrowed section, calling out that he could see old rusted traps littered with bones. "You were right, Pete. It looks like most of these have been set off already."

"Well, keep on the lookout for any big ones that haven't been."

Breanne watched closely as Paul made his way slowly through the tight crevice, the staff held in his right hand, tapping as he went. About halfway through, the staff made contact with something metal just below the surface of the dirt. So far all the traps had been small game traps, all had been triggered, and all were visible, due to having been sprung and thus pulled from their layer of cover. But not this trap. This trap was still covered, hidden under a thin layer of dirt.

"I've got something, guys – stand by."

"Be careful, Paul," Breanne said, trying to peer over Garrett's shoulder.

Breanne's heart started to pound, and she suddenly became hot as she watched Paul attempt to jam Lenny's staff under the edge of the trap to flip it up and over, away from him. She could see he was trying his best not to set the trap off on the staff.

"Almost... got it," he said, heaving the giant hunk of metal over. It was huge. Likely a bear trap. "Guys, there aren't bears in Illinois, right?" When the trap landed upside down it went off with a loud *snap!* of cracking metal. The trap lurched upright, its clenching jaws forcing it to buckle upward.

Everyone startled at the sound and Janis screamed, causing everyone to startle a second time. "Jesus! Sorry, guys. That scared the hell out of me."

"It's fine, guys," Paul called back to them. "I just set off the trap. We can keep moving."

A few minutes later Paul broke clear of the crevice. He stopped there at the mouth, assessing what he saw before him. "Check this out. I think we're here."

Breanne and the others crowded out of the crevice behind him. The space opened up quite wide and, as she shone her light forward, she could see the path ahead dropped away at a gentle slope. Several yards out, the path disappeared into an angled wall. The wall was built of giant stone blocks stacked with perfect precision, and in the center was a large rectangular doorway. The wall around it was perfectly smooth and flat. It looked familiar to her, like the many pyramids she had seen all over the world. "It's amazing! So beautiful," she said.

But then the stone wall was gone as white haze clouded her vision and something else came into focus from the corner of her eye.

Paul took a single heavy step down the slope, shifting his full weight to his falling foot.

Breanne's scream was replaced tenfold by her brother's, when in a horrible instant, rusty metal teeth snapped shut with all the force of a crocodile.

22

Below the Pyramid

Wednesday, April 6 – God Stones Day 1
Rural Chiapas State, Mexico

Gabi, Itzel, and María shared uneasy glances as Gabi's interpretation of the mural hung in the air between them.

"Magic?" Itzel said, her face dubious. "Gabi, let's be logical. Ancient wall paintings tell stories not necessarily meant to be taken literally."

"Itzel, I think this is pretty clear," María said.

"Really, María?! You too? Are you going to tell me this mural literally depicts giant stone blocks floating through the air using magic?" Itzel asked.

"No. Of course not."

"I should say of course not!" Itzel said.

"Not magic, but a technology we don't understand. Something lost long ago?" María said.

"Oh, come now, I have heard these theories. Objects being lifted with soundwaves or some such nonsense. You can't be serious!"

"Look at the wall, Itzel," María said, pointing. "The blocks of the pyramid are just floating into place. How do you explain it? How do you explain a race of giants? Would you have believed they existed if their skulls weren't sitting here in front of you?"

"No. No, I suppose not," she said quietly.

The three women approached the wall again, each taking up positions on all sides of the pyramid, their brushes dancing rhythmically as each stirred a tiny cloud of dust.

Gabi was on only the second step of her ladder, dusting underneath the painted pyramid, an area she didn't expect to contain any secrets, but suddenly something began to take shape. She cocked her head to one side as a chamber came into view. It was circular, with a spiral staircase. *That's our chamber,* she thought. Below that chamber was a long tube. *Sarah's shaft,* she thought, looking back toward the center of the room where her father and Fredy knelt by the hole.

"Mamá, look at this," she breathed, barely above a whisper, unsure of what she was seeing. But her mother didn't hear her. Her own face was creased in concentration as she gazed upon her own work.

Gabi dusted more, making sure to only apply enough pressure to remove the layer of sediment while trying to make the brush dance like her mother's. Below the long tube something else was coming into focus – something huge.

Finally, her mother announced, "Look here!"

María and Gabi stepped back again to take it in.

"This shows a single giant coming to this land and tormenting the indigenous people. See here, this looks like women were being dragged off into the jungle… Stolen!" Then she pointed. "This area depicts smaller giants. Two, then – see here? – four, then eight. They are multiplying!" She circled a different area with her brush. "Then, here we see them building this pyramid."

"Stealing the women to breed with them? María Purísima, Itzel!" María pointed now further down the wall. "Then later there was a war. I see now, we started at the end, not at the beginning. These skulls are the result of the giants that were defeated. They were placed here," Itzel said. "But see here, many escaped, retreating, but where to?"

"Yes, and why put the skulls here at all?" Itzel asked.

Finally, Gabi spoke up, pointing below the pyramid. "Mamá, look! I think they are here to warn people away from that."

They stared at the images below the pyramid.

"That can't be real!" María said.

"No, María? But like you said, neither can these skulls," Itzel said quietly.

"Mamá, we need to get Sarah."

"Ay, María Purísima… Sarah!"

23

Rusty Bite

Wednesday, April 6 – God Stones Day 1
Petersburg, Illinois

"Paul!" Garrett shouted as he ran forward.

"Garrett, wait! Stop, there could be more traps!" Pete warned.

Garrett didn't stop, not until he got to Paul. Lenny and Breanne were right on his heels. Garrett knelt beside him, noticing right away several of the bear trap's teeth bit deeply into Paul's leg just above his ankle bone. He sat yanking at the trap trying helplessly to pull it apart. "It's going to be okay, Paul," Garrett said unconvincingly.

"Get it… off me!" Paul groaned, blood flowing freely from the punctures on both sides of his leg, soaking his pant leg.

Lenny and Garrett nodded at each other, each grabbing one side of the trap.

"Keep him still, Bre. This is going to hurt like hell!" Garrett said.

"It's going to be okay, Paul. You're going to be okay," Bre said, her voice trembling.

"Just do it," Paul grunted through clenched teeth.

They pulled. It took all their strength to pry apart the trap and for a second Garrett thought the blood-slicked metal might slip from his grasp.

Paul growled, sounding more like the animal the trap was meant for as he pulled his foot clear of the steel jaws.

Pete wedged a chunk of the trap's chain in between the teeth to allow Lenny and Garrett to free their fingers as they eased the trap closed.

As soon as Paul's foot was clear, he began giving instruction. "Lenny, you still have my knife?"

"Yeah, sure," he said, producing Paul's Ka-Bar.

"Open it… quick."

Lenny flipped the tactical knife open with a nudge from his thumb.

"Good. Now… cut my pant leg… off… above the wound," he said in short breaths.

Lenny quickly cut Paul's pants. The wound was horrible. It looked like he had been attacked by a shark or something equally toothy.

Garrett's stomach turned.

"Oh Jesus, Paul!" Breanne said.

"Just stay calm. We need… to get this bleeding… under control, before I pass out," Paul said shakily.

Garrett wished they had saved some of their black belts, but what they didn't use they discarded back at the pit. Thinking quickly, he took off his dobok top and tossed it to Lenny. "Use this."

"It's not exactly warm down here, man," Lenny said.

"Yeah, so I'll be cold," Garrett said, throwing up his hands. "Look, man, the dobok is made of thick material, so it should work, right?"

"Yeah… it'll work fine… but hurry… I'm getting really dizzy here, guys." Paul looked grey as the blood drained from his face. "Lenny, cut the sleeves off and give… back the rest… keep his core warm… Besides…" – he winked weakly at Bre – "I think my sis… likes the show… too much."

"How in the hell can you make jokes at a time like this?!" Breanne tried to scold.

Paul chuckled in response.

"And how can you be laughing?" she asked.

Garrett felt a renewed urgency. It had been there all along, but now it was spurring him forward. Everyone else must have been feeling it too because they kept looking back the way they came, as if waiting for Apep to burst forth from the darkness.

"Pete, take the staff and make sure there are no more traps." Garrett nodded toward the temple entrance. Turning back to David, he said, "David keep a look out for Apep."

Garrett and Lenny wrapped Paul's ankle as tightly as they could.

Paul's eyes rolled back then snapped back into focus. "Okay, now see that keychain looking thing hanging from my pack? It's a short length of paracord. Uncoil it and cinch it tight around my leg."

Garrett uncoiled the tiny cord, wrapped Paul's ankle, and yanked.

Paul grunted, "Tighter!"

Garrett and Lenny each took an end of the knot and pulled together… hard.

"Ah!" Paul shouted. "That's good. Help me up! Let's move!"

Around the doorway were scattered bones. But these bones looked different from the ones in and around the traps. "We got human bones over here, guys!" Pete announced. "Breanne, can you have a look at these?"

Paul nodded. "Go on, sis, I'm right behind you."

Breanne approached and began examining the bones, entryway, and exposed wall. "These are human for sure and look at the angle of this exposed wall. Interesting."

"What are you thinking?" Pete asked.

"I'm thinking, the pitch of this wall screams pyramid," she said, running her hand along it. "The entryway too, the way it's built into the wall."

"Are there any more traps, Pete?" Breanne asked, hesitating before walking into the opening.

"No, well, according to Lincoln's journal anyway."

"Yeah, but it didn't mention the one outside the gap either, right?" Lenny said.

"True, but it's likely after all those years, he simply forgot he had placed one outside the crevice."

“Simply forgot? That thing nearly hacked off Paul’s foot! What else did he simply forget?” Lenny asked in annoyance.

Paul climbed to his feet. “Lenny, it’s not that bad. Let’s finish this, then I’ll get to a hospital and get it all fixed up,” he said thickly, forcing a smile. “You mind if I hang on to your staff a little longer? It makes a good crutch.”

“No, of course not, bro.”

Pete stepped hesitantly beside Breanne. “I doubt he would forget a whole other series of traps. I think this was just a one-off but, yeah, we should proceed with caution.”

“Yeah, then you go first, Pete,” Lenny said.

Garrett drew his sword. “I’ll go first.”

Pete nodded and fell in behind Garrett; Breanne and Janis fell in behind Pete, David behind the girls, and finally a hobbling Paul with assistance from Lenny fell in behind the rest. They moved from the cave into the opening. Their shuffling feet echoed off the walls.

Finally, they were in the temple or pyramid or whatever this place was. The evening had seemed so surreal, but it was all really happening. This place really did exist.

Garrett’s thoughts were heavy with the tasks the coming moments would require. He let the flashlight beam move across the blade of his sword. He was about to cut off the head of a space alien.

24

Temples and Tombs

Wednesday, April 6 – God Stones Day 1
Petersburg, Illinois

Pete broke the soft scuffle of feet with a whisper. "According to Lincoln, we should be really close to the main chamber. In the journal, he mentions a tunnel lined with racks of bones right before the main chamber."

"Racks of bones? That's very strange," Breanne said.

"Yeah, well no, not bones, skulls. Racks of skulls," Pete corrected.

Breanne flipped her light from the floor to the back of Pete's head. "Guys, on my Dad's dig site in Mexico, just before the site collapsed, we found what has to be one of the largest sets of skull racks ever discovered!" *Sarah, oh, I wish we could talk,* she thought.

"So, that's cool. I guess, right? You might find some more here," Pete said.

"No, Pete, that's not what I mean – the site in Mexico has tzompantli, Aztec skull racks. There shouldn't be any Aztec skull racks here, in central Illinois. The indigenous peoples in this area didn't make skull racks out of human heads."

"Well, maybe that's not what they are," Pete offered.

"Maybe. Yeah, I'm sure it couldn't be." She let the subject drop. They were fully inside the opening. As in a pyramid, the corridor was constructed of perfectly cut and stacked stone. The ceiling was high above their heads, and there was plenty of room to walk three wide. "If there are any seams in the stone, I sure can't see them," she said, running her hand down a wall.

They turned a corner into yet another corridor. And just as Lincoln had written, so it was. Along the walls on both sides were racks of skulls.

"No, this can't be – there's no way!" Breanne said, stopping to appraise the racks. Some had fallen apart over time but most still stood, dust-covered and fragile. It was too incredible, too impossible, too… coincidental? "This can't be here, you guys. Jesus, this can't be here! There must be dozens? Maybe hundreds?" If the circumstances were different, she would be content to spend hours – no, days – examining, measuring, and cataloging the skull racks.

What would her father say if he were here right now? Something like, *This will change everything we thought we knew about America's history, baby girl!* But her father wasn't here. She didn't even know if he was okay. And there was no time to investigate, no time to waste.

"Well, I guess we don't know what is possible – it isn't like any of us have ever been in the temple of a Native American god before," Pete said.

Garrett glanced back. "Native American god? This is a tomb."

Ahead the corridor appeared to end, showing only darkness beyond.

"Okay, tomb," Pete conceded. "But tomb or temple, what's inside is a Native American god. An evil god, but a god nonetheless."

"Pete. There's a space alien in there. One of the old ones. I thought you said you knew what was inside?" Garrett asked.

"Yeah, well, that makes sense, man. You can understand why the natives would think this thing was a god," Pete said.

They reached the end of the corridor, where a large room stretched out before them. Breanne could feel the vastness of the space in the depths of the darkness, but she couldn't see more than a dozen feet in front of her face, even with the flashlight. The chamber smelled of centuries-old musk, and the air was cold. "A god, sure, because of its magic powers or whatever."

"Powers? I don't know, maybe. But I'm talking appearance," Pete said.

"Look, at the walls," Breanne said, pointing her headlamp to both sides of the doorway they had come through. There was a ledge about shoulder high, standing a few inches off the wall, like a shelf, but it wasn't a shelf. It was more like a really long window planter box that stretched away into obscurity in both directions. "Those held a flammable fuel used to light the chamber."

"Oh, wait guys," Garrett said, retrieving James's Zippo from his pocket. He flicked the flint, and the Zippo sparked to life, a tiny flame burning steadily. "I doubt after all these years it will still light, but here goes." Garrett reached over and touched the flame to the ledge.

Instinctively Breanne shielded her eyes as the flame sprung to life, racing across the wall to stretch several feet in a flash of brilliant orange. The dancing flames continued into the depths of the chamber to circle around the entire vast room, before completing the loop all the way around to the opposite side of the door.

They had been in the dark with nothing more than flashlights for over an hour. Breanne squinted and blinked, her eyes adjusting. Suddenly she realized why she hadn't been able to see very far into the chamber with her flashlight.

"Holy shit balls!" Lenny said.

25

Lever

Wednesday, April 6 – God Stones Day 1
Rural Chiapas State, Mexico

At first the lever only moved a little. Sarah pulled harder, but still it wouldn't budge farther than a few millimeters.

She figured there were two possible outcomes after the lever finally broke loose and flipped and, truth be told, she didn't like either one. Either the bottom of this damn shaft was going to fall away, and she was going to go plummeting down into unknown depths, or this thing was a trap and would start filling with water. Why water? She didn't know, it was just a feeling. She supposed it could be anything, but water seemed simple and effective enough. She checked her figure-eight knot again with a nervous tug. "Fredy, prepare for my rope to go taut," she said through the two-way. Clicking the button again, she added, "And prepare to pull like hell on my signal."

"Okay… we're ready," Fredy answered, his voice crackling over the radio with obvious concern. Then Fredy's voice returned a moment later, mixed in with other voices. "But Sarah, why would your rope go taut when you are about to climb up?"

In the background Sarah thought she heard Itzel's voice and she sounded excited. Normally they spoke in English around her. She never asked them to. They just always did. She knew it was a gesture of respect, so that she would always understand what was being said. But through the radio it sounded like Itzel was yelling in Spanish. *They must be freaking out with worry,* she thought.

Sarah let the radio fall back against her vest, where it was clipped, then bent over and wrapped her fingers firmly around the lever between her legs. She heaved with all her strength, using her legs and back.

Slowly, slowly she felt the lever yielding.

And then, all at once, it lifted free and locked into place.

She waited, frozen like the giant stone statue a hundred feet up, her chest pinned up tight as she dared not breathe. The lid stayed below her. There was no sign of water gushing in. *So, what's this thing do?*

Suddenly, she got her answer when her whole world began to shake as the stone lid under her rotated a quarter of a turn, knocking her off balance before stopping abruptly. A loud clunk sounded, vibrating up Sarah's legs.

She looked down, searching for one of the strange notches – the ones that disappeared below the floor. There! She located one. The notch was no longer an open hole. Some sort of mechanism now protruded outward from the lid, locking into the groove. *Shit! Shit, shit, shit!* she thought, *I triggered a trap!*

26

Stoneclad and Thunderbird

Wednesday, April 6 – God Stones Day 1
Petersburg, Illinois

The chamber stretched upward, its four walls narrowing into darkness as black as obsidian. Somewhere up there, deep in the shadows above, out of sight for untold centuries, the four walls met in a perfect apex. The distance across the chamber from front to back must have been a hundred feet or more and the same side to side. The walls were painted with strange symbols. Pottery, remnants of pelts, hoards of shields, armor, and weapons were piled along a wall.

But Garrett, like everyone else, had no attention left for the size of the place or its incredible adornments. All his focus was directed toward the massive stone slab at the center of the chamber – and to the thing that lay atop it. "My god... it's huge," Garrett said.

"This can't be real!" Lenny said.

"Well, yeah, of course it's huge. It's a giant," Pete said, as if he had seen dozens of them.

Garrett struggled to find words. "But..."

"I mean, what did you expect? I thought you said you knew what was in here?" Pete said with a shrug, but the quaver in his voice betrayed the nonchalance he was trying to put up.

"I... I thought I did," Garrett said. "I mean I do. This must be the old one, right? The one I'm supposed to destroy. The one from another planet. I just didn't expect it to be so... so goddamn big! I mean this is a giant, an *actual* giant!"

"Well, when Lincoln said giant, he meant it," Pete said. "Maybe the world should have listened to the clues?"

"What the hell are you talking about?" Lenny asked.

Pete cleared his throat. *The eyes of that species of extinct giants, whose bones fill the mounds of America, have gazed on Niagara, as ours do now.* Old Abe said that all the way back in eighteen forty-eight."

Lenny shook his head. "There is something wrong with you. You know that, right? Something very wrong."

"For sure," David said.

They approached cautiously.

The giant lay only a couple dozen feet away, face up across the stone slab, which rose several feet off the floor, obstructing their view of the rest of the chamber. The giant wasn't mummified or bones, as one would expect of something that had been there for so long. No, it was flesh and blood, fully intact. It looked as if it were asleep; its one oversized eye centered in the middle of its head was closed.

"It's so big! And it looks so alive!" Breanne said.

"I've seen it all. My god, I've seen it all now," Paul said, limping forward.

"James said something about a state of suspension. Some kind of spell is keeping it preserved," Garrett said.

"Guys, um, I'm just going to hang back here by the door," David said.

Garrett heard something in David's voice. It didn't sound like fear. It sounded like something else. "David, you okay?"

"Yeah, I feel weird that's all. A little lightheaded maybe from skipping dinner. I'll be okay. If it wakes up, might be best if I'm by the door. I am probably the slowest one here," he said, leaning back on the wall.

"Don't be so sure, kid," Paul said.

Janis had the opposite reaction, suddenly running forward with reckless abandonment.

"Wait, Janis!" Pete said, giving chase.

The thing was covered in cobwebs. Janis picked a spot and quickly cleared the webs with a brush of her hand as if she were drawing back a curtain. Without hesitating, she reached out to touch its massive hand. "Guys, its skin is cold!"

"Janis, don't do that!" Pete scolded. "What if it wakes up or something?!"

Garrett and the others fell in beside her.

The hand was even with Garrett's shoulders as the body lay prone. In the reflected flames, he could see its black veins webbed under its greyish, opaque skin. "Have you ever seen a hand this big?"

"It must be as big around as a car tire!" Breanne said.

The giant wore some type of hide around its middle that seemed similar to the furry material of its boots; both were dried and decayed with age. A ragged tunic hung from its torso, riddled with tears that appeared singed along the edges. The front half of its head was completely bald. However, from the back half, beginning behind its disproportionately small ears, grew long, black hair. The coarse hair was woven into one long braid, as thick as a rope used to anchor a ship. The massive braid was adorned with stark white bones and stretched down over the giant's shoulder, the end tucked between the giant's arm and ribcage. Garrett wondered if the bones were human. "I've seen that hairstyle before on Kung Fu Theater," Garrett said, pointing toward the thing's head.

"Yeah," Lenny said, nodding. "Jet Li wears his hair like that in a bunch of his movies. Well, minus the bones. It's called a queue."

"How in the hell would you know that?" Pete asked.

"You're not the only one who knows stuff, asshat," Lenny said, flipping Pete the finger.

"A while back I actually thought about rocking it, but let's be honest my hair is just too amazing to shave half of it off."

Janis rolled her eyes.

"Besides, what if I got tired of wearing it in a braid? Then I would have a half 'fro and who in the hell has ever heard of half a 'fro? Nobody does that… not on purpose anyway."

Pete shrugged. "Maybe not nowadays, but I do know some Native Americans also wore their hair in this style. Perhaps we have old Stoneclad here to thank for ancient hairstyle similarities from one continent to another."

"Wait, did you just refer to it as Stoneclad?" Breanne asked.

"Of course," Pete responded as if the giant's name were tattooed right across the back of its massive hand for everyone to see. "According to the Potawatomi boy from Lincoln's journal, this must be Nuyunuwi, also known as the infamous Stoneclad. I was able to actually find a little info on this guy. He was a cannibalistic giant in Native American folklore who terrorized whole tribes. He killed by the dozens, stole their women for breeding, and if the natives couldn't retrieve their dead after battles Stoneclad ate them. He was a baaaaad dude."

Garrett shifted uncomfortably. He knew one thing. If half of what Pete was saying were true, he did not want this thing waking up. From the look on everyone else's faces they were suddenly feeling just as apprehensive as he was.

"Stoneclad? Sounds pretty damn indestructible," Lenny said, taking a step backward, his eyes never leaving the impossible creature.

"Yeah, according to my research, the tribes set aside their bickering to come together and defeat Stoneclad," Pete said. "Supposedly, it took six witch doctors to finally kick his ass, but they could do it only after taking his talisman. They spiked him through the wrist and feet, pinning him to the earth before burning him in a great fire that took many trees and lasted for days. Of course, these were just stories told around campfires. I mean, look guys, I don't know what I thought Lincoln really saw here, or what I expected to find, but this is… it's insane!"

Garrett lowered his voice to a whisper as if afraid he might wake the sleeping giant. "Insane, yeah, but the story makes perfect sense when you compare it to what Mr. B told us. Six sages defeated the old ones and took a God Stone from each. God Stone equals magic talisman. Sages equal witch doctors. It even looks like this thing might have been in a fire of some sort, and there is some kind of old wound on its wrist," he said, pointing.

"So, if this thing has skin like stone… how in the hell are you going to destroy it?" Paul asked.

Garrett turned to Paul, taking his eyes off Stoneclad for the first time. Paul looked bad – really bad. He must still be losing blood. Garrett needed to hurry. He swallowed, drawing his sword with a swish of metal across leather. "I'm going to cut the thing's head off with this sword."

"What?! You really think that sword is going to cut through that thing's big-ass neck? Its skin is like stone," Pete exclaimed, holding his hands palms up. "Hence the name!"

Janis turned to face Garrett and the others. "Maybe he's right, Garrett. Maybe we shouldn't."

"Yeah, I mean what if you hack at it and it just wakes it up or something," Pete said.

"Guys, Jesus Christ!" Garrett said in disbelief. "This is why we're here! There is no other way! Do you want this thing waking up!? Apep is on his way here right now, and if we don't do this, he *will* wake it up!"

No one answered.

"Now, if anyone wants to stand by me while I do this, let's go."

"I'll be right beside you, bro," Lenny said.

"You're right. Sorry, Garrett." Pete nodded, reluctantly stepping forward. "You know, Lincoln said he never actually went into the large chamber but only stood at the entryway, observing the giant by the light of his lantern. Once he was convinced of what he saw, he never returned to see it again." Pete inhaled the musty air, drawing it deep into his lungs. "Guys, we're further than any person has come since – well, since god knows when."

Quietly, afraid they might wake him, they eased alongside the thing's waist and past its chest. They couldn't see over it due to the thickness of the giant combined with the thickness of the stone slab it rested on.

"How tall do you think this thing is?" Lenny asked.

"Twenty-five feet," Pete guessed.

"No way, bro – I bet it's at least thirty, maybe more," Lenny said.

When they finally made their way to its head, Garrett sheathed his sword and climbed onto the stone slab. The giant's face was the scariest thing he had ever seen. This creature was no gentle Gulliver. No, not at all. This thing was battle-worn and menacing. Rather than resting in a peaceful sleep, the giant looked frozen in a state of rage.

"Jesus Christ, it looks seriously pissed off," Lenny said, joining Garrett.

Its lips were parted and curled in a contorted snarl. A glimmer of teeth shone beyond its parted lips, but what he could see looked wrong – more like they belonged to a shark than a – well, than a giant. But the most startling thing was that single eye, centered right in the middle of its forehead. Thankfully, it was closed. Nevertheless, Garrett couldn't shake the feeling the eye was going to pop open at any second and catch him in the act. Its brow was frozen in angry wrinkles broken by vertical scars. *Probably from ancient battles,* he thought.

"We're coming up there too," Janis said, climbing up onto the slab and scrunching in close to Lenny.

"Watch it, Janis. There is plenty of room – no need to get all frisky with my booty," Lenny said. "Better watch your girl, Petey!"

"Don't you wish, Lenny!" Janis said, punching him in the shoulder. "You couldn't get that lucky in your wettest dream!"

Pete and Breanne climbed up next.

"I'll stay here," Paul said pointing at his foot.

"I'll keep him company," David said, leaving his post by the doorway and coming closer to Paul.

Garrett caught movement out of the corner of his eye and turned to see a large rat scurrying away on the opposite side of the slab. Wondering why the rats didn't try and eat the giant, his eyes followed the rat until it disappeared into the shadows in the back half of the chamber. That's when he noticed it – something else that didn't belong – something impossible! The sight of it staggered him backward, nearly causing him to fall from the stone slab. He grabbed at Lenny's dobok sleeve and yanked. "Look! Jesus Christ, guys! What the hell is that!?" Garrett pointed toward the back of the chamber.

Only now from their perch on the slab could they behold what lay in the back half of the chamber. If they had set out to find anything more unbelievable than a giant in an underground pyramid in central Illinois, then they were looking at it.

"What do you guys see?" Paul asked.

"Well, the journal does mention it. I just didn't realize it was literal, and Lincoln wouldn't have known either if he didn't go past the door," Pete said.

"Um, hello, anybody? What the *hell* do you guys see?" Paul asked again.

"What did the journal say, Pete?" Garrett asked.

"It said the giant was guarded by the Thunderbird and that if the giant was disturbed, the Thunderbird would wake," Pete said shakily.

"That sounds like a pretty important detail, Pete!" Lenny said. "So, I'm guessing that thing is the Thunderbird!?" Not waiting for the obvious answer, he turned to Paul and David and shouted in a raspy whisper, "We got a Thunderbird over here."

"A what bird?" Paul asked.

"I don't want to sound stupid, Pete," Garrett said, "but that thing looks kinda like a pterodactyl, or wait a minute… is that a—"

"It's a dragon," Breanne interrupted.

"Balls! We got a dragon over here!" Lenny called down.

David began stepping backward toward the door again. "Did they say 'dragon'? They didn't…"

"I don't think anyone could say anything that sounds stupid given the situation. Guys, honestly, I thought the Native American kid telling Lincoln the story was speaking metaphorically," Pete said, heavy on the *r* words as all attempts at the persona of Mr. Cool slipped through the nervous cracks in his voice. "Like the Thunderbird god watches over the giant… not a freaking real-life dragon watching over a freaking real-life giant!"

They stood there for an awkward moment, gazing at the scaly beast as much in frozen terror as in awe. The dragon was huge, bigger than any animal Garrett had ever seen. Even in its current position, lying on the floor like a balled-up cat trying to keep warm, it still looked huge.

Light from the flames shimmered across its dinner plate–sized scales like sun on a mirrored glass building. Its wings ran from the base of its neck all the way down its back, but they were folded up in some strange way that made their true size impossible to judge. Knobby bones speared out from its wings and all along the dragon's back on both sides. Its head was thin and long, resting on the end of an even longer neck. Its face resembled that of an iguana but with a more pronounced cartilage ridge that ran all the way down to the tip of its nose. In the flickering light, they couldn't be sure of its true color, but Garrett guessed it was a metallic black. Its feet seemed more those of a bird than a lizard – like an eagle's but much, much larger and ending in gleaming black talons.

"Do you see that?!" Pete pointed at the dragon.

Lenny stepped up close beside him, trying to see what he was seeing. "See what?"

"Its head."

"Yeah, no shit. It's right there – if its eyes were open it would be looking directly at us," he said, pointing at the dragon's head, which sat facing them on the floor of the chamber.

"Not that head. The other one," Pete said, pointing again.

"Holy shit, it has more than one head!" Garrett had been too busy imagining the damage those massive talons could inflict to notice that it did, in fact, have two heads.

"I'm coming up – I got to get a look at this thing," Paul said.

But before he could start up, David grabbed his sleeve. "Wait, did you guys hear that?" he asked, looking back toward the corridor beyond the entrance.

No one dared breathe.

In the absolute silence of the chamber Garrett heard it, a soft sound growing louder, as the distant sound of boots slapping stone grew closer.

David gazed up at them, fresh panic in his eyes. "Guys… someone's coming."

27

The Real Apep

Wednesday, April 6 – God Stones Day 1
Petersburg, Illinois

Paul pointed to the opening. "Incoming!"

Breanne, Pete, Janis, Lenny, and Garrett all stood on top of the slab, crowded around the giant's head.

Breanne tensed. *This is it, isn't it?*

Garrett reached back over his shoulder and drew his sword and again it slid free of the scabbard, the sound cutting the silence with a *whoosh.*

A dark silhouette appeared in the opening of the chamber.

"If you're going to do it, bro, you better do it now," Lenny said in an urgent whisper.

The silhouette stepped forward and spoke. "Garrett, I wouldn't do that."

Garret gasped. "Oh, please, god, don't let it be him!"

"Garrett how – how can *he* be here?" Lenny asked, his face twitching as he tried to puzzle it out. "Unless – unless he's Apep?"

"Listen to me," the familiar voice said. "If you do it, if you cut off its head, that dragon will wake up, and if it does… it's going to kill us all."

Garrett's face contorted as though he had been gut-punched. "I trusted you! You were my friend!"

"I'm still your friend, and I'm telling you, put down that sword before you get us all killed."

Breanne could see the pain of betrayal in Garrett's eyes. She leaned in close to Lenny and whispered, "Who is he, Lenny?"

Lenny gulped hard, trying to find his voice. "Eugene."

Garrett looked like he was going to be sick. "My whole goddamn life's a lie? Nothing is real?!" he shouted, his voice echoing off the walls.

Pete flinched, then looked at the giant, the dragon, and finally back at the giant, before letting out a relieved sigh. "Well, at least we know loud noise won't wake them up."

"So, how long have you known we've had the book, Eugene?" Garrett asked. "My god, you're the one who tried to trick Lincoln. You pretended to be his friend. He wrote the journal for you, didn't he? Then something happened – he was going to give it to you, but he found you out, and hid it in… in your basement."

To Breanne, Garrett seemed to be just as surprised by his own accusations as everyone else. She watched the wheels of his mind spin behind his glistening eyes, the pain on his face as evident as the giant sprawled out before them.

"So, you bought the house to look for the book, or have you always owned it? My god – all that work, you weren't remodeling, were you, Eugene? You were searching for Lincoln's book!"

Breanne stared at Eugene. Could this be Apep? He didn't look like much with his thin arms and narrow shoulders. He was bald except for two patches of dark hair resting above his ears. Could this really be the guy who killed Jerry? Who tried to kill her family in the pit? The crazed maniac responsible for her father's coma?

Eugene began to walk forward.

"Stop right there!" Garrett shouted. He drew his sword back like a lumberjack cocking an axe. "I'll hack this thing's head off if you take one more step!"

Eugene stopped and put up his hands in surrender. "Garrett, you have to listen to me. I'm your friend, here to help keep you from making a horrible mistake. I'm not Apep."

"Really? Then who is?"

As if on cue, the sound of hurried footfalls in a dead run came echoing down the corridor.

"Well now, I think we are about to find out," Eugene said.

Breanne spun to face the opening in time to see a combat-booted man burst into the chamber, holding an assault rifle to his right shoulder. The soldier swung the rifle back and forth, frantically searching. With only a quick glance she recognized the weapon as an M4 carbine. She had shot that weapon plenty with her brothers. She didn't particularly like guns, but her brothers had insisted she know how to use them.

The man with the M4 slid to a stop. He was wearing military-issue camo BDU pants and a regulation khaki undershirt. But it was his eyes that drew her attention. His eyes looked wild in the light from the flames, like there was an untethering in them, an insanity. Breanne felt a sudden and frightening fear coalesce inside her gut as the man continued forward, searching the room.

"Coach Dagrun?" Lenny breathed.

Eugene pressed his lips together tightly and pointed a contemptuous finger. "He's your Apep."

Finding Eugene, Dagrun raised the weapon, aimed, and pulled the trigger all in one fluid motion.

Click!

Everyone flinched – even Eugene. But the gun failed to fire.

Coach Dagrun sneered at Eugene before turning to Garrett. "Goddammit, brick, what are you waiting for? An invitation? Sever that sum-bitch's head, and I mean now!"

Breanne blinked. "Lenny?"

"That's our cross-country coach," Lenny said, his eyebrows all bunched up in confusion.

Garrett tensed at the direct order, but he hesitated. He looked at Lenny then Breanne. "Something feels wrong. I… I don't know."

She looked at Eugene. He was a scrawny, ordinary-looking old guy. No cloak or trench coat like she had seen Apep wearing earlier. But he could have simply removed it. She followed Garrett's eyes to the balding guy's feet. *Were those the boots Apep wore?* Why couldn't she remember the goddamned boots? Eugene's khakis were wet up to his knees, mud-caked and filthy above that. *But what about what Garrett said about the house, and the journal?*

Then she looked at the coach guy. No cloak on him either, and he too wore boots, black combat boots. Apep's boots? Could Apep be Garrett's coach? He talked like he was military, and he had the M4. He certainly looked much more capable of picking Jerry up with one hand.

She looked at Garrett and shrugged when suddenly he gasped.

"What?" she whispered.

"Look at him. Really look. Coach Dagrun's clothes – they're… filthy and torn."

Pete narrowed his eyes, focusing his perfect vision on the coach. "Not filthy, Garrett – they look like they… like… like they've been on fire!"

"Do it, Garrett – do it now!" Dagrun yelled.

Garrett kept the sword cocked but relaxed his grip slightly. "Why are your clothes burnt, Coach?"

"What?" Dagrun's expression changed from stern command to discombobulation.

"Your clothes! Why are they burnt?" Garrett repeated with an even more accusing tone.

"I… I came to the dojo… after" – he pointed an accusing finger at Eugene – "after Apep left, but I was too late… I tried to save him – I swear, Garrett. I tried, but he was… beyond saving…"

Eugene, still holding his hands palms out, shook his head back and forth. "No. No way, Garrett. He's burnt because he's Apep. Don't listen to him! It's all a trick to get you to wake the dragon. That's what Apep wants – to burn the world. He can't wake the dragon, Garrett. Not by himself. Don't you see? It's a trick! It's all been a trick to get you to do it! It has to be you!" Eugene's pleading voice pressed, begging him to believe.

Careful to keep his sword high and at the ready, Garrett turned to

Bre and Paul. "Did either of you get a good look at him when he took the stones?"

Paul narrowed his eyes at the two men. "No. It could be either one of them."

Garrett shook his head in frustration. "I don't know what to do. Who do I trust? Bre? Can you tell which one is Apep?"

"I'm sorry, Garrett, I can't tell which one is Ap—" But before she could finish her sentence, her eyes clouded over, turning a smoky white. Then she spoke a single name. "Janis."

As the name left her lips, Garrett let out a loud *oomph!* He slammed forward, falling into her, the force causing both of them to lose their balance and tumble off the slab. She felt herself falling but couldn't see anything. The chamber's stone floor came fast. She felt a sharp pain as her elbow raked across the stone, her skin pulling away. She felt a knee or maybe an elbow dig into her side. To her right she heard a clanging of metal as Garrett's sword slid away from them into the shadows.

"Bre! You okay?" Garrett asked, untangling himself from her.

"I'm… I'm okay," she managed, blinking away the cloudiness as she pushed herself up onto her elbows just in time to catch movement from above as Pete rushed forward.

"Janis! What in god's name are you doing?" Pete shouted.

Janis quickly turned to face him.

He grabbed her by the shoulders. "Why? Why would you do that, Ja—"

Pete stopped mid-sentence, like he was frozen perfectly still.

Janis had her back to Breanne but was standing in front of Pete, blocking her view. She could only see his face, which now held a confused frown that matched Breanne's own.

Janis glanced back over her shoulder, looked right into Breanne's eyes, and winked.

"Pete!" shouted Lenny, who was still on the slab. He stepped up behind him and put a tentative hand on Pete's shoulder. "Pete, what's wrong with you? Janis, what's wrong with him?!"

Garrett stood now, pulling Breanne to her feet.

"Garrett, what's happening?!" David shouted.

Paul was in motion now, moving forward toward his sister.

Pete looked into Janis's eyes and searched for understanding but found nothing. Her eyes were as empty as an abyss, like looking into space on a starless night. He looked down then, and saw Janis holding the handle of a knife – its blade buried to the hilt in his stomach.

Pete tried to say something, but for some strange reason, words wouldn't come. He blinked and smiled, tears spilling down his cheeks, then the darkness pressed in upon him as he tipped backward off the slab.

28

The Underneath

Wednesday, April 6 – God Stones Day 1
Rural Chiapas State, Mexico

A hundred feet below, the walls around Sarah began to sink slowly, slipping downward. The sense of vertigo overtook her, and she threw her hands up as she stumbled forward, falling into the wall. Reflexively, Sarah widened her stance as if she were on a surfboard.

"Sarah! What is happening?!" Fredy yelled through the radio.

Sarah fumbled for the radio button on her vest and depressed it. "I… I don't know!" she shouted back.

"Stay calm, Sarah – we're getting you out!" Fredy's voice came back in a false calm.

The sound of grinding stone echoed all around her. Sarah realized it then. The walls were moving by even faster, but it wasn't the walls that were moving – it was her. She was rising up –fast.

"Christ – hurry, Fredy!"

Sarah was moving upward way too fast and gaining speed as she rose. She squatted down butt-to-heels, her fingertips touching the floor for balance. She didn't know if the rising floor was going to stop or continue upward, smashing her into the statue that stood straddling the hole. The irony was not lost on her. *I'm about to die by getting shoved up a giant statue's ass.* Her only hope was to try and time her arrival perfectly and jump clear before she was smashed into the statue.

~

Gabi ran on unsteady legs toward her father and Fredy as the ground beneath her trembled.

"Back! Back!" Andrés shouted, turning to Gabi and holding out his arm. "Stay back!"

Gabi stopped short and moved behind the leg of the giant, wrapping her arms around it for stability, as she heard Fredy tell Sarah they were getting her out.

Fredy released the button on the radio and with it all the false calm. "Andrés! Pull! Get Sarah out!" he shouted, grabbing hold of the rope still tied to the giant statue's ankle.

"Sarah!" Gabi screamed, but the rumbling had grown so loud she couldn't even hear her own shouts.

The floor shook violently, threatening to knock them all off their feet. Bones rattled on their wooden rods, and some of the skull racks collapsed into heaps, unable to withstand the jostling.

"Itzel! Get Gabi to the stairs!" Andrés shouted.

Gabi's mom grabbed her by the wrist. She followed numbly, her mind not on the stairs. Her mind was on the hole – on Sarah. As she followed her mother toward the promise of safety, she never took her eyes from the hole.

"¡Ay, Dios mío!" Fredy shouted, realizing that as fast as they were pulling Sarah's rope, they were only collecting slack. Fredy dropped the rope and crawled toward the edge, peering over the side as he clung to the floor, trying not to fall.

Andrés stopped pulling. "What's happening!?"

"Sarah is coming up – and fast."

Gabi sucked a sharp terrified breath that seemed to inflate her eyes rather than her lungs. As soon as Sarah broke the surface she leapt forward from the hole, launching upward and outward, narrowly missing the stone giant's crotch.

Fredy sprang forward faster than Gabi had ever seen the older man move, his arms extending like a football goalie going for the ball. As Sarah fell into Fredy's arms, the momentum sent both tumbling across the floor.

The lid stopped even with the top of the floor in an abrupt clunk of finality.

Everything went quiet.

Gabi, Itzel, and María were at the stairs. Each stopped, frozen in place. No one breathed as they listened. The quiet filled the chamber with the silence of a sanctuary.

Finally, Fredy sighed in relief. "Are you alright, Sarah?"

Sarah nodded. "I'm… I'm okay, Fredy," she said, pushing herself up onto her palms. "Is everyone else alright?"

Itzel let go of Gabi's hand and ran to Andrés, pulling him to his feet.

"Wait, Mamá," Gabi started to say, and she wanted to say more too. She wanted to say, *Come on, let's go. We have to go!* But as she opened her mouth to speak, the lid beneath the giant statue began to rotate.

"¡¿Qué diablos?!" Andrés shouted.

The lid clicked into place, and with a violent jolt the entire room dropped a full meter, knocking them all off their feet. The sound of grinding stone returned as the room began to sink.

In the center of the room the statue stood motionless, unmoving, not sinking. The lid and lip around it now formed a column.

Gabi looked up toward the scene on the wall. It was now pulling away from her as the floor sank. *She knew it now, that wasn't a lid at all.* She thought about the room. *A perfectly circular room, with a perfectly circular shaft dead center.* She shook her head, frantically trying to comprehend – to understand what was happening. They were standing on a circular platform that was dropping. *Like an elevator,* she thought. *The hollow column in the middle must somehow work as part of the mechanism.*

Fredy wasn't trying to figure out what was happening, he was shouting orders. "Andrés! María! Everyone! Get to the stairs!"

They all ran to the spiral staircase. From above lights bounced down the stairs.

Juan and Manuel appeared on the bottom step. "What is happening!?"

Andrés was the first to reach Gabi and the stairs, but the bottom step was nearly two meters high now. Her father snatched her up by the waist, lifting her in the air.

"Take her, Manuel! Take her!" Andrés begged as he held her by the waist above his head.

The two men fell to their hands and knees, reaching for Gabi.

"Reach, Gabriela! Reach!" her father screamed.

She did reach. She stretched her small hands out to the men with all she had, but the floor kept sinking and their hands pulled away. Sarah, her mother, and María all tried to jump too but none could make the grab.

Without warning, a crack opened at the bottom of the stairs. Gabi turned to see that the gap stretched all the way around the room. The floor continued to descend as the crack grew from a few centimeters into a dozen and then into a meter then more. An expanse of impenetrable darkness opened around them as cool air washed over the sinking platform. The few skull racks that remained standing tipped off the edge, the precious artifacts plummeting into the unknown.

Instinctively they all backed away from the edge.

The rumble softened as sound escaped into the vastness around them, but still they continued to descend.

"Manuel, go get rope!" Andrés shouted.

"Okay! I'll return for you, compadres!" he said, disappearing up the stairs.

Gabi's father grabbed her wrist with one hand, motioning to Itzel and María with the other. "Come on!" They ran back to where Sarah and Fredy stood near the center column, away from the edge of the platform. Her father held them tight to his chest, as if he were waiting for death itself to announce its arrival. "Sarah, what's happening?"

"It must be another trap!" Fredy asked.

Sarah answered in a voice that wasn't completely hysterical. She didn't need to yell anymore either as the rumble dissipated into the darkness beyond. "No, I don't think so, Fredy. This is too elaborate. We're descending to—"

"To the lower chamber!" Gabi burst out. "The one where the god sleeps!"

29

Judas

Wednesday, April 6 – God Stones Day 1
Petersburg, Illinois

Garrett stood on the temple floor next to Breanne, staring up at Janis. Lenny stood next to her, his own face flooded with horror. In that moment Garrett's emotions stalled. He felt like he was outside himself watching from somewhere else. This wasn't real. None of this was actually happening. He didn't just watch Janis stab Pete. He blinked, shaking his head. God, this couldn't happen. This couldn't really happen. But it was happening – it was.

Janis glared back down from the slab, her face as hard and cold as the steel blade still in her hand.

"Pete!" Lenny screamed down from the slab, his eyes going wide. "What the…?" He reached down into the small back pocket of his dobok where he had safely tucked the knife Paul had loaned him in trade for the staff – but it was gone. "Garrett! That's Paul's knife! She took it when she grabbed my ass earlier!"

Janis turned to Lenny.

The strange surrealistic feeling faded as fear clenched hold of Garrett, but it wasn't fear for himself. "Lenny! Jesus, Lenny, get out of there!" he shouted, as he and Breanne ran to Pete, who lay facedown on the slab in a pool of his own blood.

Janis turned to face Lenny, who was still standing on the slab. "Well, Lenny, what's it going to be? You can join your friends down there or bleed up here."

"For the record, I never really trusted you, Janis." Lenny threw a roundhouse kick at the girl's face.

Janis easily slipped the kick and countered with a fast, stabbing thrust, the serrated blade slicing open Lenny's dobok and the flesh of his shoulder along with it.

"Ah!" Lenny shouted, spinning away.

Janis didn't hesitate, snapping a quick kick into Lenny's back. The momentum sent him flailing off the slab.

Lenny tucked when he hit the floor, rolled, and sprang back to his feet. He spun back toward the slab, ready to give it another go, but stopped abruptly when he heard Janis start chanting. It was a low mumble at first, but as she continued, her voice became louder, more commanding.

"What the hell is she doing?" Lenny asked, craning his head to look down at his shoulder.

"I don't know, but it can't be good! Are you okay?" Garrett asked.

"Yeah, I don't think it's very deep," Lenny said.

"Help me with Pete," Garrett said, grabbing one of Pete's wrists as he nodded for Lenny to grab the other.

"I'll get his feet," Breanne said.

Pete didn't move and his arm was limp. Garrett's stomach turned.

With Lenny and Breanne's help, he dragged Pete away from the stone slab and the chanting Janis. David and Paul joined them. "This way," Garrett said. He knew they couldn't go back toward the entrance – Eugene and Dagrun were both in the way. They couldn't flee to the other side of the slab unless they wanted to risk getting closer to the sleeping dragon. They went in the only direction they could and backed themselves into the one corner void of giants, dragons, or evil wizards.

Eugene moved cautiously toward Janis as she continued to chant.

Dagrun carefully followed, matching Eugene's movements.

"Garrett, do you remember the story I told you about Sun Tzu?" Eugene yelled toward the group, without taking his eyes off Dagrun. "He wrote that book *The Art of War*. You remember?"

Garrett spotted his sword lying behind him against the chamber wall. He dropped Pete's wrist and lunged forward, grabbing his sword.

"Do you remember, my boy?"

Eugene loved to teach kids lessons, whether it be about the lord or life in general – always in a humble way, never by putting himself above others. But there was something different in his tone now, something strange in the look. Something that hinted at… contempt.

On the slab, Janis chanted faster now.

Garrett tightened his grip on the hilt and set his jaw. He had come to trust Eugene more than any other adult. In fact, he'd admired him. Garrett watched the man's face now, but it wasn't admiration he felt. Now he felt… sick. Sick because in that moment he knew he had been fooled.

"Sun Tzu taught us to subdue the enemy!" he shouted, nodding sharply to Janis.

The ground began to shake as giant spears of stalagmite broke through the floor.

"What's happening?!" Breanne shouted over the rumble.

Each spear was part of a uniform row, stretching up, gaining in height and width, until finally crashing into the ceiling one after the other. *Chunk! Chunk! Chunk!*

By the time the stalagmite spears stopped growing, they were only inches apart. Suddenly they were in a cell built of thick stone columns, each at least a couple feet in circumference. Garrett and the other five were effectively trapped, separated from Janis, Dagrun, and Eugene by large stone pillars.

Coach Dagrun ran forward.

"Stop right there or I'll burn them alive!" Eugene ordered, raising his hands up, fingers splayed. Then for effect he curled both hands into tight fists of burning grey flame. "Think I won't do it?"

Dagrun stopped.

So, there it is, I've failed, Garrett thought. *Eugene is Apep.*

Eugene paced in front of the stone cell. "Oh dear, Garrett. Oh my, you're in a real mess now. You were the last hope for your Keepers of the Light. How sad for you, how sad for your pathetic world. You can't be blamed, no, no," he said, waving a finger. "What a pathetic prophecy. Doomed from the beginning. I should know, I was here long before it was written."

Everything was spinning out of control. How was he supposed to fix this? Wasn't that what the prophecy said? He was the chosen one? Now they were trapped. Pete lay on the floor bleeding. *So much blood.* Paul had passed out too – the blood loss from his leg must have finally been too much.

"That's enough, Apep," Dagrun said. "I've been watching you for some time now, doing what you do, plotting your big comeback. Very clever, posing as an unassuming Christian do-gooder, but you've never fooled me."

Eugene pulled a face then shot Dagrun a look. "Enough? Yes, pathetic human. I suppose you're right!" He raised his skinny arm and motioned with his fingers as he mumbled some strange words Garrett had never heard. "Shirayshi, akdoe!" Shadows darted from Eugene's spread fingers toward Dagrun, taking form into something seemingly solid and pointed.

Dagrun motioned idly with his own hand, as if he were back-handing a pesky mosquito, not magic from a powerful wizard. The dark shards deflected before reaching him, falling harmlessly to the floor and dissipating back into shadow.

"Holy shit, did you see that?" Lenny said, peeking through a gap between the stalagmites.

"Yeah," Garrett said, allowing the tiniest bit of hope to seep into his voice. He knelt next to Pete, speaking in a low whisper. "Guys, we need a plan."

Eugene frowned uneasily. "I don't recognize you. What's your name, Keeper?"

"My students call me Coach Dagrun."

Eugene looked befuddled. "Dagrun?"

"That's right. It's the name I gave myself long ago."

Eugene's expression changed, taking on a suddenly uncomfortable pucker. "No," he mumbled slowly, his head beginning to shake. "That name has special meaning where I come from… it means—"

"Dragon," Coach interrupted.

"Father! Who is he?" Janis asked, uneasiness clear in her voice.

Lenny and Garrett shared a look. "Father?"

"No. It isn't possible! Syldan? You can't be here!" Eugene said, his eyes springing wide with the terror of some realization.

"But I am here," Dagrun said.

"You couldn't have opened the gate! Not without the Sound Eye!"

"No. I couldn't have. You opened it for me, Apep," Dagrun said.

"But that would mean you have been here since…?"

Dagrun pointed at the prone giant. "I've been here since you and your nephilbock opened the gate the second time."

"But… but how?" Eugene stammered.

"The portal stayed open just long enough for me to slip through before it collapsed." Dagrun stepped forward toward Eugene. "Come now, Apep, did you really think he wouldn't find out? Did you think our father would allow you to lead our enemies to another world where you could build an army unchallenged?"

"It is you!" Eugene staggered backward like he had been struck. "Brother!"

Dagrun's body began to change, to transform. His limbs, both arms and legs, stretched several inches, as did his neck. His skin changed to a bluish hue, and his ears grew to points. His eyes slanted up, then curved in a graceful arc back down. His facial features changed too, his jaw becoming more prominent and his hair transforming from a short, sandy-brown buzzcut to a long flowing sheet of black. Within a few seconds, he had completely changed into a tall, lean… what?

Garrett and Lenny tried to find an angle to see between the stone columns.

"Jesus, Garrett, what is that?" Lenny said, pointing to the thing standing where Coach had been.

"I… I can't tell for sure. But he isn't human."

The corner of Syldan's mouth turned up in what Garrett could only figure was a cross between a hateful sneer and a smile.

"That's right, Apep, twelve thousand years I've waited."

Eugene's thick brows drew together. "But—"

Syldan held up a silencing hand. "During most of my time here I allowed myself to just forget you. But over the centuries there were the nights I couldn't forget. The nights I lay awake thinking of what I might say to you in this moment. I have played it out so many times. But now that the moment is upon us, I have only questions. What is it you hope to accomplish, Apep? You are a failure. You failed our father. You failed your people. You failed your own brother, and even when you tried to kill me as I slept… still you failed. Did you think if you killed me our father would change his mind and give you the throne?

Eugene's eyes flared and looked wild. Wilder than Garrett thought possible.

"You nearly destroyed this planet with your ignorance, Apep. And what if I hadn't come? What if I hadn't intervened with the dragons you brought here? I will tell you what – they would have wiped out this whole planet. You joined with our sworn enemies and brought dragons here! To what end? You thought you could control them – *you?* I am a Dagrun Heru, Apep! You could never have controlled them!"

"Enough!" Eugene screamed, his face screwing up in disgust. "It is laughable that you have the temerity to lecture me. Do you think I cared about controlling dragons? Or about this planet? I came here to build my own army of giants. And the dragons?" he huffed. "I knew I was on the cusp of losing control of them, but it mattered not! All I needed to do was finish my work in Egypt. The pyramid was nearly complete, and then I could have opened the gate home. I wouldn't have needed to control them, they were starving – they'd have laid waste to everything in their path."

"You would destroy your own kingdom, your own people? You would have unleashed thousands more dragons into our world?"

"Yes, Syldan! Where were *our people* when father banished me? Where were *you* when father had me stripped naked and marched into the misting sand?" Eugene's face was trembling with rage as he pointed a shaking finger at the newly transformed Dagrun. "To return to

Karelia and take what is rightfully mine – I would unleash hell! I would burn it all and be king of ashes. But at least I would be king!"

"After all this time father will be long dead! Who knows if Osonian even exists?!"

Eugene smiled. "You are a bigger fool than even I could have guessed. Time is not linear, Syldan. I won't have lost a single minute from the time I last opened the portal!"

"What?"

"The heir to the throne is the eldest son. I am the eldest, Syldan! Not you! What father took from me goes against everything we are. I will enjoy looking into his eyes as the life drains from his worthless soul!"

As Eugene beat a fist into his scrawny chest for emphasis, Garrett gaped, mouth open in wide-eyed shock at the once-kind man with the shoestring arms – the bean counter, as he often referred to himself. The man who gave Garrett and his friends each a penny to make a wish. He looked at Lenny, whose feelings must have mirrored his own, because as the lighthearted Sunday school teacher continued ranting like a psychopath on the topic of destroying worlds, what Lenny said next captured Garrett's feelings perfectly.

"Garrett, if there is really a Twilight Zone, we're balls-deep in it now."

Garrett could only offer a slow nod of acknowledgment as he turned back to the gap between columns.

"Gods, I should have just killed you in Egypt, but Turek convinced me we should only imprison you and cast you into a suspended sleep. I had my people in Egypt dig you a nice deep hole and stick you behind walls so thick it should have been impossible for you to escape. But just as Turek predicted, here you are."

Eugene's clean-shaven cheek twitched as his head cocked to the side. "It was you who doomed me to that rotten hole for nearly nine thousand years! My own brother!"

Now Eugene's form began to change. No longer was he the scrawny accountant. In only seconds, Eugene was gone. In his place Apep appeared, taking on the same bluish hue in his skin as his brother Syldan, stretching to nearly seven feet tall, his frame filling out into a muscular build. His once-bald head suddenly boasted its own full head of black hair, long, silky, and dark as night. His chin became more chiseled and his nose lengthened to match his brother's. He stood up tall, pushing out his chest.

Syldan met his brother's violet eyes with his own and nodded. "It was I."

"And you would kill me for what? These humans?" Apep spat, his face contorting in bitter disgust. "We are dökkálfar! Superior in every way! Our race lives thousands of years in comparison to their paltry dozens. We are lucky to bear one child of our own, but them – they breed like Karelian morph flies, consuming everything until there's nothing left. They're a plague on their own world – roaches, vermin, meaningless insects! I will be happy to know this world is pulled apart at its fabric as I step through the portal home!"

Janis watched on, her face deadpan as if an emotionless robot dwelled behind her alien eyes.

Inside their cell, Garrett and Lenny tried to follow along. Garrett pulled his eyes away from the gap to glance back at Breanne and David. David knelt at Pete's side across from Breanne, who had her hands pressed down over Pete's stomach.

Pete was dying or maybe dead. Garrett couldn't tell, but he looked bad.

"Bre, I need to do something," David said.

Breanne's eyes darted up as she tried desperately to stop Pete's bleeding, applying pressure to the deep wound. "What?" she gasped.

David nodded, motioning her to let him take over.

She peeled her hands from Pete's gut.

Garrett tried to swallow back a wave of queasiness.

David tore open Pete's shirt and placed his hand over the slippery wound, a dark crimson seeping up between his fingers.

Garrett's heart sank at the site of the jagged puncture. *So much blood.* More than he had ever seen in real life. Time was not on their side. They needed to get out and get help for Pete. He tore his eyes from his friend to share a look of worry with Breanne. She pressed her lips into a tight line. Her brows were knitted, and Garrett realized she didn't look so good. Like she was fighting to hold it together. *Please don't lose it on me, Bre.* Somehow, he knew if she fell apart, he would follow right behind her, and then what?

As she seemed to read his face, she drew in a deep breath and turned back to David. "That's good, David, push down hard – try and stop the bleeding." Breanne changed her focus to her brother's leg, assessing the blood-soaked cloth covering his wounds. "I'm going to need to change this dressing – he's lost so much blood."

Lenny whispered to Garrett. "You're right, we need a plan, bro. Do you think you can use that focus technique to break through one of these rock pillars like you did with the patio blocks at the test?"

"No, I don't have super-strength, Lenny. There's a chance I could slow down the thing I am focusing on, but what's the use in it?"

"Well, can you slow Apep down while we think?" Lenny asked.

"I have no idea if that would even work on him. Besides, slowing things down doesn't help us get past these columns." Garrett slapped a palm against one of the giant stone stalagmites.

"Okay, well what about that sword?" Lenny said, pointing.

Garrett looked down to find he was still holding the sword in his hands.

"It was Turek's, right? Maybe it is magic or something?"

"I'm not using this sword to hack at stone columns, Lenny! What if it breaks? How the hell am I going to cut off the giant's head then?" Garrett asked.

Lenny held up his hands, waving off the idea. "Yeah, that didn't sound so stupid until I said it out loud."

Garrett sheathed his sword. "We need Paul."

On the other side of the columns, Syldan sighed heavily. "No, Apep. I won't let you destroy the humans."

Apep shifted impatiently.

"Since meeting Turek I have fought in at least a thousand wars with these humans. Waiting for the day to come – this day. Since then I've come to know them. Their lives are so short, yet maybe this is why they live so fully, so completely. You have no idea the potential of these humans. I have watched them live, love, and die. I've seen them give their lives for one another – even for me." His tone was certain. "No, brother, I won't let you destroy this world."

Janis moved close to her father.

"And you think you're going to stop me?" Apep said.

"You're aware of the prophecy of Garrett Turek?" Syldan asked.

Garrett froze at the sound of his name.

Apep laughed. "The one humans believe in so blindly they are willing to send a boy here to give me precisely what I need to wake the nephillbock!"

Syldan shook his head with an almost sorry expression. "Your vanity has no end. You think this is all about you, and so you underestimate them just like you did Turek."

"They are nothing! You speak of Turek. I killed Turek!" Apep said, his voice shrill, his patience slipping as a sword seemed to materialize in his hand from nowhere.

Syldan didn't even flinch. "You did what you were supposed to do, nothing more. Do you think the god of the humans would have died at your hand if it wasn't part of a greater plan? You played a part, Apep, and that is all."

"The god of the humans?" Apep frowned as he spun the sword in a figure eight, testing the weight of it. The sword sizzled like a searing steak as it cut through the air.

Garrett frowned.

"What did he say, Garrett? Did he say Turek was a god?" Lenny asked, his voice raspy in an urgent whisper that threatened to become much more.

"I… No. I don't think that's what he said." That couldn't be what he said. That would mean… mean what? Garrett's head spun suddenly. The prophecy, his parents, James. The Keepers of the Light. He was the light. No. He couldn't think about this. Not now.

Right now – they needed out.

30

Farewell, Brother!

Wednesday, April 6 – God Stones Day 1
Petersburg, Illinois

The tension was rising between the two men, and Garrett felt his heart racing. Behind him, he heard Breanne saying David's name over and over. On the third time, he spun, glancing back with a frown, trying to divide his attention.

David was sitting cross-legged with his eyes closed. His hand was over Pete's wound, but he wasn't pressing down.

"David, you okay?" Bre asked again.

No answer.

"David, you need to press down firmly to stop the bleeding."

No answer.

Garret glanced back again. "David, what's up, man?"

No answer.

Breanne gasped. "Garrett!"

Spinning around, Garrett saw that David was opening his eyes. And they were – glowing. "What the…"

"His eyes!" Lenny said.

David grinned widely. "Finally, I know what I'm supposed to do."

His chest began to emit a golden glow, which then migrated out from his torso, and across the rest of his body then down through his arms and legs. The glowing aura intensified, lighting the stone cell like blinds had been thrown back to reveal the morning sun. It flowed like liquid sunshine out of David's hands and into Pete's wound.

Now the glow was gone from David; the only remaining light was coming from Pete's gut. It looked like a bright lightbulb had been suddenly turned on inside him. They all watched as, slowly, the light dissipated, fading away until it too was gone.

"David?" Garrett said, watching his friend sway back and forth.

David blinked a few times. "It's okay, I… I just feel like I stood up too fast."

Garrett frowned. David hadn't stood up, but just as concerning was that his words were slurred, like that time they got into some booze during a sleepover. They'd drunk so much that, the next day, when David's father pulled out the bottle of vodka to make a Bloody Mary, he quickly realized it was mostly water, which they'd stupidly added to cover up what they'd done. David sounded just like he had that night, right before he'd hurled on his mom's favorite crocheted afghan…

David blinked again and this time his eyes rolled back in his head. He swayed forward then tipped over onto his side, unconscious.

"David!" Breanne shouted.

Apep and Syldan were still arguing. Either they didn't notice what had happened inside the stone cell or they simply didn't care.

Everyone crowded around David.

"Are you okay? David?" Lenny slapped him in the face.

Next to David, Pete opened his eyes. "Janis… Why?"

"Pete! My god, Pete!" Garrett said, frantically wiping at Pete's blood-coated stomach with the bottom of his dobok. "Your stab wound! It's gone!" All that remained was a jagged scar. It looked pink and fresh, but it was sealed.

"She stabbed me!? She tried to kill me!" Pete said, his face twisted in disbelief.

"Yeah, well, you missed the part about Apep being her dad."

"What? Apep? But…"

"Listen, Pete, we're in the shit, man. Can you move? I mean does it hurt?" Garrett asked.

Pete slowly turned and pushed himself up onto his elbow. He looked down at his stomach, still smeared with blood. "My shirt's trashed," he said, lifting one of the torn edges. "My mom's going to be pissed."

"Forget the shirt. Are you okay?" Garrett pressed.

"I… I think so," he said, blinking. "Things are just fuzzy, and I got a stomachache, but yeah, I think… I think I'm okay."

Garrett turned to Bre and Lenny. "Wake David up."

"I'm trying, bro," Lenny said.

Garrett turned back to the gap between the stones. "Well, try harder. Whatever he did to Pete he needs to do to Paul."

Bre and Lenny looked at one another in simultaneous realization. "Wake up, David! You have to wake up!"

Outside Syldan took a step toward the dragon. "I have taken precautions, Apep. Now, I am going to finish what was started."

Apep squinted his eyes. "You put the dragon in the tomb after imprisoning me?"

Syldan moved completely from Apep's path, placing a hand on the sleeping dragon. He nodded. "You slept through the dragon wars, Apep, but I didn't and, together, Turek and I killed thousands of earth-born dragons and we captured the elder seven – the seven you brought here from Karelia," he said accusingly. "Then we came back to not only this tomb, but each tomb – all seven, placing an elder dragon inside each. Turek tied each dragon to the same spell keeping the nephilbock asleep. You wake him, you wake an angry dragon."

"I've heard enough of your words, brother," Apep said, his sword beginning to glow with a radiant blue energy as a razor-sharp tentacle snaked out from the tip. Slowly the strange blade slithered back and forth as if alive before drawing up, poised to strike. Apep pointed the tip of the now-coiled sword toward Syldan. "Soon, Syldan, soon I'll build an army so immense it will devour this world and unleash hell upon ours. I will force all of Karelia into submission! The entire planet will serve one king! One god!" Apep smiled, toothy and proud.

Garrett and Lenny shared terrified looks.

"You are truly mad, Apep!" Syldan said.

"Balls!" Lenny said. "This is going to break bad, bro, I can feel it."

Despite the fact that Coach Dagrun just turned into a… drakkawhatever, Garrett still felt in his gut that he could trust him. "No, we still got Coach!"

Outside the stone cell, Syldan shouted ancient words of power in a thundering voice. "Akozak ak ff esh!" His M4 carbine changed from steel to a bright blue light then rematerialized into a brutal-looking war hammer. The head of the hammer rested on a crooked wooden handle wrapped in leather strapping. One side of the head was shining silver, blunt with smaller knobs, like an oversized meat tenderizer, while the other had a black spike that resembled one of the dragon's talons Garrett had seen a few moments ago. The two sides of the hammer blended together in a swirl of black and silver.

With his other hand Syldan drew a Colt .45. It also transformed into the strange light then materialized into a short double-edged bastard sword. The blade looked as though it was made of black onyx and the handle of ebony. Syldan smacked the two weapons together, creating a loud *crack!* followed by a brilliant burst of blue light. He ran forward, charging Apep.

Apep tossed his own sword from one hand to the other then back again as he stepped back with his right leg.

As Syldan closed the gap, Apep struck out with his sword, their weapons clashing with a crackle of energy. "You've no idea of my sacrifice. Because of you, I was forced to mate with one of these animals. I was forced to go against our own god and create an abomination. That's how committed I am, Syldan. The laws of our own gods can't even keep me from my destiny!" He pointed accusingly at Janis.

Syldan blocked with the sword and drove the war hammer down hard from overhead.

Apep side-stepped and countered.

Syldan swiped the strike away effortlessly with the bastard sword.

Flames danced in Apep's violet eyes. "You doomed me to this place… this filthy place!" He lunged again at his brother, and this time the snaking sword flexed unnaturally, finding its way around Syldan's war hammer and slicing open his face.

Syldan let out an angry war cry and attacked with both weapons, switching between the war hammer and the sword in a flurry of violent blows. The barrage of swings backed Apep across the chamber toward the sleeping giant. Syldan faked a strike with the bastard sword as he dropped to his knees, striking down on Apep's foot with the war hammer.

The spiked end impaled Apep's foot.

He shrieked in pain. "Lilith!"

Garrett and Lenny watched on in stunned shock as Janis changed. Not into the older woman they knew as Eugene's wife, Lilith, but into something between Janis and Lilith in age, yet not human either. Her skin changed from Janis's pale peach to a slightly darker blue-grey, she grew taller and more shapely, her ears became only slightly pointed, and her eyes changed to a shimmering gold – similar to Apep's but with a less pronounced angle and sweeping curve. Her hair, already dark, grew longer and her facial features became sharper – harder.

Pete was sitting fully upright now and looked to be coming to his senses. "What did I miss?"

Lenny shook his head. "Dagrun is Eugene's brother. Eugene is Apep and neither are human. They're both some kind of alien thing, and Janis is really Apep's daughter, a half-alien thing who is also Lilith. There ya go, you're all caught up!"

"What?" Pete said, crawling over next to Lenny and peering through one of the gaps in the stone. "Janis is Lilith? Janis can't be Lilith. My Janis? She can't be Lilith."

Lenny grabbed Pete by the shoulders and turned him to face him. "Bro! Did you even hear me? You've not only been making out with an old chick, but she's not even human! You were making out with an old lady space alien! Honestly, man, if we don't die, I'm *never* letting you live this down. Although, Lilith the half-alien is… kind of hot."

Pete shrugged Lenny off and pressed his face back to the gap.

Syldan looked up at Apep as a smile stretched across his face. "The power of the God Stones belongs to everyone. Just because you hold the stones doesn't make you their master!" He struck Apep hard in the face with the hilt of the bastard sword as he stood back up.

Apep covered his face and bellowed in rage.

"God, Breanne, please hurry!" Garrett said over his shoulder.

"You've no idea of my power!" Apep said, his voice rising to a screech.

In the stone cell, David opened his eyes. "Holy shit… what happened?"

"He's waking up!" Breanne shouted. "David, you passed out."

David sat up, smoothing his mustache and with it his face.

"Are you okay?" Breanne asked.

"Yeah, I think so," David said, rubbing his eyes. "Whoa, what are those?" He pointed through the columns at Syldan and Apep.

Lenny sighed and then drew in a long breath. "Dokkal-somthin's. Here's what you missed. Dagrun and Eugene are actually—"

"Dark elves?" David frowned.

"Huh?" Lenny said.

"They look like dark elves and you started to say dökkálfar. That's Norse for dark elf."

"Why do you know that?" Lenny asked, shaking his head.

"Bro, I've played every fantasy game there is. Plus, those look a whole lot like dark elves to me… maybe taller than I imagined but—"

Lenny huffed. "But this isn't a video game—"

"Everything has to come from somewhere, right? I mean we got giants, dragons, and wizards already. And didn't Mr. B say imagine everything we ever heard about magic was actually—"

"Jesus! Can we please talk about this later?" Breanne said. "David, I hate to ask this, but you need to do to Paul whatever it was you did to Pete. Can you do that?" she asked.

"What did I do?"

"You healed Pete, David!"

David blinked again. "I did?"

"You did, and I need you to do it again… please," she begged.

"Okay, I… I can try." David crawled over to Paul and placed both hands on his leg before closing his eyes.

Garrett turned back to the scene outside their prison just in time to see Apep drop to his knees, his smashed nose a fountain of magenta blood. The color was strange but no stranger than his elvish form. The hole in his foot was spilling just as much blood as his face, forming a small pool beneath him. He looked up at Syldan towering over him with his war hammer raised high above his head. "You know… brother, you've always… been a better warrior than me. But your problem is you care too much about… honor. You cling too tightly to your morals. But I say, victory goes to the one smart enough to know how to win!" Bloody purple spittle sprayed from Apep's mouth onto Syldan's now ill-fitting BDU pants.

"Goodbye, brother," Syldan said, setting his jaw and swinging the hammer toward Apep's head.

"Coach!" Garrett shouted too late.

The hammer didn't move.

Syldan hadn't noticed Lilith slip quietly behind him, and Garrett noticed too late.

The slender half-elf raised her voice from a whisper to a full-throated yell, chanting an ancient spell.

The war hammer ripped free from Syldan's hands with a sudden jerk from behind. He tried to turn and look, but his feet were fixed, bound to the floor. He looked down to find dark roots were wrapping around his legs like a great serpent in a hurry to consume him. Within an instant they were already constricting his waist.

Garrett and Lenny watched helplessly as their coach tried to pull his hand back down to fight the roots, but more roots had made their way up from behind, not only stealing his war hammer but also wrapping around his wrist and yanking his arm behind his back. Quickly, he raised his bastard sword in his only free hand in an attempt to try and hack at the roots. But as he swung, Apep blocked the strike with his own sword, giving the ever-growing tangle of roots the time they needed to snatch the wrist of the only free hand Syldan had left. The roots pulled both hands together, binding his wrists behind him.

Inside the cell David began to glow.

The roots wrapped around the throat of the now-helpless man and began to constrict. Syldan tried to speak words that would nullify the spell. "Flahoz—" he groaned but couldn't get the words out before the roots squeezed off his air.

Janis called out another word of power. Thorns protruded from the woody roots that were now beginning to look like some kind of leafless, thorn-covered vine. Thorns an inch long, then two, then three grew outward as the vine writhed.

Syldan let out a snarl of rage as the thorns pierced his flesh like sharpened nails.

Apep stood and stared into his brother's eyes. "That's why you can't beat me. Honor is for the weak and morals are for humans." Apep drew back the sword then thrust it into Syldan's gut, his wild eyes widening as he drove the blade as deep as he could force it.

"No!" Garrett screamed.

Pressing his face close to his brother's, Apep sneered as he held the sword fast. He kept it there for a long moment as the strange blade lurched back and forth.

"Look into my eyes, brother! Know that you have failed your father – failed your kingdom! Know that I have ended you!"

Syldan looked past his brother to the stone cell, finding Garrett and Lenny, his yellow orbs darting back and forth intently between the two boys.

With several feet of stone stalagmite between them and Coach, they could only look on helplessly.

"God, Lenny, he's killing him!" Garrett said as both boys refused to look away. Neither would abandon him.

Slowly the light behind Syldan's eyes faded like a rogue ember in a cool breeze. Inside Garrett a rage built. No words needed to be exchanged for the message to pass between them. It was on them now. They had to stop Apep.

Satisfied, Syldan nodded, and just before the light winked out completely, he closed his eyes and smiled.

"Farewell, brother!" Apep spat, wrenching the sword free from Syldan's flesh. The vines released their grip, withdrawing back into the earth.

Syldan's eyes rolled back into his head as he collapsed to the temple floor.

Behind Apep a stone stalagmite column cracked with a resounding pop.

31

Bound by Blood

Wednesday, April 6 – God Stones Day 1
Petersburg, Illinois

Garrett startled and spun, throwing his hands up as small bits of rock rained down around him. "Holy crap!" Paul was on his feet, both of them, moving like his leg had never been caught in that bear trap. As Paul backed up for another go, Garrett's eyes found Lenny's. Lenny made a fist and smiled. Garrett nodded and smiled back. Now they had a chance.

Apep looked back toward the stone cell, then to Lilith. "Deal with them!" He climbed up onto the slab, approaching the head of the giant.

Pressing his back against the opposite wall, Paul ran forward again, launching his whole body at the fractured stalagmite column. The chamber shook as his shoulder compressed against the dense stone. Chunks of fracturing rock exploded from the other side as even more stone rained down from the ceiling, but still the column held.

Garrett and Lenny quickly dragged a once-again unconscious David back out of the way of falling debris.

"I'm not calling this little mustached freak David anymore," Lenny said adamantly. "From now on he's Bruce Leroy."

"*The Last Dragon*?" Garrett said, digging his heels in as he baby-stepped backward, his hands clasped around David's wrist.

"Yep, and if Apep starts glowing next I'm going to start calling him Sho'nuff."

Even in this insanity, Lenny could still find a way to squeeze in an eighties movie reference. It was both inappropriate and comforting at the same time.

Paul rubbed his shoulder, a look of doubt on his face as he sized up the stone column for the third time. There was a big crack along the center, and the top had detached from the ceiling and broken off, but the giant stone column sill stood, unyielding.

As Garrett sized up the column too, a memory came to him – knowledge Mr. B had passed down to him. "Paul! Don't focus on the column! Instead, look beyond the column, past it, and go there!"

Paul's brow furrowed, then he nodded slowly as he backed up again, pressing his back against the wall. He narrowed his eyes at something beyond the column and then launched himself off the wall into a dead run, crossing their small cell in five short, fast steps. He roared as his shoulder bit into the stalagmite column.

Garrett flinched, watching but not wanting to watch. *Something was going to break… had to break.* And something did. This time Paul exploded completely through the thick stone.

Paul's momentum carried him forward in a stagger that turned into a tumble. He tucked and rolled clear of the debris only to spring back to his feet. He reached forward and touched the stone slab, then turned back toward Garrett with a sharp nod.

Garrett didn't see Lilith, but he heard her doing that creepy chanting thing again. By the time he cleared the newly opened hole with Lenny on his heels, Paul's feet were already rooted to the ground, vines winding around his legs.

Garrett reeled to his right in time to see Lilith disappearing around the corner of the slab.

"Get her, Lenny! I'm going for Apep!" Garrett shouted.

Pete and Breanne appeared from the hole next to Lenny.

Paul ripped his feet free of the vines.

Lenny gripped his staff in both hands and nodded.

"Where'd she go?" Breanne asked.

"This way," Lenny said, pointing toward the corner of the slab. "Go, Garrett. We got her!"

Garrett ran for Apep.

Apep removed the God Stones from inside his jacket, murmuring, "I have waited so long for this moment."

"I'm going to kill you, Apep!" Garrett shouted, climbing onto the slab. He drew his sword and ran toward him.

Apep waved his hand. "Eshakmue ff esh!" he said forcefully.

Garrett felt Apep's power hit him full on. It was immense, seemingly bottomless. It pressed against him like a hurricane's wind, forcing him to stop, then pushing him backward toward the edge of the slab. He was up on the balls of his feet, leaning in. He stepped back into a fighting stance to try and dig the balls of his feet in, but it was no use.

Breanne peered over her brother's shoulder as Lenny, Peter, and Paul eased close to the corner of the slab. From around the corner a shadow grew, protruding out past the edge. Longer and longer it stretched. Something was approaching from the other side where Janis had vanished. They pulled up short and waited.

Lenny stepped back into a fighting stance as he spun his staff, bringing it around to chamber in his armpit. It pointed forward, ready for whatever came next. "Here we go," he whispered.

Paul nodded. "Here we go."

Pete took a tentative step back to stand next to Breanne.

The shadow crept closer to the corner, but when it finally came into view it wasn't Janis. It was a rat. And not just a regular old river rat, but a giant river rat.

"Balls!" Lenny said.

"Back up!" Paul ordered. They all shuffled back.

The rat was huge, maybe five feet tall on all fours – and it wasn't alone. Behind it were two more rats just like it, along with a giggling

Lilith. She walked slowly toward them, her father's sword in her right hand, its tip, now rigid, dragging ominously across the floor of the chamber. "Rayzae!"

The rats attacked.

As the first one leapt, Lenny cracked it in the snout with the tip of his staff, resulting in an unnatural squeal. Paul jumped over the second one, rolled to his feet, and grabbed it by the tail. Then, straining with all he had, he pivoted and slammed the rat against the edge of the stone slab, crushing its skull.

Lilith made a pouty face, then sneered as she made some motion with her hands and spoke more ancient words.

Garrett stopped sliding before he fell over the side of the slab. Apep's power was incredible, but there was something about it – like it didn't truly belong to him. What if he was only harnessing power, rather than creating it? What had Coach said to Apep? Something like, you don't own the stones? Or maybe you don't own the power?

Apep paused. "Well now, let us see what you are made of, boy! Akdoemue oz doe!" he shouted, as he thrust his open hand out toward Garrett. Grey ribbons poured like thick smoke from his fingers, blanketing Garrett in thick shadows. Once Garrett was completely covered, Apep snapped his fingers and the ribbons of shadow surrounding him burst into flame.

Breanne looked toward the slab just in time to see the envelope of smoke covering Garrett explode in fire. "No!" she gasped.

Three more rats came scurrying from the shadows, growing larger and larger as they approached. From behind them came yet another three. Breanne's heart began to race as fear gripped her, but she refused to let it take hold. She ran to the wall, where piles of shields and weapons were stacked unceremoniously. Most were decayed beyond use. She grabbed a wooden shield that seemed to be pretty solid. She had to look a little harder for a weapon that was usable, finally settling on a stone-headed tomahawk. Now armed, she sucked in a sharp breath and ran toward Paul and the nearest rat.

She swung her stone tomahawk at a rat's head, striking it hard across the snout. The rat screeched, scurrying back. But another rat attacked.

Next to her, Paul used his bare hands and booted feet while doing his best to avoid both teeth and claws.

Breanne swung again, and again another rat attacked. Between swings she held out the old wooden shield to block the lunging bites. Occasionally her counterstrikes found purchase, parting coarse brown hair to open flesh and elicit deafening squeals. Each time, Breanne yanked her hand back and produced her own frightened shriek. But she didn't stop. She had to get to Garrett.

Garrett's vision narrowed to a single point, then expanded to a beautiful single-track forest trail flying by him at fantastic speeds, speeds he had never reached before. His blood didn't pulse, he didn't sweat, and his muscles didn't flex. The rest of his world slowed as his footfalls landed perfectly. Then the trail fell away, leaving him covered in dark grey shadows. The shadows were burning. For an instant, he thought he heard the shadows whisper to him. If his focus weren't so pure, so absolute, in the moment, he would have thought it was only the wind in his ears. But it wasn't. The shadows spoke to him. The sound was barely audible, but he heard it – a single word that was unfamiliar, and yet he understood it. It was an ancient word. It was a word of power – *Sentheye.*

Apep made another motion with his hand, commanding the flaming shadows to bring the burning boy to him.

Garrett felt his body being drawn toward Apep. He let his mind take control of the shadowy fire. The flames glowed a brilliant blue-green. He was consumed in their warmth. But they did not burn him. He didn't know how, but the flames were his now. He told the shadows to stop dragging him. He stopped moving. Next, he imagined the flames and shadows forming into a ball, and they obeyed. The flaming shadows were reduced to the size of a basketball.

"What's this?" Apep said with a look of amused interest.

Garrett held the ball of flames in his hands, his eyes suddenly going wide. He blinked. *What now? What do I do now?* His confidence began to wane as he felt his focus slip, and with it all control. The strange ball of flame suddenly felt like a wild animal in his hands. He knew it then. The Sentheye could sense his fear. Now the ball bucked terribly in his palms, stretching and lurching, the sphere becoming unstable. It was *too* hot! He had to get rid of it – now! Quickly he chucked the flaming shadow at Apep as if he were passing him the basketball in gym class.

Apep's eyes went wide as the fireball streaked toward him. He tried to stop it with a word of power, "Mue—" But he had no time. He threw his hands up and dove for cover, launching himself from the slab.

Garrett ran forward as the fireball sailed across the chamber and imploded as it slammed into a distant wall. He looked down to Paul and Bre fighting the massive rats as Lilith backed Lenny across the chamber with a flurry of kicks. He was holding his own, but if he gave up any more ground, he was going to back right into the sleeping dragon. "Behind you, Len!" Garrett shouted.

Lenny glanced back, taking his eyes off Lilith for half a second.

Lilith spun into a crouch and swept Lenny's feet from under him.

Lenny landed hard on his back, expelling all his air, the back of his head bouncing off the stone floor.

"Shit," Garrett said, preparing to jump from the slab. But then Lilith turned, running toward the spot where Apep had fallen. *Double shit*, he thought, realizing they would both be coming for him now. Garrett drew his sword.

Lilith closed the gap.

Apep had already pulled himself to his feet and was climbing back onto the slab.

Garrett looked down at the giant and sucked in a deep breath. *Now or never*, he thought as he positioned himself to strike down with the sword.

"Stop him!" Apep screamed.

Lilith shouted the words and made the gestures. "Akdoe mue flah ak zae ozoz. Zaeshi ak ff esh!" Vines emerged from the slab at Garrett's feet, but they stopped growing. Lilith frowned, forced to say the words again.

Garrett cocked the sword.

"*Akdoe* mue flah ak zae ozoz. Zaeshi ak *ff* esh!" This time she said the words with a more commanding tone and the vines obeyed, bursting forth and snaring Garrett's arms and legs. He couldn't move.

Janis collapsed to one knee, her hand outstretched.

"Focus, Lilith! Your human side is weak. You must not fail until I succeed!" Apep commanded furiously as he approached Garrett with a pointed finger. "Do you know why you are really here, Garrett?"

Garrett grappled with the vines as they snaked around his body. What happened to Coach was about to happen to him. He was panicking, fighting with all his strength, but he still had enough sense to know this wasn't going to work.

He couldn't fight the vines with his muscles, he had to fight them with his mind. He had touched Apep's energy once and turned it. He desperately needed to do that now. He tried to take control of the energy, tried to find his focus, but the more he fought the more the vines squeezed, tightening around his wrist and ankles and compressing his already bruised ribs. *Come on!* he thought, but it was no use. He couldn't grasp the power controlling the vines. He could feel the rawness of it all around him, like standing in an open field during a lightning storm, but he could no more reach out and grab hold than he could grab hold of a lightning bolt as it struck.

All he could think about was a sword to the gut.

Suddenly the roots entangled both arms, forcing them to spread, stretching them wide.

"You are untrained. You touch the Sentheye by accident, not by intention!" Apep pointed his bony index finger in Garrett's face. "Now I think it is time you learned why you're really here, boy!" The fingernail on Apep's pointed finger grew long and sharp. He grabbed Garrett by the wrist and poked the black nail forcefully into his palm.

Garrett squeezed his eyes together tight as the nail bit deep, drawing blood.

Apep squeezed Garrett's palm, ensuring a drop of blood spilled onto each God Stone, one by one. "Here is a question for you, Garrett. Why did those who claim to care most about you tell you to come here and destroy the old one?"

Garrett clenched his jaw, straining helplessly against the roots.

"I'll tell you why. Because I couldn't wake him without your blood."

Garrett stopped struggling.

Apep smirked. "That's right… Never could. Turek made sure of that. He tied his bloodline to the spell keeping the nephilbock asleep." Apep paused, letting that sink in. "You were never supposed to stop me, Garrett. Your own mother sent you here to make sure I get what I need to open the portal. To make sure I get your blood. They want me to open the portal. That's the prophecy, my boy, and this moment here and now is your only contribution."

"You're lying!" Garrett croaked.

"Your accusation lacks conviction, my boy. You know I speak the truth and now I will show you."

Below the slab Garrett caught sight of Pete as he came around the corner and pulled up short at the sight of Janis.

"Janis, stop! Don't do this! I know you care about me. I know somewhere inside what we had over this past week was real. Tell me it was real!"

Lilith stretched out a hand toward him.

Pete smiled.

But then Lilith pressed her lips together into a sneer and closed the hand into a tight fist. As she squeezed, so too did the roots squeeze around Garrett's neck and torso, constricting ever tighter.

Garrett tried to groan but no sound came. It felt as though any second his ribs would start popping one by one like popcorn, and he would no longer be able to breathe.

Apep began reciting ageless words – words that Garrett somehow knew were the language of the gods. One by one the God Stones started to spin, suspended in the air, each glowing in oscillating, opaque colors before settling on a strange new color, a color Garrett couldn't form words to describe and couldn't look upon directly. He couldn't pull in a breath, and the edges of his vision began to close in.

Spreading his arms wide, Apep smiled. "Yes! The time has come!" he shouted, his voice echoing off the chamber walls. "Thank you, my boy! Thank you, Garrett!"

Darkness pressed in on Garrett as he fought to keep his eyes from rolling back into his head. He looked down at the face of the giant as Apep's voice, along with the shouts from Pete and battle cries from the rat fight, all faded into the background. The last thing he saw before the darkness took him was the giant's large oblong eyelid as it popped open.

32

Sounds in the Dark

Wednesday, April 6 – God Stones Day 1
Rural Chiapas State, Mexico

Grinding stone reverberated through Gabi's feet as the platform continued its long descent into darkness.

"What is she talking about? What lower chamber?" Fredy asked, his voice unnerved.

"The one painted on the wall. We were trying to tell you, Sarah, but then all hell broke loose," Itzel said.

Sarah blinked. "This is major!" She grabbed Fredy by the shoulders. "It's major, Fredy."

Gabi noticed movement near the edge of her vision and turned just in time to see a massive stone block moving upward, outside the circular platform. Quickly she spun around, noticing three more blocks moving upward past the platform. "Look!" she pointed.

"¡Dios mío! Counterweights!" Fredy said as he grabbed the lighting tripod from the floor and pointed it up.

They craned their heads upward, the spotlight revealing a large expanse of domed ceiling. It was as if they were descending from the roof of an ancient cathedral. They could see it now – they had descended out of an oculus centered in the dome above. The giant column Sarah had been inside of stretched up all the way to the top of the dome and into the center of the hole, like an oversized fireman's pole.

Gabi stood, neck bent backward, studying the ceiling's shape. The half-globed arc with the stone column was just like what she had uncovered on the wall painting. Then she heard a distant sound from way off in the darkness. *What was that?* It was barely audible over the soft rumbling of stone sliding on stone, but it was there. Looking at her mom told Gabi that Itzel had heard it too.

The others stood still, each straining to hear the sound again.

The hair stood up on the back of Gabi's neck.

"What was that?" Itzel asked, pushing herself out of Andrés's arms to meet his eyes.

Gabi's father shook his head. "I don't know, but it can't be what it sounded like." His curious unease twisted into fear as his brows furrowed.

It was María who finally said it. "It sounded like someone talking."

"That's ridiculous. No one could be down here," Sarah said.

They looked out into the blackness, searching for the source of the mysterious sound, but beyond the platform was only darkness.

As they continued to descend, Gabi's mind spun with possibilities. *Are we alone? What if some race of giant things are living down here? What if the skulls were placed on the racks as a warning for them not to come back up?* Then there was what she had seen on the wall under the pyramid. *But that couldn't have been real… there couldn't be a—*

With a bone-jarring thud, Gabi fell onto her bottom. The platform hadn't slowed before touching down hard, pulling her back into the moment with a jolt. Just like the sudden start had knocked them off their feet, the sudden stop did the same. With the exception of a startled scream from María and grunts from the others, the chamber was eerily silent. They stood, brushing themselves off and taking in the scene around them.

They had settled at the bottom of a large domed cavern. As they shined their lights over the side of the platform, the first thing Gabi noticed was water – water everywhere. Their platform seemed to be an island. Fredy worked the tripod light, shining it across the expanse, searching for any clues of what this place was.

"Over here, Fredy, look." Sarah was shining her headlamp at a stone pathway leading off the island across the water toward a wall. "Focus your light at that far wall!"

They all joined Sarah and Fredy. Fredy aimed the light across the stone pathway, following it to the wall, then searching along it.

That's when they saw it. A giant arched opening was set into the left wall of the massive cavern, a couple hundred meters down the path.

"An adjacent room!" Andrés said.

The opening itself was enormous, but what was more amazing were the megalithic sculptures stretching up the entire height of the cavern on either side of the opening.

"That's it! Do you see it?! Look, there are carvings, Fredy!" Sarah jumped off the circular platform onto the stone pathway.

"Sarah! Wait! There could be traps!" Fredy shouted. But it was too late – she was already on the path.

Suddenly they heard the sound again, coming from the direction of the opening. Everyone froze, including Sarah.

Gabi's heart pounded in her throat as she squeezed her mother's hand. There could be no denying it *was* a voice.

The voice thundered out across the water in a language Gabi didn't recognize. She was still a bit of a novice in her language studies, but she would have at least recognized Hebrew, Lithuanian, Farsi, or a number of other languages, even if she couldn't have understood them, but this was something completely unlike anything she had ever heard.

"Sarah! Come back," Fredy urged.

Sarah's eyes were flexed wide as she stood stone still, either trying to comprehend the strange language or frozen in fear – Gabi couldn't tell which.

"Mamá," Gabi managed as she gave her mother's hand a tug. "Please, we need to go."

Andrés focused a light upward, looking for a rope from Manuel, but saw nothing. "Come on, Manuel."

Across the chamber came another sound. A terrible screech that at first sounded like dying pigs. Gabi squinted her eyes and covered her ears. "Mamá, please!" she urged.

The screeching rose and fell strangely. "Andrés, listen to it," Itzel said. "Those are words, not just screams. A second voice speaking to the other?"

Fredy set the light down and jumped down onto the path next to Sarah. "We need to get out of here!" he said, grabbing her by the wrist. Consumed by fear, he began forcefully pulling her back toward the platform, like she was a disobedient child being pulled from a playground.

Suddenly the screeching voice distorted into a violent roar so deep and loud it reminded Gabi of the black howler monkey.

Everyone instinctively covered their ears.

As the roar grew it became so loud that, even with their ears covered, it created a piercing pain. Gabi screamed – maybe everyone screamed – but nothing penetrated the incredible roar.

The ground began to pulse. *BOOM! BOOM! BOOM! BOOM!*

Gabi pressed her hands tight to her ears. She wanted so bad to shut her eyes up tight, but she forced herself to look. Sarah was still down on the path with Fredy, bathed in the glow of the tripod light. She could see Fredy's lips moving, only he wasn't speaking. His mouth moved, opening and shutting like a goldfish with no sound coming out. Finally finding words, he mouthed, "¡Ay, Dios mío!"

BOOM! BOOM! BOOM! BOOM! The booming grew closer until suddenly a figure burst through the opening in a panicked run. Beyond the shadowed figure, the room it emerged from began to glow.

Gabi knew what she was looking at, though what she was looking at was impossible. She couldn't speak. Couldn't move. She was fixed like a stone.

The giant stood taller than a house, easily ten meters high. It was clothed in a tattered tunic and loincloth, with a headdress fixed atop its head. It was the statue from up above come to life. *No,* Gabi thought. *This was even bigger.* It held something in its right hand, but it was hidden in shadow. The giant paused for the briefest second, its head swinging left then right, before abruptly lunging, throwing itself against the wall in what appeared to be an attempt to take cover behind the carved monolith.

It's true – what I saw on the wall under the pyramid, it's all true! But that means not just the giant, but what comes next. Oh María Purísima, it was all painted right there on the wall!

Before anyone could register what they were seeing, the roar from beyond the opening reached a pinnacle, and the glow turned into flame. The flame poured from the room in a strange-colored liquid fire, lighting up the entire chamber in unnatural greenish-orange light.

Gabi stood paralyzed on the spot, ignoring the fire to stare at the giant, who stood facing them with his back against the wall. In the light, she caught a glimpse of its face. *Only one eye?*

The massive fireball continued through the chamber, rolling across the water, not stopping – and heading right for them.

Fredy let go of Sarah's wrist, then pushed her off the stone path into the water. Sarah gasped, sucking in a breath as she plunged into the frigid liquid.

Gabi felt a shove from behind her as her father shouted something she couldn't make out. She was falling now. She turned in time to see her father grab María and her mother's hands as he leapt from the edge. The water was cold, and she wanted to gasp but she held her breath as she rolled onto her back. Near her, bodies crashed into the water. For a brief second everything was dark. Gabi kicked her legs and broke the surface, stealing only a single gasp of air before her vision filled with flames. She pushed herself under as far from the surface as she could get with a few quick waves of her palms. Then as if the sun itself had leapt out from hiding and rolled over them, everything exploded in fiery light.

Distorted flames glowed above them as the seconds passed. The ominous roar was now muffled under the water, but then a new sound replaced it as the water near the surface began to boil. They were trapped under fire.

Instinctively Gabi pushed herself even deeper. But as she looked for the others, she could see María was too close to the surface. Her father was there grabbing María by the ankle, pulling her down with a sudden desperate jerk, trying to get her away from the surface, away from the superheated water. María let out a gargled scream, releasing what little air she had as she began rubbing frantically at her arm.

Gabi watched as her mother swam to María, grabbing her flailing arms. She tried to pull the woman close, tried to calm her. But it was a futile effort; María kicked at her and flailed, desperate for air, until finally she broke free. In a strange, emerald-yellow distortion of light cast by the flames from above, Gabi watched in horror as young María swam upward as hard as she could. *Oh no, please, María! Please! Don't!*

Gabi slammed her eyes shut, unable to watch.

33

Love Inferno

Wednesday, April 6 – God Stones Day 1
Petersburg, Illinois

"Wait, Pete!" Breanne shouted, but Pete didn't wait. Instead he closed the gap between he and Lilith, his face saying it all. His heart was leading him now, compelling him to her.

Breanne thought, *God, after what she's done!*

"Janis. Please, don't kill him." Pete held his open palms up, pleading. "If you care about me – if any of our talks, any of the time we spent meant anything, please… stop this!" He turned his palms down, willing Janis to calm down. "Please, Janis, you're killing him! I beg you, please!"

"Careful, Pete!" Breanne yelled, swinging the tomahawk at a rat's face but missing. "Paul, can you handle this? I have to help Garrett."

Paul nodded over his shoulder. "Go! Help the kid. I got this," he said, spinning as a rat lunged forward. He snatched the rat by the tail and began dragging it. "Come here, big fella!" The rat screeched as two others closed in.

Above them the giant sucked in a long, slow breath, blinked, blinked again, and then set his strange egg-shaped eye on Apep.

Breanne ran for the slab. She had to try and stop Janis.

Then Apep shouted and Breanne gasped.

"Lilith! Finish the boy now!"

"Yes, father."

As Breanne approached, she watched Lilith hesitate. Something in her eyes was different. For the briefest second, she struggled in thought. Breanne prepared to take the moment and attack but then, atop the slab, the roots fell away, and Garrett collapsed.

"You worthless girl!" Apep shouted at his daughter. "You pathetic human failure!"

"Get him down, Pete!" Breanne said, turning her attention to Lilith. Breanne met the girl's strange eyes and what she found was a deep sadness. Instead of attacking her she felt compelled to reach for Lilith's hand.

Lilith narrowed her eyes.

"Lilith, you *are not* worthless! You have friends! You have Pete! Help us, please!" Breanne begged.

Lilith's sharp features softened as she took Breanne's hand in hers and nodded shyly. "Janis. Call me Janis. That's the name my mother wanted me to have." She glared back up at Apep. "I hate the name he gave me!"

"Okay… Janis." Breanne nodded.

On the slab, Apep was speaking triumphantly in an incomprehensible language.

"I don't know what he's saying, but it must be bad! Please, Janis. We need your help."

"He will kill me, and all of you… Petey too," Janis said, tears building in her golden eyes. Then turning to meet Breanne's gaze, her face hardened once again. "Unless I kill him first!" Still holding Breanne's hand, she reached out with her other, placing it atop Breanne's own as she spoke the words of power, "Mueeshshi esh ak akdoemue."

Breanne felt a strange tickle in her mind.

Apep spoke in the same incomprehensible language but now something had changed. Breanne could understand. Now the words unscrambled in her mind's eye, and they made sense.

"Balor, I have awoken you!" Apep said.

Across the chamber, four more eyes opened as the dragon raised both its scaly heads.

Breanne's eyes sprung wide as the heads looked at each other, then turned to face Apep and the giant. The dragon seemed to take in the scene as it stood and stretched its wings, then pulled them back to its side. Its black-scaled heads stretched up high above, vanishing as they blended into the shadows of the massive chamber. As the dragon rose to its full height, the chamber suddenly seemed very small to Breanne.

"Janis!" Breanne pointed.

"Go! Help the others!" Janis turned away, then turned back. "Thank you, Bre." She turned away again and this time she didn't look back as she ran to face the dragon.

Behind Breanne, Balor spoke in the same odd dialect as Apep. The chamber rumbled at the sound of his voice. "How long have I slept?"

Apep answered, "Thousands of years too long, but I've kept my promise."

The dragon spoke now, their voice coming in a strange hiss, each word emerging from one head then the other, but the speech was fluid, as if one mind controlled the thought. "Dökkálfar Apep and nephilbock Balor! What is the trickery that brings us to this place... This place of our enemies?" The dragon didn't wait for an answer as both heads began to roar, loud at first, but rising to ear-piercing volume within seconds.

Inside the stone prison, David woke to a large rat licking his face. He screamed, scrambling backward on his butt, trying to put distance between himself and the massive rat. Quickly he found himself trapped between the rat and the chamber wall. David would have given anything for a different magical power in that moment.

There was nowhere to go. He closed his eyes tightly, turning his face away as he thrust out his arms to stop the rat's advance. For the second time in his life he was so frightened his bladder released. The rat's open jowls came close to his face, clamping down hard with a loud *Snap!* as hot rancid breath washed over David's face. He gasped in the rank air, his fingers sinking into the rat's coarse hair as he squeezed it in fistfuls, trying desperately to hold back its pressing weight. The rat was strong and heavy. David's arms shook as they began to fold, the rat's teeth coming so close. He couldn't hold it back.

"Help! Please, someone help me!" he croaked. But no one came.

As the rat inched ever forward, David's hand slipped further down its neck and into something wet.

The rat shrieked from the pain of David's hand sinking into the deep wound. The rat hissed in rage, pressing harder than ever. It opened its jaw and prepared to lunge again at David's face. David jerked his head back so hard it bounced off the chamber wall. He didn't think about what happened next. It just happened.

David began to glow.

Breanne got to Garrett right as Pete dragged him off the slab, and both tumbled down onto the temple floor. Balor rolled his giant frame off the stone slab too, landing hard, shaking the chamber.

Pete sprang into action, scooping up Garrett's sword from the floor. "We have to kill the giant now before he gets up!"

Garrett lay on the ground, holding his head in one hand and his throat with the other, still coughing and gasping for breath. "No, Pete… Wait!" he rasped, reaching for his friend, but it was no use – Pete was heading straight for Balor.

Breanne pulled Garrett to his feet. "Jesus, look at her, I think she's controlling it! She's talking to it. Can you hear her in your mind, Garrett?"

"Hear her?" he asked, brows furrowing as he searched for Pete.

Janis closed both her hands, and the dragon closed both its mouths. "That's right, Sylanth, good dragon. You don't really want to burn me, do you? No, you want to make the one who put you here pay," she said in a soothing voice as she slowly walked toward the calming beast.

Sylanth settled their focus on her. "Where are we, child? How have we come to this place?" The dragon's questions were no longer angry but curious.

Breanne turned to see the giant was starting to push himself upright as Pete appeared behind the slab next to the giant's head, Garrett's sword cocked and ready to strike.

"Pete!" Garrett shouted.

Apep shouted a warning to the giant.

Pete swung the sword.

Balor must have caught the movement of flashing steel in the firelight because he flinched away, the sword missing his neck and instead cutting a deep gash along his jawbone. The razor-sharp blade continued its severing of flesh across his entire face, just missing the oval eye before glancing off his forehead.

"Oh, father!" Janis shouted from across the chamber. "I guess my worthless human side takes after uncle Syldan after all." A sly smile stretching across her face, she pointed at Apep. "He imprisoned you here, my dear Sylanth! Kill him!"

Sylanth's two toothy mouths opened, each saying one word, "Dökkálfar Apep!"

Apep's eyes darted to the dragon then to Pete as he shouted ancient words of power, "Shirayshi, Esh akoz, oz akdoe!" Ribbons of Sentheye yanked Pete from the floor and several feet into the air. Apep held him there suspended between himself and the dragon. The squeeze of shadows forced Pete to drop the sword as he struggled just to breathe. The shadowy tangles of Sentheye began drawing the life from him.

"Kill the beast, girl! Kill them or he dies!"

"Oh, no! Pete!" Breanne yelled.

Pete looked down at her, his terror-stricken eyes pleading for help.

Balor screamed in rage, pressing one of his huge six-fingered hands against his wounded face before turning his attention to Pete.

"I'm coming, Pete!" Garrett shouted, but Balor swung out with the back of his hand, connecting with Garrett's side and sending him tumbling in a backward roll toward the chamber wall.

Breanne scanned the area around her for something to throw. She saw Lenny coming to his senses after hitting his head during his fight with Janis. He pushed himself to his feet, rubbing the back of his head with a look of confusion. When he finally looked up, his face swiveled from the giant to the dragon realizing with horror both were awake.

"Lenny, help Pete!" Breanne yelled.

Lenny hardened his face with determination, set his jaw tight, and ran toward Apep.

Breanne picked up a chunk of small stone from the broken column and hurled it at the giant. The throw flew true and cracked the giant on the back of the head.

Balor rolled to his hands and knees and pushed himself up, his one bulbous eye searching until he located the source of this new pain.

Breanne stood in front of the giant, weaponless.

Garrett got to his feet. "I'm coming, Bre!"

Apep spotted Lenny before he could get to him.

Lenny shouted a war cry that sounded a lot to Breanne like, "Baaaaaaalllllllsss!"

Reaching out with his other hand, Apep grabbed Lenny with shadows, lifting him off his feet too.

Flames built in the dragon's throat.

"No! Sylanth, wait!" Janis ordered.

Garrett got to Breanne just as the giant was picking up his foot, intent on stomping her down. There was nowhere to run. They were trapped between a giant and the wall. *We're going to die.*

Just then Paul came skidding toward them from between the giant's legs. In a smooth motion, he turned, facing the giant and reaching above his head just in time to catch the giant's foot in both hands as it stomped down.

Paul wrestled with the giant's foot as the beast fought for balance. He shouted up at the giant as he gave the foot a final shove, "Not today!"

The giant launched airborne, both upward and backward, his other foot coming off the ground.

"Holy shit!" Garrett cheered.

The giant fell back, landing awkwardly across the stone slab.

"Thanks, Paul," Breanne started, but a different rumble pulled her attention away from the giant. She turned to find Janis staring down Apep in a now too familiar mumbling chant. With tears cutting wet trails down her face, she screamed the last of her chant. A violent eruption of roots burst from the floor beneath Apep, consuming his feet, then quickly spreading over the rest of his body. In the same instant, more roots came from the shadowed ceiling far above, tangling around his neck and wrists. Then the roots began receding, but they didn't let go. Apep's body was pulled taut as if he were on a medieval rack.

"What is this?!" Apep gagged out as his eyes ignited with rage.

Pete dropped to the floor, and Lenny dropped to his knees, gasping hungrily for air.

Behind Janis the false veil of confusion cleared from Sylanth's mind like smoke on a windy day, and his voice echoed in Breanne's mind. "Treachery!" both heads of the dragon gasped in unison as they sucked in long angry breaths of air. Their necks began to glow.

"Janis!" Pete croaked as he limped toward her, holding his side.

But she could no more hear Pete than she could the dragon behind her. Breanne screamed too and so did Lenny and Garrett, but it was no use.

Janis began to turn deep blueish red as she focused all her rage and power on her father. The roots wrapped Apep from head to toe, then came the thorns.

Breanne's relief for the falling giant turned to terror as she watched Pete break into a staggering run across the chamber.

Garrett shouted, "No! Oh god, Pete! No! Doesn't he see the dragon?!"

Breanne knew he only saw one thing – Janis.

Lenny began to run. "Pete!"

"Janis!" Pete shouted again.

This time Janis heard him, and all the rage fell from her face as Pete reached her. Breanne watched in horror as they opened their arms to each other, colliding in a hard embrace. Pete lifted her, spinning her in a circle. "I love you, Janis… I love you so goddamn much!"

Fire built in Sylanth's throats.

She smiled back at him, hugging him just as tight. "I love you too, Petey!"

Breanne blinked slowly. In this moment no one else existed. There were no evil dark elf wizards, giants, or dragons. There was only Petey and Janis. As the same strange light began to build in both the dragons' throats, Breanne knew no one could get to them in time. They might as well have been on the other side of the planet.

But then Pete's face changed as he finally saw what Breanne saw. He saw the nightmare of glowing dragon throats and mouths stretched open. He saw the reason Garrett was screaming and why Lenny was frantically waving his arms. He saw dragon fire.

With her back to Sylanth, Janis couldn't see dragon fire, but she didn't need to. She saw the look on Pete's face. In a second so impossibly brief she must have understood – she no longer held command over Sylanth. Janis forced a smile at Pete, one for him to remember her by. With a hard shove she pushed him back, creating enough space for what came next.

"No! Janis!" he shouted as he lunged for her, but she kicked him in the midsection, sending him careening backward several feet and onto his ass to slide even further away from her.

From both heads Sylanth's open mouths exhaled out something far worse than hellfire, engulfing Janis in a concentrated torrent of brilliantly colored dragon fire.

Pete screamed.

Breanne dropped to her knees. "Oh, Janis. Oh, god no."

34

Don't Look Back

Wednesday, April 6 – God Stones Day 1
Rural Chiapas State, Mexico

Gabi wanted to scream but knew she would be just as dead as María if she did. Instead she floated in horrified weightlessness as María's body drifted somewhere in the distance, sinking slowly into the shadows below.

Then her mother and father were beside her. Her mother's eyes spoke to her, saying so much without ever saying anything. *Don't breathe, Gabi – no matter what, don't breathe.* It had only been thirty seconds, maybe forty-five, and she could hold her breath for several minutes, at least three. But her heart was beating so fast now.

The glow above them dissipated and once again they were in darkness. They waited as long as they could stand it before swimming up. Her father went first, breaking the surface and motioning Gabi and her mom up. They sucked in air, gasping for breath. The air smelled like rotting eggs and tasted even worse, but they drank it in greedily and they didn't die.

A few meters away near the walkway, Fredy and Sarah treaded water, pulling long breaths.

Gabi startled as her mother choked out a sob. "María, she's dead! I saw her die! Why wouldn't she listen to me!? I tried – I swear I tried, but she wouldn't listen!"

"Oh no, god, Itzel, no!" Sarah said.

Gabi felt her father's strong, callused hand take hers as he led her and her mother toward the path. "You couldn't do anything, Itzel. It isn't your fault." He turned to the others. "Everyone, swim to the footpath near the wall and let's try to find cover."

With the elevated platform and the walkway leading to the wall blocking her view, Gabi couldn't see anything. Then her father pulled her onto the walkway. She stared, unable to look away as her eyes found the giant, who now stood motionless against the wall as if waiting for something. Waiting for something else Gabi had seen on the wall painting.

No sooner did they get their footing then the source of the fire showed itself. Gabi's legs buckled at the sight of it and she collapsed, skinning her knees on the stone. A creature that looked like a giant dinosaur with wings burst through the opening, screeching in a voice that sounded both intelligent and completely incomprehensible. The thing was monstrous and just as tall as the giant, which leapt from behind the wall, swinging what looked like an enormous axe at the creature.

Everyone jolted into motion when Sarah screamed a word as impossible as the creatures standing before them, "Dragon!"

They ran for the wall, Gabi's father dragging her like a limp sack of potatoes. "Get your feet under you, Gabi! We have to move!"

The dragon ducked its head under the swing of the giant's axe, before belching out a roar of flame.

Firelight reflected off the dragon's ebony scales, sparkling like a chain mail coat made of onyx diamonds. The creature was as beautiful as it was terrifying.

The water came only to the giant's knees. Even so it dove out of the way of the flame, belly flopping into the water. The flame hit the wall, then deflected in both directions, leaving pieces of the stone monolith burning.

Fortunately for Gabi and the others, the flames dissipated before crossing the distance to them. Instead of fire they were consumed in a wave of hot wind, hot enough to force them to shield their faces.

The giant grabbed the dragon's front leg as he stood and flipped the beast backward, sending it scrambling to find its feet. The domed cavern rumbled, shaking beneath them.

Sarah ran down the path, reaching the wall. "I don't see cover!"

"Sarah! Everyone! We have to move closer, we are too open here!" Fredy shouted.

"Look up ahead – the wall juts out a little. Maybe we can hide there," Andrés said.

The giant spoke again, its voice a deep baritone of unintelligible sounds, then it swung at the dragon with its axe.

The dragon roared, swinging its tail into the giant, knocking it on its bottom before belching out another torrent of fire.

The giant bellowed an angry pained cry as it pushed itself under the water to wait out the flames. When it rose, the back of the giant's tunic was burnt away. It lunged at the dragon, clipping its side with the axe.

Now it was the dragon who screamed in rage.

The giant ran toward the platform – toward Gabi. She pressed herself to the wall so hard it hurt and slammed her eyes shut. "Please!" she screamed as it ran by.

When the giant reached the platform, it wrapped its arms and legs around the center column and began scaling it.

Andrés watched in stunned amazement. "It's trying to flee!" As he looked up, he noticed something else. A rope. "Look! Manuel dropped us a rope! That's it! That's our way out!"

Gabi forced herself to look.

Sarah looked at Andrés like he had just suggested they climb on the giant's back and have him carry them out. "What about the giant?!"

Gabi was no longer paying attention to the rope or the giant. The dragon had her full attention now. It spread its wings, then, leaping into the air, it flew fast toward the giant. Even though she could barely see the black-scaled beast when it wasn't breathing fire, the burning columns gave off enough light she could see its silhouette gliding silently through the darkness. "¡Papá!" she screamed, giving her father's hand a yank. A second later the dragon collided with the giant.

The column exploded as both beasts tumbled across the chamber into the water beyond the platform. Massive chunks of the stone column flew in every direction. From above, the stone giant that had stood sentinel for unknown centuries dropped, breaking into pieces along with the column. The entire dome shook violently as a scream pierced through the chaos.

Gabi's head snapped up toward the oculus for the source of the scream. Manuel was in a freefall. She turned away, slamming her eyes closed and covering her ears.

"Manuel!" Sarah screamed.

"We have to move!" Andrés shouted, grabbing Gabi's and Itzel's hands. They ran along the wall, Fredy and Sarah on their heels. "We have to try and get to the other room. Maybe there's another way out!"

"The room is still so far!" Fredy shouted back.

"We have no choice! Fifty meters, Fredy! We can do it! We have to!"

The dragon spoke again in its strange, high-pitched screech. Then it roared.

"Don't look back, Gabi," her mother said.

But Gabi did look back. Just for a second, just long enough to see the beast open its mouth and exhale another gush of strange, blue-green fire. She could feel the heat instantly. She had her legs fully under her now, running as hard as she could run.

Behind them, the giant squatted near a large chunk of the stone column as the flames poured over it. When the flames passed, he stood once again, the stone he had used for cover now burning like a giant torch.

Sarah fell, landing hard on her stomach.

Itzel stopped and turned back, grabbing Sarah by the elbow and pulling her to her feet.

Gabi tried to stop too.

"No, Gabi! Run, dammit!" her father shouted.

The flame was too close. "Jump in the water, Sarah!" her mother yelled as she threw herself over the side. Sarah followed. They both disappeared below the water just before it erupted in a superheated boil.

Gabi was six steps ahead of her father when she heard him say, "Keep running, Gabi! You will make it!" She spared a glance back to see Fredy and her father jump over the side.

Gabi didn't jump. She did what her father said, and she ran. She ran faster than ever, faster than even she thought possible. She was almost there, and as the heat pressed against her she rounded the corner of the smoldering monolith and into the second room.

The flames passed by, and she quickly stepped back around the corner to find the others. Startled, she choked in a rancid breath. Sarah, Fredy, and her parents were still in the water. The giant was in a full-on run right toward them. Gabi's heart slammed against her chest. She found her voice and began shouting. "The giant is coming! Look out, Papá! Look out, Mamá!" Without thinking, she ran from the safety of the next room and back down the path.

Still shouting, Gabi watched in dismay as the giant stomped over them. It stepped down so close to Fredy that the suction pulled him under. Gabi arrived in time to help her mother pull Sarah from the water back onto the path while her father retrieved Fredy, dragging him onto the path.

"Damn you, girl!" her father scolded. "Why didn't you stay safe?"

Gabi didn't try to answer. She had never seen her father so scared.

"Will he be okay?" Itzel asked.

"He's hurt. Fredy, wake up, compadre, this is no time to be taking a siesta," her father said, eyeballing the giant, who stood between them and the opening to the next chamber. "We're only twenty meters from the opening, but now he is blocking our way."

"If we wait, we may be burned by the next burst of fire from the dragon," Sarah said.

Gabi spared a glance back toward the way they had come. The chamber was silent, but the dragon was out there somewhere in the darkness.

"Look, the giant is waiting for the dragon to attack." Andrés pointed past the giant. "We have to go for it!"

Fredy opened his eyes. "My leg. I think it's broken. I can't make it. You go."

"No, Fredy!" Sarah cried out.

"Sí, no way we're leaving you!" Andrés nodded to Itzel and Sarah. They nodded back, each taking an arm. Andrés grabbed Fredy's legs. "I'm sorry, compadre, this is going to hurt like hell but no screaming." He looked up at Gabi. "Stay in front. If the dragon comes you leave all of us and get to the room, find a way out." With only about twenty meters to the archway, they started pulling.

As soon as Andrés lifted Fredy's busted leg, he screamed, drawing the attention of the giant. Its massive head tilted toward them as it gave them a sideways glance with one oblong eye.

"¡Mierda!" Andrés said. "Don't stop! Just go!"

Behind them the dragon stalked forward out of the shadows, screeching in its strange tongue again.

The giant glanced away from them, focusing its attention back on the dragon.

The dragon leapt into the air above the giant, flapping its massive wings. Then, angling its body so that its head pointed down, the dragon roared.

Flame rained down at the giant. The giant saw the opening and took it, running underneath the dragon and avoiding the flames.

The fire dispersed out across the water and onto the walkway. Fredy continued to scream in pain as they pulled and ran as fast as they could. But it was not fast enough.

"Go, Gabi!" her father urged. "Run! Don't look back! Please, no matter what, don't look! Itzel! Don't look, just—"

Heat from the dragon fire pressed against Gabi's back. Behind her she heard a body hit the water with a splash. *Oh, please be okay, Papá!*

Her mother screamed as she continued to pull Fredy along by the wrist.

Gabi didn't look back, but she could hear Fredy shouting. "Let go of me!" he demanded. "I'm not going to make it!" Suddenly his voice went into a high-pitched scream of pain. "Now run! Save yourselves! Run as fast—"

35

Click

Wednesday, April 6 – God Stones Day 1
Petersburg, Illinois

Next to Garrett, Breanne screamed, but he couldn't hear her over his own.

The heat was so intense they had to turn away from the fire and the horror beneath it. Even then it was nearly unbearable. Within seconds the temperature of the entire tomb had risen beyond that of a hot summer day.

For a fleeting moment, the air had been electric with the hope of an impossible love. Now the air was void of hope, and in its place hung the rancid stench of burning skin, hair, and rotting vapors.

Sylanth exhaled the last of their burning breath, inhaled, and turned their heads toward the next closest target.

Pete, looking shocked and heartbroken, was collapsed in a heap nearby. He looked up at the dragon and screamed, "You son of a bitch!"

Garrett and Breanne shared a look, but it was Lenny who made the first move.

"Dammit, Pete!" Lenny shouted as he picked himself up and ran toward his friend, and right toward the dragon.

"Crap! Lenny, no!" Garrett shouted, running for the sword lying where Pete had dropped it. The giant was just feet away, maneuvering his enormous frame to a sitting position. *Great!* He didn't have time to deal with the giant. But it turned out he didn't have to – Paul was on him.

Garrett dove, rolled, and grabbed the sword. He glanced back as Apep began a cast, "Shirayshi, Esh akoz—" But before Apep could get the fourth word out of his mouth, Breanne was there with Lenny's staff in hand. She swung, cracking him over the back of the head. Apep staggered forward, falling to his hands and knees.

"That's for my dad, you son of a bitch!" Breanne reared back again.

Garrett spun back toward the dragon.

Across the chamber, Sylanth drew in another breath and the two heads spoke. Garrett didn't know what the thing said but when the dragon began to roar, he knew it was bad. All four eyes were locked on Pete and Lenny.

No! You're not getting them too, you bastard! Garrett ran toward Lenny, watching helplessly as his best friend in the world slid to a stop at the feet of the dragon. Lenny grabbed Pete under the arms and started pulling him back. Pete didn't seem to resist, but he wasn't helping either.

The dragon's heads parted, taking up position on either side of Lenny and Pete. They were trapped. There was no way they were going to make it!

Garrett pushed his body as hard as he could. "No! Over here! Right here!" he screamed as he ran, but it was no use. It was like the dragon didn't hear him or didn't care. The thing's necks started to glow as a deep throaty roar began to build. Garrett realized there was no way he could stop this. This was real. And his friends were about to die just like Janis had.

Lenny must have realized he wasn't going to make it too because he stopped pulling Pete. Instead, he stepped right in front of Pete. Lenny didn't cower, and he didn't flee. He lifted his chin in defiance, looked at one head, then the other and shouted into the roar, "Well, what are you waiting for, you overgrown gecko?"

The dragon's roar increased as they opened their mouths, revealing the furnace within.

Garrett was close now. But close wasn't enough.

The dragon's roar turned to a scream as both heads jolted up toward the ceiling in a wailing cry.

Lenny flinched back at the screech, nearly falling backward over Pete as he waited for the burn, but the burn didn't come. He cautiously opened one eye, raised an eyebrow, then opened both, his fear replaced with disbelief. "You got to be kidding me! Mr. Mustache?!"

Off to the dragon's side stood David, holding Coach's bastard sword, which was now fully embedded in Sylanth's rear leg. David looked as shocked as Lenny.

"Well, don't just stand there – run!" Garrett shouted.

David let go of the sword and staggered back. He and Lenny shared a "holy shit" look, grabbed Pete under each arm, and began to retreat. "Come on, Garrett!" Lenny shouted.

Garrett could have turned and run too, but he knew it was now or never – if he didn't act the dragon was going to kill them all.

In a psychotic fury, Sylanth lowered their heads, their scaly jowls trembling with rage as they searched, intent on finding the source of their pain and incinerating it.

As the first head lowered to better scan for the trespasser, Garrett took three running steps toward it, his sword raised and cocked over his shoulder.

Sylanth reeled their other head toward their injured leg, biting hold of the sword and tearing it free.

As the dragon's right head swung around toward Garrett, he fell back onto his thigh, letting his feet lead like he was sliding into home plate. The dragon's head passed just over him. Once clear of the dragon's head, he sprung up and spun around, set his feet, and before Sylanth could turn their head to find him he swung for the fences, hacking into the dragon's neck with a savage swing.

Sylanth's right head toppled to the floor, while its remaining head let out another pained, ear-piercing scream. Copious amounts of viscous blood pumped from the severed neck, washing over Garrett and pooling under his feet.

Sylanth spat fire from his remaining head along with seething shrieks of agony.

Lenny punched a fist into the air. "Did you see that?!"

But Garrett wasn't finished. He was committed to the cause – this bastard had killed their friend. There was only one way this was going to end: one of them was going to die.

"Paul! Help," Breanne shouted as she continued to whack Apep across the back with Lenny's staff. She risked a look over and found that Paul had his hands full.

Before Balor could get back to his feet, Paul grabbed his ankle with both hands and yanked.

Balor fell again onto his back and began kicking at Paul with his other leg.

Ducking the giant's foot, Paul ran in between its legs, leaping up onto its stomach. Breanne's hopes rose as Paul then tried to jump again to the slab, but they sank just as fast as Balor caught him in his fist.

Breanne hit Apep twice more across the back before he scrambled into a position where he could defend himself. "And that one was for Janis!"

Finally, Apep turned on Breanne. "Foolish girl!" He ripped the staff from her hands with an unseen force, pulling it to him. Drawing it back he swung at Breanne, striking her hard.

She staggered backward, grabbing her shoulder.

"Leave… her… alone!" Paul managed from the grip of the giant. He pulled his arms free, grabbed the giant's thumb, and pulled it back unnaturally. The thumb emitted a loud snap. The giant bellowed out in agony. Its hand popped open, dropping Paul to the floor.

Paul disappeared below the slab and a second later the giant's legs came out from under him with such force that both legs flew into the air as the giant toppled, its head striking the back of the chamber hard enough to fracture the temple wall.

Water sprayed from the newly formed fracture.

Breanne backpedaled away from Apep as he reared back for another swing.

Paul appeared on the slab in a full-on run toward Breanne and Apep. He didn't slow as he approached, and he didn't stop when he arrived. He hit Apep in a full run. Lenny's staff went flying from Apep's hands as he fell backward.

Breanne's eyes clouded over, rolling back as she saw what was to come. *No! Please! No!*

Distantly, as the vision took hold, she sensed Paul and Apep fighting desperately. But it didn't matter because now she knew how this fight would end. *Oh god, she knew!*

Water continued to gush through the fractured wall.

Apep tried frantically to shield his battered face from Paul. Finally finding his wits between strikes, he shouted in a voice somewhere between anger and terror, "Enough! Rayzae!"

Breanne's mind cleared in time to watch helplessly as Paul's body lifted, launching high into the air. He hit the ground below the slab with horrible force, sliding headfirst into the wall of the chamber. Water rushed all around him. She was sure she watched her brother die… she knew she was sure because she had already seen it.

Across the chamber Sylanth swung his remaining head back and forth, dowsing the area in front of him in brilliant, blue-green fire, his panicked eyes searching feverishly for the offender.

Garrett was sure he was going to die as the flames washed over his blood-covered body. He braced himself for the pain. When the flames hit him – and they did hit him – he felt only a warmth as the dragon blood covering him started to sizzle like fish in a fryer. But he did not burn.

Outside the envelope of fire, his friends screamed.

"Shit, David, do you see Garrett? I can't see him!" Lenny was shouting.

"I think he's in the fire!" David shouted. "Jesus, Len! I think he's burning up!"

Not waiting around to figure out *why* he did not burn, Garrett scrambled to get away from the flames, quickly rolling under the dragon. Lying on his back beneath the beast's great belly, he found the spot where he assumed the heart would be and, rolling over, he got to his feet in a squat. Pulling in a deep breath he gritted his teeth and thrust the sword upward, being sure to drive the weapon all the way to the hilt.

The dragon reared up on his back legs like a horse. But try as he might, the dragon couldn't escape the bite of steel.

Garrett leapt up and grabbed the hilt of the sword, hanging his full weight from it, but it held fast, not budging. As the dragon fell back to his feet, Garrett ripped the sword from his chest, more blood pouring over his hands and arms.

Sylanth staggered, the dragon fire dissipating as he gasped in short, pained breaths.

Garrett stole the opportunity, diving into a reckless roll between the dragon's front legs. Then, springing upward he swung for the throat attached to the remaining head. Garrett's sword found the beast, but with his blood-slicked hands, he couldn't get a solid strike like with the first head. Still, the sword bit down, slicing the dragon's throat.

With its last gargled breath, Sylanth found Garrett, his eyes boring into him. The ill wishes in the dragon's eyes were too little too late – he would have no revenge.

Garrett never broke eye contact with the dragon, holding his stare until the head rested on the floor and the last of his life faded. Garrett wanted Sylanth to know who had destroyed them. It was the least he could do for Janis.

~

As Apep pulled himself back to his feet he gingerly touched his broken nose. He wanted to heal himself and stop the pain the Moore boy had inflicted on his face, but there was no time, not when he was so close. Wiping his sleeve across his bleeding nose, he turned to Balor. "If you agree to keep our truce and take me to King Ogliosh I give my word that our treaty will be upheld when I sit on the throne of Osonian. The others will all be awake now, Balor. By waking one, I have woken all seven of you!"

"Yes, I can feel the others. All have risen. All will converge on King Ogliosh. We must go to him," Balor said.

"Yes. But first show me how to assemble the stones. This world is different now, Balor. They have new weapons, new… energy. If I assemble the God Stones into the Sound Eye, their world will change. Their energy won't work."

Balor stood looking down at Apep, hesitating – perhaps contemplating whether to trust the elvish wizard. "It is dangerous to assemble the Sound Eye before the portal's conductor is ready. This world is not meant for such power."

"Balor! You must trust me. If the humans' power isn't nullified, we will be in for a battle. We did this your way last time! I waited a thousand years for my army and look where it got us! The world is different now. We have to assemble them! Show me!"

Balor stared down, his one big eye unblinking. Finally, he held out his hand. "Give them to me and I will assembly them."

Now it was Apep who faltered.

Across the chamber, Pete stood under his own power, tears still streaming down his face, as Garrett ran toward them.

Garrett stood in front of him. "I'm sorry, Pete."

Pete threw his arms around Garrett and hugged him, and Lenny and David piled on. The moment was broken when they heard Breanne scream.

"That's Bre!" Garrett said, water splashing over his feet as he turned toward Breanne's voice.

"Yeah, and she's yelling for me! Oh, this can't be good!" David said.

"Come on!" Garrett said, splashing forward.

The others followed.

Pete wiped tears from his face and squinted in the direction of Breanne's screams. "That water isn't good. It can only be coming from one place."

Lenny frowned. "We can't be anywhere close to the Sangamon?"

"Not the Sangamon, Lenny. We must be under Lake Petersburg," Pete said.

The three boys ran across the back of the chamber and around to the opposite side of the slab. Apep was atop the slab, speaking to the giant. As they rounded the slab, they found Breanne kneeling next to Paul.

"Jesus, what happened?" Lenny asked.

"Please, David. Please help him," Breanne begged.

"I'll try," David said, kneeling next to her.

"Garrett… come… come here," Paul managed through clenched teeth.

Garrett knelt down.

Paul reached up, grabbing his collar.

David placed his hands on Paul's chest and closed his eyes.

Paul pulled Garrett close, whispering in his ear, "Take care… of… her… Garrett."

"No, Paul! Get up! Please just get up!" Breanne begged.

Garrett's throat constricted – he could only nod.

David started to glow.

Apep looked down on them from atop the slab.

Breanne sobbed. She looked up, her eyes finding Apep's. "It isn't going to work. He isn't going to let it work!"

"Shall I finish them?" Balor asked, turning to the group crowded around Paul.

"No… leave them, they're all about to die anyway." Then he motioned with his hand, "Eshesh esh zaeray!"

"No! Leave him alone!" Breanne screamed. But it was too late – the words were spoken. Reflexively Paul's body arched, forcing his back off the floor as his whole body seized. Finally, his muscles relaxed, and his body went limp.

Paul's heart stopped beating.

"Oh god, no! Please! Please, Paul, no!" Breanne screamed.

David's glow faded away prematurely. The mustached boy swayed, but he didn't pass out. He refocused and tried again, but the golden glow wouldn't come. He turned to Breanne with tear-filled eyes. "I'm so sorry, Breanne."

But Breanne was somewhere else. Pulled away to a place deep in her own mind – deep into her past. Her mother was telling her not to worry. It was going to be okay. They would just go back and get her violin, and if they were late for the Christmas recital at all, it would only be a few minutes. But Breanne wasn't having it. She was arguing about how embarrassed she would be showing up late in front of all her friends and that she couldn't believe her mother had let her forget her violin. They probably wouldn't even let her play. She was so mad, and all she could think was she would never forgive her mother for forgetting her violin. And so, her mother drove faster. On the radio "Rudolph the Red-Nosed Reindeer" played. In her mind she replayed the moment, crossing her arms over her chest and glaring at her mother, *I'll never forgive you for this! Never!* The words came hot and fast – and more words too! And, oh god, how she didn't mean them! She wanted so bad to take them back!

Outside her mind was shouting that she couldn't hear.

"Bre! Get away from him!" Garrett shouted.

"Bre, run!" David shouted.

She also couldn't hear Lenny beating his fists on Paul's chest and shouting, "You can't die! You *can't* die!" over and over. "I owe you a knife! How can I give you your damn knife if you die!" She wouldn't know part of Lenny's strange stepparent's training had required he learn several first aid techniques, including CPR. She wouldn't see Lenny begin giving her brother chest compressions. She wouldn't hear him counting off, "One one-thousand, two one-thousand, three one-thousand!"

No, Breanne's world was now consumed with a shattering windshield, crushing metal, and the sound of her own heart as it broke. She couldn't even feel the ribbons of shadow as they wrapped around her arms like cold, dead fingers. Reality was more like a dream as she became weightless, drawn up onto the slab, where she was dropped at the feet of Apep only to be snatched up again. This time the fingers that wrapped around her arm were very real – yet still, she barely noticed.

~

Garrett stood, pointed his sword, then started toward Apep. "You're going to die, Apep!"

Apep smiled from atop the stone slab, "In the words of your dead friend, 'Not today.'"

Apep turned and said something to the giant.

Balor took two strides forward and kicked the wall near the fracture.

The wall split open, pouring more water into the chamber.

Behind Garrett, Paul gasped for breath.

"He's aliv—" Lenny tried to shout, but the sudden gush surged into the kids, knocking them over and washing them across the chamber.

Lenny scrambled for Paul, grabbing him by the collar. "We have to get out of here or we're all going to drown."

"But he has Bre! I won't leave her!" Garrett argued, as he began wading against the current back toward Apep.

Paul's face was full of confusion as he tried to speak in what sounded to the boys like a drunken slur. "Oh… my god… It's Oak Island all over… but now I'm Ed… now…"

Apep glared down at Garrett, a condescending smile on his face. He handed the God Stones to Balor.

Balor turned his back to them, not allowing anyone to see him assemble the stones.

"He's connecting them!" Garrett shouted, his eyes going wide as he pushed forward against the rising current.

"Goddammit, Garrett! We have to go now!" Lenny said, pushing

David to go as he dragged Paul through the shallow water toward the entrance to the chamber.

Garrett waved a hand. “Go, Lenny, get them out. I have to stop them!”

But Garrett couldn’t stop Balor, who had just one movement left to complete the assembly of the God Stones into the Sound Eye.

With a single, unremarkable click, the entire world changed.

In that instant, intense energy spilled forth, spreading like a shock wave, permeating everything – saturating the world.

36

End Game

Wednesday, April 6 – God Stones Day 1
Petersburg, Illinois

Garrett could feel the increase of power, the supreme energy. It was thick in the air, pulsing in everything around him – amazing and ominous at the same time. Mr. B's story of the great flood came rushing back to him. The last time the earth was exposed to the Sound Eye, it was used to tear open a hole in the fabric of space, nearly destroying the world in the process.

Balor looked down at Apep, who was shouting at the giant and holding out his hand. The giant said something with unflinching finality. He did not give the Sound Eye back to Apep.

The next words Garrett understood as they were in English.

"After what I went through to wake you! You would dare to betray me?!" Then came the words of power, "Rayesh ak eshmue, Esh akoz oz flahmue!"

Balor turned on Apep, hammering his big fist downward to try and crush the elf before he could cast. But Apep was too fast, lurching out of the way and nearly yanking Breanne's arm out of its socket in the process.

The spell hit Balor, freezing the water around his feet. Garrett saw it, but the giant didn't realize it until he tried to take a step. He fell forward off balance, instinctively reaching out with his hands…

The Sound Eye dropped onto the slab as Balor flailed, the ice now climbing up his legs.

Garrett waded forward. This was his chance. The giant was trapped. He had to get the Sound Eye before Apep, then he could rescue Bre.

~

In the tunnel, Paul grabbed Lenny by the arm. "No, Lenny, we can't… leave without them!"

"Right now, I got to get you out of here! I promised Garrett," Lenny said, dragging Paul forward through the thigh-deep water.

"And didn't you promise…" Paul struggled to get the words out. "You promised Mr. B you would take care of him… Lenny, you have to go back and help him save my sister."

David was holding Lenny's staff and flailing it wildly. "We're out of time. If we don't go now, we won't make it. That wall is going!" His voice was high and panicked. "And when it does, we're screwed. I don't want to drown! Lake Petersburg is over sixty feet deep. I know, I've fished it plenty with my dad. Do you even realize how much pressure that is?!"

Paul continued to hold Lenny's gaze as water rushed past them. Away from the fire-lit chamber, the only light was coming from Paul's headlamp. Finally, he tried to speak again. "I can't do it, Lenny. My head is messed up… and my body isn't working right. I need you. Garrett and Bre need you! Jesus, Lenny, if I lose my sister…" He swallowed before continuing, "You know it's more though – if we lose Garrett, I think I lose my pops, but I also think the whole world loses."

Lenny turned to David and Pete. "Get him out of here."

"What? You're actually going back?" David said.

"I was always going back, David, but I told Garrett I would get you guys out. Garrett didn't say out of what. You're out of the chamber. Now you two take it from here and get him the rest of the way."

"Going back in there is suicide for sure," David shouted. "But fine! If that's how you want it, Lenny, just… Fine!"

Lenny could see David's mustache twitch in the dim light of Paul's headlamp.

David spun, shoving the staff into Lenny's hands. "I should have known I was going to die in this rotten place! Not enough I nearly fell in the river getting in, then almost fell in that death trap of a pit when I was attacked by that disgusting bat! Son of bitch, Lenny! Not enough a rat nearly ate my face!"

"Ate your face—?"

"Shut up!" David shouted. "That's right! My face! Not enough I stabbed a freaking dragon to save your ass! No!" David pointed at Lenny. "Now, I finally get to leave, and I find out we got to go back in!"

"David, you can wait here until I get—"

"Shut up, Lenny! Just you shut up right now! After what happened to Janis! I got to go back in! Shit's sake, Lenny, I gotta make sure you don't die! Make sure Garrett and Bre don't die!" David turned and started marching back into the chamber. "The truth is we're probably all going to die in this rotten place, Lenny! So, come on! Let's go die… you dick!"

Lenny raised both eyebrows and looked at Pete.

"Whatever. Let's just get this over with," Pete said, turning to follow David.

Paul handed Lenny his headlamp, then leaned up against the side of the tunnel, bracing himself against the rising water. "Just get them out, Lenny. Just get them out."

The Sound Eye was much closer to Apep than it was to Garrett but in a split-second decision Garrett launched himself headfirst, hoping against hope he could close the gap by making the first move.

Apep released his grip on Breanne and lunged, landing hard on his stomach. The lanky elf sprawled across the slab, frantically trying to grab the Sound Eye before it slid off.

Garrett scrambled on his belly too, stretching out only inches away. He was almost there when long blue-grey fingers filled his vision and a sharp elbow collided with his eye.

Apep quickly scooped up the Sound Eye with both hands. He stood, raising the round object high above his head triumphantly. Then he began laughing, like a child who had just been given a ticket to an amusement park. His laughter quickly turned into a different sound full of gluttonous avidity, the sound of unbearable thirst being quenched. "Ah! Finally, it's mine!"

"Bre! Run!" Garrett shouted. But she didn't run. She didn't move. *What the hell was wrong with her?* Apep stood between them, still goggling the Sound Eye, still laughing. Garrett felt like he had been gut punched, but it was the sound of fracturing ice that startled him from his misery. The giant was nearly free of the ice spell.

Apep spun.

Balor smashed frantically at his one remaining foot still frozen in place.

"Garrett!" came a rasping voice from behind him.

Garrett turned, looking for the source of the voice.

Down on the chamber floor, propped against one of the columns Janis had conjured, was Coach. He was somehow still alive! But only barely, his blue skin an ashen grey in the firelight.

"Garrett, run! Run now!" Syldan ordered.

"But, Coach! Apep has the stones and Bre!"

Apep had taken Breanne by the upper arm and was backing away toward the opposite end of the slab, closer to the source of the water.

"Goddammit, brick, you got no time. Get out of here before you can't!"

"But… the old one, Apep. We can't let them escape! I have to stop them."

"Listen to me. You did exactly what you were supposed to do. You came in the tomb and Apep is leaving with the stones. I'm trying to save you from the next part! The next part will be the worst of it! But maybe… if you just go!"

He isn't making any damn sense, Garrett thought.

From the opening to the chamber the light from a headlamp bounced toward him. It was Lenny, David, and Pete.

"What the hell are you guys doing back?" Garrett asked, glancing back to see Apep tugging Bre along. She wasn't even resisting. *He must have her in some kind of trance,* Garrett thought.

"Coach?" Lenny asked in surprise.

"Lenny, you were supposed to get them out!" Garrett said, wading away from them and toward the slab.

"We're not leaving without you!" Lenny said.

"And I'm not leaving without her!" Garrett said.

With a final grunt the last of the ice holding Balor shattered, freeing the giant's foot from its frozen shackle.

"You guys, figure this shit out, would you? I got Coach!" David shouted as he grabbed Coach by the wrist and started pulling.

"Dammit, brick, get your head on straight! You can't save me, there's no time and there's no point! Just go," the elvish coach protested as he tried unsuccessfully to pull his arm back.

David continued to slosh forward, ignoring the strange pointy-eared elf barking at him like a drill sergeant.

As Syldan's body stretched out, he made a horrible groan then muttered, "Jesus H. Christ," and passed out.

"What's the move, Garrett?" Lenny said.

Apep began chanting at the wall. He held the round Sound Eye out in front, and it began to glow.

"The giant's loose and he looks pissed!" Garrett pointed at Balor.

"I bet he goes after Apep!" Lenny shouted back.

Garrett nodded. "Yeah, and when he does you grab Bre, I'll grab the Sound Eye, and we bail."

But Balor didn't attack Apep. Instead he turned toward them and ran like hell toward the exit – the exit that was on the other side of Garrett and Lenny. The space between the slab and the wall wasn't necessarily narrow, but with a thirty-foot giant running toward him it seemed to close in really quick.

"Garrett!" Lenny shouted, falling into a fighting stance.

"This is bad!" Garrett shouted through gritted teeth as he drew his sword.

"You think!" Lenny said.

"It's freaking out! I think it's trying to make a run for it!"

"It can't fit through the tunnel!"

"It doesn't know that!" As Garrett watched the giant advance, a suicidal plan blossomed from a single thought. Although it was not human, it had legs and feet, just bigger, so it was reasonable to assume it had an Achilles tendon running down the back of its foot as well.

Suicidal is fine for me but not Lenny. But Garrett knew Lenny wouldn't leave him. "Run, Lenny, I'm right behind you! Go! Go! Go!" he shouted, slapping his hands against the water, and with that Lenny took off.

Garrett turned back to the giant as it bore down on him. With only three long strides the giant was on him. Every ounce of Garrett's being told him to move, but he tightened his grip on his sword, set his jaw, and held fast.

The giant's foot descended overhead.

Just a half second more.

When Garrett felt the wind off the giant's foot, he made his move, spinning away as the foot splashed down. He swung the sword blindly through an explosion of erupting water. The long sweeping arc of the blade encountered very little resistance as it bit deep into the back of Balor's foot, cutting through the flesh and tendon, until finally scraping across bone.

Although Garrett felt all of it through the hilt of his sword, he knew beyond doubt his strike had been true when the giant's slack foot rose from the water. He had severed the giant's Achilles tendon. The big beast's foot came back down, landing toes first and then rolling unnaturally with an audible crunch.

The giant fell hard, face-planting into the water.

On top of the slab, Breanne blinked away the past to find herself in the very real present, consumed instantly in heartache and loss. Paul was dead. His heart had stopped beating, and even David couldn't fix him. Sobs came and through them she heard Apep's voice chanting a strange combination of syllables. This was the language of the God Stones. Even with Janis's spell, she couldn't understand it. She felt Apep's hand under her arm, yanking it awkwardly like a parent snatching up a child about to get into trouble. His grip was painful as he pulled her, but she deserved it. She deserved whatever came next because she knew this was all her fault. She dragged her brother here to this town, to this impossible place deep under the ground. Earlier he told her she couldn't keep blaming herself and that what happened to her mother wasn't her fault. But wasn't it? Wasn't it also her fault she couldn't stop her father from opening that damned chest, and look what happened? So many people were dead! Now Paul was dead! God, not Paul! Her father… Jesus, her father would probably die! She looked across the chamber. The giant was running and then falling. She saw Garrett and from the looks of it he would be dead soon enough. Suddenly she knew what she had to do.

As soon as the giant hit the water, Garrett went into motion, finding the back of its other foot. He swallowed hard, rearing back to hack just above the thing's heel. He chopped down as hard as he could, as if he were trying to split wood with a sword. This time he had leverage and when the sword bit in, it sank deeper than he thought possible.

Balor bellowed something incomprehensible and pulled his legs beneath him. He tried to stand but failed, letting out a cry of rage and falling back on his ass. He searched for the source of his agony and reached for Garrett with his good hand, the one with all six fingers still working.

From across the chamber Breanne screamed his name and Garrett froze, his heart knotted. He had to get to her. He tried to dodge the hand, back-pedaling in the waist-deep water, but he wasn't fast enough. "Kiai!" Garrett yelled, slashing with his sword.

Balor yanked his hand back too slowly, costing him the tips of three of his fingers.

Garrett shuffled back.

The enraged giant's eye went wide with fear as his attention shifted to something beyond Garrett. He pushed himself away, dragging himself backward toward the chamber's opening.

Despite the pain Garrett had inflicted, he realized the giant didn't fear him – it was Apep's chant he feared. Garrett turned back to the slab and climbed. "I'm coming!"

Breanne held out her hand and shook her head. "No, Garrett! No! Get out now!"

Garrett froze, confused. He was at the opposite end, still a good thirty feet away.

"Just run, Garrett!"

"No! Apep, listen to me. Take the stones! You can have them! Just please, let her go!" Garrett's eyes welled and threatened to spill over. The bastard killed Mr. B and Phillip. He felt the rage pushing him to the brink of losing himself. He wanted to attack, but what if Apep killed her? He couldn't lose Bre too… he couldn't. He knew it then and there. The God Stones, Apep – damn it all to hell. He just didn't want to lose Bre. "Just leave, Apep! Take the stupid stones and go! Just go!" he commanded.

The air between them hummed with an electric energy.

Thirty feet away Apep fell one word short of completing the cast. He placed the Sound Eye on his head like a crown, smiled at Garrett, then laughed. He narrowed his eyes as his voice turned serious. "You dare to command me?" His voice rose again as he pointed at Garrett, "You get nothing! You lose!"

Breanne's face was a tearful grimace as the bastard squeezed her arm too tight. It was too much. Garrett squeezed the hilt of his sword so tight his fingers ached. Her eyes still told him to run, but he only wanted to run to her.

Apep sucked a calming breath between bloody lips. "But I will leave you with this thought. You won't find this one in *The Art of War*, Garrett. Another way to subdue the enemy is to offer them a gift. One thing about humans – giants love to eat them… alive." His smirk returned. "Something for you to ponder while you sulk in your final moments."

"No!" Garrett screamed and bolted forward, raising his sword high to strike.

Twenty-five feet.

"So long, my boy." With a flourish of his free hand he spoke the final word.

Twenty feet.

Garrett had to shield his eyes as the energy around him coalesced into a blinding glow encompassing both Apep and Breanne in a perfect sphere. Still he ran.

Ten feet.

As the light intensified, heat radiated out from the sphere in a wave so strong his eyebrows singed. But it didn't matter – he would run blind through fire if he had to.

"Breanne!" Garrett screamed, the heat filling his mouth and throat as he pulled in a breath. He had to be close to her. Had to be! There! He could hear her in front of him.

"Gar… rett!"

Five feet.

Then the light was gone along with Apep – and Breanne.

"No!" Garrett screamed, dropping to his knees. "No!"

For a single heartbeat, the chamber fell silent and Garrett wanted to die. Despite the insanity of it, until this moment he'd had hope and that hope fueled him to fight. But hope was truly lost, and it twisted his insides.

Somewhere in the darkness a rat squeaked.

Another breath and another heartbeat passed before it came, but it came and when it did it was deafening. A loud crack that vibrated through his bones. He raised his head and blinked away the bright spots still floating across his corneas.

His vision returned just in time to see the entire back wall of the ancient tomb collapse.

37

¡Eres el Amor de Mi Vida!

Wednesday, April 6 – God Stones Day 1
Rural Chiapas State, Mexico

Gabi didn't look back. She couldn't. Her mother's scream and Fredy's pleas told her everything. *Oh god, please! María Purísima, please! Please, no!* The heat of grotesque fire too close warmed her back, but she did not look. To look was to die. She made the corner for the second time.

A split-second later, Itzel and Sarah rounded the sculptured corner just as the flames passed.

Itzel fell into Gabi's arms as both collapsed in a heap, stunned and sobbing. "I think Andrés made it to the water! María Purísima! I saw him catch fire, but I know he went into the water!" Itzel screamed in near hysteria as she pushed herself up.

"No, Itzel! You can't!" Sarah said.

Itzel reached beneath her shirt, pulled out the necklace Sarah had given her, and yanked it free from her neck. Her eyes were wild with terror as she tried to force a final smile. She shoved the ring and necklace into her daughter's hand. "I love you, Gabriela. You are noconetzin." She turned to Sarah. "Please! Get my daughter out of here, Sarah! Promise me!"

"I… I promise," Sarah said, grabbing her arm. "But Itzel, please."

Itzel wrestled her arm free of Sarah's grasp and was gone.

"Mamá, no!"

~

Back in the large chamber, Andrés poked his head above the water in time to see the dragon, which was standing right next to him, let out a last hateful gush of flame toward the giant. As flame gave chase, the giant ran past the broken platform, where the water deepened. When the giant was nearly waist deep, it spared a glance over its shoulder, gasped in a deep breath, and disappeared under the water for a final time.

The back of Andrés's body stung like the skin had been completely burned off. Perhaps it had. He fought to stay conscious through the pain as he pulled himself onto the platform. He had to get to Gabi and Itzel; he had to make sure they were safe.

The dragon turned its massive, horned head and watched as he pulled himself slowly out of the water. He could feel it staring at him and, though he didn't want to, he slowly risked a cautious look over his shoulder, careful to move slowly.

The dragon was smiling. And then it spoke in a strange feminine voice he couldn't understand.

Andrés turned to face her, still on his knees at the edge of the water.

Twisting her thick neck, she lowered her head all the way down to meet the human's eyes and spoke again.

Andrés shut his eyes up tight, like two guillotines dropping, as hot, rancid breath washed over his face. He groped blindly for the knife he always carried at his side, slowly drawing it out from its leather sheath. The dragon was speaking to him in a dialect unlike anything he had ever heard. It seemed as though there were two separate voices talking at the same time, one high and one low, neither matching the other nor making any sense.

He forced himself to look and instantly wished he hadn't. The thing's head reminded him of a massive black iguana but with horns. Only it was so, so much bigger and darker. Its jaws looked strong and its head muscular. The dragon's mouth was open slightly, showing a row of saliva-soaked teeth. As Andrés looked into its eyes, he realized he didn't need to understand its words to know what came next.

He forced himself up onto his knees and met the dragon's eyes, telling himself not to blink. Large orbs swirled with brilliant emerald flecks and starburst of amber that reminded him of fire, and they too stared back unblinking, bottomless with ageless wisdom and an incredible intelligence. There was something else there too. Andrés frowned – *what is it?* He felt like he could be swallowed by those eyes, that he might fall off the ledge and into a bottomless maelstrom of fire. His whole body began to shake uncontrollably. Above all else, clear and true, he saw the dragon's insatiable hunger.

Andrés tightened his jaw until it ached. It was now or never.

To his left Itzel screamed out, "No!"

"No, Itzel! Go back!" Andrés yelled, extending his left hand out to the side, motioning her back. In the other he squeezed the handle of the knife as though it were the only thing worth holding onto in the world. With a sudden jerk he raised the knife high above his head and shouted fearlessly into the dragon's face. "Eres el amor de mi vida! I'll be with you always, Itzel!"

"Andrés!" Itzel screamed.

Andrés thrust the knife toward the dragon's eye.

Azazel lunged forward, her mouth snapping shut to chomp down on the upper half of the human's body. Metal clattered to the stone floor as she drew back. The human's bottom half sat motionless, still kneeling there on the stone path.

From her right she found the source of the pained cry. Another human sat whimpering. Waiting to be devoured. *Hmm, good. As it should be.* But that one would have to wait. The queen of queens stretched forward a second time, finishing the lower half of the human. She swallowed, closing her eyes to relish every taste. Stretching her neck, she lapped at the stone with her long, forked tongue, like a hungry dog licking clean the bowl, careful to leave nothing behind.

Azazel sighed, her wide nostrils flaring out as her breath stirred plumes of smoky dust from the walkway. She turned her head to the whimpering one, and again she was satisfied.

She heard another scream. *Ah, more humans – and close.* This was very good indeed.

38

Not Today

Wednesday, April 6 – God Stones Day 1
Petersburg, Illinois

Lenny caught up to the others at the end of the corridor, where the floor dropped away into the cave. David and Pete had made good time – Coach might even be proud of their efforts considering they both nearly failed his P.E. class – and Paul had kept up with them. Water spilled off the ledge, filling the stretch between the mouth of the tomb and the tight crevice they had come through earlier. They would somehow have to swim it with an unconscious Coach and a wounded Paul.

"Let's go, guys, we are going to have to swim it."

"What? With them?" David gestured to Coach and Paul. "And what about Garrett and Breanne?"

For the first time, Lenny turned and looked back down the corridor. "That dick didn't follow me out!" Lenny slapped the water. "If he doesn't get himself killed, I'm going to kill him myself!"

"What about my sister, Lenny?" Paul slurred, his body shivering from the cold water.

For the first time Lenny realized Paul's left arm was hanging oddly and his head was bleeding pretty bad. *What the hell did Apep do to him?* He couldn't think about that now. "Look, Garrett's a big boy. He will get her. You guys are hurt, and we are running out of time. You said it yourself, David, Lake Petersburg is on the other side of that cracked wall. If it goes, how are we supposed to make it out then?"

Even as he said the words, he felt a stab of guilt at the thought of leaving Garrett. But they couldn't wait. Garrett would get Bre and the God Stones, and he would catch up. At least that's what Lenny had to tell himself. "Get in the water and I will slide Paul and Coach in, then I will follow, and we will pull them across. Maybe it isn't over our heads yet."

"Okay, Lenny." David's voice cracked in a way that said this plan was anything but okay.

Pete climbed in without a word, and Lenny began to think the poor kid might be in shock.

A sudden roar from the tunnel caused Lenny to jump.

David shouted and fell backward into the water. He stood up, his feet barely touching the bottom. "What the shit was that!?"

From deep inside the corridor came the sounds of splashing and pained grunts.

Lenny pointed the headlamp down the corridor, illuminating the seated giant pushing himself along with its hands. "Balls!"

"It's the giant, isn't it? The godforsaken giant! Lenny, dammit! Tell me it isn't!"

"It is!"

David screamed, grabbed Coach, pulled him off the ledge, and made for the crevice.

"Go, Pete!" Lenny said as he grabbed Paul by the collar. A sudden, bright golden glow filled the corridor, as if the sun had somehow risen inside the tomb. The grunting giant silhouetted in the glow roared again, redoubling its efforts to escape.

"What the…" Lenny's words were overtaken by a new sound. It was low at first, but quickly built into a loud rumble – *water?* The corridor began to shake.

~

When the wall collapsed, Garrett turned and ran as hard as he could down the slab toward the tomb's exit. He reached back and sheathed his sword on the run and when he was as close as he could get, he dove headfirst off the slab and into the water. He didn't look back. He just kicked and paddled harder than he ever had.

Behind him water surged around the slab, quickly swallowing it and reaching high enough on the wall to squelch the firelight, leaving the chamber in total darkness.

The full force of Lake Petersburg's silty water hit him right as he entered the tunnel. He had no choice now but to fight to stay upright and go with the surge. The water carried him, blind as a bat, down the tunnel toward the crevice. If he could get to the crevice without drowning, he had a chance. Then, over the rushing water he heard deep grunts. *The giant?! Oh come on!*

Suddenly, he slammed into the beast. Garrett flipped upside down then, and for a terrifying second, he was pushed down beneath it as both rolled in the wave. Garrett kicked in sheer panic, his instinct to survive taking over as he fought desperately not to be crushed underneath its massive bulk. Scrambling forward, he kicked and kicked, occasionally finding purchase, whether on a wall, the floor, or the giant itself.

Unsure which way was up, Garrett held his hands out in front of him, fighting the urge to breathe, when he suddenly slammed into a wall and was promptly pulled sideways and into a tighter tunnel, where the current pushed him with a newfound force. *This has to be it! God, please, this has to be the crevice,* he thought. A moment later he spilled out the other side to the sound of voices.

"Look, it's Garrett!" Lenny shouted.

"Swim to us, Garrett!" David yelled.

"Ah!" Garrett shouted, covering his head as the cavern shook and chunks of the ceiling fell all around him. From the crevice came a gargled roar. The gushing water rose, pushing Garrett forward. The entire lake was pushing its way through the tunnel with fierce relentlessness.

Garrett reached the group. "Go! Go! Go!" he screamed as if there were hope. It wasn't the giant he worried about. He was pretty sure it wouldn't fit through the crevice. He just didn't see how they had any chance of making it a mile with the water rising so fast, and he was sure when the chamber filled to the top the water was going to come even faster. In seconds the tunnel would be filled. None of them could hold their breath for a mile. They would all drown, and then they'd be flushed into the Sangamon River. Their bodies wouldn't be found for days, if at all.

"What the shit, Garrett!" David shouted.

"The wall caved in! We got to hurry before the whole tunn..." Garrett stopped, gasping, and frowned. The water had slowed like a faucet being turned down to a trickle.

As the water slowed, so did the group.

Lenny glanced back, shining the headlamp into the darkness. "Why did the water slow down?"

"The giant must be stuck where the tunnel narrowed," Garrett said, trying to catch his breath.

"Oh! Perfect! You think he'll get through?" David asked.

"Settle down, David. I don't think it could fit through," Garrett tried to reassure him.

"But you're not sure! Jesus, we gotta move!"

"Settle down, Yosemite Sam, you little mustached freak," Lenny said.

"Don't you tell me to settle down with a giant on its way to kill us! You settle down, Lenny! You settle do—"

"Enough!" Pete shouted. "It won't fit through. It's way too big."

"Well, hello, Petey!" Lenny said, slapping him on the shoulder. "Good to have you back."

"Lenny, don't ever call me Petey again. Janis called me that."

"Sorry, man. Seriously. I'm sorry."

Pete nodded. "I know. Thanks, Lenny."

Lenny spun on Garrett. "What the hell happened back there? I thought you were with me!"

"Lenny, I'm—"

"Garrett, where's my sister?" Paul asked.

Garrett hesitated, choking on the words.

"Where is she?!" Paul demanded again, his face twisting in anguish.

"She's gone, Paul," Garrett said quietly.

Lenny placed a hand on Paul's shoulder.

"What do you mean, gone! Are you saying she's… No!" Paul shouted, shrugging off Lenny's hand. "No! She can't be… she can't be…" But he couldn't say the word. "I'm going back!"

"No! Paul, she isn't dead, but Apep took her. I couldn't get to her. I tried. Honest, I tried!"

"Took her? Took her how? Took her where? For what?" His face contorted, screwing up in confusion.

"I… I don't know. They just vanished in a ball of light," he said, knowing it would do Paul no good to know what Apep had said. "I tried to get her, Paul."

Paul sagged back against the cavern wall, unable to speak.

"That must have been the light we saw in the corridor," Lenny said.

Behind them came another loud roar and the sound of falling stone.

"I knew it! Oh, man! The giant is forcing its way through the crevice! We're so screwed!" David said, taking off down the tunnel with Coach in tow.

"Let's just get out of here and then we will figure out what to do. There is no going back and nothing to go back for," Garrett said.

"I'm going back," Paul said flatly.

"Paul, this is crazy. I already told you there's nothing to go back for, and even if there was, that giant—"

"Garrett, listen to me – if that giant pushes through, that whole lake is coming with him. If that happens, we're all dead, just like that," Paul said, snapping the fingers of his working hand. "I *will* stop him, at least long enough for you guys to get out. But you have to promise me. Promise right now, in front of god and your best friend, you will find my sister and you will save her from that bastard!"

"Paul, you can't! You're hurt—"

"Promise me, Garrett!" he shouted.

Behind them came the sounds of stones scraping and splashing into water.

Garrett nodded. "If it is the last thing I do, I *will* find her. I promise I will. I swear it. Whether you make it or not. I swear it!"

Paul thrust his hand into Garrett's and pulled him into his shoulder, then let go of his hand and pounded a fist on his back. "I believe you."

"Let me heal you at least!" David said.

"So you can pass out? Sorry, kid, but I appreciate the offer."

"Paul, come with us," Lenny begged.

Paul grabbed Lenny next, pulled him in, and pounded a fist on his back too. "That folder I gave you, still got it?"

"Folder?" Lenny asked, then shook his head. "Oh, right, the knife? I do," he said, choking back a sob. He dug into his back dobok pocket and pulled out the knife, which was clean and free of Pete's blood.

"Lenny, don't worry about me. I'll kick this asshole's pecker into the dirt and catch up with you boys in a few minutes." He shoved Lenny's staff toward him and took his knife and the headlamp. "Now get moving."

Paul turned away, pointing the headlamp back down the corridor, and started limping down the tunnel. He never looked back, and Garrett wondered silently if he would ever see him again.

The giant had managed to get his massive shoulders free of the crevice by the time Paul approached, which meant the damn thing's arms were both free. There was no sneaking up on the thing either because if the giant couldn't see in the dark, he would have at least seen his headlamp as he approached. Paul tried to move his left arm, but it was completely dislocated.

The giant spoke loud and deep, swiping a hand out from the crevice toward Paul.

Paul dodged, flicking open his knife with a click. "Whatever you got to say, you may as well save it, big guy." He ran forward as best he could with pain shooting through his hip, falling forward into the giant's face.

The giant roared, reaching back toward his own face as Paul stuck him in his eye.

Paul felt a warm fluid run down onto his arm as the roar escalated into a high-pitched scream, but he didn't relent, stabbing again and again.

Again, the giant flailed his hand back toward his face.

This time Paul couldn't get away. The giant wrapped his fingers around him and squeezed, then shoved him underwater. But before the giant could get him away from his face Paul plunged his arm deep into the giant's eye – as deep as he could. All the way to the back. As the giant shoved Paul under, Paul pulled the big bastard's face underwater by a fistful of optic nerves. He twisted his fist to wrap the nerves around his own hand, holding on as if they were a lifeline. If he were to lose his grip on the slimy rope of nerves now, the giant would lift his face out of the water, grab a breath, and surely crush Paul to death. Worse than that, he would make it out of the crevice and Garrett and the others would die – and his sister would die. *No! Not today!*

I'm going to… pull your brain… out through your eye if that's what it takes!

But the harder Paul pulled, the harder the giant squeezed. He was being crushed to death and he knew it, but he had one thing going for him. He was a warrior. He might not be able to hold his breath longer than his brother Ed, but he could outlast this shitstain – he had to.

Paul did the only thing he could. He held on and he held his breath. He held it for his mom to make her proud, he held it for his pops and Ed because he never left a man behind. Mostly though, he held it for his baby sister because if he saved Garrett, Garrett would keep his promise – he would save Bre.

Paul released a rage-filled roar and with it all the air he had left. With a final superhuman yank, the nerves that wound their way all the way to the back of the giant's brain ripped loose.

The giant's massive body bucked. Wedged in the crevice, his giant eyeball ripped from his head and his face forced under the water, the giant screamed out all of his remaining air, sucked water deep into his giant lungs, and died.

The massive fingers around Paul loosened. He pushed up, breaking the surface of the water, and he breathed. Paul sagged back heavily against the wall and laughed. The laugh turned into a bloody cough. "I told you… Not today."

Paul knew there would be no leaving this place, not alive anyway, and he had made his peace with it. The water was still rising but only slowly thanks to the giant filling most of the crevice. The important thing was he had given Garrett and the others the time they needed.

He leaned back, closed his eyes, and rested his head against the stone wall. Then he heard something. *What the?* He stiffened. It was coming from the other side of the crevice, and it sounded like… chewing.

Then he heard a rat squeak.

39

Move

Wednesday, April 6 – God Stones Day 1
Rural Chiapas State, Mexico

Sarah spun toward Gabi, tearing her eyes from her view around the corner. The look on her face was total devastation.

"Do you see them?" Gabi asked.

Sarah knelt down. Tears poured down her face. "Gabi. We have to run. We have to run now!"

"But Mamá and Papá?" she asked, knowing the answer.

"We have to run, Gabi!"

Suddenly all sound faded away. She might have screamed. The singular gut-wrenching scream of someone who has just lost everything. Nothing else mattered to her now. She no longer wanted to fight for her life. She couldn't hear her own screams. She couldn't hear anything. Gabi was numb.

Gabi had no idea she was even moving. But she was moving, being pulled by something… no… someone. Sarah was pulling her. Sound began to return to her ears.

"Run, Gabi! We have to run!" Sarah cried.

Somehow Gabi's legs were moving under her. The ground below

her feet was dry. She looked up, her headlamp pointing forward. She blinked. Beneath her the ground shook.

"Look!" Sarah said.

But Gabi didn't look. She just blinked and ran.

"There. See it!? It's a giant slab of stone. C'mon, Gabi! Twenty-five meters! You can do it! Run!"

The stone slab must have been nearly two meters thick and a dozen long.

Sarah threw herself behind the slab, dragging Gabi down with her.

Heavy footsteps shook the floor as the dragon ran toward them. The roar came so loud Gabi felt it through her chest, and she knew she was about to die, just like her father and her mother. With her back pressed to the slab, she covered her ears. Oh, dear María Purísima, she knew what came next. Behind her the monster's roar became impossibly loud. In front of her the chamber wall suddenly glowed with emerald firelight. Then came the fire. The dragon fire struck the slab as they pressed their bodies against it, scrunching themselves into tight balls. Green flame whooshed over the top of the stone, changing to a blue-orange as it passed. Gabi screamed a silent scream drowned out by the dragon's roar. Heat, horrible and rank, pressed down on them.

Sarah screamed too, but she was actually screaming words and motioning. "We can't stay here! We have to move!" Sarah pulled on her arm.

The ground beneath began shaking again. The dragon was moving closer. Near the far wall, several small fires were now burning.

She watched numbly as Sarah scanned the wall for something.

"There! That shadow. Come on, Gabi!" Sarah pointed. "Let's move!"

Sarah grabbed her hand and pulled, but she was frozen with fear.

"Gabi. Please, we move now, or we die! I won't go without you, so if we stay, we die together!"

Gabi blinked again. *No. She didn't want to die. She didn't want Sarah to die.* She managed to get to her feet.

"That's it, Gabi! Now run!"

She did, and together they ran for the wall.

"Oh god! Oh god! Please let this be more than a shadow!" Sarah said as they approached the wall.

Behind them the dragon leapt onto the now burning stone slab and roared. There was nothing between the dragon and them. The wall lit up from behind them with a radiant greenish glow. Gabi felt the back of her shirt get hot, too hot, as she and Sarah ran full speed into the shadow. She put her hands up in front of her, unsure if she was running into a void or straight into the wall.

Gabi's back began to burn.

40

I Won't Let You Down

Wednesday, April 6 – God Stones Day 1
Petersburg, Illinois

As cold lake water overwhelmed everything inside the darkened tomb, one creature still stirred. An oversized rat with a long scar across her left shoulder swam for her life. She swam out of the stone cell, across the chamber, slipping into the corridor. She needed air. She had to find the air.

She paddled through the darkness like she was born of water, like a natural, her oversized paws kicking rhythmically. Had she been a normal-sized rat she could have held her breath for three minutes tops, but with her size came the ability to hold her breath even longer. She swam down the corridor and into the cave.

Once in the cave she couldn't find a way out, but she could feel it. The water was pulling past her. She followed it down into a crevice where the water moved fast. *Yes,* she thought, *this must be the way.* But then there was no way! A large fleshy creature blocked the way!

But something else was happening. Her mind was clearer than it had ever been. She was thinking and she knew things too. She knew something made her grow big. A strange creature, named Janis. Yes, and she knew other words too, like 'human.' She knew the one who made her big had died. She died at the same time a human boy… David? Yes, David. Janis died while David was putting the sunshine inside her.

That's when the thinking started, that's when her mind became different, when she was trying to eat his face. She didn't want to eat his face now though. David fixed her. He took the pain back… and something else? He put something inside her. The sunshine. Yes, that, but something else too. When others yelled the name Janis and the room lit with fire, David thought of Janis, the girl died, and the healing went in. Now she was aware and thinking, and she knew things, but most of all she knew she didn't want to die.

Her instincts told her she had to get past the fleshy thing to get out, but first she needed air. She swam up and found there was a small pocket of space between the ceiling and the water. Just enough space to stick her snout. Filling her lungs, she dove back down and went to work. She would gnaw and chew through the big fleshy thing, but she had hurry.

Feverishly, yet easily, she chewed through the flesh, tendons, and cartilage of the dead thing. She let her instinct guide her. Her powerful jaws compressed sharp incisors, effortlessly separating limbs at the joints. After several minutes of holding her breath she swam up to the small pocket of space at the ceiling of the cave, sucked in a breath, then dove back down to resume chewing on the only thing standing between her and freedom.

"Guys, I found the edge of the pit," Lenny said, probing with his staff. "The drop-off is right here. We will have to swim across."

Garrett moved to ease himself in when something large bumped into his back. As he reached out to push it away, he realized it was the giant's arm. "What the…" *Paul must have torn the giant's arm off trying to keep it in the crevice?* Then a second limb hit him, along with a sudden rise in the water. He was pretty sure it was part of the giant's leg. He shone the light on where the leg had been severed. It looked like it had been chewed on. No, not chewed on… chewed through? Suddenly, comprehension clicked in his mind. *The giant rats? They weren't all dead after all, and they must be trying to get out!* "Guys! Oh god! Guys, we need to hurry!"

"What now?" David shouted. Then he yelped, "What is that?! Is that a piece of the giant's leg?"

Foregoing caution, Garrett dove in and swam the gap across the pit. Once across, he shouted, "Guys, go! Hurry!"

They rounded the bend back to Lincoln's brick wall. But it was different from how they had left it. Before, the hole they had climbed through had been high up, but now a huge section of the wall had collapsed. Water rolled over the lower half of the remaining wall, down into the drainage tunnel below.

The drainage tunnel. Garrett didn't need to see into it to know they were in trouble. The violent roar of gushing water told him his worst fears were realized. It must still be pouring outside.

They approached the drainage tunnel cautiously. The water rushing past them was moving like whitewater.

"Guys, we have to go for it," Garrett said.

"What do you mean, go for it?" Lenny asked. "Because I know you can't mean jump into… that!" He pointed toward the rapids below.

"We have to jump in. Let the water take us."

"Have you lost your shit!?" David asked. "You want the water to take us where, Garrett? To the bottom of a brush pile? Over the dam, which you know is a damn death sentence in itself? And what about Coach? You think we can swim and still hold onto him – in the river? If we go in that river, we're all as good as dead!" David yelled frantically over the roar of water blasting through the drainage tunnel.

Lenny stepped up next to David. "There has to be another way. David's right – it's pitch black out there. We won't even be able to see once we're in the water."

Garrett looked at his friends. Lenny hugged himself, shaking uncontrollably from the cold water. David's mustache bounced as his jaw shivered, his fist full of Coach's collar, the only thing preventing Coach from being pulled over the small wall. And Pete was present physically, but clearly his thoughts were still back in the temple – with

Janis. The idea of asking his friends to willingly throw themselves into the freezing cold Sangamon River, a mere quarter mile from the busted dam, was insanity. Add darkness, a storm, and an unconscious man, and the already bad plan escalated to one of pure stupidity.

Another chunk of giant floated past them, quickly disappearing into the drainage tunnel. Garrett couldn't tell if it was a leg or an arm. The tunnel was filling, and time was running out. *Shit, we have to go,* he thought. He turned to David. "You remember back in the dojo when you said you believe in me, but that I need to believe in myself?"

David's eyebrows stitched together.

This was it. There would be no second chances. "You remember when you guys said you would follow me, even into fire? Well, this isn't fire, but I'm asking you to trust me, to believe in me now." Garrett turned back to David, his eyes shimmering in the low light of the headlamp. "I know you're scared, David. We're all scared, but believe in me now. We have to try! There's no other way! Something is tearing that giant apart, and we're about to get flushed." He put his hand on David's shoulder and pressed his lips into a flat line. "Follow me, David! I won't let you down."

David pressed his palms against the sides of his head. "Alright. Ah!" He nodded. "This is nuts, man! This is *the* craziest shit ever, but alright." He sucked in a breath and clenched his fist, trying to control the fear. "What's the plan?"

Garrett looked at Lenny and Pete.

Lenny forced a weak smile. "Balls."

Pete shrugged.

Garrett let out a single relieved exhale. He didn't know why he was relieved. He had just convinced his friends to follow him into a plunge to their deaths.

They positioned Coach on the edge next to the rushing water of the drainage tunnel, careful not to let him get washed away. "Okay, everyone grab ahold of Coach, and no matter what, don't let go of him. He will be the link that keeps us all together. When you hit the river, swim like crazy for the bank and whatever you do, don't let go of Coach."

Everyone nodded, reluctantly working their way into position.

"Wait," Lenny said, holding up a hand for quiet. "Did you hear that?"

Everyone froze, trying to listen for whatever Lenny had heard over the roar from the drainage tunnel. Then they all heard it. The shrieking of a rat being tossed about by a wave of crashing water heading right toward them.

"Guys, there's nothing blocking that crevice anymore!" David shouted.

But then they heard something else – a voice. "Steady now! Stay... steady!"

"That's Paul!"

"Now! Go!" Garrett yelled, grabbing ahold of Coach's arm as he jumped into the drainage tunnel. Simultaneously everyone else did the same. David hugged one of Coach's legs, Pete grabbed the other, and Lenny latched onto the arm opposite Garrett's with one hand and his staff with the other.

Instantly they were swept away with a rush.

41

Into the River

Wednesday, April 6 – God Stones Day 1
Petersburg, Illinois

Underwater, Garrett's ears filled with the roar of churning water mixed with high-pitched screeches as he and the others tangled and tumbled with the giant rat.

To and fro, Garrett was tossed before suddenly he was slammed against the bottom of the drainage pipe, a great furry weight crushing him then scrambling over him. For a brief instant, he thought all the air would be forced from his lungs, and in that moment, Garrett was sure he would die. Bre flashed through his mind. The thought of not keeping his word to Paul hurt more than the heavy rat squishing him. He wanted to live. To see them all, to keep his promise to Paul – to save Bre. He fought the urge to breathe, visualizing Bre's eyes, her smile – her beauty. He was so close to giving in to the urge when he realized something. He had never heard Bre laugh. Oh, it must be a beautiful laugh. Probably the most beautiful sound god had ever created. He wanted so bad to know that laugh.

Garrett squeezed Coach's arm for dear life, nearly losing it, but holding on. Then he was weightless, falling, ejected from the drainage pipe like so much refuse, and sent hurling through the wet night air. Time around him seemed to slow, but he wasn't doing it. The moment was just so surreal. He sucked in a short gasp of air, aware of the rat, water, his friends, and even Paul – all falling weightless with him. Sightless in the night, he could only feel their consciousnesses around him. He gasped in again, shallowly, as he smashed into the river below, landing hard on his back amongst a tangle of knees and elbows, the river stealing the air from his lungs.

When Garrett's body struck the water, he was ripped away from Coach. He moved with the current, frantically gasping for breath that wouldn't come as he searched around for Coach and the others. But he was alone. He wanted to yell, and now that his head was above water, he should have been able to breathe, but his body wouldn't let him. His diaphragm had tensed in spasms from the impact. He had had the wind knocked out of him before, but this felt so much worse than he had remembered. He heard a voice. *Lenny!* Garrett spun in a circle and found Lenny's headlamp glowing in the distance.

"Garrett! Garrett!" Lenny shouted.

"Leeennnnnnyyy!" Garrett rasped, barely above a whisper. He sucked in short pulls of air as he fought the current. Something below him tugged. In his mind he told himself it was the current – only the current. Finally, through the short wheezing breaths, air was getting in. He kept his eye on Lenny's headlamp as he tried to swim toward him, his legs heavy as if his ankles were wrapped in chains.

As Garrett approached the headlamp, his heart filled with relief when he saw Lenny and Pete still clutching Coach. Then as fast as hope rose it sank again. "Where's David?!"

"What happened… to not letting go of Coach?" Lenny said through shivers.

"Lenny, David? Did you see what happened."

"I don't… know, I haven't seen… him since the tunnel. We need to get out of this water, Garrett… I can't feel my feet or hands," Lenny said.

"He let go in the tunnel. I tried to grab him, but he kicked me in the face," Pete said.

"Swim, guys, we got to get to the bank," Garrett said through clenched teeth.

Together they pushed and kicked, somehow avoiding any brush piles. A few moments later they dragged Coach's body onto the muddy bank of the Sangamon and collapsed.

Garrett pushed himself onto his hands and knees, the cold mud pushing between his fingers. They had somehow made it out of this nightmare, but where was David?

Lenny placed his head on Coach's chest. "I think he's dead, man."

"Help! God, please… I… I can't hold on!"

"That's David!" Lenny announced.

"David! Where are you?" Garrett shouted back at the dark river.

David returned the shout, his voice difficult to hear over the rumble of the dam. "I'm slipping, man! I'm in a brush pile and I can't hang on! It's pulling me under! I don't want to die! God, please! I don't want to die! Not like this… not like this!"

Pete squinted in the direction of the shouts. "He's pinned under a brush pile on the other side of the river!"

"I'm going in!" Garrett said, turning to Lenny, both on their feet now.

"You'll never be able to cross it before you're washed over!" Lenny argued.

"I have no choice! David trusted me!" Garrett shouted. He was so pissed at himself. He had given that damn speech about trust and believing in him, and now David was alone fighting for his life. *If you ever believed in me, believe in me now… what a joke.* "I asked him to follow me out of that stupid-ass pipe, Lenny!" Garrett stepped into the edge of the water. "I'm going," he said with finality. Turning in the direction of David's voice, he shouted into the night, "I'm coming, David!"

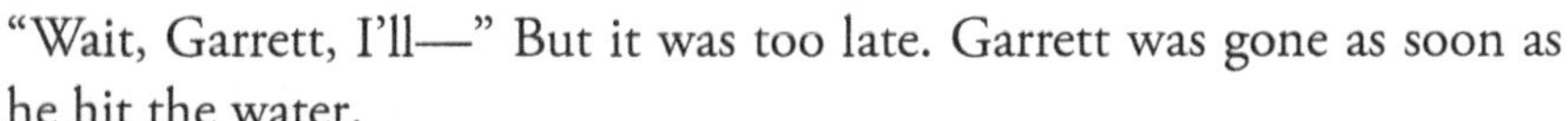

"Wait, Garrett, I'll—" But it was too late. Garrett was gone as soon as he hit the water.

"Hey," croaked a voice from behind him.

"What the!" Lenny spun, falling back onto the muddy bank. "Coach?"

"Where's Garrett?" Coach asked, barely able to speak.

"I… I don't know. He went back into the river to get David." Lenny stood and shouted, "Garrett!"

"Damn that brick!" Coach growled. "I tried to save him from the worst part. I tried, dammit!"

Lenny frowned. "What are you talking about?" He turned back to the river uneasily, worry gripping his face like a mask as he searched the darkness. "Garrett!" he shouted in desperation. *Where is he?*

"The prophecy, Lenny. 'The serpent shall swallow my son, delivering him to his death,'" Coach said, pointing his long elvish finger at the river. "I was stupid to interfere. Stupid to think I could keep him from dying."

"What? You're saying he's going to die!?" Pete turned back to the dark water.

Lenny's eyes sprung wide. "What! Die?!"

The elf nodded, but he was nodding to empty air – because Lenny was gone.

Lenny was on the same side of the river as the tunnel they had been spit out of. He was running to beat hell – no, to beat death. The shoreline between the tunnel and the dam was practically nonexistent, rising up dozens of feet at an unclimbable, near-vertical grade. What riverbank there was between Lenny all the way to the dam was littered with busted-up trees and broken slabs of concrete, some chunks as big as living room furniture – a preventive measure to reduce erosion on the town side of the river.

Garrett couldn't die. What kind of *f*'ed-up prophecy kills off the guy who's supposed to defeat the bad guy and get the God Stones back? But they hadn't got the God Stones back, and they hadn't stopped the bad guy, had they? What the hell was going on? He didn't know, but he knew his best friend in the whole world couldn't freaking die!

Lenny maneuvered on the uneven surface with a speed that should not have been possible. Not on a moonless night, not on the bank of the Sangamon, especially on this specific stretch. Hell, not even on a sunny day, with his body well rested, should the ease with which he negotiated the terrain be possible. The thought niggled there, at the back of his mind, but Lenny was focused on one thing – Garrett.

Gracefully, almost artfully, he bounded over stuff small enough to jump, danced with short steps across stuff too big to jump, and made hairpin pivots around stuff too big to cross, and he did it with nothing more than a single headlamp beam to guide him through the seemingly impenetrable darkness. In less than two minutes, Lenny was at the broken dam.

As it turned out, they hadn't been too far away. Lenny guessed maybe a quarter mile. This was not necessarily good though. How was Garrett going to get to David before being swept over?

Lenny ran out onto the dam. "Garrett!" he screamed, trying to get his voice above the roar of water.

The dam had been a derelict structure doomed from the start. Like at some point the city decided they would create a dam by taking the busted-up concrete or maybe even bricks from the old cobblestone streets they had replaced with blacktop and pile it across the river then, for good measure, pour a thick layer of concrete over the top. It was no wonder the dam had breached long ago, leaving a wide space in the middle where water raged through. You could venture out for a good twenty yards before reaching the spot that was broken. On the upstream side of the river, the concrete dam wasn't much higher than the water level, but on the downside the water dropped a good six feet.

As Lenny reached the broken section, water gushed over the jutting rocks in a whitecapped furry, breaking violently in sporadic sprays as it churned through the gauntlet of jagged rocks, no doubt splintering any debris that might pass through before plunging powerfully down on the opposite side, dragging any remaining pieces deep below the surface in the undertow. Just standing next to the break was frightening, as to fall in here meant certain death.

Kids said the water had been digging its way down in that spot way before the dam was ever built. They said kids had been dying in there way before America was even a thought. They said it just kept getting deeper and deeper, over hundreds maybe even thousands of years. Lenny had even heard other kids say there was no bottom at all.

Lenny didn't think it was bottomless, but he believed the thousands of years part. Hell, he'd fished it, they all had, and it didn't matter how much weight he put on a line or how much string he cast out, it would just sink and sink.

All this flashed through Lenny's mind as he drew up to the edge of the break, and he couldn't help but hate the Sangamon – the river Abraham Lincoln so loved. He hated it for the kids it killed, and for the friends he feared he couldn't save.

Lenny bit down hard on his lip, knowing he was about to flirt with a danger of the incredibly stupid kind. He might as well be standing back in that temple with the dragon about to light his ass up. He squeezed his staff in both fists harder than he realized. If Garrett and David went over this dam, he would never see them alive again.

He looked upstream into the night and screamed Garrett's name.

42

Breathe

Wednesday, April 6 – God Stones Day 1
Rural Chiapas State, Mexico

As Gabi entered the shadow the ground disappeared beneath her feet and she fell, tumbling forward down what felt like stairs. A second later she hit water. Fully immersed, she scrambled to right herself as Sarah landed with a hard splash next to her.

Jade flames followed them, rolling down the stairs in a great ball of death, filling every bit of the void. Underwater, Gabi squinted as the world above was suddenly blindingly bright with fire. There was no time to allow herself to feel the pain of the fall, no time to scream out, no time to pull in a breath. This time it was Gabi who grabbed Sarah and pulled her underwater. The flames rolled over them.

They tumbled, clinging to each other as a strong current dragged them away from the dragon and the fire and into the unknown. They were being swept downward into an underground river or stream. *Not a stream, streams are outside. We are in a cave.* This was bad. Gabi's heart slammed against her chest as the darkness swallowed them once again. She kicked her legs in a panic. *What if she couldn't surface!? What if the water went all the way to the ceiling!?* Gabi kicked and kicked as she screamed out all the air she had, exhaling as she broke the surface. She gasped again and again. The ceiling above her was low, her head nearly scraping the surface. Sarah broke the surface next to her, flailing for breath.

Behind them the dragon roared something. This sound was different. It had meaning. This wasn't the roar that preceded the flame; this was an angry scream. The dragon was saying something to them – yelling something *at* them. Then after came the roar of fire, a final burst of it – a last hope of incineration.

Behind them the cave glowed, but they were moving fast and were far out of reach.

Their heads were bumping against the ceiling now, and Gabi could barely keep her mouth above water.

"We need to get out," Sarah said in a gargled rasp as they swam for the edge, but the walls were sheer to the ceiling. There was no place to get out. The ceiling pressed even lower now.

"This is bad!" Sarah said. "Hold your breath, Gabi."

That's all they could do – hold their breath. They would be pulled under and never seen again. After all this… they were going to drown. *Mamá, Papá, I'm coming to you.* Gabi drew in a deep breath as the ceiling met the water.

Blindly they drifted forward, the water cold and the darkness absolute. Underground rivers could run for miles and miles. Some never surfaced at all.

Gabi rolled onto her back, face up, dragging her hands along the ceiling, hoping against hope to find an air pocket. Even a small one, just something to allow her a breath. But there was nothing. *Why couldn't I have just died with my family? María Purísima! Please. I don't want to drown!* Then she saw something. A light. This was it. This was death. The other side. Heaven. Her parents would be there, waiting for her. She just needed to let go, breathe the water in and let go. Then she felt Sarah pulling on her. Pulling urgently. *Sarah*, Gabi frowned. She could still see. Not very well but a little. The absolute darkness was no longer absolute, there *was* a light. Now she realized it wasn't the other side… it was coming from somewhere else. *But where?* This light wasn't sunlight. The color was wrong, and it couldn't be daylight out – not yet. *Then what?* She rolled around in the water looking for the source. The silhouette of Sarah was motioning frantically now, pushing her toward the light. She realized now there was a fork. The left side was light, the right side was complete darkness – death. If she didn't make it to the left tunnel she was going to die. She swam with everything she had, harder than she had ever swum. Death pulled at her, trying to drag her down into the depths, and she was sure at any second a serpent would lunge forward from the darkness and pull her under.

When Gabi reached the small shaft of white light, she felt Sarah pushing her from behind and suddenly she wondered if Sarah was panicking, about to run out of breath. *Oh please, Sarah! Please don't!* She couldn't lose Sarah too. She couldn't be alone.

It was a tight squeeze, but she managed to squirm inside. She had enough room to reach up and pull herself. She grabbed at anything she could, dragging herself along by her fingertips for what seemed like forever. Her heart raced as the light became brighter and the sensation to draw breath burned in her chest.

Finally, Gabi pulled herself free, emerging from beneath a partially submerged rock outcrop. Once she wriggled clear of the overhang, she planted her feet and pushed herself up. Her face broke the surface of the water and she gasped greedily at the night air, two breaths, then three, then four. The water was shallow, coming only to her waist.

Sarah burst from the water next to her, choking.

"Sarah! Are you okay?"

Sarah held out her hand, waving her off as she bent and retched violently into the water. A moment later she spoke. "Gabi… I almost made it but then I couldn't… I couldn't hold it any longer," she coughed again, still gasping for breath. "I must have swallowed a gallon of water!"

Gabi gasped sharply, her breath catching.

"What?" Sarah asked, following Gabi's gaze skyward.

"María Purísima," Gabi whispered. With the exception of the water moving gently across the palms of her hands, the tiny gorge was frozen in absolute stillness as if captured in a single frame outside of time. But it was the full moon, swollen and imposing, that drew her attention. Its mellow radiance spilled over everything, bathing the small gorge in magic silver light.

Without words both women gazed at the glowing orb as if for the first time in their lives. They didn't need to speak to know each other's thoughts. For only rare moments, and only when the moon was full, would it be positioned in such a way to shine underneath the rock outcropping and the long shaft they had escaped through. For them to pass by when they did, when the light from the moon was just so – the odds had to be astronomical. Had they passed by minutes from now or minutes earlier, the position would be different, and the way out would be invisible.

Gabi knew without a doubt this was a gift from her parents. She thought the strange light she had seen in the water was the other side – heaven – but her parents were not bringing her to be with them. They were taking her away – away to live.

Sarah turned and grabbed her, pulling her into her arms, wrapping her in them and squeezing. Gabi hugged her back with all she had. They stood there in the water for a long time, holding each other and sobbing.

43

Serpent

Wednesday, April 6 – God Stones Day 1
Petersburg, Illinois

Garrett struggled to push his battered body across the current toward the sound of David's voice. He was breathing hard as he pushed against the volume of water moving beneath him. It felt like a massive living creature, immensely powerful and completely unstoppable. In the dark, he couldn't be sure how fast he was moving, but his instincts told him he was moving fast.

In the distance he heard a low rumble that could only be water rushing through the busted dam. A strange hopelessness surrounded him. It felt as though any moment he would be swallowed. He wished he had a light. God, what he would give to be able to just see. Then he heard David's voice again, but only barely – a gargled cry in the storm. He kicked even harder, a sharp pain forming in the back of his leg, deep in his hamstring.

His greatest fear was that he would be washed over the dam before he made it to David, and that his friend would never know he had at least tried to save him. He tried to shout at David to just hold on, but his own shout was gargled as he sucked in the nasty river water. He gagged and coughed, then suddenly his hands struck mud below him. He had made it across.

Unlike the opposite side of the river, this side tapered up gradually, disappearing into a small forest separating the river flood zone from viable farmland. Garrett scrambled to his feet, which were quickly drawn down into the mud. The river was making one last effort to keep him prisoner. He fought to break the clasp of invisible hands, each foot reluctantly pulling loose from the soul-sucking grasp of the mud. He finally made his way up onto more solid ground and bent forward to stretch as he shouted, "David! Where are you?"

"I'm here!" David managed from somewhere upstream.

Garrett stumbled forward toward David's voice, finally finding the kid stuck several feet offshore, his whole body caught under a tangle of branches protruding from the water.

"I'm here, David! I'm here. It's going to be okay."

"Ah! Not okay!" David screamed, losing his grip on the branch.

Garrett heard twigs snapping as David flailed to find purchase. Then nothing. Then a gasp. "Oh, please, Garrett! I can't hold on!" He choked and gasped and began crying. "Please!" he moaned.

Garrett stepped forward into the mud and began climbing out onto the brush pile, grabbing blindly for protruding branches as he worked his way slowly forward, David's gargled sobs and the occasional flash of lightning guiding him. He was right over David when a flash illuminated his mustached face and little fingers as they grasped tight to a twig that shouldn't have held. David's face was a visage of terror, poking up just above the waterline.

"Hold on, David! Jesus, just hold on. I'm coming for you, bro." Garrett scrambled forward on waterlogged limbs. Smaller twigs cracked and snapped, breaking beneath him as he reached for David's hands. "I got you!"

"I thought I was a goner!" David wept. Then without warning, something crashed into the brush pile.

Garrett was knocked off balance, lost his footing, and plunged through the pile.

David slipped from his grip as both boys were cast back into the river.

Garrett flailed his arms, fighting with all his strength to swim against the current, but it was like trying to win a tug-of-war contest with a locomotive. He had nothing left. He had already dug down deep all the way to the bottom, and the cramp in his left leg came back with vengeance, completely locking it up.

A thought occurred to him then, and for whatever reason it struck him as funny. It wasn't going to be giants, dragons, or elf wizards that killed him. It wasn't going to be giant rats, the God Stones, or Lincoln's booby traps. It wasn't going to be any of the things his parents *didn't* warn him about. No, it was going to be the one thing his parents had *always* warned him about. His whole life, it was the one thing they said to stay away from – the goddamn Sangamon River. Now that was irony. Garrett laughed. Actually laughed. He swallowed about a half-gallon of rancid river water as he did, but what did that matter? He laughed so damn hard he must have lost his mind.

On the dam Lenny heard the shouting, but he strained to see upriver. His headlamp couldn't penetrate farther than directly in front of him, so he ripped it off and squinted into the night, hoping to see something – anything. Then a strange thing happened. The night changed and it wasn't night anymore. It wasn't daytime either, but it was suddenly somehow different. The night had turned into a bizarre twilight. The moonlight was radiant, with an electric shimmer, but even brighter – a supercharged moonlight. But there was no moon nor stars on this night, only silver rain, lightning, and storm clouds thick as dirt.

Was this what Janis saw when she looked into the dark? As Lenny's eyes adjusted, he began to see movement fighting against the current just upriver.

In his most optimistic of hopes he had prayed that Garrett would cross close enough to his side that he could reach his staff out at just the right moment and Garrett would grab on before being washed over, but now his heart sank. He was still above the water, but he was floating facedown and about to be pulled over the dam on the far side of the break, a good thirty yards away and nowhere near Lenny.

"I'm going!" Lenny said to no one. Then as loud as he could yell, "I'm coming, Garrett!"

As water crashed over rocks that refused to breach the surface, the Sangamon roared a never-ending warning, loud enough to rival that of a dragon about to breathe fire.

Stay away or die!

To do what Lenny was about to do was suicide.

Lenny took three steps back, then positioned his right leg behind him as he fixed his eyes upstream. Bouncing on his toes twice, he flexed his fingers around his staff.

Goddammit, Lennard Wade, what are you doing?! "Going to get my friend!" he screamed as he took off running straight for the breach.

Lenny jumped.

He soared several feet out over the broken dam, over the fast current and jagged rocks. Then he dropped like a stone before reaching a dozen feet. As he leapt into the gauntlet of jagged rocks, the laws of gravity would only allow for one outcome. When his feet made contact with the water, they were sure to be ripped out from under him by millions of gallons of angry river. The stone teeth of the broken dam would chew him up like a hungry shark, and finally, he would be swallowed by the undertow and consumed into the bowels of the Sangamon.

Garrett drew in too much water; it choked him, sucking what little strength he had left out of his limbs. He was drowning. His face was under water, and he couldn't even fight it. In a final effort to breathe, he pushed his face above the water line one last time. Lightning flashed and in the corner of his vision he saw something so ridiculous it couldn't be real. A glimpse of a scene so absurd it had to be a hallucination brought on by lack of oxygen to his brain. But there it was – several yards in the distance David clung to a giant rat's tail as it pulled him through the water. But stranger still, the rat was being ridden by Paul.

The burst of lightning switched off, leaving Garrett surrounded by darkness once again. All around him the great serpent tugged, unwilling to let go.

Garrett slipped quietly under the black water and died.

44

Pressing On

Wednesday, April 6 – God Stones Day 1
Rural Chiapas State, Mexico

Once Sarah and Gabi had rested for a few minutes, they waded across what turned out to be a small, shallow stream and pulled themselves from the water.

Gabi looked back from the direction they had come, her voice barely a mutter. "We're off the mountain." She looked at the moon again. "We must be on the back side of it now."

Sarah followed her gaze. "We could be miles away from base camp, but once we get out of this gorge, we should be able to get our bearings and get back. We need to get help. Juan and his crew will still be there trying to figure out what happened. Maybe they have already called for help."

As they hiked through the dense foliage around the mountain, neither spoke. Gabi staggered along, lost in thoughts of her mother and father, periodically collapsing into a heap of tears. Sarah never pressed her or rushed her. Instead, each time she lost it, Sarah lost it with her, and together they cried. And each time they picked themselves up after a moment and pressed on.

Hours passed as night turned to morning and the sun rose, casting its harsh rays on their already fire-seared backs. As the heat began to press, Gabi's thoughts drifted to what they had seen, and she couldn't help but wonder how they were going to explain all this to anyone who hadn't been there to see it. No one would believe it. When the authorities came to investigate would the dragon still be inside, and if so would they be killed too? Soon her question was answered for her. The dragon would not be below, waiting for whoever came.

Overhead, a loud shriek rang out across the mountain. It was terrible and angry and could only belong to one thing – the murderer of her parents.

Gabi winced, throwing her hands over her ears and herself onto the ground. Beside her Sarah did the same.

Above them a large shadow appeared, momentarily blotting out the sun. The dragon flew over them, flapping its massive wings and belting out a torrent of fire as it disappeared into the midmorning sun. In the distant southwest, the forest combusted in unnatural colors. Acres upon acres ignited in flame so quickly it was as if the sun had lunged forward and kissed the mountains with one single fiery caress. They felt the heat right away, but the flames were nowhere near them.

"It didn't see us," Gabi said hopefully, but beneath her relief she felt a surprising rage building inside her.

"Come on, Gabi, we have to be close."

They turned away from the dragon as it continued southwest, deep into the Sierra Madre de Chiapas mountains, screaming and breathing fire.

Finally, they made it back around the mouth of the gorge leading to the entry point of the site, but base camp was deserted.

"Everyone is gone!" Gabi said.

"No, they wouldn't have left us unless they went for help, but the vehicles are still here," Sarah said. "First things first." Sarah retrieved two bottles of water from the supply. "We need to hydrate. Juan and his team must be inside trying to get us out." Sarah took a pull of water and nodded toward the trail leading into the gorge. "I will go tell them we are here. You can wait here and get some food in you. You must be starving."

"Sarah, don't leave me. I will go with you," Gabi said, her eyes tearing up. She did not want to be left alone but more than that they still didn't know what happened to the giant.

"Okay, come on," Sarah said, her eyes softening. "I won't leave you, Gabi. I won't ever leave you."

Gabi nodded.

As they approached the crevice Gabi's stomach twisted. The whole thing was sealed with rubble. It had collapsed again.

Sarah dropped to her knees. "Jesus, they were all inside. They must have been."

"Maybe they are still alive! Maybe it's only the opening that collapsed!" Gabi said, hope filling her voice.

Sarah nodded, forcing a smile. "Come on, let's get back to the vehicles and call for help."

Once back at camp, Gabi jumped into one of the three Jeeps and turned the key… nothing. "It's completely dead!"

Sarah tried one of the others. "Dammit! This one won't start either! Gabi, try the satellite phone! It should be in the back!" she shouted as she ran toward the equipment truck.

Gabi pulled the satellite phone from the backseat. It was dead too. "No, no, no! This can't be!" She continued desperately pressing buttons to no avail. "It isn't working, Sarah!" From the truck she heard Sarah scream out in frustration. She climbed out of the Jeep and stood facing Sarah, the satellite phone hanging loose in one hand. "What do we do?"

Sarah wiped her sleeve across her brow. "All the vehicles are dead and the phone too. What the hell is going on!?" It was nearing noon and already getting incredibly warm under the hot Mexico sun. "With no power to start the vehicles, the CB radios won't work even if someone was within range to hear them. Without Fredy or your dad, I don't think I can get us back."

Gabi pointed toward the jungle in a northerly direction. "I know the way back, but it would be a long hike before we reach help."

Sarah's eyes followed the pointing finger. "We need to rest and eat first. We should try and sleep some too."

Gabi had no appetite to eat and knew she would not sleep but agreed anyway. She knew she had to at least try to eat and rest if they were going to get out of there.

They thought of starting a fire but neither had the energy. So they sat, leaning against one of the Jeeps, and force fed themselves cold canned beans and rations.

Smoke billowed in the distance as Gabi finished off the last of her freeze-dried scrambled egg rations. "Sarah, do you think we are safe to stay and rest? What if the fire works itself this way?"

"I don't think it will. The wind seems to be carrying it in the opposite direction. I can't even smell the smoke now," Sarah said. Then, brightening a little, she turned to face the girl. "But maybe it will draw authorities to fight the fire and we can get help."

Gabi nodded.

"But first we rest," Sarah said, glancing toward the camp tents, an unease spreading across her face.

Gabi followed her gaze. There was no way she would be able to close her eyes with nothing more than a zipper separating her from only María Purísima knew what.

"We'll rest in the Jeep. Come on."

They climbed into the cab of the Jeep covered by the most shade and locked the doors. Gabi was sure she wouldn't sleep but as soon as she leaned back and closed her eyes, she slipped into a fitful nightmare of fire-breathing dragons and her parents' screams.

Sometime later Gabi woke with a start. The entire Jeep had jolted, tossing her to the opposite seat. "What!" Her eyes went wide as she struggled to orient herself. *Where am I?* Then the horror of the earlier events came rushing back. Four shots rang out in fast succession. Gabi threw herself down, scrambling off the seat and onto the floorboard. "Oh! María Purísima! What's happening?" She screamed for Sarah, but Sarah was gone. She was alone in the Jeep. She pushed on the driver's side door handle, but the door wouldn't budge. Crawling to the other side, she pushed open the door and fell out onto the dirt. "Sarah! Where are you? Sarah!" There was a loud crash of smashing metal as the Jeep jolted again, tipping up onto two wheels, threatening to tip over, crushing her, but it slowly lurched back the other way, settling onto all four tires again.

She still couldn't see what was happening. More gun shots. She screamed again and pressed herself against the nearest tire. Were they being shot at? Who was shooting at them? Gabi's mind raced for a logical answer. *It could be the cartel,* she thought.

More gunfire.

More shouting. Gabi's English was good, but the words Sarah was screaming weren't familiar.

A large boulder rolled passed the front of the Jeep, crashing into the jungle behind her. *Sarah!* Suddenly hiding behind the Jeep didn't seem like such a good idea. If that boulder had hit the Jeep, it might have flipped it right on top of her. Gabi pushed herself into a squat and peeked carefully over the hood. Her mouth fell open.

The giant was midway up the mountain, standing on a newly cleared flat section. He was pulling large chunks of rock from behind him and tossing them idly down the mountain. The base camp was right in the line of fire. Gabi caught movement to her right and quickly found the source of the gunshots. Sarah was reloading an assault rifle, which must have been in one of the Jeeps. Another boulder came dangerously close. It was only a matter of time before her luck ran out.

Gabi ran from behind the Jeep, dodging a smaller boulder as it bounded by. "Sarah! What are you doing?"

"Get in the truck, Gabi!" she shouted, pointing the rifle up the mountain, the stock tight against her shoulder as she squinted one eye closed and squeezed the trigger repetitively. A burst of rapid cracks echoed off the mountains. "Yes! I hit him! Gabi, I got him!"

The giant stopped and turned, peering down the mountain.

Gabi's eyes went wide. "No! Sarah, please!"

Another burst of gunfire rang out, followed by a metallic click. Sarah dropped her head and began loading the gun again.

Gabi headed toward the truck but didn't take her eyes off the giant as he leapt from the flat area of the mountain, landing on the steep slope as if he were on an invisible skateboard. Rocks, shrubs, and small trees tore loose from the ground as he began a reckless slide, his feet churning up the loose earth as gravity pulled him toward them.

"Sarah! It's coming!" she shouted. She reached Sarah and grabbed her by the sleeve.

Sarah jerked her head up as she staggered forward off balance, her eyes flashing with panic. She dropped the rifle to the ground with a clatter. "Oh no! What have I done!" She started for the truck.

Gabi had started to flee too, but she stopped when she heard the gun fall to the ground. She didn't know why but for some instinctual reason she would never understand she made a knee-jerk decision, turned, and went for the gun.

"No, Gabi, forget it! Just get in the truck!" Sarah dove in through the window, not bothering with the door.

Rocks and boulders careened down the mountain. Within seconds the giant was on them.

There was no time, and she didn't know much about guns. Sarah had managed to get the magazine back in before she dropped it, but she hadn't pulled the thing back. Frantically, Gabi searched for the thing she needed to pull to get a round into the rifle. She yanked it back with a click and it snapped back with a clack. She turned to point the long gun with hands trembling. She had shot before but only targets, never a living thing.

"No, Gabi! Get away! Run!"

The giant slid to a stop in the clearing between Gabi and the vehicles. His one giant eye searched the vehicles for the source of the shouts. The big eye fixed itself on Sarah, and the giant stepped forward.

Gabi took aim.

The giant roared.

"No!" Gabi screamed, firing the rifle into the giant's back.

The giant turned, reaching for her.

Gabi stepped back and fell, striking her head hard on a stone.

The giant turned away from her and kicked the utility truck.

Sarah screamed as the truck flipped off the clearing and down into the jungle, crashing apart as it rolled into the gorge far below.

Gabi tried to sit up, but the world spun.

As darkness closed in, the last thing she saw was an enormous blurry eye hovering over her.

45

Reborn of Dragon Fire and Blood

Saturday, April 16 – God Stones Day 10
Petersburg, Illinois

Long blades of prairie grass swooshed, like waves in a vast ocean, as a gentle breeze pushed across an open field. The blue sky was cloudless as the sun shone warmly on Garrett's face. It seemed like a perfect day. He closed his eyes, inhaling long and deep as the smell of prairie sage, aster, and columbine permeated his senses, intermixing in an exotic bouquet of fragrances.

When he opened his eyes again the whole world erupted in flame.

At least Garrett's world did, and all he could see around him was burning. He spun. *What's happening?* The sky was darker now, blotted out by smoke. The breeze no longer felt good across his face; instead it felt hot, dry, and hard to breathe. He was still standing in the field on top of a rolling hill of dry prairie grass. The field overlooked a valley and beyond this was a forest as far as his eyes could see. A forest on fire. He didn't need to wonder where the flames came from – dragons. He couldn't see them, but he could hear them in the distance all around him. Hungry screams of dragons as they set the earth ablaze.

Garrett held out a palm to try and shield his face from the heat. At the opposite end of the field stood a man in a long, white robe. Garrett ran across the field. He didn't know why he felt compelled to run to him, but he did, and as he reached him, the robed man turned to face him. His long hair and beard were light grey in contrast to his dark skin. He smiled at Garrett.

"I am proud of you, my son."

Garrett looked up at the man, old and weathered, like a man who'd lived his whole life under a scornful sun. He had kind eyes hooded by brows etched in wrinkles set deep into his leathery skin. "But I failed. I didn't stop Apep, and now the whole world will burn." Saying it made Garrett's heart ache and his throat constrict.

The flames closed tighter around them. Garrett caught movement behind the man. Others were standing in the distance, though he could only see their silhouettes. But silhouettes were like signatures, and Garrett could read each one. "Mr. B! And my dad!" He longed for them, longed to push past the robed man and run to them.

Then the robed man spoke again. "Blood of my blood, flesh of my flesh, you and yours have not failed. You fulfilled my prophecy, but your journey has only just begun. You have much to do."

"I don't understand. What am I supposed to do?"

"You must set right what has long been wrong. This is the only way to save humankind."

"What does that mean?" Garrett asked.

"You will know," the man said reassuringly.

"But how will I know?"

The man smiled, "Because I gave you a heart. All you have to do is follow it." He turned away toward the dragons and the flames, and Garrett sensed his time was short.

Wait! "Are you… Are you god?"

The man turned back to him and appraised him for a long moment, then said, "I created humankind."

Garrett thought about this, his brows furrowing. Finally, he asked, "Did you create everything?"

The man smiled and it was the warmest smile Garrett had ever seen. It was full and bright and most of all it was proud, and Garrett knew the smile was for the question. The silver bearded man's head nodded sagely. But the nod was not an answer to the question. Rather, it signaled approval of the question.

"No. I am one of seven creators."

Garrett's furrow deepened. He suddenly had dozens of questions swimming through his mind, and he thought he could easily fire them off, one after another, like a five-year-old asking why over and over, but something instinctively told him he only had one shot at this. He needed to make the next question count. "Who created you? Who is god?"

The man bent lower to meet Garrett's eyes. He was still smiling, and now Garrett could see something danced in his eyes – a spark of silver-blue flame.

"The mother. The one who clapped her hands and created something when there was nothing." He stood erect and pointed a finger down at Garrett. All expressions of warmth had fallen away.

The fire closed in around them. "You are hereby reborn of the dragon blood and fire. And Garrett?"

"Yes, sir?"

"Be sure and follow your heart."

Garrett swallowed and nodded.

The flames closed over his head.

"Now wake, my child, the journey lies ahead of you."

Garrett opened his eyes and gasped. He was back in the river. Everything was out of focus. The murky water must be clouding his vision. He started to panic. He had to swim! Swim to the surface and find air! He flailed his arms, waiting for water to burn his lungs. But the burn never came. Then he felt a hand on his chest.

"Easy, Garrett, easy. Take it slow," a voice said.

He recognized the voice as Breanne's. The warmth from her hand and soft voice calmed him, and he knew then he was no longer in the river. He settled back into a pillow; blinking rapidly, he fought to clear his fuzzy vision. He couldn't think of anyone he would rather have seen when he woke. His heart began to pound as he took in her beauty. Her braids were pulled back in a ponytail, revealing her perfect skin, dark and smooth. She wore no makeup, and he doubted she ever did. *Why would she?* She had a natural beauty that makeup would be wasted on. She was breathtaking. Garrett's heart began to beat even faster as he held her stare.

"Jesus, Bre, I thought I lost you… I thought… I thought Apep took you away. Bre! Oh, Bre! Thank god!" The words came in a croak rather than a shout as he fought forward through the tangle of blankets to embrace her.

"Honey, please, settle down. You're okay, I am here."

Garrett's vision went blurry again and he blinked. The voice was no longer Bre's. "What's happening! Bre!"

"Garrett, honey, it's your mother. Calm down. You are safe now," Elaine said, placing her hand back on his chest.

Still confused, he settled back. As his surroundings came into focus, he could see he was in a small room, plain and windowless. The ceiling was low, and there was no light other than what shone from two gas lanterns. The floor was plain concrete, and the walls appeared to be made of concrete block with no windows. Worst of all, there was no Bre. Slowly his eyes glanced up the block wall, coming to rest on the ceiling. Garrett cocked his head, his eyes knitting together as he realized he was looking up at exposed joist. The air around him was cool and clammy too, as if he were underground. *What is this place?*

Elaine drew her hand back from his chest. "Welcome back."

Garrett tried to speak. "Where… where am…" But his throat was dry, and now he realized just how bad speaking hurt.

She reached for a glass of water from on top of a wood crate that had been tipped onto its side, now posing as a nightstand. "You don't have to talk, Garrett. I know you have questions for me, but all in time." She placed the glass to his lips, tipping it carefully. "Right now, I think you want to know what happened?"

He took a long pull from the glass and nodded.

Elaine sat the water down and turned to Lenny, who Garrett hadn't even noticed was sitting in an overstuffed chair across the tiny room. "Lenny never left your side, Garrett. He should be the one to tell you what happened. Now, Lenny, I am going to leave you two alone while I get Garrett some food. You must be starved," Elaine said, standing. "Oh, Garrett, we are so proud of you." She smiled.

Garrett saw it then, the false smile. A smile created to conceal a truth, but it was thin as paper, as transparent as window glass. Behind the smile was stress. But more, there was a deep exhaustion like she hadn't slept in days. "Mom?"

"Yes?"

"You okay?" he asked, realizing too late how stupid the question was.

"I am now," she reassured him. Then nodding she said, "Talk to your friend. I'll be back."

Lenny stood and grabbed the small wooden chair Elaine had occupied, spun it around, and straddled it. "Bro, that was seriously awkward listening to you confuse your mom with a hot chick you clearly want to hook up with. I would give you crap, but considering we have a shit ton to cover I'm going to let it slide!" Lenny laughed and rubbed his hands together. "Alright, let's start with rat boy. Apparently back when we were in the chamber, a rat cornered David. He woke up with the thing licking his face." Lenny shivered involuntarily and pulled a face. "Anyway, David says he 'freaked out,'" – Lenny gave the words air quotes – "and screamed, and I mean, who could blame him, right? Yeah, well, whatever. Little mustached creep probably liked it. David tries to push it off and as he does his hand slips into a bloody cut on the side of the rat. Nasty, right!? Well, without even trying he gets the Bruce Leroy glow and he heals the rat. David said with everything happening so fast he didn't have time to think about it and just got the hell out of there. But later when he was drowning under the brush pile, he said the rat crashed into it, knocking him off. And, bro, here's the best part! Paul was on the rat's back! He's alive, bro! He yells at David, 'Grab on!' So David grabs the thing's tail! Can you believe that shit!? Rats are great swimmers and apparently giant rats are even better. The rat walked right up onto the bank and then laid down so Paul could climb off! Un-freaking believable!"

"No. Not unbelievable. The last thing I remember before I went under was seeing Paul, David, and the rat," Garrett said huskily.

"Well, there you go! Here, take another drink – you sound like ass."

Garrett took a drink. "Where is Pete?"

"Well, he hasn't exactly been himself, but he is starting to come around, I think. Anyway, and this is kind of weird, Paul said the rat had the same golden eyes as Janis. He also said the rat seemed to know him. After it squeezed though the crevice it swam under Paul and lifted him to the top of the water. He rode the thing out!"

"Crazy," Garrett said.

"Crazier than a shithouse rat! So, Petey has been down at the river every day trying to find it. I told him to just leave the thing alone before he ends up with rabies. I mean the dude already made out with a space alien elf chick – who knows what he will do if he finds that rat!" Lenny laughed.

"Len," he began hoarsely, "how am I alive? I was going over the dam, I know I was… it was right there… but then I… I think I died."

The door flew open and David burst in, clean-shaven except for his mustache, which seemed strangely longer, with twisted ends. "I heard you were awake!" he said, approaching the bed and slapping Garrett on the shoulder.

Garrett grimaced involuntarily. The friendly pat sent a shock wave through his body, lighting up all the soreness from worn muscles down through his aching chest and bruised ribs before settling into his strained legs.

"We were just talking about you, rat boy," Lenny said.

"I told you not to call me that, Lenny." David's eyes narrowed.

"Take it easy. I Just finished telling the part about how you healed the rat that you and Paul rode out of the river."

"Oh, did you tell the part about how you saved him yet? You didn't, did you? Oh, let me! You told my part – come on, let me tell yours!"

Lenny held up his hands. "Go ahead, it would be weird for me to tell it anyway."

David flopped down on the edge of the bed. "Right. So check this, Lenny got some superpower at the last minute and could see you out in the river, heading right for the dam. You were already… well, you weren't moving. I mean you were moving down river, but *you* weren't moving."

"Jesus, David, he knows what you mean," Lenny said.

Garrett pushed up onto his elbows, winced, and fell back into the pillow. "You got night vision? Wait, like Janis said she had?"

"Yep, and then—"

"Anyway!" One horn of David's mustache rose higher than the other in a threatening sneer. "I'm telling it. So, suddenly Lenny figures what he has to do and takes off running right for the busted part of the dam. Then you know what this guy does?" He paused for dramatic effect. "He jumps in!"

Garrett looked at Lenny in disbelief. "Into the busted dam, Len?"

Lenny shrugged.

"I know, right?! He doesn't land in the water per se, he sort of…" He paused again – this time not for effect but to find a way to tell it. "Okay, you ever see those martial arts movies where the kung fu guys run across the treetops?"

Garrett nodded. Silly question – he and Lenny had seen just about every kung fu movie ever made.

"Well, that's what he did. He landed on the water – then he ran across it, feather light." David waved his hand in a long arc while wiggling his fingers. "His feet barely made contact with the water. It was insane, just like in those kung fu movies. I was on the opposite side of the river, the side you found me on, Garrett. So I didn't see him jump in, but I heard Lenny's voice shout this, I dunno, war cry from across the dam. So I turn, like, what the hell? The next thing I see is the silhouette of Lenny running on top of the water! Then just as you start to go over, Lenny reaches down with his staff, hooks you by the collar, and takes – oh what, Lenny? about three more strides? – while dragging you through the water." He doesn't wait for Lenny to respond. "Laws of physics be dammed, next thing I know Lenny's pulling you off the dam and laying you out on the shore. I stood there frozen for a minute. I couldn't believe it. Once you were on the bank, we laid you out flat on your back."

"You healed me?" Garrett asked.

David looked down and shook his head gravely. "Heck no,

Garrett. There wasn't nothing for me to heal. You were gone. Dead as a doornail."

Garrett frowned and looked at Lenny.

"He's telling the truth. You didn't have a pulse, bro. I thought for sure I lost my best friend." Lenny placed a hand on Garrett's arm.

"Then how am I… how am I here?"

"Well, just because you were dead, wasn't either one of us ready to give up," David said, a smile stretching back across his face. "I tried to heal you with the glow a few times, but with you being dead it wouldn't come." He turned to Lenny, frowning now. "And no matter how many times this dickhole threatened to kill me if I didn't save you, the glow still wouldn't come. Like I tried to explain in the moment, there has to be life to heal and *you* didn't have any. But Lenny wasn't hearing it, so he starts giving you CPR and, for the record, I may have had to lip lock with you." David waggled his eyebrows, which made his mustache twitch creepily.

"And for the record, I think he liked it. He had that 'stache all up in your mouth," Lenny added.

"So anyway," David said, frowning, "we gave you CPR for what seemed like, I don't know, forever." He took a deep breath, casting his eyes down at the floor, and tears began to well.

Garrett scrunched his brows together. "What is it?"

"I told Lenny you were gone – that you were dead. I grabbed him by the shoulders and pulled him back. I told him I was sorry but there was nothing more we could do. Don't you see, Garrett? I gave up on you." He raised his watery eyes. "Lenny shrugged me off. He screamed at you. He told you that you weren't allowed to die – that you were just getting started. He said he needed you – that the world needed you. He got right in your face and screamed that Bre needed you, and then he started beating on your chest. I knew it was desperate and hopeless, and I just started crying. Then you know what? Your eyes sprang open, Garrett! And then you ralphed river water all over Lenny! It was the best thing I ever saw!"

Garrett looked over at Lenny, smiled, and nodded. "Thanks, bro."

Lenny grabbed Garrett and wrapped his arms around him in a huge hug that was incredibly painful, but he didn't care.

David was crying. "You never gave up on me. You crossed the river and came back for me, and what did I do? I gave up too soon."

"David, you're looking at this all wrong," Garrett said. "You didn't give up. You were just trying to help another friend accept an awful truth. I don't blame you for that!"

David smiled and threw himself onto Garrett.

As the laughter quieted, David took on an all-too-serious expression. "Seriously, Garrett, you came back for me. I'll never forget that, not as long as we live. Never."

Garrett nodded and then shot David a smirk. "Well, if I'd known you were going to get curbside service from Paul riding a rat, I would've kept my ass grounded." But somehow, he knew the river would have just found another way to pull him in. "Hey, where is Paul?"

"Normally he isn't far from your bedside. Pacing back and forth, waiting for you wake up," Lenny said.

"He's feeling better then?"

"All healed up thanks to yours truly," David said.

"And Coach?" Garrett asked.

"Once we got you guys back across, David healed him then passed out right after—"

Garrett cut him off. "What! You healed him, David! He's alive?"

David's eyes fell to the floor. "I been trying, Garrett, and he did regain consciousness yesterday, but I don't think I had much to do with it. I don't know why, but it feels different when I try to heal him, like he is resisting it somehow. I wasn't even healing him when he woke up. I think it's because he isn't human."

Garrett's heart sank. He had known Coach was in bad shape, but he had hoped he would somehow be okay. He had so many questions that he was sure Coach could have answered. A heavy sadness hung in the air. "I want to see him."

David nodded. "I will take you there when you're ready."

Garrett sighed and pushed himself up onto his elbows, wincing. "So where is here anyway? I feel like I'm in a basement or something."

His mother reappeared with a tray of food. The small room filled with the aromas of fresh-made bread coated in butter and jam, fresh pineapple, and cured meats. A tall glass of bright orange juice thick with pulp sat on the tray. She set the tray carefully onto Garrett's lap. "Take it slow, Garrett – you haven't eaten anything in days. You've been getting all your nutrition intravenously."

Intravenously? Whatever that meant. Garrett grabbed the juice and gulped half of it down. Juice had never tasted better. "This is amazing. Thank you!" He sighed in satisfaction as he reached for a piece of bread.

"Slow, Garrett. Now, I need to see James and let him know you are awake. I will leave you boys to finish catching up but, Lenny, you make sure he takes his time with this food." Elaine bent and kissed Garrett on the forehead.

As the door pulled closed Garrett said, "You were about to tell me where we are?"

Lenny nodded. "You're under the dojo."

"Under the dojo, but it burnt down?"

Lenny stood up. "Yeah, well under isn't exactly right. One of the entrances to this place is under the dojo, but you're probably a block to the east, under the old hotel on the other side of Route 6. There is a whole underground labyrinth down here."

Garrett looked around the small room with renewed curiosity. Suddenly his mind shifted gears. *Why am I in a basement? Why is it lit by lanterns when there is a perfectly fine light fixture with a pull chain mounted in the middle of the ceiling?* "Guys… what's going on?"

"Right, well after we got you guys out of the river, we were all borderline hypothermic." Lenny shivered at the memory. "I hadn't even had a chance to think about how we were going to all get back across the river when suddenly dozens of people showed up on the dam with lanterns. A few minutes later a john boat paddled up to shore with James at the helm. They wrapped us all in blankets, loaded us up, and brought us here." Lenny sat back down. "I was too cold and tired to think about it at the time, but now I'm pretty sure the Keepers were watching us, waiting to let it all play out before they interfered. By the time we all got to the square, dozens more people were there waiting for us – waiting for you."

"Dozens of Keepers?" Garrett asked.

Lenny reached toward Garrett's tray. "Hundreds, Garrett! People we've known all our lives."

David slapped Lenny's hand. "Don't even think about it."

"What? Like who?" Garrett asked.

Lenny pulled his hand back and shot David a look. "Ms. Harris, Mr. Bloomer, Mr. Holly, Tony from the bait shop, Mr. Bowman from the drugstore and his wife and kid, George. Who else? Oh—"

"Wait, Mr. Holly, the principal, is a Keeper?" Garrett asked.

David laughed. "I know, right? I always hated that guy!"

"Man, I'm just getting started. You got Officer Cullen; the librarian, Ms. Cleary; Ben, the bartender – you remember that guy? Oh! And our high school secretary, Thomas; Mayor Bedfield… Well, you get the point. There are a lot of them."

"All of them!" Garrett said, sitting up too fast, nearly spilling his juice. His head spun and he slumped back down.

Lenny waved his hands in concern. "Easy, bro. You've been sleeping for a while, best to go slow."

"Right. How long have I been asleep?"

Lenny and David looked at each other, then back at Garrett.

"Ten days now," David said.

"Ten days!" He bolted upright again.

Lenny was ready this time and snatched the juice glass from the tray before it toppled.

Again, Garrett's head spun, but he stayed sitting up, waiting for it to pass. "We have to get started."

Lenny and David looked at each other and smiled.

"We know, Garrett, and we will be ready when you are. But first your people are waiting to see you," David said.

"My people? What are you talking about?" Garrett didn't like this at all. He could clearly see the looks they were sharing like they had some big secret they weren't spilling.

"Garrett, there is a book you need to read – well, not a book as much as a…" Lenny looked up, searching for the word as if he expected it to be stamped on the ceiling.

Garrett looked up too. "What?"

"Oh shit, man, just tell him already," David said, unable to stand the suspense any longer. "Dude, you're going to get so many chicks."

Lenny shook his head. "You're kind of a big deal now, man. Turns out this book of Turek's told how all this would go. The whole prophecy thing, remember? But it is way more than just what happened in the temple. I don't want to ruin the end for you, but it tells us what we're supposed to do next. Says we're going to set things right, and you're going to lead us."

46

The Giant King

Thursday, April 7 – God Stones Day 2
Rural Chiapas State, Mexico

The sound of stone scraping across stone raked pain through Gabi's skull. She forced open her eyes to a vision of blurred beige. Near her, she heard a great grunt and the ground beneath her shook. She blinked her eyes until the blur cleared to reveal she was surrounded by limestone. *Where am I?* Carefully she pushed herself up onto her palms and looked for the source of the sound.

Her heart caught when she saw the massive giant lifting a large chunk of stone, hugging it to his chest like a burlap bag of fresh-picked coffee. It seemed to pay her no attention as it walked toward an opening and out onto some kind of ledge. She understood now, she was no longer in camp. She was up the mountain, inside the opening the giant had come from. *The entrance to the pyramid?* She looked the other way, down the newly unclogged corridor. It was only partially cleared – that was what the giant was doing, she realized, clearing the stone that filled the corridor. *María Purísima, her head hurt!* Carefully she touched the lump on the back of her head and inspected her hand, expecting to see blood, but there was none. She looked at the ceiling.

It was made of smoothly worked stone that spanned the width of the corridor, with flawless seams every meter or so. This meant the rubble the giant was removing wasn't a collapse – it was placed here intentionally. *To hide this place. Why else?*

The giant tossed the boulder over the side then turned back to face her. He took three long strides toward her.

Gabi pushed herself back against the cool stone wall. Her heart was beating so fast now. It was going to kill her! She lifted her hands, palms out, as if she could push him away.

The giant, easily over three meters tall, bent toward her, its big, black eye coming close to her. "You fear me?"

Gabi froze. *It's speaking to… to me? But its lips didn't move – did they?*

The giant rose back to its full height. "You are in pain?" he asked, and the single orb in the middle of its face blinked. "Please, let me help."

Suddenly a warmth, like warm water, filled her head, then her neck and back. It wasn't the feeling of water being poured over her head, but a wet warmth *in her head.* It felt wonderful. Then, as the feeling of warm water faded, her pain went with it. She blinked and rubbed the back of her head. The lump was gone, and her back no longer stung.

"I'm afraid only time can heal the pain in your heart," the giant said, then it paused as if listening for something. "Ah, beneath your fear is something else… anger. But you misplace your hate. You are not angry with me, human girl. Your anger is with Azazel. Why do you attack me with the magic weapon?"

Strangely Gabi could understand the words, but she wasn't sure how that could be. Yet she could. Its voice was calm, and its words were clear. Gabi spoke Spanish and English perfectly. She spoke the Maya language Tzotzil pretty well too, but the giant wasn't speaking any language she knew. *Or, wait, was it speaking all of them?* The thing's mouth wasn't moving when it spoke. She realized she wasn't hearing him with her ears; she was hearing him *in* her mind. There was something else in that voice though, something strangely familiar. His voice had a fatherly tone. It was so unexpected. No, there was something else – his voice was not just fatherly, but was that of her own father, Andrés. *It's my papa!* Her heart ached at the sound of her father's voice, and the realization nearly broke her.

"I've upset you with this voice? I'm sorry. I thought it would be familiar… comfortable. I can change it."

"No." Her throat constricted with emotion. "Please don't." She answered quickly, not understanding why, only knowing she wanted to hear her father's voice more than anything.

The giant stood, looming over her. "I am King Ogliosh of the nephilbock. Mine are peaceful people from a time long ago. We seek only to open the door that takes us home. Your Andrés was killed not by me but by my enemy."

She hadn't said her father's name, but she had thought it. It must be somehow reading her thoughts. The mention of her father and the word *killed* in the same sentence caused her heart to catch. *Its enemy? The dragon?* She looked up, noticing it was looking down expectantly, as if waiting for her to speak, but before she could, her father's voice returned.

"Yes, that's right – my enemy is what you call a dragon." Ogliosh nodded sagely. "I know your pain, Gabi. I am sorry for your loss. I only wish I could have stopped the soulless beast, but I was fleeing for my own life after waking to find Azazel trying to kill me."

So it was reading her mind.

Her father's soothing voice rang out in her mind again as the giant continued. "Gabi, I am listening to your thoughts. Everything you think, I hear. Your mind is like a room with a door. The door is open, but you *can* close it. Focus your thoughts on my voice. Feel me inside your mind. Can you feel my presence?"

Gabi thought back, *Yes.*

"Good. Now push the door to your mind closed. It should feel like a pressure. But before you do, understand when you feel me press against your mind you will need to open the door for us to communicate. If you don't open the door, I can't come in. Try it now."

Gabi focused on the giant's presence in her mind and immediately she could feel it in her head. As directed, she thought about the room and the door. Her brows furrowed as she concentrated, visualizing the door shutting. Suddenly the giant was gone from her mind and everything was still. Her thoughts were hers and hers alone. Outside of Gabi's mind, she felt the giant pressing on the door. Now she pictured herself opening it.

"Excellent! You see, when we are not talking or when you want to think about something you don't want me to hear, simply shut the door. If I want to talk to you, I can press on the door. If you want to talk to me just think to me. Excuse me now," Ogliosh said. Turning, he walked back and picked up another large boulder and brought it back to the opening.

Gabi felt the boulder hit the ground after the giant let it fall from his arms. King Ogliosh turned back to face her, ambled over, and peered down at her with his strange oblong eye. Slowly he knelt; his giant knees popped, echoing through the corridor. Then he placed one of his large six-digit hands flat onto the floor and shifted into a sitting position, crossing his large legs. He rested the strange hands on his knees as if preparing to meditate. Even sitting he was still much, much taller than her.

Her heart began to slow as the feeling of imminent danger passed. With the giant sitting down and the late-day sun pouring into the opening, Gabi could really look at the strange being. She stared at its odd six-digit hands resting on its knees. Black veins spiderwebbed just under the surface of its waxy, pale skin. She wondered oddly if its blood was black too. Most of its skin was bare, except for his loincloth of what she guessed was jaguar hides and a tunic made of what almost looked like lizard or snakeskin. But she couldn't imagine the size of the creature necessary to make a tunic this large, and there were no visible seams in the garment. Some form of leather hides, wrapped and stitched, covered his massive feet. He was covered in scars – old battle wounds, she guessed. She let her eyes wander to his face, which was also scarred and wrinkled. His lower jaw protruded with a bad underbite, and his mouth seemed to be overcrowded with teeth. Then, suddenly and quite terribly, he smiled. The crow's feet on each side of the giant's eye folded up like the bellows of an accordion. But it was the smile that made her want to run out of the opening and jump from the mountainside. Every tooth in his enormous mouth was large, sharp, and stained the brown color of old rusty blood.

Seeming to sense her discomfort, he closed his mouth.

King Ogliosh looked nothing like he sounded in her mind, and as she gazed upon him, she could only see horror – until, that is, she let her eyes meet his. There, surrounded by unbearable ugliness, she found something so beautiful it must have been fueled by magic. The long oval orb shone brightly with colors spun in different shades of blue, like Vincent Van Gogh's *Starry Night* come to life.

The giant was sitting. She could run. She could take off and run for the opening right now before it was too late. She could find Sarah. *Sarah! Where was Sarah?* She could go now before he ate her or smashed her. But she didn't move.

"I'm not going to hurt you… or eat you for that matter. Your mind is fuzzy, and you don't remember exactly what happened to you or to your friend Sarah," the giant said in her father's soothing voice.

Her face flushed as she realized she had thought all this with her mind open. She felt almost guilty as the giant continued in the same tone her father had used when she was little and afraid to sleep alone – the tone he used to convince her it was going to be okay and there was nothing to fear.

"It's going to be okay, Gabi – let me explain. Your Sarah was using the magic weapon against me, which is understandable – she was scared. I tried to stop her while being careful not to hurt her. You were scared too. You backed away, fell, and hit your head. Your friend ran off into the woods. I assume she went to get help – that's what I would do."

Was that what happened? Gabi wasn't sure. No matter how hard she concentrated, she couldn't remember how she got here. She remembered Sarah shouting and gunshots, but then everything went fuzzy. She was so confused and scared, but if the giant was going to hurt her, he would have already done it, right? She wanted her parents back, and she wanted the dragon that killed them to die for what it did, and where was Sarah? What if she didn't come back? She tried to hold back tears, but they spilled over, running down her face as she began to shudder.

"Your friend will get help and come for you. In the meantime, you are safe here with me. The day is late, and darkness will soon follow.

The jungle at night is no place for a young girl alone. For now, tell me about your world, Gabi. Tell me of this magic you wield and what other magic your kind possesses. In return I will tell you of Azazel and how she can be killed." Then his voice changed to one of sympathy. "I can feel your pain. Stay with me and your parents' deaths will be avenged. I don't know how, but the God Stones have been assembled into the Sound Eye. Others are coming, and I must prepare for their arrival. We can talk while I work."

She didn't understand that last part, but she knew she didn't want to go off alone into the jungle, especially not at night. She also didn't know why, but she trusted this… creature. And she wanted to know more. She wanted to know what he knew, and she wanted to know about the dragon.

~

Sarah felt hands under her arms and the sensation of being pulled.

"Sarah! Sarah, can you hear me?" a voice whispered urgently.

"What's happening?" she moaned and tried to open her eyes, but they wouldn't respond. Without warning, as if being plugged into an outlet, her mind connected with her body in a flood of pain and her eyes flung open.

Sarah screamed.

"Sarah! Please don't scream. It will be okay," the voice whispered.

But Sarah didn't care… couldn't care, and she screamed again. Then a hand clamped over her mouth, stifling her scream to a horrible moan.

"Sarah! Listen to me! It's Juan! I am going to help you. You are injured, and we are going to need to set some bones and get you to help, but right now you must not scream."

Agony. White-hot agony seemed to come from every part of her. One of Sarah's eyes opened, and she fixed it on her tormenter, screaming beneath his hand. His face was panicked, and he spoke in rapid-fire Spanish. She couldn't understand it all, but it sounded like he was asking for a syringe from the med kit. She tried to turn her head, not wanting to see herself. Instead she saw what was left of the utility truck – a broken cab resting upside down against a tree, almost unrecognizable in its twisted shape.

Around her, others spoke with a quiet urgency. “Give her two,” she heard a voice say as everything began to close in. The pain became distant as her consciousness began to slip away. She reached up with the hand that still worked and grabbed a fistful of Juan’s shirt. Her jaw hung strange and slack. But she forced the words. “Ga… Gabi! Please! Oh god… Juan! It has… Gabi!”

Sarah’s eyes rolled back, showing only the whites as her hand fell slack to her side.

47

I Thought This Was the End

Saturday, April 16 – God Stones Day 10
Petersburg, Illinois

"What do you mean, ruin the end?! I thought this was the end!" But Garrett knew better. As quickly as the words left his mouth, he knew this *was not* the end. He suddenly felt sick. Not sick, different. Physically something felt different, but he wasn't sure what it was.

"No way, bro! No – you know this isn't the end. You just said it yourself a second ago – we have to get started."

The strange sensation was in Garrett's hands. It started as a tingling, but now the sensation was all the way to his elbows and his hands were burning. Not painfully, but enough to notice. He held up his hands, looking at them for the first time. His skin was a dark charcoal color, like it had been burnt. They all stared in silence at his strange hands and arms, his grey-black skin fading as it disappeared under his short sleeve tee shirt, but no one else looked surprised – only him. "What the..."

He felt his heart suddenly racing. The dragon! Had he been burnt and hadn't realized it? He rubbed the top of his hand briskly with the palm of his other. A section of the grey-black skin peeled off, revealing something else underneath – markings of some kind. It was hard to tell in the low lantern light, but his skin was definitely lighter in color underneath. However, there were thin red and black lines crisscrossing in some strange designs. Garrett reflected back on the dream, then finally spoke. "You are hereby reborn of dragon blood and fire."

Lenny and David looked at each other, wide-eyed.

"Holy crap, guys... Holy crap!" David thrust two fists in the air. "It's all true!"

"Where did you hear that?" Lenny asked quietly.

"I dreamt it," Garrett said, still staring at his hands as he flipped them over and back, again and again. He couldn't believe how different they looked. It was frightening. He squeezed them into a fist then flexed his fingers out, expecting it to cause pain, but he only felt the tingling. "Why, what do you think it means?"

"We know what it means, Garrett," Lenny said, standing to pace. "That's what we need to tell you. Turek's prophecy told of everything that happened. It said you and your sages would kill a great giant and slay a dragon." He drew in a hesitant breath. "But then the chosen one would die in the depths of an ancient river, only to be reborn of the dragon blood and fire."

Time seemed to stop as the small room fell completely silent.

Garrett finally spoke. "Turek's book says that? Specifically, that?"

David nodded, examining the strange patterns on Garrett's hand where the burnt skin had flaked away. "Yes, and so much more. These marks, I think they are runes. I wish Pete were back – he would know for sure, but I have seen similar ones in some of the fantasy video games I've played."

"Fantasy video games?" Garrett asked.

"Hey, everything comes from somewhere, right? I mean I've seen giants, dragons, elves, and magic in video games too, and who would have thought any of it was real until now?"

Lenny stopped pacing and turned to Garrett. "The people here, the Keepers, they believe Turek—"

"Wait, Lenny," David said. "Just stop – this will be easier if we show him." He turned to Garrett. "You think you can walk?"

Garrett handed the tray off to David and threw back his blanket to find he had a pair of shorts on. A clear tube protruded from his lower leg, connected to a large bag of liquid hanging from what looked like an old wooden coat rack near the head of his bed. He wondered how he hadn't noticed it before. "What the hell is this doing in my leg?"

"It's an IV," David said. "It's how we kept you alive for the last ten days. Normally it would go in your arm but, well, they weren't sure that was such a good idea given the burns."

"You sure he's ready?" Lenny asked.

Garrett reached down and ripped the tape off his leg then proceeded to yank the IV out, which hurt way more than he thought it would, but he did his best not to let it show. "So, let's go see whatever this is you need me to see. I have to know what's going on."

"Slow down, buddy!" Lenny said.

But it was too late. He was already swinging his legs off the side of the bed. "I need to get up. I need to understand, and I need to see James. And why in the hell are we using lanterns? What's wrong with the lights?"

Lenny grabbed Garrett's arm and steadied him as he stood. "No power, man."

"Because of the fire on the square?" Garrett asked, swaying as his head swam.

David moved forward to help. "No, no power anywhere. As far as we know, the whole world could be without power."

"Maybe I should throw a little golden glow at you and see if we can get you tip top?" David said.

"Does it still make you pass out?" Garrett asked.

"Oh, hell yeah. I have no control over it. The glow comes and it's lights out. Now, granted, I haven't been using it much over the last ten days. People have to be hurt, so I just been trying to help Coach, since they don't seem to care much for him anyway. Oh, and I do any basic healing for the others when there is a need. But these dicks didn't trust me to try it on you. Afraid I would interfere with the natural order of things. But hell, now that you're awake we can give it a go?"

"No, not right now. Let me do this – besides, I don't want you passed out. I want you with me."

David beamed a bright mustached smile as he and Lenny helped Garrett get dressed.

It was nice to be out of the dobok and in a pair of real pants. The pants weren't his from before – he supposed everything he ever owned was gone – but the green cargo pants were a perfect fit, loose and comfortable. Lenny handed him a tee shirt and a brown, hooded knit sweater. Moments later he made his way out of the room and into a hall or tunnel. He really didn't like being underground. He had had enough of tunnels to last him a lifetime, and he longed for the sun.

After a short walk they reached a doorway where a man stood on guard. Garrett didn't recognize the older man with a scruffy greying beard. He assumed he was a guard by the rifle slung over his shoulder. The man looked flustered at the sight of Garrett. Garrett didn't think much of it at first, figuring he was just surprised to see him awake, but then the man did something unexpected, something Garrett found very odd. The man dropped to his knees and bowed, placing his forehead on the ground.

"Are you okay?" Garrett asked, kneeling down to check on him. The man looked up in surprise, then his eyes settled on Garrett's hands. The man quickly ducked away, pressing his head back to the floor. Garrett frowned. He was a second-degree black belt – he had been bowed to plenty, but not like this. No one had ever got down on their knees and put their head on the floor. *That was weird.*

They exited the hall and crossed a plain-looking room, filled with several tables and chairs. *A cafeteria maybe?* Then they made their way into yet another hall. Two turns later they were standing in front of an unassuming, gunmetal-grey double door.

"You ready for this?" Lenny asked with a wry smile.

Garrett crinkled his brows. *Ready for what, exactly,* he wanted to ask, but they were being so secret about it he thought it easier to play along. "I guess so."

David pushed open the doors.

They entered an expansive room lit with lanterns that hung from hooks mounted on the cinder block walls. Row upon row of chairs were lined up, all facing him. Judging from the podium before him, he had entered onto a makeshift stage. The chairs were empty but the room was not. It was full of people. They were grabbing the chairs and stacking them in a corner, clearing the room as if preparing for a dance. Some people Garrett recognized as classmates, neighbors, and other members of the community, but others Garrett didn't recognize at all. As soon as they noticed his entrance, all motion stopped and the room fell eerily silent. Everyone stared at him. The only motion now was from the opposite side of the room, where people continued to quietly flood in. Within seconds the underground auditorium became packed with people.

Garrett suddenly felt an uncomfortableness akin to one of those dreams where you find you're standing alone in the middle of your school gymnasium, the bleachers are packed with the entire school, and everyone is laughing and pointing. You wonder what the hell is so funny, what they are all looking at. Following the pointing fingers, you look down to find you're naked from the waist down, and the cause of everyone's laughter is your bait and tackle dangling in full view for the entire world, or at least the entire school, to see. Then suddenly you wake up, flushed. But this wasn't a dream, and Garrett wasn't waking up.

The people before him were looking at him strangely. He couldn't quite place the meaning in their eyes. It wasn't fear or pity, not like you look at someone who just found out they were dying of cancer or had been in a horrible accident. There was no laughter either, but just to be safe he looked down and, yes, he still had his pants on. No, these people looked at him as if he were… were what? A ghost? He leaned over and whispered into Lenny's ear. "Dude, what the *f* is going on?"

James pushed forward through the crowd, an uncharacteristically bright smile on his face. "I never doubted you, little brother."

"What's going on, James?" Garrett asked.

James continued to smile, nodding. "I never doubted you! And I know father never did either."

"James? What is this?" Garrett asked quietly. His brother's smile was strange, full of pride. Then, like the man in the hall, James – the big brother who had banished Garrett from his room, twisted his arm to the point of nearly breaking it on numerous occasions, and squeezed his shoulder muscle until he screamed uncle – took a knee and bowed his head.

Following his cue, everyone in the crowd dropped to their knees and bowed, pressing their heads to the cold concrete floor.

Garrett neither liked nor understood what was happening. Had he been named king of the basement while he was sleeping and no one told him?

Lenny smiled a serious smile and spoke into Garrett's ear. "This is what you had to see to believe. The Keepers of the Light weren't just hiding the bloodline of Turek the ancient wizard or the descendant of an old Templar knight. They were protecting something far more important. They were protecting the bloodline of god, Garrett. And not just the bloodline, but the chosen one. The descendant of the bloodline is to fulfill a prophecy so incredible it's unthinkable."

Garrett looked at him blankly, but his mind was reeling inside. The conversation he overheard in the temple with Coach and Apep, and the dream where he asked Turek if he was god. Turek said he created humankind, but there were seven creators and the mother was god. *What did that mean?*

In typical David fashion, he put it in layman's terms. "You're the descendant of a freaking god, dude! You're like Hercules or some shit!"

James lifted his head and shot David a cutting look.

He was whispering excitedly, but too loudly. "I'm sorry, but c'mon! That's what we're saying! That's what he is, man! There's no sense sugar-coating it."

A god? The god of humans? His mind continued spinning in search of some kind of reason. He supposed all sorts of people believed in all sorts of gods. And, to be honest, they were certainly dealing with some epic weirdness. Space aliens, dragons, and giants, but god… we're talking creation. Garrett closed his eyes and pinched the bridge of his nose. His knees felt suddenly weak, and the wonderful food he had eaten moments earlier threatened to come back up.

"Garrett?" Lenny reached out and grabbed his arm. "Are you okay?"

He opened his eyes. "Jesus, can you please make them stand back up? They don't need to bow like that." He hated this. It felt… wrong. He had only gotten lucky – sure, very lucky, but still. For crap's sake, he had almost died a dozen times. He didn't know what was happening, but he knew one thing: whatever this Turek guy was – *Garrett* was no god.

James stood. "Garrett. You are the descendant of the god of humans. They are bowing to you in the kowtow, showing you the respect and love that's due to a god."

Garrett winced and frowned. "Please stop saying that."

From the crowd Elaine rose and walked toward them. Her sandy-brown hair was braided into a long plait that lay over her shoulder. Her long white dress trailed behind her as she stepped carefully through the narrow spaces between the kneeling, bowing people.

Garrett saw his mother and ran to her. They embraced. He squeezed her, hugging her as tight as he could. He never wanted to let go – the embrace felt like the safest place in the world.

Elaine pushed him back to an arm's length and looked him in the eyes. "Tell them to rise."

Garrett shook his head. "What?"

She spread her arms over the crowd. "Tell them to rise."

Garrett turned to the crowd, hesitantly clearing his throat. "Everyone," he started, "you can stop doing that now."

The crowd of people sat fidgeting, unsure, as they looked from Garrett to James.

"Command them, Garrett, and they will obey," James said.

He didn't want to command anyone, and he certainly didn't want people obeying him. "Please, everyone, stand up. Thank you, but you don't have to do that – ever."

Elaine cupped his face in her hands. "You have made me so proud. You have defeated a giant, slain a dragon, and died in an ancient river only to be reborn of dragon blood and fire. You've done everything just as foretold." She grabbed his hands and held them up for everyone to see.

Garrett looked out over the crowd from the makeshift platform. The surreal moment moved slowly, too slowly… too strangely. The crowd repeated after her in an even chant, "You have been reborn of dragon blood and fire!" They bowed again, placing their heads back down onto the floor.

"Stop!" Garrett said. He wanted nothing more than to hide underneath something.

"Garrett? Please be respectful to your followers," his mother said.

He pulled a face and looked to Lenny with pleading eyes. "Get me out of here."

Lenny nodded. "Where to?"

"Coach. Where is he?"

His mother placed a hand on his arm. "Wait, Garrett. Your people—"

Garrett didn't wait. He turned and followed Lenny and David toward the back of the stage.

As they spilled back through the heavy door and into the corridor, James was right on their heels. "Syldan? We have him locked up under around-the-clock guard in another wing."

Garrett spun on his brother. "Locked up! Why?"

James drew in a deep breath. "We knew from Turek's writings that Apep wasn't from this world, but the fact that he was elvish – well, that was enlightening. Then we learn Apep apparently had an older brother named Syldan. This wasn't in any of Turek's writings. He has been here all along, right under our noses, watching us." James clenched his hand into a fist. "Garrett, we aren't sure of his intentions or whether he is evil but—"

"Coach isn't evil, James!" Garrett interrupted. "I order him released immediately." As much as he rejected the thought, he *was* supposed to be some relation to god now, right? So then James had to obey. Jesus Christ, the thought felt blasphemous. Nevertheless, whether he believed it or not, his brother did. "You have to obey me, right?"

Usually speaking to James this way might get him twisted into a pretzel, but he wasn't that Garrett anymore and James… James wasn't that same older brother.

James stared at him for a long three-count. "I am the last of Turek's original disciples, Garrett. I am the only one left who lived when he lived. I remember his death like it was yesterday – the day my own flesh burned. I have lost my father, John, and everyone else who lived then – everyone who knew Turek on this earth. They are all dead." James thrust a finger into Garrett's chest. "You ask what I *have* to do? What I *have* to do is protect the Light, and its Keepers. Even when that means protecting a foolish boy from himself."

Garrett felt his ears getting hot. "James, you have—"

James held up a hand and sighed. "Listen, it isn't like he can go anywhere. He can't even walk."

"Then why is he imprisoned?'

"He is locked away for his own protection as much as for ours. He's Apep's brother, Garrett, and although you believe he's on our side, it may be very difficult for others to believe his motives are pure. Until we decide what to do with him, I just want to ensure everyone is safe, including him. Besides, it may not be much of a decision. He seems to be dying. I'm actually surprised he lasted this long."

Garrett rubbed his face. "He saved us back in that temple. We would all be dead if it wasn't for him."

"I'm sorry, Garrett, but I don't believe that either. His interference did nothing to change the prophecy."

"Yeah, well, you weren't there, were you? Oh, that's right, you were busy sending me off to die!" The comment was intended to cut, but James didn't blink.

"No, I wasn't, and he shouldn't have been either. If he wasn't a Keeper and he wasn't in alliance with his brother, then how did he know so damn much?"

"You didn't tell him, Lenny? You didn't tell him he knew Turek? That after the giants were defeated, he helped capture the elder dragons and imprison them? We're talking thousands of years back, before Apep was locked away."

"I told him," Lenny said matter-of-factly.

"Yeah, and all we have is Apep's brother's story to go on!"

"Well, that's good enough for me, James!"

"Well, it isn't for me!"

The two locked eyes as the tension thickened like cold honey, but there was no sweetness to it.

"Just take me to him, James. Take me or stand aside!" Garrett ordered, holding James's stare, no longer the little brother who screamed uncle. Not blinking, Garrett could feel as much as see in his peripheral vision that David and Lenny exchanged looks of concern. For a breath, Garrett thought James might actually lunge at him. But instead he tipped his head to the side and spoke.

"Alright, Garrett." James nodded, the angry red color draining from his face. The tight, serious line of his lips faltered as the corners turned ever so slowly upward – perhaps a twinge of old big brother still stirred inside him. "I will take you to him, and I will be in the room with you. This is nonnegotiable. Follow me." He bowed at the waist.

Garrett let out a breath as they fell in behind James, walking in silence. They made their way through a maze of corridors; it was like leaving the good part of town and entering the slums. The silence was broken only by the sounds of dripping water and their feet scuffing across the rough surface as the corridor became tighter, damper, and dimmer. They hit a section of tunnel that was holding a couple inches of water, which they were forced to pass through, soaking their feet. It was becoming even more obvious to Garrett that the entire underground— underground what? Bunker? Compound? He wasn't sure what to call it, but it was massive.

After a few minutes of walking, Lenny cleared his throat. "James, why don't you explain to Garrett what this place is."

James nodded sagely. "This underground complex was built long before you were born as a place for the Keepers of the Light and the Light itself" – he motioned back at Garrett with a hooked thumb – "to take refuge when end days came and to prepare for what comes next. We already know from the prophecy the world will go crazy in the coming weeks. Now you only need to flip a light switch to see the evidence. There's no electricity since the God Stones were united, and it is likely there won't be. Imagine a massive electromagnetic pulse going off, but instead of taking out electricity in an area it knocks out the entire world – and, worse, it continues to go off. My men…" He paused. "Rather *your* men, Garrett. Anyway, they report compasses don't work either – they just spin. As long as the God Stones are loose in the world, the magnetic fields are going to be all jacked up."

My men, Garrett thought uncomfortably.

James ducked under a low pipe. "Watch your heads," he said, pointing up. "Over the past ten days our scouts have ventured as far southwest as Springfield and as far north as Havana. In the next day or two I expect scouts to be returning from Peoria and Lincoln, but I expect more of the same."

"What are they saying?" Garrett asked.

"Disturbing news. Folks in Springfield are under house arrest. The National Guard has been deployed, but without electricity all communication has failed. There is no transportation, hence no commerce. The only food in the city is what they had when the power went out. So it's no wonder riots have begun. We can assume St. Louis and Chicago are in a dire state, as is the rest of the country and probably the world. It's only a matter of days before people start killing one another, if they haven't already. But as bad as this sounds, it's only the beginning. It's going to get really nasty when the world begins to burn. Once that starts, people fighting one another will be the least of our concerns."

Garrett stopped at the mention of the world burning. Although James had not actually said it, Garrett knew what would be coming – what would be burning the world.

"What is it?" James asked, glancing back over his shoulder.

"You're talking about dragons? I've seen the fire in my dreams. I've heard their roars. I've heard people screaming as they burn, James. I've heard it."

James turned to him and nodded. "Yeah, the dragons will rise again. That was written too."

"But aren't there only seven?" David asked. "How can seven dragons burn the world?"

"Six now, after the one Garrett killed," Lenny reminded them.

"We don't know, David, but honestly, who knows what they are capable of? I mean, how many dragons have you seen?" James said.

"One more than you, and I can tell you they scare the hell out of me," David retorted.

"Bro, everything scares the hell out of you," Lenny said. "But this one time, I'm with you. They scare the hell out of me too."

"There is something else happening," James said hesitantly. He stopped and turned to face Garrett. "It's the trees."

"The trees?" Garrett asked.

James nodded. "We think they're moving."

48

A Friend and Ally

Saturday, April 9 –
God Stones Day 4, six days before Garrett awakes
Rural Chiapas State, Mexico

Gabi woke to the sound of King Ogliosh speaking in her mind. She blinked her eyes, stretched, and opened the door to the Jeep. She climbed out onto the ledge and stretched again. Sleeping in the Jeep was horribly uncomfortable, but it was better than the stone floor and warmer too. She had told Ogliosh she was hungry, and he'd asked where he could get her food, to which she replied there were rations and water in the Jeep. When Ogliosh disappeared down the mountain she hadn't expected him to bring the whole Jeep back, but a few moments later he reappeared, dragging the Jeep behind him like a child dragging its favorite doll by the arm.

Gabi looked out across the jungle, but the view was just the same. Two days had passed, and no one had come for her. Her parents were dead. Manuel, María, and Fredy were dead. Where was Sarah? Was Sarah lost in the jungle? What if she got lost running for help?

"I have removed the last of the stones," King Ogliosh said now. "The inner door is open. Come, I will show you."

Gabi hastily pulled on her boots and followed King Ogliosh down the corridor. The mountain, she now knew for sure, was no mountain at all but a hidden pyramid – larger than any known pyramid on earth. King Ogliosh had not only told her what it was, he had told her what it was for. He'd said he had come to earth on a mission with six of his people some twelve thousand years ago to teach humans about agriculture, society, and language. The king told amazing stories explaining the pyramids and how they were assembled. He spoke of five cities, the first cities of the world, and explained it was he and his six who saved humanity from a great flood. It was mind-blowing. Even at her age she understood what this meant to humankind. Now humanity would know their true history.

But the king didn't stop there – he told her of his own world and how his race of people ruled through peace and sharing, how all species worked together to ensure a peaceful society. He explained it was only dragons who caused problems. King Ogliosh told of how the dragons followed him to earth and tried to kill him, using magic against him and finally casting him into a deep sleep to be guarded for all eternity by an evil dragon called Azazel. This was her dragon – the dragon who killed her parents.

He promised her before he left this world he would help her kill Azazel. He wouldn't leave the dragons to wreak hell on earth. After all, he wanted revenge for having been put to sleep and imprisoned for thousands of years. The other giants would be here soon – how many he didn't say, only that he could feel them coming. Soon the giants would take their vengeance on the dragons, open the gate, and go back home.

Gabi could tell King Ogliosh was sad and in pain. He had been away from his home planet, and many of his friends and family had been killed by the dragons. Her pain was new and fresh, but it was so deep and real and wrong. She felt a bond in their pain. He would help her realize justice for her parents. In return she answered all his questions without hesitation, telling him anything he wanted to know. After all, her parents' homeschooling had been thorough, and she was able to answer his questions, which were mostly about geography and the location of pyramids. He seemed to know about the pyramids in

Mesoamerica and Egypt, but she'd explained that there were supposedly pyramids in Bosnia, China, and even Antarctica, retrieving a map from the Jeep's glove compartment and showing him the locations. He was also interested in technology and weaponry; she told him about everything from the invention of gunpowder to nuclear weapons, as well as electricity, engines, and space flight.

King Ogliosh explained his race was heavily centered around the movement of celestial bodies. They didn't have weapons like hers, they didn't use electricity, or power anything with nuclear power. But despite his world not having the modern advances Gabi's had, it soon became clear Ogliosh understood mathematics on a level well beyond her own. Ogliosh tried to explain his world was a world of magic and that the laws of the universe work differently where magic is present.

Could there really be magic? As quick as she asked herself the question, she answered it. Yes, of course there could be magic. If there could be dragons, giants, and telepathy why not magic? The best she could understand was that magic took math to a whole different level. Honestly, she didn't get it… not even a little. Maybe magic was its own type of science or math or whatever.

Finally Ogliosh said, "Our worlds are both governed by mathematical law. That's why math is one of the first things I taught your people long ago – math is universal. But magic distorts mathematical law, bends it, and in some cases even circumvents it altogether."

After that she knew she couldn't understand his math and she decided she didn't care to. As long as the end result was justice for her parents, she never needed to understand.

Now, finally, Gabi was going into the pyramid to see how it worked – how he would use it to open the gate to his world. And although he hadn't said it and she hadn't asked, something told her she could choose to go with him and leave this horrible place behind. This place that had nothing left for her. The more time she spent with Ogliosh, her giant, her friend, the more she didn't want him to go without her. She walked quickly down the long corridor, dodging smaller rocks as she took five or six steps to the king's one lumbering stride.

Before reaching the end of the corridor, Ogliosh stopped abruptly.

"What's wrong?" Gabi asked.

"We have a guest, Gabi."

"The other giants?" she asked.

"No, something else."

49

Cooperate or Die!

Saturday, April 9 – God Stones Day 4
Rural Chiapas State, Mexico

Breanne's palms pressed into the dry earth as she retched. Her head spun wildly, as if she had been turned in circles repeatedly, and she wasn't sure if she was on the ground or falling off it. Her stomach twisted and she retched again, but nothing came up. The horrible spinning had happened eight times, she thought. *Eight times? Nine times?* She wasn't sure, but each time Apep spoke the strange words, unconsciousness had followed, for how long she couldn't say. She was sure days had gone by, and she hadn't eaten anything. She blinked at the dry ground cast in the shadow of her tormentor, the cloaked man looming over her. No, not a man – *a murderer.*

"You make this hard, Breanne. You make this hard, and my patience is growing thin. We can keep doing this until you die, or you can simply point toward the location of your father's dig site. Given time, I will find it anyway."

She swiveled her head up to look upon Apep's face, but she didn't meet his eyes. He looked so different in the sun. His sharp ears were almost translucent, an opaque blue-grey, like discolored rice paper. His facial features were sharp too; his skin there was a darker, unblemished blue-grey. Sweat beaded on his forehead, and it was here she focused. There was something mortal about the fact he was sweating. If he could sweat, he could die. And she wanted nothing more in this world than to kill him.

Apep shook a bottle of water at her. "Drink, Breanne."

She took the bottle with a shaky hand and tipped it back, gulping the water down. When the bottle was empty, she tossed it to the ground and wiped her mouth across her sleeve. "You're an evil bastard! I'm not helping you!"

"That's what you think? I am evil. Is that it? You have no idea what has been taken from me. You have no idea what your kind has done to me. No idea what my own people – my own family – have done. No, but you aren't capable of comprehending time in any meaningful way, so how could you understand my suffering? I am righteous in my convictions."

"You killed my brother! I will never help you!" she choked.

"Then you no longer have value!" Apep shouted as he kicked her in the ribs.

Breanne fell over onto her side, away from him, and groaned.

Apep took a step closer. "What about your father and your other brother – the bigger one, Ed? I can assume, like you, they made it out of the pit?"

She didn't answer. She pressed her face into the hot, sandy dirt, choking out sobs between gasps.

"Ask yourself this, Breanne. Would the brother you still have alive want you to die? Would the father who still lives want you to die? Or would they want you to cooperate and live?"

She didn't want to die. She thought of her dad and knew what her death would do to him. Besides, if she died now, she couldn't kill Apep. And if Breanne Moore was nothing else, she was determined to watch him die.

"I know your father's site was somewhere in Chiapas. I am growing tired of randomly teleporting. We are just outside Palenque, Breanne, and I know we can't be that far from the site. I can only teleport to places I have seen before or can see now. I am going to lift you up high above this place. Point me in the direction of the site. If you refuse, or mislead me, we will randomly teleport over and over until it kills you! Do you understand?!" Apep shouted, grabbing her by the wrist and yanking her onto her feet.

Breanne shouted in pain again, but reluctantly she nodded.

"Good," Apep said.

Then, as the elf began shouting a command in some strange words, the earth fell away from her feet with a *whoosh* as hot wind blew across her face, forcing her eyes closed. Suddenly she was hovering high above Palenque.

"Now point, Breanne, and remember – the closer you get, the fewer times we will need to do this."

The sun was high and bright. Far to the east were the Sierra Madre del Sur mountains. Breanne looked to the southwest, found the general area she was searching for, and pointed.

"Ah, good!" Apep said.

Her world spun again and this time she woke on top of a mountain, a foot striking her back. Again, her stomach was wrecked, and she tried to vomit but couldn't. Then she heard his voice.

"I have been waiting for you to wake," Apep said, as if this was her fault. "You humans are pathetically fragile. We are where you pointed. Now get up and show me where the pyramid is," he demanded.

She tried to stand but fell backward, her equilibrium completely out of sorts. She felt like she was trying to stand atop a merry-go-round. Her head was pounding harder than ever, and she wasn't sure she could or should open her eyes.

Apep grabbed her by the wrist once again and yanked her to her feet. She blinked rapidly, trying to get her eyes to focus, but before she could look around, she was off the ground again soaring upward.

"Point!"

She squinted. She knew it had to be right there, right there in the cluster of mountains a little further south. "There." She pointed, hating what came next.

She woke up some time later. This time Apep didn't wait for her to get her bearings. As soon as she started to dry heave, he yanked her up into the air again.

“Point me to the…” Apep began to say but trailed off. “What’s this?”

Breanne squinted, trying to focus as she followed Apep’s gaze. A few miles to the south, maybe less, she saw what he saw. There was a mountain with a large cavern opening several meters from the top. The opening appeared to spill out onto a ledge. Did she see a vehicle on the ledge? Below the opening, far down the mountain, were more vehicles. One was on its side and the others had rocks piled against them. Below the vehicles was a deep gorge. The only way she could be sure it was a gorge at all was because the jungle had been drawn back, shredded by falling boulders that she could only guess were pulled from the opening in the mountain. She wasn’t sure what was going on, but she was sure this was her mountain.

Then Apep said the words. Her gut twisted and, before she could even scream, everything went black.

50

Guests

Wednesday, April 9 – God Stones Day 4
Rural Chiapas State, Mexico

Gabi spun around to see the silhouette of a tall man standing on the opposite side of the ledge from the Jeep. Something was heaped in a pile next to him, but she couldn't tell what it was.

Ogliosh moved past her. "Stay behind me, Gabi. When we get close, get inside the Jeep."

"Who is that?" she asked.

Ogliosh didn't answer as he strode forward.

As they drew close, the tall man pulled something that looked like a jagged crown from his cloak and placed it on his own head. Gabi felt a pressure in her head; the closer she drew, the worse the pressure became. Still, she stared at the crown, unable to take her eyes off of it. The object was radiating beautiful colors until finally one appeared she had never seen! The harder she looked, the worse it hurt – but the color! She couldn't look away.

The pressure in her head turned to pain that turned to an unbearable anguish. Blood began to trickle from her nose. Everything became muffled and then something wet ran down both sides of her neck. The colors changed from one to another, then to another still, until she once again saw the color she couldn't understand. Both her eyes began to bulge, and everything took on a blood-red tint. Bloody tears ran from her eyes and her stomach began to curl.

Gabi tried to scream, but her mouth went dry and her throat constricted so tight she couldn't draw a breath. She doubled over as her stomach surged, but nothing could come up. Just when she thought she was going to pass out, she felt something inside her head pop with a loud crack like a snapping branch. She sat down hard on her bottom and fell over onto her side.

Slowly, too slowly, the pain started to pass. She wiped her bloody eyes and nose and looked at her hand covered in wet crimson. Her heart pounded against her chest. Ay, María Purísima, she was bleeding! She stretched her jaw and her ear popped, allowing her to hear again. Gabi sat up shakily, still nauseous as she began pushing herself backward toward the wall, trying to catch her breath.

Leaning back against the wall of the pyramid, she observed the two creatures talking through blurry eyes. As her senses returned, it appeared King Ogliosh might kill the other creature. She was sure it wasn't human, though it wasn't a giant either. But now they seemed to be just staring at each other. Suddenly Ogliosh pointed at her and both began walking toward her. She realized he wasn't pointing at her, but beyond her, toward the back of the corridor. As they passed, the tall man looked over at her with a sneer. She gasped. She could feel his hatred toward her and, for a second, she thought he might kill her. Soon the two disappeared from her view, moving deeper into the pyramid.

As the pain in Gabi's head subsided, she realized something was different. Two and a half days she had spent with the king and most of that time was spent speaking to each other with their minds. So far, she had only been able to hear what he wanted her to hear, but now something was different. There was some other noise, some kind of buzzing…

Her thought was interrupted as the soothing voice of her father spoke in her mind. "Gabi, you have been exposed to the Sound Eye. Most humans would not survive such an exposure. You are lucky to be alive. I must deal with this creature. I will explain soon – go to the Jeep if you can, and rest," Ogliosh said.

She never really got used to that voice coming from him. "What is a Sound Eye?" she asked.

"The key to the doorway home. Now, when you can stand and walk, I want you to go and rest."

She wanted to ask a million questions, but she knew this wasn't the time. *Okay,* she thought back. She wrinkled her brow, hearing that *something else* again. This new buzzing sensation mingled into the presence of Ogliosh.

She sat a moment longer trying to catch her breath, trying to understand the fuzzy noise in her mind. It was coming from far in the background of her mind, like static from a radio. Not the kind where you can't listen to a song, but the kind that is just slightly annoying. She focused on the sound, pushing her mind into the static, trying to hear it. She frowned. There was something there alright, she was sure of it.

Gabi let her mind wade deeper into the fuzzy noise until it was completely submerged. *What is this?* she wondered as the strange static changed to something else. Gabi cocked her head to the side, listening as she instinctively tuned the frequency of thought until what came into focus was a muffled conversation. The static now formed into words.

At first, the words didn't make any sense. It wasn't her father's voice, and it wasn't speaking Spanish nor English. She couldn't understand it at all, but she could hear it clearly now. She took the words and pulled on them, stretching them. Then she pushed them, working the words into something pliable. As she worked, she found she could almost shape them, like when she helped her mom make tortillas for the entire dig team. The memory of sitting by the campfire and working the masa dough broke her concentration and sent a pang through her heart.

Determined, Gabi pushed the pain down and refocused on the

words. They came easily now, but she still couldn't understand what she was hearing. She twisted them, bent them, and even folded them in upon themselves, only to stretch them back out again just like the masa dough. Somehow, she knew this was solvable. And then *it* happened. Gabi's heart raced as an invisible cog slid into some place in her mind, completing the puzzle. And with that she understood! It made no sense how, but she understood!

There were two voices. One called himself Apep and the other was King Ogliosh, but he no longer sounded like her father. Now, she realized with a gasp, she was eavesdropping on a conversation happening in a language she shouldn't understand. The conversation was taking place somewhere deep inside the pyramid between Ogliosh and this new creature.

"The interior structure will need some work, and the sub-level stone water column was destroyed by Azazel, but the rest has been preserved well and is mostly intact." The giant king's voice was no longer warm and kind. Instead his voice had a grim, gravelly tone – still deep and heavy like a vast ocean, but no longer smooth or soothing.

The creature called Apep spoke next, and she noticed right away that he sounded like he should be a king. His voice had a regal tone to it. "Fine. How long before the others arrive?"

"The others, yes. First tell me again, what happened to General Balor?"

"I already told you, it was chaos. The humans beat me to the chamber and were about to cut off Balor's head when I stopped them. I was able to break the spell, but Sylanth woke too and everything went bad. Balor assembled the Sound Eye, knowing it was our only hope to make it out, but Turek's descendant killed him while I was dealing with the dragon."

"Humans killed my general?" Ogliosh asked, and Gabi could feel mistrust in the question.

"That's what I said."

Gabi felt sudden annoyance with the giant. It was a strange sensation to become annoyed over something she didn't understand.

"I find it hard to believe a few humans killed my general all by themselves. You – what were you doing to help Balor? You had the Sound Eye, did you not?"

Gabi felt skeptical, as if she had just been told a lie she could see right through.

"I already told you, I was dealing with the dragon, which is now dead! Turek and the ones who killed Balor are all dead! I've told you what happened, Ogliosh – let's move on. You will have vengeance on the humans soon enough."

Vengeance on humans? But Ogliosh doesn't hate humans, he wants to help them, she thought. She didn't like the conversation, and she didn't like this Apep either.

"Turek?" Ogliosh said in surprise. "One of the seven?"

"Seven what? Mages of old? No, he is the descendant of the old mage. Rather, *was* before he died," Apep said simply.

"Not mages. Turek is a very old name not spoken on Karelia since the humans were banished. It is the true name of the humans' god."

"What are you talking about? I am speaking of the descendant of the human mage of old. The one who cast the spell on you. That Turek."

"The descendant of the god Turek then?"

"Why do you keep calling him a god? I killed the human mage hundreds of years ago. His bones are submerged over a hundred feet underground on an island, so he couldn't very well be a god now, could he? This was some prophecy he concocted to try and keep the humans following him even after death. All part of their plan to try and keep me from the God Stones!"

"Prophecy?" Ogliosh asked, and Gabi was consumed with a deep dread.

"Yes, a last-ditch effort, a Hail Mary, a pathetic last line of defense. Humans are quite dramatic that way."

"Last ditch? What is a last ditch?"

"Never mind!"

"If the human god is interfering on this planet, we should be very concerned. Creating a prophecy, allowing you to kill him – you should be asking yourself why, Apep. What is the human god planning? Are you positive the human descendant is dead? You saw him die?"

"Yes, now let's move on to more pressing matters than that of human children and false gods! Did the others survive their awakening with the dragons? How close are they? We've an army to build!" The anger poured off Apep and washed over Gabi, overwhelming her until she too became angry.

The conversation stopped and her mind became abruptly quiet. She could feel Ogliosh stare down the smaller creature. In the silent pause, Gabi realized these rapidly shifting emotions were not hers. They swirled strangely inside her, two separate creatures feeling different emotions at the same moment, and she was feeling both while also feeling her own. Annoyance, anger, and impatience from Apep, while skepticism and mistrust radiated from Ogliosh.

Finally, the king said, "Some I feel are very close, the others have to cross the ocean. All five survived their awakenings with the dragons and should be here within a few days. The main army will take much longer to make the journey."

"What main army? What journey?!" Apep asked.

Gabi's mind exploded in a burst of confusion.

"My army, Apep. Did you think all was lost? Did you think I was not smarter than humans? When the sages came to put us down, do you not think I had a back-up plan? My army is secure. I led only a hundred into battle – the rest I sent away to multiply and prepare in case we were to fall. By now they will number in the tens of thousands. We are nephilbock!" the king said, and pride filled Gabi's chest.

"That's impossible! There is nowhere you could have hidden an army that size for thousands of years!"

Then, as Ogliosh formed the thoughts, she gasped in horror. The army wasn't hidden on earth, it was hidden *inside* the earth. Deep inside. Her mind reeled. *Why? His people were astrologists, they were teachers! Why did he need an army?*

"Inside, Apep! My army waits, deep in the bowels of the earth!"

"Inner earth?" Apep scoffed. "I knew it could be possible. After all, legends say Karelia has an inner world, but earth? Interesting… And you're sure it was large enough and habitable for an army this size?"

"Of course, I am sure. The inner core is made up of liquid iron quartz. It is like an internal sun and provides for photosynthesis. The inner world is quite sustainable." Gabi could feel Ogliosh's impatience with Apep's questions. "There is an opening not far from here in South America, in what is now called the Amazon. It is guarded by a native tribe of humans. They were to wait for the one phrase to be spoken. Once the phrase was spoken, they were to go and summon my people."

"The Amazon in South America? How do you know these modern terms, Ogliosh?" Apep asked.

"I have a human. I have read through her mind and learned everything useful. She is a young human, but knowledgeable."

Gabi felt her stomach tighten as she realized something was very wrong.

"Ah, the small one we walked past. Yes, very good." Apep's thoughts returned immediately to the army. "Do you understand how much time this will save us? You have ensured I have an army! If this army is as big as you say, you have done well, Ogliosh! Well indeed! For your efforts, let me offer a modest gift. I also have a human girl. Take her! She is young, but she is very intelligent for a human. She will be beneficial in furthering your knowledge. When you finish with her, have her for lunch, or whatever you like – just make sure she dies." Apep laughed.

Apep was so suddenly happy that Gabi felt like giggling, but then Ogliosh spoke and his words left her feeling twisted again.

"Yes, I am quite hungry, and I expect my army will hunger for humans too."

Gabi felt the giant's hunger pangs as if they were her own. Tears filled her eyes. She couldn't believe what she was hearing, she didn't want to believe. The shock racked her body, and she began to shake as she fought back sobs. He wasn't going to help her. He wasn't going to kill the dragon for her. Worse, he was going to kill her and… eat her! All this time, he was only pretending? He had been lying all along. He was supposed to be her friend! Ay, María Purísima, if he lied about this, what about Sarah? Had he eaten Sarah?

"Well, good. These two will get you started then! Mine is called Breanne. She is well educated. She was favored by the descendant of the mage who imprisoned you, and she helped kill your general. Make sure she suffers," Apep said evenly.

Gabi's breath came in rapid pants as panic set in and the tears stung her eyes. She couldn't breathe. Ogliosh was going to check in on her any second and find out she had been listening. She just knew it! She was going to die! Her face was hot, and her vision narrowed. *Think, Gabi! What had Apep said? Mine is called Breanne… Breanne? Sarah's Breanne? Could that be?* She looked over toward the heap crumpled on the platform. It was unmoving, exposed under the hot sun. She had to do something. She pushed herself up onto wobbly feet as the conversation in her head continued.

"What is the phrase that must be spoken to call forth my army?" Apep asked.

"Why does it matter to you, Apep?"

"I will go and speak the words while you do what needs to be done here. We need the army moving now," Apep said as if the question were stupid. "How can you even be sure after thousands of years the humans you have entrusted will still be there? Will they still know the phrase?"

"They worship the nephilbock as gods. We are their religion. They will be there," Ogliosh said confidently.

"We are wasting time!" Apep countered.

"You were never supposed to hold the stones in their assembled form. That was our agreement. The nephilbock were to be the keepers of the stones. We would assemble the Sound Eye only when it was time to return. The power is too great… too tempting for a—"

Apep's crazy laugh flooded her mind. "For a dökkálfar? Is that you were about to say, Ogliosh?"

Gabi staggered past the Jeep and out onto the ledge. Something stirred inside her – inside Apep. It was a hateful feeling and she didn't like it.

"You think me a fool, Apep. You think my army would follow you without the nephilbock to lead. Would you be so arrogant to try and cut us out? Would you try and leave us here? Or maybe you would try and turn my army against us? But you forget, Apep, you must place the Sound Eye atop the pyramid to open the gate. The words must be spoken, and you don't know how. Don't you forget that!"

"And once the gate closes, the Sound Eye comes back to the one who placed it atop the pyramid. Don't you forget that, Ogliosh!"

"We have a treaty! You signed it in your own blood. When you rule Osonian there will be peace between dökkálfar, nephilbock, and dragons. That is why we all came, Apep. That's the promise!"

"Yes! And that hasn't changed! Once I overthrow my father, I will keep my word," Apep said.

"And the nephilbock will be standing next to you all along the way, ensuring you keep your word. And ensuring you return to us our God Stone."

"Of course," Apep said. "Now allow me to go signal them so we can get on with this."

"I would never allow an elf to call forth my army!"

"Careful with these new words you have learned, Ogliosh! Do you think it wise to insult me?" Apep said.

Gabi felt the Sound Eye begin to react to the Apep's anger, and her own chest grew hot with rage. The rage she felt from the two creatures was flooding her mind and was almost too much to control as she reached the unconscious girl.

Gabi shook the girl. "Wake up, Breanne! Please, please wake up!" The sudden thought of kicking the sleeping girl in the ribs sprang forth in her mind. The angry emotions were not her own, and, amidst the rage that wasn't hers, she felt ashamed for thinking of hurting her. She threw her palms to both sides of her head, shutting her eyes up tight, trying to somehow force the feelings away. She wanted to scream. She shook the girl again. "Wake up!" she shouted.

Breanne moaned and opened her eyes, fixing them on her with confusion.

"Your service is not required, Apep. It has already been taken care of!"

"What! How?" Apep asked.

"I ordered one of my five to give the signal before reporting here. So you see, it is done!"

"Well, good! Then I can get on with more pressing matters."

"I still don't believe you, Apep. Just like I don't believe Balor was so easily convinced to obey you, nor that he was destroyed by a tiny human boy."

Gabi sensed Apep's anger turn to something else, and she didn't fully understand the emotion, but it terrified her.

"You would be best to remember your place. You can think whatever you want but understand this. You and all your half-breeds are mine to command until this is over, and I am on the throne. Do we have an understanding?"

Ogliosh hesitated only briefly. The decision lingered between them. Finally, he nodded.

"Good. Now, how long before they arrive?"

"Three months hence, maybe longer. Now, perhaps you should deal with Azazel? I am sure she will be making her own plans."

"Just leave her to me. Her dragons will have plenty of humans to feed on, with plenty more to enslave. You have no idea how their population has grown over the millennia."

"My human has informed me of the population among other things," King Ogliosh said.

The king thought of Gabi in that moment, and she froze, gasping sharply. She grabbed the girl's shirt in fistfuls and shook her desperately. "Get up, get up, get up, Breanne!"

Breanne sat up, blinking. "Where am I, and who are you?"

"I'm Gabi. We've got to go. Can you walk?"

"Gabi? Sarah's Gabi? I… I think so."

Gabi nodded. "Come on!"

"I know what Azazel will be doing and where she and hers will gather. I have known for a long time. When the time comes, all you need to do is make sure the door is open and stable," Apep said confidently. "Azazel will want to go home to her people as much as we do. I will go to her. I have a proposition she won't be able to refuse. This is all coming together so much easier than last time. You should have allowed me to assemble the stones in the first place."

Gabi pulled on Breanne's arm in a frantic jerk. "We need to hurry, Bre!" she begged. Then as she tried to speak again, a sudden smugness washed over her. "Get in the Jeep, stupid girl, or do you want to die?" She gasped at her own words, covering her mouth in shock.

In that same moment Ogliosh spoke with a smug finality. "Even with the Sound Eye, you can't control dragons."

Breanne, still clearly disoriented, turned to look at her with furrowed brows. "What? No! Of course I don't want to die!"

"I'm sorry! I wasn't … I didn't mean…" Gabi pleaded as she led her to the Jeep and yanked open the door.

Apep's voice screeched in her mind, and she felt this new agitation rake down her spine. She balled her fist. "María Purísima, please!"

Apep snapped back at the giant. "I don't need to control them, I just need Azazel to follow orders!"

"You have no idea what assembling the Sound Eye is doing to this world. You have put us on a timeline, Apep. This tiny world wasn't made for the power of the Sound Eye. In time it will destroy itself, but before it does the creatures of this world – humans and others, the ones that are capable – they will feed on the Sentheye! What do you think will happen when those creatures find out you wish to open the portal home and take the power from this world? Do you think they will want to give up the Sentheye after they have tasted it? There is an awakening happening, and they will all want what you have."

"Then you better get to work, King Ogliosh. Now I suggest you stop! Stop trying to get into my head!" Apep said.

The Sound Eye began to glow.

"I'm not in your head! Wait! What is this!?"

Gabi tried to slam the door of her mind, but it wouldn't close. "Seat belt, Breanne!" she yelled, pulling the emergency brake.

Breanne pulled on her belt, clasping it into place with a click. "Do you know what you're doing?"

"No!" Gabi yelled, as the Jeep rolled forward toward the edge of the ledge.

"Gabi!" the giant yelled in her mind.

"The human!?" Apep said.

Pressure pushed against her mind, and a door slammed with a sharp pain. Apep was gone. Now she could only hear Ogliosh. "You should not have been listening, human girl."

The voice was not her father, it was the ugly voice of betrayal. The ground shook as an angry roar filled the tunnel. Gabi gripped the wheel of the Jeep for dear life. She looked in the side mirror in time to see Ogliosh appear behind them, coming fast.

"What the hell is that?!" Breanne yelled as the Jeep tipped over the edge of the platform and down onto the mountain.

Both girls screamed.

51

Feast and Grow!

Wednesday, April 9 – God Stones Day 4
Rural Chiapas State, Mexico

Apep and Ogliosh arrived at the edge of the ledge just in time to see the Jeep bounce across the uneven terrain, crash through the camp near the base of the mountain, and vanish into the gorge below.

Apep laughed. "You fool. You've let them escape."

"Careful, Apep," King Ogliosh said, tightening his eye, "I don't bow before you. You aspire to be a king, but you forget I am already a king."

Apep spun on him, staring skyward, trying to meet the giant's eye. "It is you who should be careful – I possess the Sound Eye," he snapped.

"You possess nothing, you only hold it."

Apep frowned. "Either way – hold it, possess it. The point is, Ogliosh, I could smite you with its power."

The giant stared back, his one eye unblinking. "The humans are of no matter," he said flatly. "There will be more, many more, to harvest."

Apep hated giants – not as much as humans, but still he hated them. They were big and dangerous, worthless if not for their size and impossibly long lives. The truth was he didn't know how long they lived – perhaps forever. And they never seemed to forget anything. While humans were cursed with incredibly short lives and were too stupid to remember yesterday, nephilbock remembered it all. The dökkálfars were the perfect race, and he was the perfect dökkálfar. Perhaps he would take the dökkálfar goddess Ereshkigal as his own wife when this was over. Yes, she would make the perfect queen.

Apep shook away the thought. All in due time. Everything that was owed would be paid. "You will be vulnerable to humans and their weapons should they find out about you and send armed forces. Two birds, one stone. I will clean up this mess with these two escapees and provide you with some protection while I am gone!" *And show this nephilbock why he should fear me in the process,* Apep thought, as he began to chant words and the Sound Eye began to glow. Blue-grey ribbons the color of Apep's skin poured forth in thick bands. The elf stepped to the edge of the ledge.

King Ogliosh backed away from Apep toward the mouth of the pyramid.

Apep opened his palms to the sky and gazed out from the ledge, down the mountain to the jungle beyond. The ribbons of power dissipated into a fog, flowing down over the mountain, following Apep's gaze as it spread across everything in sight. He chanted more words and the Sentheye obeyed, moving with a purpose, his purpose. He was one with the Sentheye, seeing through it.

The jungle floor teemed with life. Just in his span of reach were thousands of insects – mosquitoes, ants, flies, and larger bugs too. There were scorpions, spiders, and some sort of strange giant beetle nearly as big as Apep's hand. Then he detected even more substantial life. Iguanas sunned themselves on the warm rock shelves while others fought amongst themselves over females and territory. Further down the steep slope he sensed a lynx and her young. She was nursing a litter under the shade of a rock outcropping. He reached even further and deeper, groping with the Sentheye, finding even more creatures – poisonous vipers, wild dogs, something like a racoon but not a racoon. *What a strange thing.* The Sentheye led him to dozens of small black monkeys. There were so many of them, the trees seemed full of them.

"What are you doing, Apep!?" Ogliosh asked, his massive brow wrinkling.

Ignoring the giant, Apep cocked his head to the side. *Yes, I see you, I see all of you.* He sucked in a deep breath and extended his hands outward, splaying his fingers. How strange he must look, dressed in human clothes, boots, and a long duster with his magical crown slightly askew atop his midnight hair. He supposed he looked almost comical, but what came next no one would find amusing – except him of course.

He chanted the words over and over, shouting them as loud as he could shout. "Flah oz zaeshi ff mue, flah oz zaeshi! Flah oz zaeshi!" More Sentheye poured from his hands as dense as smoke from burning car tires. The Sentheye supercharged the liquid grey fog until it too became impossibly thick, heavy like liquid given shape, given purpose. But this was not smoke, nor shadow, nor liquid. No, this was power – magic – Sentheye.

"Now eat! Feast upon the Sentheye and grow!" Apep shouted triumphantly.

The Sentheye found its way to all the creatures, and as the creatures fed on the Sentheye, the Sentheye consumed them, then changed them. From the thick smoke a giant snake slithered, iguanas lifted their heads above the fog, a jaguar roared, trees swayed and bowed under the weight of giant monkeys. Wasps, mosquitoes, and even biting gnats could be seen from a distance.

Apep dropped his hands to his side, his vision becoming narrow as he swayed on his feet. Just as quickly as it had begun, it was over. He blinked back the darkness, surprised at the exhaustion he felt.

"What have you done?" the king demanded as he leaned his great girth over the mountainside for a better look.

"I am cleaning up your mess. If the human females lived through that little stunt they pulled, these creatures will ensure they don't for long. You will be vulnerable while you work. If word gets out about you being here, they could send military. My new pets will take care of them," Apep said, brushing his hands together in satisfaction. He turned back to the giant. "You're welcome."

Below, giant insects buzzed around noisily. A few iguanas darted off – the rest, about a dozen or so, were all easily visible due to their newly acquired monstrous size. They were seemingly unaware of how they had grown as they went back to sunning themselves or fighting one another for space. "You can command them?" Ogliosh asked skeptically, pointing down the mountain at a viper easily forty feet in length as it slithered through base camp.

Apep didn't answer; instead he focused his mind on imposing his will, compelling the animals and insects to obey him. Excitement consumed him. *All these new creatures to command. I can add to my army with the sorry creatures of this planet! Make them into the fierce monsters they should have been if a real god had created them… a dökkálfar god. Yes, of course, it will be perfect,* he thought, as the huge snake worked its way across the rocks and between vehicles. *Yes! Come to me, my children. Come to me and obey!*

The giant snake paused briefly, turning its head toward them.

"That's right. Yes, come to me." Apep beckoned with his hand. The Sound Eye crown atop his head began to glow once again. "Come to me!"

The viper stretched upward several feet off the ground, its long tongue flicking at the air. What followed was a defiant hiss that could be heard all the way up the mountain.

Apep frowned. Despite all his focus the creatures *did not* obey. Not even one of the biting gnats and certainly not the snake. They were *not* his creatures. He had seen his own daughter grow and command rats but he couldn't bend a bug to his will? He, with more power than anyone in the universe. He, with more power than the gods themselves – couldn't make them obey? He could use the Sound Eye to physically change them, but he couldn't do what a pathetic half-breed could do with a few rats!

"What's wrong?" Ogliosh asked.

"C'est la vie." Apep sighed.

Ogliosh laughed and then he laughed even harder, holding his massive belly as it shook. "Of course, you can't command them, can you?"

"What do you mean 'of course'?" Apep asked, feeling blood flush to his face as anger built inside him.

"It isn't in your nature to control creatures. The Sound Eye hasn't changed that. It will only enhance your attributes, mage, not give you new ones."

In the distance, one of the raccoon things tried to scurry up a tree, but the tree wouldn't hold, cracking with a loud pop under the beast's newfound weight. The beast startled and took off like a shot, running wildly into the jungle, wrecking foliage and toppling trees as it went.

Apep raised a long finger toward the giant. "Just prepare, Ogliosh. If humans come snooping, they will be in for a surprise."

"As will my nephilbock, when they arrive," he said disapprovingly.

"Oh, come now, I don't think a few giant monkeys and some overgrown mosquitos are anything your nephilbock can't handle," Apep said. "Now, if you excuse me, I've a dragon queen to see."

"Perhaps you should stay and rest. The Sound Eye is taking its toll on you," Ogliosh said as he backed away, never taking his ostrich egg–sized eye off Apep.

"Nonsense. I have never felt better in my life!" He closed his eyes and pictured the place he wanted to go. The place he knew Azazel would be. It had been many years, but the memory was solid. The Sound Eye glowed bright, so bright it swallowed him in its light. Then he was gone.

52

Old Guilt

Saturday, April 9 – God Stones Day 4
Rural Chiapas State, Mexico

Somehow the Jeep managed to stay upright as it careened down the mountain and through base camp. Breanne screamed, one hand gripping the dashboard handle, and the other clinging for dear life to the handle above the door. As her body locked up, horrible memories flashed through her mind of the last car accident she was in, the one that stole her mother, the one that she caused. Now this girl, this strange girl, trying to save her was going to die! She needed to stay present. She had to stay here… now.

The girl in the driver's seat was squeezing the steering wheel, her eyes wider than she thought possible. When the Jeep hit the edge of the gorge, Breanne felt a weightlessness as everything smoothed out. They were flying. The ground beneath them was gone, and the only sound remaining were their screams. A moment later they hit the ground hard. Even belted in, it was all she could do to keep her head from slamming into the roof of the Jeep. The other girl, Gabi, wasn't so lucky. Breanne saw her hit her head and her body go slack, but before she could grab the wheel the Jeep turned abruptly and flipped onto the driver's side. Breanne watched in horror as Gabi fell limp toward the ground the Jeep was sliding along. She lunged for the girl, trying to pull her back. The Jeep slid for what seemed like forever, ripping through foliage and small trees before finally stopping abruptly against a large tree.

The girl opened her eyes. "Mamá, my head," she moaned.

"Gabi? Are you okay?" Breanne asked.

The girl lay there for a long moment as if listening for something. "Yes, I think so. I don't hear them anymore."

"Hear who?" Breanne asked, bracing her feet against the dash. She unclipped her seat belt and lowered herself to straddle the girl.

"Ogliosh and Apep. I'm not in their heads anymore." Gabi shook her head side to side.

"Listen, Gabi, I am going to assume Ogi—"

"King Ogliosh, the giant."

"Right, Ogliosh. I'm going to assume he is going to try and kill us, and I for sure know Apep will. Can you get up?" Breanne extended her hand to the girl. Gabi's hand was small but strong. Breanne took it and pulled the girl to her feet. They climbed up and out of the passenger side window.

Breanne jumped down, the dry foliage crunching under her feet as she landed. "Is your head okay? I think you were knocked out there for a second."

Gabi swung her leg over the side of the Jeep door. "Hurts a little. But I am getting used to it."

The girl jumped down next to her, and for the first time Breanne had a chance to *really* look at her. She was about a foot shorter than Breanne, with long jet-black hair parted down the middle and braided into two matching pigtails. Her clothes were torn and filthy. She looked really young, but something was off. It was in her eyes. Something horrible had happened to her. And after the way she had screamed at Breanne on the mountain and talked about being in *their* heads, she wondered if the poor thing wasn't broken. "Where is Sarah, Gabi?" she asked softly.

"I… I don't know. I think she's dead," Gabi whispered.

Breanne's heart sank into her stomach. Memories came in a rush, flashing through her mind of a time when she was even younger than Gabi, squatting down over a shallow hole on a dig site, brushing strata away from objects buried centuries earlier, talking girl stuff with Sarah and laughing. "Are you sure?" she tried to ask, her voice cracking.

"What?" Gabi said distantly.

"Gabi, are you sure? You said you think. Are you sure!"

"No. But I think the giant killed her, maybe even ate her."

"But you're not—"

Above them something crashed through the trees.

Breanne looked up just as a large black mass scrambled down the gorge not thirty yards away. She grabbed Gabi by the arm and pulled her back against the bottom of the overturned Jeep, pressing her own back into it. She squatted down and peered beneath the protruding tire of the Jeep.

The monkey howled so loud Breanne had to cover her ears. She grabbed Gabi and pulled her down into a squat. The monkey stood facing away from them, swaying on its feet.

"That's a howler monkey," Gabi said.

Breanne knew what it was, but this monkey was way, way too big to be a monkey at all. Yet there it was, with its long tail reaching high up over its head as if searching for something. Then, as Breanne watched, the man-sized monkey grew another three feet.

Breanne looked back up the wall of the steep gorge where the monkey had come from and gasped. "Gabi, can you run?"

"Sure, I can run," Gabi said flatly.

Blue-grey fog spilled over the top of the gorge from above.

The monkey staggered forward, taking several steps away from them.

Breanne pulled Gabi up by the hand, fearful the girl was in some kind of shock. "Okay, we have to make a run for it, Gabi."

Breanne pointed further down into the gorge away from the monkey. As they prepared to run, something clacked off the Jeep above them. Then again, again, and again. Maybe some kind of landslide from above? Then a fire ant landed in front of them. It was the size of a football. "Run, Gabi!"

Gabi bolted forward as if a starting gun had gone off.

Ants were landing all around them. Breanne leapt over one as she gave chase. Gabi wasn't kidding – she could run. Breanne pushed hard to keep up, her body dehydrated and threatening to cramp. Two minutes later and a good distance away, she yelled for Gabi to stop. Sweat soaked her shirt, pasting it to her back. She gasped for breath. "Gabi, do you know how to get out of here? How to get to a road or, better yet, a town? And where is everyone else from the dig?" She hesitated before asking but then said, "Your parents? Where are they?"

Tears filled Gabi's eyes and spilled down her dirt-streaked cheeks. She shook her head. She reached forward, taking hold of Breanne's hand.

Breanne dropped to one knee as a memory forced itself into her mind. She was in a large cavern with a dragon and a giant. Sarah was there with others, and all around her people were screaming and running. She could hear herself screaming too. "Mamá! Papá!" A woman pushed something into her hand. She looked down and saw it was a familiar chain, her own father's chain, and on it was a wedding ring with a small diamond. The woman, she knew somehow she was Gabi's mother, turned and ran away… and died.

Breanne grabbed the girl by the shoulders. "Oh, Gabi! I'm sorry!"

Gabi shook her head and said in a voice that was barely a whisper, "Gone. They are all gone."

Breanne hugged the girl to her chest and squeezed her with all she had. She knew this vision wasn't hers. It felt different and, besides, she had never seen a vision of the past before – only the future. She had no idea how the girl had shared this memory with her, but she knew what she had seen, and she knew what *gone* meant. Her brother was *gone*. Her mother was *gone* and her father… she didn't know. God, she didn't know. She didn't know about Garrett or the others, were they… *gone*? This girl, this little girl, taking her hand in hers did something to Breanne. This young girl Sarah had talked about. The girl who was to be like a little sister to her when she was able to join the dig during breaks from college. Now they were together fighting for their lives. She couldn't speak, didn't know what to say if she could, but then it was Gabi who spoke.

The girl pushed herself back far enough to look at Breanne. She was holding the chain with her mother's ring. "This chain was your father's?"

"Yes. Did Sarah tell you?"

"No, you told me."

Breanne frowned – she hadn't said anything.

Gabi started to slide the ring off the chain when Breanne put her hand on top of the girl's. "Hang onto it for me? Please?"

Gabi forced a weak smile. "Thank you," she said, stuffing the chain and ring back into her front pocket before wiping her eyes with dirty sleeves. She looked away and pointed behind Breanne. "There is a town, but it is over an hour's drive. The road isn't that far though, and there is a farming village a few miles down once we get to the road. That's where Fredy hired the laborers from. We will have to cross back through the gorge though. If we don't, we will get lost for sure."

With their hands clasped tight together they began to walk. "Okay, listen to me Gabi. We are going to go wide on the far side of the gorge. Did you see that bluish fog?"

Gabi shook her head side to side. "No."

"Well, I think that is what's making the ants and the monkey and god only know what else grow. If we see that fog, we have to avoid it and anything else we might see." She stopped and pulled Gabi toward her, hugging her again. "Just stay close to me. We are going to get out of here, Gabi. I promise." And she meant it. She meant it from the bottom of her heart. "Come on, we need to get to that road before the sun sets."

Together they raced down deeper into the gorge, crossed the worn dirt path that led back to base camp, and over to the far side until it became too steep and thick to traverse. From there they began working their way along the gorge, horizontal to the trail. As they moved, they heard buzzing insects too loud to be normal. They foraged some long branches to use to bat any that came too close but so far none did. They did see more ants, some large beetles, and one butterfly the size of a dinner plate. They stepped carefully and as quietly as they could, always giving the insects a wide berth.

"Breanne! Look!" Gabi said, pointing.

They had come upon a utility truck, or what was left of it. Some of the cab attached to a twisted frame and one wheel was all that remained of the upside-down vehicle. It had torn a pretty good path through the jungle heading back toward base camp.

"I remember, Sarah jumped into this car right before I blacked out. Ogliosh told me she ran away."

Breanne ran to the cab and squatted down to peer inside through the busted window. There was no sign of Sarah, but there was plenty of blood. "She's not here but stay back and keep an eye out," Breanne said instinctively, not wanting the girl to see the blood. She crawled into the cab, searching for anything useful but finding only a khaki work shirt, a wide brimmed hat, and half a bottle of water mixed among a scatter of other debris. She lifted the door to the glovebox and reached in to find a pistol stuffed into a leather holster with a spare magazine and a plastic box of 9mm ammunition. She grabbed it all and scooted herself backward out the window of the truck. She emptied the box of rounds into the cargo pocket on her thigh and clipped the holster onto her waistline. She didn't want to shoot the gun, but not because she was afraid to or didn't know how. Her brothers were military and they'd insisted she knew how, but she didn't want to draw attention. Better to have it and not need it.

"Gabi, when the sun goes down it's going to get cold," she said, draping the shirt over her shoulders and placing the hat atop her head.

Gabi pushed her arms into the long sleeves of the oversized shirt and adjusted the hat. "Maybe Sarah is okay?" she said with a slight glimmer of hope.

"Maybe," Breanne said, less hopeful. There had been so much blood. Too much. "Come on, let's get to the road."

They were cautious as they crept along, barely daring to speak as they made their way through the dense jungle gorge. Once they were off the mountain, they followed the same narrow trail that had been blazed to get the vehicles to base camp. The trail ultimately broke free of the jungle to a single-lane dirt road where they were able to jog. When they were too tired to run, they walked as fast as their tired legs would carry them. As they slowed Gabi began to tell Breanne everything about her time with Ogliosh. Once she got started, she didn't stop until it was all out. She told her about the promise he had made her, and all the lies. She told her how after she saw the Sound Eye, she could get in Ogliosh and Apep's heads, feel their emotions, listen to their thoughts. Then she told her about Apep's plan, and Ogliosh's army.

The inner earth? Middle earth? The same inner earth the space alien nuts talk about? Breanne thought.

"Yes, the same one. I know how it sounds. But he said there's an army that's been waiting and multiplying over thousands of years, a race of half-breed giants like the skulls we found on the tzompantli skull racks in the circular chamber—"

"Wait a minute, Gabi, are you listening to my thoughts?" Breanne asked, stopping to face the girl.

"I'm sorry. I didn't mean it, Bre."

She hadn't told Gabi she preferred to be called Bre over Breanne. "Can you control it?" Bre asked.

"I don't know. I'm really sorry." Gabi looked at the ground.

"Don't be sorry for something you can't help."

She looked up and smiled shyly. "I'm really glad you're here, Bre."

Gabi threw her arms around her and hugged her so tight Breanne could feel the girl's soul. For the first time she didn't feel doom and sorrow. For the first time she felt hope. And for the first time, as strange as it was, and as bad as she missed her father, her brothers and, oddly, the boy Garrett who she had only known for a few hours, she felt like she was where she was supposed to be. Gabi needed her. She had to protect her. Now she just had to figure out the rest of it. "Now go on, Gabi, tell me about the army."

They began to walk again. "Sarah said some of them could be as big as twelve feet tall, maybe even bigger! Don't you see, those skulls on the racks were part of his army before they were killed, and Ogliosh was put to sleep by the mages. He lied and told me it was the dragons, but it wasn't, it was us. Humans imprisoned him and now Ogliosh's army, Apep, and the dragons are gathering to open the gate back to their planet. Apep said he is going to overthrow his father, but I was in his head – he wants more, he wants to rule everything. He wants to be a god. And this place, Bre! This place, this mountain – it's a pyramid.

The whole thing is a pyramid bigger than any on earth and, even worse, it's the portal!"

Ahead they saw a dark tree trunk lying across the road. Except this tree trunk was moving. "What the hell is that?" Breanne asked. Then beside them, just off the road, they heard the hiss.

Before Breanne could reach for the gun or even react, the giant snake darted forward from its hiding place and struck Gabi in the face. Gabi flailed and tried to scream but she couldn't. The snake retracted, dragging her body back into the jungle as it coiled around her. Breanne's body began to shake uncontrollably, and her vision narrowed. In the broken part of her mind, Christmas music played, a car crashed, and her mother died.

53

Farewell, Prince

Saturday, April 16 – God Stones Day 10
Petersburg, Illinois

"What do you mean trees are moving?" Lenny asked. "What kind of moving? We talking swaying back and forth or walking around?"

James shook his head. "Not walking per se but dragging themselves. And it's not all of them. It just seems to be the big ones or maybe the older ones. Look, no one has seen them move, but trees are out of place and they leave a trail of churned-up earth."

"How?" Garrett asked.

"We think they are pulling themselves along by their roots."

"No, I mean how in the hell can trees be moving?"

"Oh, simple, it has to be the God Stones. They are altering things," James said.

"Have you asked Coach about it?" Garrett asked.

"Well, oddly enough, he only woke yesterday. I tried to talk to him, but he said he would only talk to you and to leave him be until you woke. Except his language was a bit more – colorful. I thought about torturing him and perhaps if you hadn't woken up today, I might have lost patience and ripped off one of the bastard's pointy ears," James said flatly.

Garrett looked back over his shoulder at Lenny, who held out his palms and shrugged.

They came to a room with two guards standing on either side of a large steel door. The guards dropped to their knees and bowed immediately upon seeing Garrett. Garrett recognized one of the guards as Darnell, but he went by Yogi. Yogi was several years older than Garrett and had always been a complete dick; now he wondered if that was all part of the plan. Part of his training? Another lie to add to the long list of deceits. Either way, he didn't like the older boy bowing to him. He paused at the door before entering. "Please stand up, guys."

The men stood. Yogi, looking at the floor, shoved a key in a padlock, and unclasped the door.

The smell of moldy basement, damp and cold, hit Garrett's senses as soon as he entered the room. There were some folding chairs, a crate like the one Garrett had in the small room he woke up in, and the cot Coach lay across. The walls in this room were stacked stone, and the ceiling had rough-hewn wood beams. It wasn't that the room looked old, just rough, like it was intended to be a food cellar or a horse stall, not a bedroom. Garrett let his gaze fall to Coach. Even in the unfamiliar elven form, Garrett could see he looked bad, really bad.

"Coach? Can you hear me?" Garrett asked.

No response.

Garrett approached the cot. Now that he wasn't fleeing for his life, he had time to actually take in the strange appearance of the creature. He was so different, with his blue-grey skin and strangely shaped eyes and ears. They looked as though they belonged to a wolf not a human. Even stranger were his eyelids, shaped like a sideways *s*, that swooped out and faded away where his crow's feet should be. His eyebrows, nose, and jawline were defined, with hard edges. He didn't look particularly like any elf Garrett had ever seen in movies or books. He was very tall, not short, and his skin color didn't fit that of any elves he had seen depicted either. Only his pointed ears fit Garrett's conception of an elf.

Garrett leaned forward and touched Coach lightly on his shoulder. No response.

James frowned. "Careful, Garrett."

Garrett frowned back and shook Syldan gently. "I'm here, Coach. I'm here."

Syldan opened his eyes and smiled weakly. "Brick."

James hurried forward to take up position next to Garrett.

Syldan shifted his golden yellow eyes toward James. "Ah, your… brother… he doesn't like me."

The others came forward too.

Lenny offered Syldan a drink from a glass that sat on the crate.

"Thanks," he said, taking a small pull as he appraised Garrett and cleared his throat. "You look good for a dead kid." Syldan smiled, weakly. "You know I tried… Garrett, I tried to save you from the worst of it… but I guess your Keepers had it right after all… Whatever was going to happen was going to happen no matter… no matter what."

James leaned in. "How do you know about the Keepers of the Light? How do you know about the prophecy?"

"Back off, James," Garrett said, putting a hand against his chest.

"It's okay, Garrett," Syldan said fixing his golden eyes on James. "James is a good man… a good brother. You are lucky to have him in this. You need to understand his mistrust. After all, my own brother almost killed him once before. But I am a friend. You see, long ago… I was a friend to Turek … when he walked the earth before the Keepers of the Light ever formed, before the Knights Templar, even before Egypt was Egypt and the word *pharaoh* was ever spoken. I helped Turek cast Apep into darkness. I placed the Elder Dragons in the seven tombs. I listened as Turek cast the spells that tied his blood" – he pointed a long finger – "your blood, Garrett, to the nephilbock and the dragons."

James's eyes grew wide.

"That's right, James, I heard Turek's plan from his own mouth thousands of years before you were even a tingle in your papa's pants. I have been here since the beginning. Not idly waiting either. No, I have lived thousands of human lives on this planet, all the while wondering why the gods wouldn't let me age, wouldn't let me just grow old and die." Suddenly Coach squeezed his eyes shut and grunted out a pained cry.

"Coach!" Garrett shouted.

"The pain will… pass." He winced, then drawing a few slow breaths, he continued. "By the gods, a death in battle with my men would have been the sweetest death. I have served in thousands of armies and fought hundreds of wars. But as time continued its relentless tick tock… I began… I began to think it wasn't the gods keeping me here. It was one god, Turek. I started to think he wanted me here for the day Apep finally unearthed the God Stones and broke the spell waking the nephilbock and the dragons. I convinced myself he wanted me here to save you from the worst of it. Now, after what happened and what my brother told me in that temple, I understand the reason I never died and still live now."

"Why?" James pressed.

"In the tomb, Apep said time isn't linear and that no time will have passed on my world since the last time the gate was opened. That was over twelve thousand years ago! This means my father will still be alive. My bloodline will still be in power. I am the rightful heir to the throne."

"I don't understand," Garrett said.

"It's okay, Garrett, in time you will. What I am about to give you, you must believe it… all of it." He slipped his long-fingered hand beneath his blanket and retrieved a crudely folded piece of parchment. With a shaky hand, he pushed it toward Garrett.

Garrett reached out and gently grasped the paper. As the parchment slipped from Syldan's hand, what remaining color he had drained from his face and his visage took on a new grimace of pain.

Syldan turned his attention back to James. "You feel… you failed… failed Turek when you could not… save him from… my brother."

"Of course I do! He died because we couldn't stop Apep!" James said angrily.

Syldan reached for James. Extending a long arm and finding James's wrist, he squeezed it assuredly. "Let go of it, James. You did not fail… Turek died, but he did so by choice… so that one day *his* people… led by *his* descendent… the blood of *his* blood… the one reborn of dragon… blood and fire, could, with the help of his own chosen sages one day set right… a wrong from long ago. That's what this is about, James. It's about taking your people home and fixing the wrong." Syldan gasped and began coughing uncontrollably as he turned his gaze to Garrett's hands. In his fit of hacking, blood began to seep from the corner of his mouth, a bright trail of violet making its way down onto his chin.

Finally, bringing the coughing fit under control, he drew in a slow, shaky breath and studied the runes on Garrett's hands like a medium might study the lines of a person's palms before telling them their future. "Very good."

"You know what they mean?" Garrett asked hopefully.

"What do they mean? They mean a great deal… they are dragon runes… that I know of… no human has ever… been marked with… with dragon runes."

Garrett wanted to scream. He had had enough of riddles with the journal and enough of mystery with the God Stones. He just wanted some straight answers, but Coach was clearly in a great deal of pain.

But Syldan only nodded and closed his eyes. "All of you, listen to me," he said, forcing his hand to lift, to beckon them close.

David and James knelt down next to Garrett and Lenny, who had already taken a knee. The single lantern lighting the room cast a portentous glow that reflected a strange hue off the face of the elf.

Syldan drew in a long breath and looked at each of them in turn as he spoke. "The prophecy was only the beginning. The ushering in of the events to come. I would never have guessed Apep would assemble the stones so soon. Only two times were the stones assembled. Only two times, but both times they were used to open the gate soon after. Now it seems my brother will use them to do much more. I am not sure how the Sound Eye will react over time on this planet or how this planet is reacting to the Sound Eye even in this very moment. I know what the prophecy says comes next. At some point in the coming months my brother will open the portal home, and you must be there when he does." He settled his eyes on James. "Let go of your burden,

James. You… have a new… burden to bear now. Do for your brother what… I could not do for mine… help him follow his path."

James swallowed and nodded.

Syldan's strange yellow eyes bore into Garrett's own as he held his gaze. "I'm… afraid I can't… stay any longer…" He shifted his eyes to David and smiled. "Thanks for trying to fix this old soldier, David, but I have fought my last battle."

Tears spilled freely down David's cheeks despite his efforts to keep them in check.

"Listen to me, all of you," he said, his eyes now fixed on Lenny. "You boys must do this together… Win or lose, the sages stay together… no matter how bad it gets. You are all Turek's chosen. Remember that… all of you. Syldan grabbed at Lenny and pulled him close. "Lenny," he rasped, his own eyes filling with tears now, "I am so proud of you. Never forget that." The dökkálfar smiled and squeezed Lenny's hand. Then he closed his eyes. "I'm going… home."

Lenny's mouth pressed tight, but his brow hinted at confusion.

Garrett's eyebrows knitted together. "Coach! Wait! Please!"

Coach Dagrun – the dökkálfar elf, Prince Syldan, son of King Vulmon Loravaris, named heir to the throne of Osonian, Dragon Master, military war hero, and cross-country coach – exhaled his final breath and died.

James pulled the blanket up and gently covered Syldan's face.

Except for the soft sound of David's muffled sobs, the room fell into a heavy silence.

Garrett finally broke the stillness by unfolding the paper Coach had given him. Inside the folded parchment was what looked like a large gold dollar coin. It was round and golden but way thicker than a coin. On both sides were weird markings.

"Let me see it, Garrett?" David asked, pawing at his eyes. He studied the object for a moment, flipping it over in his hand. "It's covered in runes like your arms."

"What does it mean?" Lenny asked.

David's mustache, wet with tears, twitched. "I have no idea. I can't read elvish runes. But I bet it is a magical item of some kind."

Lenny snatched it from David, frowning as he studied the strange symbols. "Maybe the note says something about it." He nodded toward the paper.

Garret began to read.

Garrett,

I don't know how much longer I can hold on, so I write you now in case I don't make it to see you again. I live on the corner of North Twelfth and Harris. In the basement of my home, on the east wall, is a tunnel that was part of the Underground Railroad. It's covered by wood paneling that you will have to remove to gain access. Go inside and follow the tunnel as far as you can. There is a small room at the back. In the room, next to a desk, you will find an old trunk and inside it a diary. I want you to have it.

I began writing it some time ago in the hopes I could pass it on to my own child someday. I see now this will never be, so I ask that you take it. It will contain many answers you seek. But be warned, you will discover truths inside that may change your opinion of me. I won't make excuses for everything I've done and can only say I have made difficult decisions that I thought were in the best interest of those involved. Keep what you learn to yourself until the time is right. When that time comes, I know you will do the right thing.

The Eyra of Tunga is one of the few items I brought with me to this world. Someday, you and your sages may find it useful.

—Coach

The room fell quiet for a moment that seemed to stretch out. Garrett reflected on the time he had spent with Coach. The first day he met him, and just a few days ago when he'd made him captain of the cross-country team. Finally, he raised his head, "Goodbye, Coach."

"Bye, Coach," Lenny repeated.

"Bye, Coach," David choked out.

Lenny drew in a deep breath and rubbed a hand across his face. "Well, that letter was pretty ominous."

David sniffed. "So we have to go back into a tunnel to get another book. One that you probably won't like reading. You're kidding, right? This sucks ass!"

"Well, we found out the name of this Eyra of Tunga thing," Lenny said, turning the golden object over in his hand, "but we didn't get any answers."

James nodded. "True, but it tells you where to find them. We still have time before dark if we go now. Well? Anyone up for a trip across town, Keeper of the Light style?"

"Garrett, you up for it?" Lenny asked.

"Yeah," Garrett said, glancing back at Coach, his still shape unmoving under the sheet.

"Don't worry, I will have his body carefully removed and prepared for a funeral pyre," James said. "It's what he requested."

They filed back out into the hallway, where the two guards were talking to a large man dressed in camo BDUs and white tee shirt.

"Paul!" Garrett shouted.

The two clasped hands and pulled each other into a bro hug.

"I heard you were awake! Are you all caught up on what happened?" Before Garrett could answer, Paul looked to James. "I finished my assessment of the Undertown's rear quadrant. It isn't bad but I see a few things we could implement immediately that would make a big difference." He turned back to Garrett.

Garrett nodded. "Yeah, I think so."

"Good. I am hoping you can tell me your plan for finding my sister," Paul said in a serious tone. "I have been bouncing off the walls waiting for you to wake up. Do you know where she is?"

Garrett blinked. "I… I…"

James held out a hand. "He just woke up, Paul, and Syldan just died. Give him some time."

Paul frowned, a protest building in his eyes.

"We are going to Coach's place. He left a diary there. Maybe it will contain answers. Join us."

Paul nodded. "A diary? Yes. That could be helpful."

James led them through what Paul had referred to simply as Undertown. The catacombs wove under not only a good part of downtown Petersburg, but also snaked back into the bluffs as well. James explained, "Many of the narrow tunnels lead to the Keepers' homes. This allows us to move in secret, meet up, strategize, and prepare without being noticed."

"And keep an eye on me?" Garrett asked pointedly.

"Protect you," James countered.

Garrett decided to let that go for now. "But why the secrecy? Isn't the whole town in on this?"

"No," David answered quickly. "Pete's mom wasn't and neither was my dad."

"My parents were. That's why I was being trained at night too," Lenny said.

Garrett thought this made sense since Lenny had to train but Pete didn't. He assumed now David didn't either. "Wait a minute, David, so where does your dad think you are?"

"Oh, he knows now. Now that I'm one of your sages, James had him brought into the fold."

"And he was good with it? Just like that?"

"No, he took some convincing, but with the world going crazy out there and our even crazier story, he is convinced. At least convinced enough to stay."

"What about Pete's mom?"

James shook his head sadly. "You know Pete's mom is engaged to Jack's dad. Pete went to her and tried to tell her the story. I think she wanted to believe Pete, but Jack's dad wasn't hearing it. Pete ran off. We found him and brought him in. As for his mom, she ended up going to the police. But the ones who aren't Keepers or aren't already dead from their run-in with Apep have their hands full out there. They don't have time or resources to worry about a missing kid right now. The last report we had on her, she had gone to live with Jack's dad, and we haven't heard from her since."

Jack – there was a name he hadn't thought of since waking up. "Has anyone heard from Jack or his brother?"

"I had some of your men scouring the river. They found two older men dead a couple miles past the dam. No sign of Jack or his brother. It isn't likely they made it either, Garrett. The Sangamon tends to hold on to its dead. Frankly, I was surprised it gave up the others so soon," James said.

A cold chill ran down Garrett's back. *Thanks to Lenny, it hadn't held onto him.* It would be fine by him if he never saw the Sangamon again as long as he lived.

James stopped, motioning toward a ladder. "Here we are. North Rutledge is about as close as I can get us to Syldan's. We are going to have to hoof it from here. Once we get topside, stay close and follow me."

It was the first time the sun had touched Garrett's face in over ten days. They beat feet through a yard and into the woods, where an old set of tracks used to run through but had been pulled up long ago, leaving only a gravelly trail.

"This way," James said, but then drew up short. "There!" he pointed. "You see what I mean?" Cutting across the old railroad tracks was a swath of turned-up earth about fifteen feet across. "That's got to be a tree trail," James whispered. "C'mon, let's keep moving."

Off to their left they could hear the sound of breaking limbs and rustling leaves.

James held up a hand and they stopped again.

They stayed still, listening, but the sound seemed to be moving away from them.

"Let's go!" James whispered urgently.

"I don't like this," Paul announced.

"Yeah, this is freaking me out, man," David said.

"Eyes up front, David. Don't look back," James said as they ran forward.

A few minutes later they climbed the stairs to Coach's. They tried the door and it opened. The house wasn't very big, but it was old. They didn't need to go past the mud room to find the entrance to the basement and once in the basement they found a false wall. They ripped the paneling away, revealing the entrance to the old tunnel. The tunnel was small, and they had to duck their heads to navigate it, but they didn't need to go far to find the little room. Just as Coach said, there was a small trunk. Garrett opened the trunk and, sitting right on top of some framed war commendations, sat a plain-looking notebook. It was old, probably as old as Garrett, but in comparison to Coach it was written yesterday.

"Okay, let's get out of here," James said.

Soon they had crossed back through the woods and over the railroad tracks. This time all was quiet, but the tension was still thick. Once in the tunnel they began to wind their way back toward the heart of Undertown.

"James, what is the wrong I am supposed to set right exactly?" Garrett asked.

"Thank you! That question has been eating at me," Lenny said.

"Me three," David said.

James stopped and turned completely around to face them. "You have to lead your people to the portal, Garrett, and then you have to lead them home."

"Then what?" Garrett asked.

"Apep will open the gate with the God Stones. When he does you will lead us through, back home to Karelia. Karelia is the planet we came from, but long ago something happened. Something bad enough it must of pissed off all the other gods because Turek fled with whatever humans he could from Karelia to Earth."

"But why? Why did he leave?" Lenny asked.

"From what we know, something happened between Turek and the other gods. A disagreement. Garrett, you are the one who will lead us home and set things right."

"Um, James, does the prophecy say what exactly I am supposed to do? Do you know where this portal even is? Am I just supposed to start walking and you guys are all going to follow me? Tell me you have a better plan than that? Because that sounds like a stupid plan."

James frowned. "Don't mock Turek, Garrett."

Garrett was tired and he had no interest in fighting with his brother again. "James, honestly, bro, I'm not mocking anyone – I'm just saying I don't understand this. You lied to me, told me I was supposed to stop Apep, when you really knew I was going to die! Now you tell me you want me to lead all these Keepers to another world and we don't know where the door is? Then what? We walk through? Pretty sure Apep will be there along with a massive army of giants and dragons. So then what, James? Does going through the portal just fix things? Does that 'set things right'? I just want to understand the plan, James."

"Faith, Garrett. We wait for a sign. Perhaps you will have a dream, or a feeling, and you will know what to do."

"What? Everyone is going to sit around and wait for me to have a feeling? You realize he took Bre? Right? You realize right now she is with him if he hasn't… hasn't…"

"Don't you dare say it!" Paul said. "You were asleep for ten days! You didn't have one dream about Bre?"

"Well, he was talking to her when he woke up, but I don't think that's the kind of dream we're talking about here," Lenny offered.

Garrett flushed. "You want me to sit here under the ground and wait for a sign!? I can't do that, James!"

"You promised me, Garrett. You promised you would find her," Paul said.

"I know what I promised, but I don't know where she is, Paul!" He didn't mean to yell, but the frustration and the weight was too much.

In the distance, from a connecting corridor, feet clapped off stones, getting louder as a runner approached. From around the corner a man appeared. Garrett instantly recognized him as Yogi, who had been guarding Coach's room earlier.

Yogi slid to a stop, breathing hard as he bowed. "Sir! Our men brought someone in. Two someones actually. They are asking for Garrett," Yogi said, his eyes flicking to Garrett, then to Paul, then back to James.

"Well, who are they?" James demanded.

"Two Black men, sir. The younger guy is jacked and looks military. He's with an older guy in a fedora, his dad I think. He claims to be Breanne's father. He is demanding to speak to Garrett. Sir… he says he knows where Apep is!" Yogi said, his eyes flicking nervously back to Paul.

"My pops is here!?" Paul said, pushing past them.

James nodded, turned to Garrett, and smiled. "I told you, little brother – faith."

54

Forgive

Saturday, April 9 – God Stones Day 4
Rural Chiapas State, Mexico

Breanne was in an all-too-familiar place – a frozen moment of horror. The worst song in the world played on the radio as cold winter air blew across crimson crystals of shattered glass. Her mother had been hurrying because Breanne had forgotten her stupid violin and they had to go back. Why? Because Breanne was throwing a fit. She absolutely couldn't be late for this recital. She would be devastated. All her friends would see her show up late. She was yelling at her mother, "God, Mom, just hurry, would you!"

"Young lady, you're overreacting. It will be fine! We won't be *that* late."

"No! No, it won't be fine, Mom! I can't be late! I can't believe you forgot my violin!" Breanne shouted.

"Breanne! You are responsible for remembering your instrument. Now, I won't have you speaking to me like this. I will turn this car around right now!" her mother said, taking her eyes off the road long enough to give Breanne *the look.* But before her mother looked back to the road, something happened – the car lost traction and slid. Her mother gasped and yanked the wheel hard – too hard. The car went into a spin and suddenly Breanne was upside down, metal was scraping, and she and her mom screamed as windows shattered, peppering her with broken glass.

When her world finally stopped coming apart, her own scream faded and everything went quiet until all she could hear was a cold wind blowing through the car, that horrible song, and her ragged breaths as her heart beat out of her chest. Dazed, she stared down at the roof of the car as she hung there, suspended by the seat belt. She couldn't understand where all the red diamonds scattered across the roof came from. But as she watched, the red diamonds became lost in a quickly growing pool of red liquid. "Mom?" she moaned, twisting her head to look across the narrow space between them.

She shouldn't have looked, but she looked, and she saw, and she could never unsee her mother's eyes staring back at her, unmoving, fixed in death – a death she caused over a stupid middle school recital that no one would remember.

Breanne had lived this moment over and over in her nightmares for the last five years. The two of them suspended upside down by seatbelts, the cold wind, the red diamonds, her mother's lifeless body draining of its blood. She slammed her eyes shut, refusing to look. She had looked once, and it had ruined her. "God! Why? Why did you take her! Why didn't you let me die! Oh god, why! Why?!"

These were the questions she had begged to have answered over and over for five years.

Then something very unexpected happened. A voice *answered.* But the voice wasn't god.

No, Breanne. This wasn't your fault. Do you think this is what your mom would have wanted? Would she have wanted you to blame yourself for an accident? People need you here… now. I need you, Bre!

The seatbelt cut into her neck, and she couldn't breathe. *Gabi? Is that you?*

Tell her, Bre! Look at her and tell her!

She didn't want to open her eyes. She didn't want to feel her guts eaten raw by the guilt of it. "God, please!" she begged, but the same god who let her mother die then didn't answer now. Somehow, in her silent agony, she knew the answer – she had to open her eyes. She had to face it straight away – and so she did. She forced her eyelids to peel back and look into her mother's dead eyes. "I'm sorry!" Breanne screamed. "I'm sorry for making you rush. I'm… I'm sorry for what happened… for what I did! God, I'm so sorry!"

Her mother's eyes, clouded in death, blinked slowly, clearing to find her in their focus. "Oh, Bre," the dead woman said. "You never needed my forgiveness. You just need to forgive yourself. I love you. I always loved you. You need to live. You have too much ahead, too much depends on you. Now go, leave this place in the past where it belongs, and don't come back!"

"I love you too, Mom!" Breanne said, the words echoing as the moment became somehow less real and more dream.

The woman hanging next to her smiled. "Oh, my little Yanni, my baby, of course you do. Now go!"

The present moment rushed back. Breanne blinked, gasping in short bursts, tears running down her face. Her knees felt weak and for a second, she thought she might go down.

"Are you okay, Bre?" Gabi said from beside her. "Did I say something wrong?"

"No." She breathed, finding her legs. She looked over at the girl's face. She was fine. Gabi was fine. "Gabi, I just had a flash." She shook her head in confusion. "A flash of the future, but this time it was so strange… this time I think you…" She trailed off, noticing a fallen tree lying across their path.

"The future? This time? What do you—"

Breanne held up a hand, silencing her as she frowned at the long shape. This was no sensation of déjà vu – this was more. This was the vision from before. "Gabi," she said quietly, "that isn't a tree."

As the words left her mouth they were drowned out by a loud hiss from off trail on the other side of Gabi. Breanne gasped sharply. Her heart leapt as fear grabbed her, but she didn't hesitate, not for one second. No car crashed and no horrible Christmas song played. There was no shattering glass and no red diamonds.

Breanne grabbed Gabi, jerking the girl back with one hand as she stepped in front of her and ripped the pistol from its leather holster.

The giant snake struck out, it's mouth opening to reveal curved, spiked fangs dripping with venom.

The 9mm rose upward in one smooth motion as Breanne covered it with her left hand and racked the slide. Leveling the gun, she fired as fast as she could pull the trigger.

Bullets ripped through the snake's mouth and out the back of its head as its forward momentum carried it into Breanne, knocking her off her feet.

Breanne kicked at the viper's scaly face, pushing herself back as she scrambled to her feet. She released the spent magazine into the dirt and fumbled with the other magazine, finally shoving it into place with a click. She leveled the gun at the snake again, but it was over. The snake was dead.

Overcome with emotion she dropped her shaking gun hand to her side and began to cry. It wasn't the brush with death pulling her tears. She didn't freeze up! She kept Gabi safe and she didn't freeze!

Gabi took her hand. "Thank you, Bre. You saved me," she whispered.

Breanne looked at her with knitted brows. "Gabi… were you… were you in my… my memory?"

Gabi returned her confused look.

In the distance a door slammed, and dogs barked.

"Did you hear that?" Gabi asked, looking down the dirt road. "I think that's the farm up ahead."

Breanne thumbed the safety on the pistol before sliding it back into the leather holster. "Jesus, we made it," she said, smiling. But in the back of her mind the question still nagged. Was Gabi there, in her memory somehow, or was it a creation of her own mind?

"Bre?"

"Yeah?"

"Will you tell me about your mom sometime?"

Breanne gasped, searching the girl's eyes as if they would reveal the answers to a thousand blossoming questions. Finally, she drew in a deep breath, letting it out slowly, and smiled. Then she said something she would never have thought she would ever hear herself say. “I’d like that, Gabi. I’d like that a lot, but only if you tell me about yours.”

Gabi smiled shyly and nodded.

Not for the first time nor the last, Breanne grabbed Gabi and embraced her in a tight hug. “Come on. Let’s get the hell out of here.”

The two girls ran toward the sound of the barking dogs and hope.

55

Family Reunion

Saturday, April 9 – God Stones Day 4
Rural Chiapas State, Mexico

The girls cautiously made their way up a rutted drive toward a small farmhouse. Somewhere, far beyond them, the evening sun disappeared behind the mountains and into the Pacific. The small home was framed in red brick arches and stucco walls painted yellow. The whole thing was topped with corrugated tin sheeting that carried through onto the porch, which was held up by rough-cut oak timbers.

On the porch stood a slight-statured, mustached man, silhouetted in candlelight cast from the open door behind him. His expression was that of suspicious curiosity. He looked to be in his seventies, slender but sturdy. As the candlelight spilled out onto the porch so did wonderful aromas of cooked meat, spices, and warm tortillas. Breanne had not realized until that very moment just how hungry she was.

The man yelled something back over his shoulder. Breanne didn't catch it all, but she caught the name Juan and then Gabi.

Gabi ran forward and onto the porch just as another man appeared. This man looked like a younger version of the older man.

Gabi and the man embraced in a hug, followed by a flurry of Spanish Breanne couldn't keep up with. The man looked at her, then at the gun on her hip, and began speaking fast again. Gabi went into some explanation, the man nodded, then she caught another name – Sarah – and that's when Gabi burst into tears.

"What is it, Gabi?! What about Sarah?! What did he say about Sarah?" Breanne begged, stepping up onto the porch. There was another flurry of words.

"It's Sarah! Breanne, she is alive! She is alive!"

Breanne smiled and turned to the younger man.

"I'm sorry, Breanne, right?" Juan asked. "I have heard Sarah speak of you, and Fredy…" He trailed off for a moment, looking away. He drew in a breath. "Fredy used to talk about your father often. This is my father, Carlos," he said, pointing at the elderly man.

His English was very good. Way better than her Spanish, she thought. "It's nice to meet you, Juan. Do you have a phone?" she asked.

Juan shook his head sadly. "Yes, we have one, but it is of no use. There is no power for anything electrical. Nothing works, not the vehicles, the home electricity, phone… nothing."

Breanne and Gabi exchanged worried looks.

"It's the God Stones," Gabi said. "They are interfering with the magnetic fields of this planet. It will be this way everywhere."

"God Stones?" Juan asked.

"Ogliosh told me about them. He said the longer our planet is exposed to them the worse things could get, and since Apep connected them to… what did he call it? A Sound… Sound Eye! That's it! It's going to happen even faster. Connecting them increases their power and he should only have done that when the pyramid was ready for them to open the portal."

"Ogliosh," Juan said slowly, testing the word. "Who is this?"

"The giant in the pyramid," Gabi said matter-of-factly.

To Breanne's surprise, Juan nodded. "Every time Sarah wakes, she only wants to know about you, if we've found you. When she talks, she tells of the dragon and giant and you, always you. She said the last she knew you were up on the mountain with the giant," he said, pointing. "As hard as it is to believe I knew she was telling the truth. I didn't see the giant or dragon for myself, but when things below the mountain went bad, the whole place sounded as though it was coming apart. Manuel appeared, screaming for rope. He ran back in and we tried to follow, but before I could get down the stairs we heard the dragon roar. Heat plumed up from below, and I thought everyone down there must be dead. We got out just before the whole place came down." Juan looked down at his feet. "Manuel didn't make it out."

"I know, I saw him fall…" Gabi said quietly.

An uncomfortable quiet grew between them.

"How is Sarah?" Breanne asked.

"She's hurt pretty bad. Broke both legs, one of her arms, and some ribs. Mamá said she thinks she bruised some organs too, and she isn't sure about internal bleeding. She says it's too soon to rule it out. That would be the biggest worry – well, that and fever. We set the broken bones best we could as soon as we got her back here, and she has been in and out since."

Juan's mother, Rosa, a weathered woman, hardened and lean from years of farm work, appeared on the porch, wearing a long skirt and colorful blouse. She smiled politely at the two girls, then looked at Carlos and Juan disapprovingly, pointing at both of them as she rattled off words Breanne knew were scolding.

"Mamá says we are being rude. Please come in, you must be starving. Besides it isn't safe out here. We have been seeing… well, strange insects flying around all afternoon."

"Strange how?" Breanne asked, fearing she already knew the answer.

"Much bigger than they should be. Now please, come inside."

As Breanne stepped inside, she and Gabi shared knowing looks.

"Juan, can we see Sarah?" Gabi asked.

"She is in a room in the back resting. I will take you to her, but let's get you two washed up and fed first."

As the girls went to wash, Rosa disappeared and soon the smells of more food being prepared fill the air. Almost everything Rosa served was grown, harvested, and processed from the farm. She had soaked the farm-grown maize in a water and lime mix before grinding it into masa and forming the tortillas by hand. Breanne watched her as she squatted in front of the stone hearth, dipping each tortilla in water before dropping it into the cast-iron skillet. With practiced precision, she carefully charred each side to perfection before flipping it and repeating the toasting process on the opposite side. Next, she loaded it with beans that she had reduced into a smooth creamy deliciousness earlier in the day. On the side, she served a spicy salsa topped with fresh avocado and cilantro, and rice flavored with tomato, garlic, and onion. The main course was goat meat that had been cooked down in a pot of unknown ingredients until it was tender, practically melting in Breanne's mouth. Despite the spicy heat of the chiles, she couldn't stop eating.

Once the two had eaten themselves practically sick Rosa ushered them off, not even allowing them to help clean up.

"Come, I will take you to Sarah," Juan said.

"Sarah?" Breanne said, stepping softly through the doorway. The room was small, with a wood-planked floor. A small wooden table with a single candle sat casting a flickering glow over a still form.

As Breanne and Gabi approached, the woman's head turned slightly. Breanne tried not to show a reaction to seeing Sarah's face. She was almost unrecognizable. Half her face was badly bruised, her nose was slightly twisted, and one eye was swollen shut.

"Oh! Breanne?! Gabi?! Is that really you? No, no of course this can't be real, you can't both be here. Not unless… unless I'm dead? Yes, and you are my angels. Oh, god, please let this be heaven!"

The woman's voice came in a slur, whether from some medication or the swollen face Breanne couldn't tell, but the sight of Sarah brought both girls to tears. "Sarah, we are really here, and we are going to get you help!"

"Gabi, I thought for sure… I thought…" Abandoning the

thought, her eye darted back to Breanne. "If you're here, then your father? Where is your father, Bre? Oh please, I want to see him too!"

"He isn't here, Sarah. He's… Well, he's… It's hard to explain, but he isn't here."

Half of Sarah's face frowned in confusion, and she turned to Gabi. "I'm sorry. Gabi, I'm sorry I couldn't save them! Sorry I was in such a damn hurry to know! God, I'm sorry!" Sarah said, her open eye blinking back tears.

"No, Sarah. This is no more your fault then it is mine. We were all right where we wanted to be. No one could have known. The ones to blame are the dragon… and the giant," Gabi said, a hardness in her voice.

Breanne looked at the girl anew. There was something in Gabi's tone, something she hadn't seen until now – a hatred, deep and angry.

Sarah tried to smile at them. "You are really here?"

Gabi fished into her pocket and pulled out the long gold chain with her mother's ring on it. She slid the ring off, stuffed it back into her pocket, and held out the chain.

Sarah lifted her unbandaged hand shakily, gently clasping the chain. Then she looked at Breanne. "Do you know who this belonged to?"

Breanne nodded, reaching out to touch the chain. "My father – he gave it to you when we were in Egypt. I was with him when he bought it." She smiled at the memory. "I remember he was so nervous, Sarah. We must have spent the whole day looking for the perfect necklace for you."

"Yes. God, I miss him. I remember that day he gave it to me…" She shifted in the bed. "Did you feel that?"

Breanne's eyes knitted together. "Yes! What was that? Gabi, did you feel… There! I felt it again!"

Gabi let go of the chain.

"It's so weird. It's gone now but for a second it felt like…" Breanne shook her head. Then for some reason she thought of the snake and the memory of her mother and Gabi talking to her. An idea occurred to her. "Gabi, take the chain again, please!"

Gabi reached out and put her hand around the chain, right

between Sarah and Breanne's. "There it is again! I feel… I feel my dad! Like he is sitting right next to me!"

"I feel him too!" Sarah said.

Gabi sat still for a long moment with her eyes pressed tight. She opened her eyes and looked from Sarah to Breanne. "He said he is glad we are all safe, and wants to know how you got here and where your brother Paul is?"

56

Band of Holes

Saturday, April 9 – God Stones Day 4
Pisco Valley, Peru

Bright light faded from Apep's vision to reveal a barren landscape of loose, rocky soil. He found himself in the Pisco Valley, staring up at one of the most mysterious places on earth, the Band of Holes.

Just another of the many forgotten details of human history, the Band of Holes consisted of over six thousand holes, a meter deep and a meter wide, placed in neat rows of eight that marched up the side of the remote mountain the Spanish had named Serpent Mountain. A fitting name for something humans had no memory of creating.

The holes stretched back before recorded time, leaving the short-lived humans to come up with all kinds of preposterous theories, like that it was a mass grave. Their stupidity was almost comical, Apep thought. *How does one conclude six thousand open holes are graves when not a single one has a bone in it?* The explanation was so obvious. For a species that had been so close to complete annihilation to forget what it was that had almost destroyed them and where they came from was, well, idiotic.

The humans spent hundreds of years investigating empty holes, but did they ever once think to look around at the other mountains in the valley? Of course not. If only they had picked a mountainside, in any direction, and dug. They wouldn't have even had to excavate very deep. But what did they do? They dug in empty holes. Fools.

Apep could have teleported the mile to the top of the mountain but instead he decided to walk. He wanted to think. Something was nagging him. Besides, the tips of his fingers were tingling and his joints felt like they were… stinging. He had been using so much power there were bound to be some – well, minor side effects. Nothing to worry about, but perhaps it was better he saved his energy for what was to come.

After waking from his long, forced nap in Egypt in 1050, he spent years fighting the mage Turek until finally killing him but not before he'd hidden the God Stones out of reach. He spent several hundred years whispering in the ears of humans like Tesla and Einstein, helping them advance. Later still he funded the creation of a massive mining and construction equipment company, pouring money into their research and development department, so he would have the technology he needed to retrieve the God Stones once he learned where Turek had hidden them. But even with the best equipment money could buy, he knew he needed more than technology. Turek had been clever for a human. He had hidden the stones deep inside the bedrock itself. Still, Apep had been smarter. He hired his own clever human, Dr. Moore, and then finally the God Stones were his. Then came the boy – the descendant of the mage and his ridiculous prophecy of a chosen one. But he had killed him too, hadn't he?

This was Ogliosh's fault. All his talk about the human being one of the gods. Could he be right? Could Turek really have been one of the seven gods? The god of humans? "Then why would the human god let you kill him? That's what you should be asking yourself, Apep," Ogliosh had said. Syldan had mentioned this too. *Suppose there was truth to it. Then what is Turek playing at? If he were one of the seven gods, he could have just killed me years ago. He could have killed the dragons and the nephilbock. Why the dramatics? No, this can't be… mustn't be.* Yet still the thought nagged.

As soon as Apep reached the top of the mountain he found what he was looking for. *It seems all the dragons managed to escape their prisons with the giant. Well, except for Sylanth, the one Garrett killed.*

The great scaly beasts were spread out across a stretch of steeply sloped mountainside. Each dragon exhaled bursts of flame onto the barren ground – ground already devoid of all moisture and life. It reminded Apep of the nightshade desert on Karelia, minus the shadow creatures that lived in the loose soil. Gods, he hated this place.

Azazel and the others had wasted no time getting to work heating the soil and raising it to impossible temperatures. What lay dormant beneath the soil, undisturbed and undiscovered for centuries, would only stir under the perfect conditions.

Long ago when Apep first led them through the portal, the dragons and their queen sought out a perfect place to lay and hide thousands of dragon eggs. As it had turned out, the rocky soil combined with the perfect altitude and climate of Peru's Pisco Valley formed the ideal place to bury, incubate, and hatch dragon eggs. And so, with the enslavement of over a thousand indigenous humans, the dragons buried tens of thousands of eggs. Unlike egg-laying creatures of earth, dragon eggs were fertilized by the male's dragon fire. With the conditions perfect, over time the dragons began to hatch – and grow. Once the dragons learned to fly, they began to feed insatiably, ushering in a dark period in humanity's history known then as the Dragon Wars – a period that, of course, humans didn't remember.

Such a shame, Apep thought. He would have so enjoyed seeing the Dragon Wars at their peak, but he'd slept through it. What he deduced, based on the open holes stretching up the mountain, was that nearly seven thousand dragons must have hatched and been roaming the earth at the height of the Dragon Wars. What he never understood was how the humans bested them. His working theory was that the dragons were exposed to something on this world and had succumbed to it. Perhaps some kind of deadly virus. Of course, now he knew the truth. The dragons' defeat was only achieved with the help of his own brother… Syldan. Thinking about the deceit made him feel foolish. To think, he'd actually believed it possible that humans had somehow managed to defeat dragons on their own. He could see now the idea was ridiculous.

The walk up the slope, the fresh air, the time to think and reflect, left him feeling good. He knew what needed to be done and he was ready. He spoke the words of power, and the light consumed him, transporting him two peaks over, a safe distance away from Queen Azazel's breath should she try and annihilate him on sight.

At the sight of Apep the dragons stopped their work, rushing up the slope to take up positions on both sides of Azazel, ready to defend their queen.

The light around him faded as the elven wizard fell into a casual walk toward Azazel.

"What do you want, dökkálfar?" Azazel asked in her strange dual voice.

Apep held up his hands. "I came here to help you, Queen Azazel."

The queen's forked tongue flicked out like a snake tasting the air. "And why, pray tell, do you think I require your help?"

The other dragons hissed and cursed. "Kill him!" one said in a voice that sounded as though it belonged to a snake.

"Yes! Smite him, my queen!" another said, its voice filled with strange, cackling laughter, as if something hysterically funny had taken place.

"Smite the dökkálfar with fire and watch him burn," another said. This one's voice was strangely musical and angelic, as if the heavens opened and an angel began to sing. But the voice was a stark contrast to the menacing monster's appearance as it sneered with its long, yellowed teeth, dripping saliva.

Apep felt himself becoming annoyed. The Sound Eye crown atop his head began to glow. "Before you try and cast me away with your pathetic dragon fire, you should know I have united the God Stones and now possess the Sound Eye!"

"Yes – we feel the power, but you should know, you cannot possess the Sound Eye, dökkálfar! You can only hold it," Queen Azazel said.

Apep swept his arm out, gesturing at the assembled dragons. "Well, *I* hold it! And with it I can destroy you all."

The dragons slowly formed a circle around him. "Are you sure, dökkálfar?" Queen Azazel asked. "Are you sure you can destroy us? I feel the Sentheye surging in me too… What's to stop me from just reaching out and taking it from you?"

The other dragons laughed and urged their queen to take the Sound Eye.

Let her try! Apep thought, staring at the queen unflinchingly. By freeing the queen and a handful of others from slavery under his father's rule and bringing them here, he thought they would obey him, but they had not. They had built their army and attacked the humans, but not at his bidding. *It's of no matter. Damn them all. I will kill them all if I have to. By the gods I swear, no one will take the crown from atop my head.*

He turned, focusing his attention on the dragon closest to him, still laughing and cursing. He vaguely remembered this one from Karelia, but its name escaped him. It was a magnificent beast, the largest of the six dragons, even larger than Queen Azazel. Its scales sparkled a brilliant metallic blue. Apep narrowed his eyes at the dragon, allowing his own face to contort as he sent the Sentheye forward in a dense gush toward the dragon. The thick liquid shadow wrapped around the dragon's neck like an oversized lasso. Suddenly its toothy face became a wash of sheer terror as its eyes bulged under the ever-tightening squeeze of Sentheye.

But the Sentheye didn't stop constricting. Once any hope of capturing a breath was stolen, Apep held out both fists and twisted them in opposite directions as if ringing an invisible rag. "What's the matter? You've stopped laughing. Am I no longer funny!?" The Sentheye began to twist the beast's neck unnaturally, and its head began slowly turning backward. The dragon tried to scream as blood vessels in its eyes burst – but no sound came.

On Apep's opposite side a red-scaled dragon screamed. Its scream was not a pained cry, but one of pure rage, building to an angry roar that could only mean one thing. The Sound Eye glowed bright, alternating colors as it appeared to distort his own face. Apep held out an open palm in the direction of the red beast. Fire shot from the angry dragon's mouth like water shooting from an oversized fire hydrant. The blast of liquid fire churned a trench into the ground as it swept toward Apep, set to swallow him in an all-consuming flash. Nothing on earth

– whether manmade molten iron from a foundry ladle, nor natural lava from the heart of a volcano – could compare with the liquid hell barreling toward him.

Yet the elven mage did not panic, or flee… or burn. Instead, the dragon fire changed shape, narrowing into a fine stream thick as a sturdy rope. The rope of spectacular dragon fire streamed into the wizard's hand, disappearing as easily as a long ribbon in the hands of a magician. But this was no sleight of hand with a ribbon.

The midnight-blue dragon's eyes rolled back in its head as its neck continued to twist.

Without releasing his grip on the Sentheye, Apep reeled on the fire-breathing dragon, seething. He would teach these insolent beasts to dare breathe fire in his direction. He opened his mouth and roared until the fire he had absorbed through his hand burst from his mouth in a crescendo of grey-blue flame – dragon fire laced with Sentheye.

All the dragons' eyes went wide as the red-scaled dragon scrambled backward, trying to escape the flame – but it could not. In a panic, it halted its retreat, opting instead to use its own wing to shield itself. But the wing caught fire and the dragon cried out in agony, falling to the ground atop its wing in an attempt to smother its burning flesh.

"Enough!" Azazel shouted.

Apep shot Azazel a smug sneer as the ground around him smoldered, casting him in smoky shadows. His vision blurred, his hands tingled, and his whole body felt strangely – what? Singed. He felt the weight of the crown pressing down, resting heavily against his ears. The Sound Eye – so much power sat atop his head, but it was all his. He alone was destined for greatness. Destined to be the most powerful being in the universe.

Apep turned back to the midnight-blue dragon, continuing to twist. He wanted to keep twisting until its insolent head separated from its body.

"I said enough!" Azazel shouted again.

Apep released the blue dragon from the grip of the Sentheye.

The dragon collapsed to the ground in a heavy heap, dry soil clouding up around him as he released his breath into the dirt and began gasping greedily for air.

Apep stepped forward through the fog of smoke smoldering up from the scorched earth and spoke in a stern voice. "Queen Azazel, if you want to live, I implore you to listen to my next words very carefully."

The dragons circling Apep froze in place, motionless. No longer did they taunt. No longer did they laugh. They were silent now. Their queen too was silent. Apep looked from one to the next, taking time to lock eyes with each. Each looked at him in return, then turned their gazes down to the dirt. They were afraid – as they should be.

There could never be peace between his people and dragons, nor did he ever wish it. As such, he knew better than to try and make promises of peace with them now. "You will listen to me and you *will* do as I say, or I will strike you down here and now!" he bellowed, his voice echoing down the mountain. "In a few months' time I will open the portal back to our world. I will overthrow my father with an army of overwhelming force!"

Apep began pacing. "On our planet, many of your kind are slaves to mine. If you want to free them you will bring your army of dragons through the portal and wage war against my kingdom. Once my kingdom is defeated, your kind will be freed and you will go, leaving my kingdom forever, or so help you I will use the power of the Sound Eye to rid Karelia of dragons for all time. I am not threatening you, queen of queens. I am promising you." Apep paused for effect.

Azazel's nostrils flared.

"But it needn't be that way," Apep said, softening his tone. "Karelia is big enough for all of us, but you must obey me now. What happened in the past is the past. My brother Syldan caused you this grief. He and the human mage destroyed your dragons and placed you in the deep sleep with your enemies. I too was cast in sleep. I escaped, I took the God Stones back, and I freed all of you. Most importantly, I killed the mage and… I killed my brother."

The dragons shared unsure looks.

The queen's eyes narrowed as she leaned forward. "Dökkálfar Syldan is dead?"

Apep nodded. "So you see, you have no reason not to trust what I am telling you." Apep held his palms out, then clenched them into fists. "However, you also have no reason not to believe I will do whatever it takes to claim my kingdom."

As all eyes fell to Azazel as she stood silent for a long moment. "And what of our God Stone, dökkálfar? Am I to believe you will return it to me when you are king?"

Apep forced a wide smile to stretch across the sharp features of his face. "Of course. When this is over and I am king, your God Stone shall be returned."

"We want to go back to Karelia – to our kind, to our home. We want our dragons freed. However, what you ask is impossible – we cannot wage a war on the dökkálfar army in mere months. We would need years to prepare. We have thousands of eggs here. We must incubate them and then grow our young. If we go in only months, our young would not be hatched. We would have to abandon them. Your people will use enslaved dragons against us. With only six of us, your army will lose, and we will die or become enslaved. No, dökkálfar. I think not. We will stay here. There are many more humans here now for us to feed on. No, we will rule here."

Apep couldn't contain his smile and beamed ear-to-ear. "Queen Azazel, what if I told you I can offer you both an army of dragons in a few short months and this whole world to feed them with?"

Azazel flexed her long wings wide and then folded them in upon themselves. "Explain yourself!"

"Perhaps it would be better if I showed you." He stepped toward the slope and the dragons parted. As he drew near he felt the heat from the soil penetrating his boots. Closing his eyes he spread his arms wide and began to chant. Despite the pain in his joints and tingling in his hands, the Sentheye came forth when called and snaked from his fingertips down toward the ground, forcing its shadowy blue-grey tentacles into the earth.

The dragons gathered behind him, watching quietly as the ground began to quake. A sound like that of breaking bone rang out. First one loud crack, then another, then more. The dirt began to move down the slope as dragon hatchlings pushed free of their shells and up through the rocky soil. First two rows of eight, followed by four more rows, then six, then eight, then ten. The sound of the fracturing eggs changed to the sound of screeching young.

Apep stopped chanting when one hundred hatchlings had broken the surface.

Azazel looked to the Sound Eye crown atop Apep's head. "You can do this with all my young?"

"I can do better," he said, beginning a new chant. The Sentheye came rushing from him as it had in Mexico, blue-grey fog drifting down the slope. The hatchlings stopped screeching, breathing in the Sentheye, feeding on it. In seconds they had grown to fledglings – then, stretching their wings, they became juveniles.

A juvenile in the fourth row spit fire, flapped its wings, and lifted off the ground.

Apep involuntarily dropped to one knee as exhaustion overtook him. He quickly forced himself to his feet, hoping the distraction of what he had just done was enough to keep the dragons from noticing, as it wouldn't be wise to show weakness in front of the queen of queens.

Azazel turned to him. "Impressive. Can you hatch them all?"

Apep nodded. "Not all at once but, yes, over the next few weeks I can grow your army."

Azazel turned to a silver dragon. "Ahi, rally the juveniles and take them to town to feed. After, gather as many humans as they can carry and bring them back here. It's time we start enslaving our own humans."

Ahi nodded. "Yes, my queen." He flapped his wings as he lifted from the ground.

Azazel turned to Apep. "Why did we not do this from the start?"

"You know why, Azazel. The nephilbock would not allow me to join the God Stones until it was time to open the portal," Apep said, shielding his eyes from the dust stirred by Ahi.

"But they have changed their mind now?"

"They have seen the wisdom of my decision."

"And you can build them an army too? They don't have eggs. Can you simply turn humans into slave monsters for your army?"

No, only you can turn humans into obedient slave monsters, Apep thought, knowing he couldn't command creatures by simply altering them. But Azazel didn't need to know that. "I don't need to. They have an army in the tens of thousands and they are already at my command."

"Interesting. And where is this army hiding?"

"Azazel, that is of no matter to you. You serve me. They serve me. If you want to war with the nephilbock, you will wait until after I have my kingdom. Now, do you want me to grow you an army and lead your dragons into war and out of slavery, or will you settle for this tiny world while your dragons back on Karelia stay enslaved to me for your failure to obey?"

Azazel's hateful eyes bore through him. "I will join you in this campaign, young king, but I serve no one less than the god Typhon herself!"

"Whatever," Apep said, waving a hand. "I need one more thing."

"What do you want, dökkálfar?"

"Your general, Sylanth, wasn't killed by the nephilbock it was bound to but by a young human boy. I believe I killed him, in turn, but I need you to send a dragon to be sure."

Azazel lowered her head down to meet Apep's eyes. "You expect me to believe a human child killed my general? Even if that were possible, you were there, and you did nothing?!"

"Careful, queen," Apep said, taking a step forward. "I was there and I did plenty, but I was dealing with many other humans and an angry nephilbock. Sylanth wasn't exactly in a good mood when they woke either. The boy who killed Sylanth was the descendant of the mage who helped my brother imprison you. His name was Turek. Do you know that name?"

"Yes. He was the mage of old, the one we battled."

"Yes, but had you heard that name before coming to this planet?" Apep asked.

Azazel hesitated, then said, "No. Not before this planet."

"You hesitated. Are you sure, Azazel? You never heard the name before coming here?"

"That's what I said!" Azazel looked away into the distance and her next words came softer than Apep had ever heard her speak. "Sylanth was a rare two-headed dragon. In their own way they were like a queen, very rare. Only one born in five thousand." She turned back to Apep, her voice now sharp as a steel blade. "Where is this boy who killed my dragon general?"

"I killed him," Apep said. "But there was a lot of commotion and I didn't see his body in death. I need to be sure."

"What do you require?" Azazel asked coldly.

"I need you to send a dragon to make sure. I want you to torture every human in the town if you have to and when you finish, I want it burned to ash. If the boy is found alive, I want him killed and laid at my feet so I can see for myself. After, he is yours to consume."

"And if he is already dead?"

"If you find the body, bring it to me. I want to see it. Either way, feast on the town. Leave no one left alive. For good measure burn every town around that one while you are at it."

"Repair Goch's wing and I will send him and six juveniles. We will find this boy if he lives, and we will kill, eat, and burn everything else."

Apep frowned at the red dragon and his shriveled wing devoid of all scales, his flesh charred to the bone.

"Kings must be good for more than destruction," Azazel said.

Apep rubbed his fingers together and called upon the Sentheye to repair the wing, much like he had used it to repair himself over the last few days of battle. Everything was coming together better than he could have hoped. He would stay here, let the dragons deal with Petersburg. He had a dragon army to grow. In the meantime, Ogliosh would prepare the pyramid and his army would work their way up from the center of the earth.

With the nephilbock at his command, Queen Azazel falling in line, and his earthly enemies defeated, there was nothing to prevent him from opening the portal and going home to claim his birthright and take his place on the throne of Osonian.

I'll be home soon, father. I'll be home soon.

57

Follow Your Heart

Saturday, April 16 – God Stones Day 10
Petersburg, Illinois

Garrett entered the "war room" as his brother called it, to find a rotund older man sitting next to a younger guy who he recognized instantly to be an older, more muscular version of Paul. Both men sat on the far side of the really long table in the otherwise stark room. They looked like they had belly-crawled through hell to get here. Neither had seen a razor in some time, and their clothes were tattered, as if they had been living on the street for months.

Elaine was there, sipping a cup of tea and chatting with the men. She turned to the door as he entered the room. "Garrett, do you know who these men are?" she asked, motioning to them.

Garrett nodded, wide eyed. "You must be Dr. Moore, Bre's dad! And that means you must be her other brother, Ed!"

From behind Garrett, Paul entered the room.

The two men lurched upward as chairs toppled.

"Paul! Jesus Christ, boy! You're alive!" the older man shouted, throwing his arms around Paul.

The younger man threw his own giant arms around both of them.

"Bre said you were dead," he said, his eyes glistening and threatening to spill over.

"What? Breanne! You've talked to her? Is she with you?!" Garrett asked, searching the men's faces.

Dr. Moore shook his head, trying to catch his breath. "Slow down, everyone, just slow down." He wiped his eyes. "So you're Garrett. *The* Garrett. You don't have to call me doctor or mister, you just call me plain old Charles." He turned back to Paul, both hands on his son's shoulders. He squeezed them. "I… I never thought I would see you again, son."

"I'm okay, Pops," Paul said.

Charles looked back to Garrett. "And this is my oldest son, Ed."

Garrett looked at Ed and nodded, but there was something about the way Ed looked at Garrett that made him feel like he didn't like him… not at all.

"Who are your friends?" Charles asked.

"This is Lenny and David. They know Bre too," Garrett said sheepishly. "Did you say you talked to Bre?"

Ed cut in. "I want you to tell me what happened that night, Garrett. I want you to tell me in your own words what happened." He pointed accusingly across the table. "I want to know how you let Bre get taken by that psycho if you're supposed to be some kind of chosen one!? That's what I want to know!"

Paul spoke up. "Now hold on, Ed, you weren't there. Garrett went back for her, he tried—"

"And what about you, Paul? Bre thinks you're dead. How could you leave without her?" Ed asked.

"Like I said, you weren't there. Once Apep magicked himself out, there wasn't really shit we could do but try not to die and live long enough to find Bre after!" Paul said.

Garrett looked from Paul to Ed, focusing on a vein bulging from the side of his neck like a swollen garden hose about to burst.

"Ed. Stop. We talked about this," Charles said.

"Stop?! How can you—"

"Who opened the ark, Ed?" Charles asked. "When Bre begged me not to, who opened it!? If you want to blame someone for all this, you blame me, dammit!"

Garrett blinked back tears as Breanne's father's eyes filled and dumped wet trails down his face.

"I'm sorry!" Garrett shouted. "I never wanted any of this. I tried to get to her. I tried to get her to run to me, but she wouldn't or couldn't." He shook his head back and forth in frustration and looked to Paul. "I… I begged Paul not to go back, but he wouldn't listen to me and if he had listened, we would all be dead too! I couldn't save our friend Janis when the dragon burned her alive, I couldn't save Mr. B, I couldn't save my dad! I couldn't save anyone! Now he's got Bre and I don't know where he is! I don't know what I am supposed to do!" Garrett slammed his fist down on the table as the tears came and flowed openly. He forced himself to look up and meet Ed's eyes. "I'm sorry, I'm sorry for all of it."

Elaine made her way around the table to comfort him. Garrett waved her off.

"I believe you did everything you could do," Charles choked out.

Ed's face fell and he sat back in his chair.

Garrett looked up and met the man's eyes. "When you saw Paul, you said Bre said he was dead. What did you mean?"

"I know where my daughter is," Charles said, looking at Garrett.

Garrett lifted his head and traded glances with Lenny. "What? Where? Is she alright? Does Apep still have her? Is she far? Is she hurt? Is she—"

"Alright, slow down, Garrett," Charles said. "Let me start from the beginning, and I will tell you everything. For me this starts in a hospital bed in Nova Scotia the night Apep connected the stones and the whole world went dark. For some reason I don't understand, when those stones connected, I woke up. Albeit with a horrible headache, a fuzzy memory, and a quickly fading dream, but I was back. We didn't know what to do next. Ed's compound fracture healed within twenty-four hours of being broken. Some effect of the God Stones." He gave Ed a sideways glance. "So, my only thought was getting out and finding Bre and Paul. Ed remembered hearing them mention the land of Lincoln, Petersburg, and a kid named Garrett, and so we got out of there and started for Illinois."

"But how did you get here so quickly on foot?" James asked.

"We weren't on foot so to speak. Look, I would rather not get into it, but let's just say the ability to heal isn't the only thing that Ed here ended up acquiring from the God Stones."

"I can sort of fly," Ed said.

"You can fly, Ed?" Paul asked.

"Wait, what does that mean, 'sort of fly'?" David asked, making no effort to hide his excitement.

"It means not very long, not very high, and not very good," Charles said.

"I got us here, didn't I?" Ed said defensively. "Besides if it wasn't for me, we would never had made it past the dragons."

"Dragons?!" James said.

"Dammit, you're getting ahead, Ed. Tell it right or let me tell it," Charles said.

Ed motioned for his dad to continue, and everyone else leaned forward.

"I hadn't been on a bike in years, but you know what they say, it's like riding a bike. When we were on the long stretches of clear road, Ed was able to fly a foot or two off the ground with a rope tied from him to the bike and we hit some incredibly dangerous speeds. We hit the dirt a few times too, trying to figure it out but, luckily, we were able to get here in one piece and in pretty decent time. We could have been here sooner, but we had to use the river to sneak past the dragons. If it wasn't for Ed's ability, I'm sure I would have drowned."

"What are you talking about dragons? We haven't seen any dragons," James said.

"Are you people not sending scouts out?" Ed asked.

"Of course but... Well, to be honest, we haven't had any return in the last several days. I expected this, what with the trees moving and their orders to go further out, but what are you saying?" James asked.

"I'm saying we didn't see any dragons until we got to within fifty miles, then we saw our first and we tried to go around, then we saw our second, so we went further afield. Then we saw our third, and that's when we realized they are surrounding this town. They are closing in and burning surrounding towns. You are being surrounded and cut off from everything. It's only a matter of days before they reach this place."

Paul and James shared a look.

"Haven't you guys seen the smoke in the far-off distance?" Charles asked.

"The world has gone crazy without power, so we figured riots in Springfield could be the cause of the smoke. I sent a two-man team to check it out," James said.

"Well, your two-man team is probably dragon food," Charles said.

"And that's if the trees don't kill them first," Ed said.

James's eyes widened. "The trees? We've seen them moving, but they are attacking?"

"Have you been down in this hole too long or what?" Ed asked.

"Ed, knock it off. These folks have actually created a pretty defendable and sustainable bunker down here," Paul said.

"The trees haven't attacked, at least not in mass, not yet, but they are mobilizing and if I were a tree come to life, I don't think I would care too much for humans," Charles said.

Uneasy looks traveled around the table.

"Trees are alive and mobilizing?!" David shook his head.

Garrett absently listened to the information about the dragons and the trees. Everyone was talking all at once, asking questions, but his mind was somewhere else. All he wanted to know about was Bre. "Mr. Moore?"

Everyone fell silent.

"Just Charles," he said.

"Where is Bre and how do you know where she is?" he asked.

Charles nodded sagely. "There is this girl, Gabi. She was exposed to the God Stones after Apep left Petersburg. She has the ability to take an object that two people have possessed, or I don't know maybe even just touched, and somehow connect them." Charles held up his hands and interlocked his fingers. He launched into the whole story, telling Garrett and the others all about Gabi, Ogliosh, Apep, Azazel, Sarah, and Bre. When he was finished, he sat back and said, "I've talked to my daughter every day for the last seven nights. Sarah is getting worse. She is bedridden and has come down with a fever. She needs antibiotics and pain medicine, but Bre tells me they have nothing there and the area is overrun with giant bugs, snakes, monkeys – you name it."

"But how is that possible?" Lenny asked.

"Apep. The last Breanne knew he was on the mountain with Ogliosh. During her escape she saw a blue-grey fog, then she noticed the bugs and had a run-in with a giant snake. She described howler monkeys larger than any gorilla in existence."

"Great, just what we need – a bunch of King Kongs!" David said.

"The night before last, she said an iguana attacked and killed one of the ranch hands," Charles said, his forehead creasing. "Last night for the first time in seven nights, she didn't communicate. I'm worried sick. Listen, Garrett, I don't know what you have planned but Apep is going to open the portal using that pyramid in Mexico. I don't know how much longer Sarah can hold out and I don't know how long my baby girl can fend off all these… all these dangers. I would like to know your plan and how soon you are going to make your move."

Elaine placed her cup of tea on the table. "We are prepared to weather all of it – dragons, giants, trees, and whatever else Apep tries to put in our path. We have over a thousand followers, ready to march behind the chosen, the one reborn of dragon fire and blood." She pointed at Garrett and smiled. "Show him your arms, Garrett."

Garrett's face reddened as he turned to James. "How long before we can go?"

"Your call, Garrett. When we leave is up to you, but if what Mr. Moore is telling us is true, we should wait until the dragons finish their search and move on. In a couple weeks when it's safe, we can move out. This will give us time to prepare for the journey. We have horses in underground stalls. Enough for those who can't walk. We have wagons too, to sustain us for the long journey."

"You can't be serious!?" Ed shouted.

Charles held up his hands for calm. "What my son is saying is surely you don't plan to wait weeks after what we just told you? My daughter is in imminent danger! Sarah may die if we don't get medicine to her soon. The journey will take weeks, maybe months. And you want to wait even longer!"

"Please, Charles, try and understand this is bigger than us. It's bigger than all of us!" Elaine said.

"Bigger than two little girls that have already lost so much?!" Charles replied.

"I knew this was a mistake, Pops! We wasted too much time on this!" Edward said, standing up from the table.

Paul stood. "Everyone, just calm down."

"There is no time for this, son. Your sister needs you!" Charles said.

"Please, don't be foolish!" James said. "Stay with us and we will go together."

"Didn't you hear anything we said?!" Edward's face was flushed with anger again. "My sister will be dead before we get there!"

Garrett's face furrowed. He looked at Lenny, who wore the same confused expression. It was like looking in the mirror.

"I don't see what more there is to discuss." Charles stood. "Edward, Paul, go – get your sister, Gabi, and Sarah."

"And what about you?" Edward said.

"I will stay here and travel with this group."

"But Pops!" Ed started.

"Ed, I won't make it. I barely made it here. I am too damn old and slow. Besides, to get to that part of Mexico, they may need a guide. It's up to you. Just get your sister and help Sarah."

"We will stock you with provisions, provide you meds, and arm you. I am afraid that's all I can offer," James said. "You should get some rest now and leave when it's dark."

Ed nodded, then looked at Garrett. He didn't speak and if Garrett thought the giant man didn't like him before, he was sure now.

Paul looked at Garrett expectantly.

Garrett couldn't hold his stare, and he didn't know what to say. This all felt wrong, but it was happening so fast.

"This is the right decision," his mother said, placing a hand on Garrett's shoulder. "Your people need you, Garrett."

"Come with me – I will show you where you can rest," James said, nodding towards the Moores as he headed for the door.

Garrett glanced up in time to see Paul shake his head and turn away. He felt sick.

The two other Moores followed.

"Boys, leave Garrett and I for a moment, please," Elaine said.

When Lenny and David were gone, Elaine turned to her son. "Close the door."

Garrett closed the door and returned to the table, sitting back down across from his mother. She picked up her cup and took a sip.

"You know this is the first time we have really been alone since you woke up this morning. So much has happened. Did you get the item you sought from Syldan's?" she asked.

Garrett laid the diary on the table. "Yeah, I got it."

"Already, today, you have woken, Syldan has died, and the Moores have shown up, disclosing the location of Apep and with it the destiny of mankind." She paused to look sideways at him. She placed a finger on the rim of the cup and began to move it slowly around the lip. "How are you?"

Garrett frowned at the absurdity of the question. He thought about that for a long moment. How was he? He was pissed off. He wanted to yell at her, *I am damned pissed!* He wanted to tell her she was horrible for doing this to him. Horrible for lying to him. He wanted to tell her that he didn't trust her, that he didn't trust any of this.

Yet somehow, he knew the prophecy was real. He knew this was all really happening. He thought about Breanne. If her own brothers didn't save her, she would be dead long before he got there. And what would she think of him then? The boy who didn't try to save her. His stomach turned as a voice spoke in his mind. It was a memory from the cave… when he thought he would never see Paul again. *Promise right now, that if I don't make it, you will find my sister and you will save her from that bastard!*

Garrett had made that promise not understanding the burden he now carried for a thousand others. *If it is the last thing I do I will find her. I promise I will. I swear it. Whether you make it or not. I swear it!* He had known Breanne for one evening but it felt like he'd known her his whole life, and now she might die because he couldn't save her in the cave and he couldn't save her now.

"Garrett?" his mother said.

Garrett blinked up at her. "Sorry… I… I was just thinking."

"Care to share?"

"What exactly does the prophecy say I will do?"

Elaine looked curiously at him. "It says you will lead your people home. Back to the planet we were cast away from."

Lead my people home? "It says that specifically?" Garrett asked.

His mother's frown deepened. "No, it says, *The one of me, flesh and blood of my flesh and blood, the only male descendant of me. The one named Garrett. The one who died and was reborn of dragon fire and blood. The one who is reborn bearing the mark will lead his people through the portal and put right what was made wrong so long ago.* There, satisfied?" his mother said. "That's word for word."

"What does put right the wrong mean?"

"Ah, yes, that is the question. No one knows. It isn't written. Perhaps leading us home rights the wrong done to humanity and nothing else will be required."

"Or there will be more to this," Garrett said.

"Perhaps, but you will know what to do when the time comes."

"But how?"

His mother smiled and for a moment it felt like it used to, before he knew she was someone else. "Your heart will lead you."

Garrett nodded slowly and stood from the table. "I'm tired, Mom. I think I should get some rest."

"You sure you are okay?"

"Just tired – it's all overwhelming."

"Of course."

He turned to leave when his mom said, "Garrett?"

"Yeah?"

"I love you."

"I love you too, Mom."

Garrett found Lenny, David, and Pete waiting outside.

"Pete!" Garrett said, throwing his arms around the boy.

Pete hugged him back and smiled. "Glad to see you decided to wake up."

"Are you okay? I mean, I heard about your mom and stuff."

Pete shrugged. "It is what it is."

But Garrett could tell it wasn't okay. There was something different about Pete – something besides the fact he didn't wear glasses anymore.

"You find your rat today?"

Pete looked at Lenny and shook his head side to side, then back to Garrett. "Who were those guys I saw walking with Paul?"

"They were his brother and dad. Turns out Bre has been talking to them through some telepathic girl," David said.

"Seriously?" Pete asked, raising an eyebrow.

"Seriously. So come on, Garrett, out with it. What's the plan?" Lenny asked.

"You know the plan. You heard it. In a couple weeks we leave and get these people safely to the portal. When Apep opens it, everyone is going home."

"What? Look, I'm all for exploring a new world, but what about Bre?! What about the promise you made Paul!" Lenny said.

Garrett glanced uneasily over his shoulder. "Go get some rest, guys. We'll talk more tomorrow." He turned and began walking.

Lenny grabbed Garrett by the shoulder and spun him around. "You're just going to let her die? How could you!"

"What do you want me to do, Len? Her brother is bigger than the three of us put together, he apparently heals super-fast and can fly. He has Paul, who has super-strength. I think they have a better chance than I do! I am needed here for this! What do you want me to do!?"

"Just when I thought you were starting to grow a sack, you go all coward on me! I want you to find your balls, Garrett – that's what I want!"

"I got to go," Garrett said, glancing at David.

David looked away.

"Yeah, whatever!" Lenny said.

When Garrett was almost to his room, Charles Moore stepped out from a shadowed nook. "Garrett, can I have a word?"

Garrett's stomach tightened. "Sure."

"I didn't want to say it in front of the others, but Breanne wanted me to make sure you knew her being taken wasn't your fault. She told me all she needed to do was run to you, but she couldn't. She froze. It wasn't your fault. You see, something happened to her a long time ago and sometimes she freezes up. She doesn't talk about it... ever. But she wanted me to tell you. He mother died when she was eleven years old in a car accident."

Garrett looked down and shook his head. "I should have got to her. Whether she was frozen up or not, I should have got to her." Garrett looked up. "I'm really sorry about her mom."

Charles shook his head. "Yeah, me too. Garrett, listen, my Bre, she knows something about guilt and how it can eat you up. She wanted me to tell you this for a reason, and she doesn't talk to anyone about what happened to her mom, not even family."

Garrett nodded. "Thanks, Dr. Moore. I best be getting some rest."

"Um, Garrett. One more thing." Charles looked both directions down the corridor.

Garrett frowned.

"When I was in a coma, I had a dream about the Templar we found in one of the caverns on Oak Island. He called himself Turek. Then he asked me to give you a message. To say the least, it was odd being asked to deliver a message to a kid I never met from a dead Templar in a dream, but here we are."

"What did he say?" Garrett asked eagerly.

Charles took off his fedora and ran a hand through his curly hair. "He told me to tell you to follow your heart, and your heart would lead you down the right path." He put the hat back on his head and tipped the brim toward Garrett. "Best get some rest."

Garrett continued to frown, but nodded. "Take care, Dr. Moore."

"Just Charles," the man said, turning away.

Garrett didn't stop at his room and instead went past it – towards the utility and supply stores James had shown him earlier. But before he got there a door opened. Garrett started to hide but then he realized it was Pete.

"Pete?"

"Isn't your room back that way?" Pete asked.

"Yep, hey you sure you're okay?"

"I'm going to tell you something, Garrett, but don't tell the guys."

"Okay sure, Pete."

"I been down to that river every day looking for that rat. Paul told me it had golden eyes like Janis. And it carried him out of the tunnel. I don't know – I just thought if I could find it, maybe she is trapped in the rat somehow… and maybe, just maybe, we could find someone who could change her back." He looked up, then back down. "Sounds stupid, right?"

"No, Pete. It doesn't sound stupid at all."

Pete smiled thinly. "Well, today you woke up and today I found that rat."

"And what happened, Pete?"

"It had strange golden eyes just like Paul said. I tried to talk to it. To see if maybe it would talk back."

"And did it?"

Pete shook his head. "No, and you know what else?"

"What?"

"The damn thing hissed at me."

"So not Janis?"

"No, that's just it," he said, taking a step closer. "It was. At least some part of it was."

"I don't get it, Pete."

"She wanted me to stop, Garrett. She wanted me to let her go. Don't you see? Because if I couldn't let her go, I might not be able to do what comes next. And do you know when I was sure? When I walked in and found out that the same moment I found her, you were opening your eyes for the first time in ten days."

Garrett swallowed and took a deep breath and let it out. *What comes next,* he thought.

Pete smiled and it wasn't thin or forced. It was a bright smile, a true smile and it was good to see. "So, should I go get the guys?"

Garrett returned the smile and nodded. "Yes, you should absolutely go get the guys."

"Where we meeting up?"

"The supply room."

Pete nodded and headed off down the hall.

The sun would set soon and a few hours later Ed and Paul would be heading out into the night. Garrett rummaged through the supplies, retrieving a tactical backpack, clothing, and rations. He packed a fire-starter, a few maps, and a water bladder. He found tactical military-issued running boots too. He had never worn boots like these running before but figured if they were good enough for the military, they would be good enough for him.

The door to the supply room burst open.

"You son of a bitch!" Lenny shouted, running into the room with David and Pete on his heels. "I thought you were really going to let Paul and Ed go it alone!"

"I wanted to tell you, but I couldn't be sure who might be listening. Listen, I know you guys are all excited about this, but it is going to be incredibly difficult and we are going to need to move fast."

David's mustache twitched disapprovingly. "I get it, I'm not the fastest, but I am one of your sages too, Garrett, plus this Sarah lady needs me. If we can get there, I can heal her just like that," he said, snapping his fingers. "And what if you get hurt along the way? Did you even think about that? Suppose you twist an ankle or worse. What then, you going to limp to Mexico?"

Garrett waved his hand. "David, if I have learned anything, it's that we have to stick together. All of us! No more of me running off on my own." He slapped David on the shoulder. "It has to be all of us or none of us!"

David wrapped him in a hug, pressing his mustache against Garrett's shoulder.

"You better mean that," Lenny said, "because I haven't forgot how you ditched me in the tunnel. I'm still going to bust you in the balls for that. You won't know when, but it's coming." Lenny stepped up, hugging both boys. "Get in here, Pete. David, you little freak, keep your hands where I can see them."

Pete piled on and the four hugged. And it was in that moment the knot in Garrett's stomach went away and he knew he was following his heart.

When Garrett opened his eyes, James was standing in the doorway. "What do you think you are doing, Garrett?"

The four broke apart.

"You know what I'm doing, James."

"You're supposed to lead us to the portal and back to our home—"

"Yeah, please stop," Garrett said, cutting him off. "Mom told me word for word what I am supposed to do, James."

"So, what the hell are you doing?"

"The prophecy says I am supposed to lead them *through* the portal not *to* the portal," Garrett said, slinging the backpack over his shoulder.

The others went to the shelves and started packing their own gear.

"Are you trying to play semantics, Garrett?! These people won't make it to southern Mexico if you aren't with them!"

"Yes, James, they will make it. Because they will have you leading them."

"What?"

"You're a leader, James. You always have been. I have been awake one day, and I would have to be blind not to see it. James, these people will follow you anywhere. I mean, crap, I would follow you anywhere. Just do your nine-hundred-year-old James thing and you will be fine, and they will be fine. And if this prophecy is legit, we will all meet up at the portal, but I can't wait. I *can't wait*, James. Everything inside me is screaming at me to go! I have to listen to my heart. I have to go today… Right now!"

"It's the girl, isn't it? You are doing this for some girl you knew for a day?"

"James, she's way more than that. She is one of my sages. She is one of the seven who pledged to follow me. I made promises – promises nothing is going to stop me from keeping! So, you have to lead them – you have to get them to the portal safely."

"Garrett, I don't know how to do that!"

"Yes, you do. Stick to your plan and wait out the dragons and then make for Mexico. You have been planning this out for hundreds of years – Undertown, horses, wagons, provisions."

James shook his head. "You're really going?"

"Yes. What do you think me leading would look like? Let me tell you. I would have been saying, James, which way? James, should we stop and camp or keep pushing? James—"

James's serious face broke into a smile and he laughed. "Yeah, for sure you would have."

"Now just pretend I'm there with you, asking the dumb questions, and before you know it we will be in Mexico together." Garrett extended his hand out to his brother.

James reached past Garrett's hand, grabbed his forearm, and squeezed. "See, hundreds of years ago this was a proper handshake."

Garrett smiled, clasping his brother's forearm in return.

Then James yanked his brother forward and hugged him tight. "But this has always been a proper hug."

Garrett embraced his brother and slapped his back. "Mom is going to freak out."

"Yes. But once you're gone, I will help her understand. Nothing changes. We will meet you there."

"Can you wake Ed and Paul and let him know we're leaving?"

James nodded. "Anything else?"

"Can you get us out of here without Mom seeing us?"

James smiled. "I think I can handle that, little brother."

The four friends, born and raised in Petersburg, Illinois, prepared for the journey of their lifetime, an adventure that promised to take them across two countries and to the portal to another world.

No one knew how this was going to end, but Garrett knew, for the first time since this whole thing started, this decision was his and nobody was making it for him. Right or wrong it was his. Standing there in the low light of the supply room, watching his friends stuff gear into packs, it felt pretty damn right.

"Alright then, boys, let's go to Mexico."

Epilogue: Jack

Sunday, April 17 – God Stones Day 11
The Sangamon River, Petersburg, Illinois

Jack pushed the stick into the small fire and flipped the branch over. He grabbed another from the stack and tossed it on before sitting back down. Eleven days since that night. The night Garrett killed his brother. At first, he thought Danny *must* have made it out. After he'd dragged himself from the water, he screamed for Danny, screamed and screamed, but his brother didn't answer. He figured he must have gotten washed further down, that's all. So, when the pain settled and he could get to his feet, he started walking.

By the time Jack had gotten to the old busted dam, his throat hurt from screaming. He was freezing. He knew he had to find Danny, and fast, except he musta got washed over the dam and he ain't heard of no one living through that. But then no one was tougher than Danny, and if he knew anything it was that if he'd made it out, his big brother made it out too.

Making his way past the dam he'd forced his raw throat to keep on screaming. His whole body was shivering and the pain in his head was bad, but nothing compared to the pain in his testicles. That bastard Garrett might have broken one of his nuts.

He had rounded the bend in the river and made his way under the Highway 123 overpass, more than a mile from where they had gone in and still nothing. "Dan-ny!" he screamed out over the dark water as the tears began to come. He couldn't stop the tears, and he couldn't keep going. It was pitch black. His only source of light was the strange, lightning-filled sky, but it only came in strobing flashes. The rain was falling in sheets. He couldn't see for shit, and he had fallen repeatedly.

Without a plan Jack had found a relatively dry spot under the overpass where he could curl up in a ball. He couldn't go home, not without Danny. What would he tell his dad? Besides, he just couldn't do it. Home was a good two-mile walk. He was so cold. Somehow his lower lip was healed, but his face was still throbbing, and everything hurt. That night, he had been more scared than he had ever been in his life as he lay there and cried.

Morning had arrived, along with a strange dog licking his face. He forced opened his eyes in a squint of pain. It was a chocolate lab with a bright red collar. He blinked, realizing his legs and arms had practically gone numb from the cold. "Get away, mutt," he had said, as he reached out and put his frozen hand on the dog to push him back.

Something happened.

The dog cried out in a high-pitched yelp, but it froze in place.

Jack felt a warmth pull into his hand, like he had just reached into a warm bath. His hand stayed on the dog and the warmth drew up his arm and across his chest. The shirt he wore went from wet to dry as the warmth spread.

The dog whimpered softly.

Jack didn't pay any attention to the dog as he closed his eyes, feeling the warmth move up his swollen and bruised neck and into his head, while at the same time spreading down his torso and into his testicles. As the warmth radiated through his body, all his pain melted away. A moment passed and the dog quieted, and he felt… amazing.

Jack drew in a deep breath, let it out, and opened his eyes. He gasped in horror, yanking his hand back away from the dog. It didn't look much like a dog anymore. A good part of the lab's coat was missing, replaced with rotted patches of raw flesh, one of its eyes was dried up, and its teeth… Jesus, its teeth had fallen out.

The lab fell over, unable to stand. It looked like loose, rotting fur draped over bones. Jack stared, not understanding what had happened. The dog took a last labored breath and died. Jack looked down at his hand and back to the carcass. He pushed himself back away from it, got to his feet, and ran.

He ran as fast as he could along the bank of the river. He couldn't think about that dog and whatever… *that* was. He had to find Danny. That's all that mattered. Danny would know what to do. His voice was strong now and the sun was up. He yelled for Danny for the next seven miles, never once taking his eyes off the river. But as the hours passed with no sign of his brother, he feared he would have to turn back and go home. *That's it,* he had thought. *Maybe Danny went home? Maybe I missed him somehow.* The more he ran, the more he knew that must have been what happened, he simply missed him. He decided he would round the next bend and then turn back.

Looking back, he wished he would never have rounded that bend.

Something pale and bloated was poking out of a brush pile on his side of the river. It didn't look like a person though, not at first. But the closer he got the more his guts began to twist. When he was fifty feet away, he knew it *was* a person. But it couldn't be Danny – it had to be one of his brother's friends… not Danny.

At thirty feet away the water was moving so fast it looked like it might rip the body out of the brush pile. The body had Danny's hair color, but it couldn't be Danny! Tears began to flow down Jack's face as he walked numbly forward.

At ten feet away Jack could see the bloated and bruised face of his brother, and he dropped to his knees and screamed. "Danny! God, Danny, please! Wake up! Get up, Danny!"

Jack pushed himself up and waded into the current, grabbing his brother's bloated body and jerking him free of the brush. The Sangamon pulled back, sucking them into the current.

The next several miles, Jack had clung to Danny's body with all he had. He fought the river, trying not to get pulled under, but eventually the river won the battle, forcing him to let go of his brother or drown. Jack flailed frantically, screaming, "Danny!"

He would never forget the image of Danny's body as it rolled over in the current one last time and disappeared.

Jack had spent the next several days trying to find Danny again. He slept in the woods along the river, built fires, and ate what small critters he could find. He discovered that he could focus on animals such as squirrels and fish, and, if he did it right, he could infect their brain or their heart without tainting their meat. He ruined a few, turning them completely rotten, but it didn't take long for him to get the knack at targeting their organs once he puzzled it out.

After a while he knew, he was never going to find Danny. He also knew he never wanted to go home. Once his father found out Danny was dead, it would just be another reason for him to drink and beat on him. No, he wasn't going home.

Then, mourning the loss of Danny shifted his thoughts to Garrett. Garrett, who had humiliated him and killed the one person in the world he loved, Danny. At first, Jack didn't want to live, but now, eleven days later, he lived for one purpose – to kill Garrett. But he wouldn't just kill him straightaway. No, he didn't deserve mercy. Garrett needed to feel what he had felt. He would kill everyone he loved first.

Sanity had departed days ago, and what was left now was vengeful and broken. In the late evening of the eleventh day, Jack sat on a sandbar stoking a fire and talking with Danny. He wasn't sure when talking out loud to Danny had started or how it happened. "I'm going back, Danny! You hear me! I'm going back to find that son of a bitch Garrett Turek and his friends, and I'm going to make them pay! Lenny, Pete, and those outsiders too! All of 'em are going to pay for what they did to you, Danny! Garrett's mom, his brother, anyone who ever smiled at him, Danny! They are all going to die, and he is going to live to see it. Then I'm going to kill Garrett slow, starting by rotting his balls off!" he screamed out over the river, his voice cracking in rage as spittle flew from his mouth.

Behind him, beyond the sandbar, the trees stirred.

Jack spun. "Who's there!" he shouted.

Silence.

"I know you are there, by god – I heard you plain as day!"

From the woods a tree rushed toward him, its roots churning through the dirt as it pulled itself forward with surprising speed.

"Je-sus!" Jack shouted, backpedaling past his fire and into the river up to his knees.

The tree stopped in the center of the sandbar. "Boy!"

Jack spun around in a circle, looking for the source of the voice.

"Boy, where is Garrett Turek?" the voice said.

Jack looked up into the tree, trying to see if a person was in the branches, but then he realized the voice was coming from the tree itself.

"What? I… I don't know," Jack said, standing still in the water.

"Did you not yell his name twice? Did you not state your intentions to kill him?" the tree asked, its branches moving in multiple directions all at once as its newly budding leaves shook.

"He… Yes, but…" Jack straightened. "Yeah, that's right. I said I'm going to kill him and everything he loves. What's it any business of yours, tree?"

"Where is he? I have business with this human."

"What business do you got?" Jack asked.

"My queen desires an audience with him," the tree said.

The tree sounded real proper, like big city proper, and Jack didn't care for it. "Look, tree, if you want to kill him, you better get in line. And if you don't want to kill him, you best get out the way." Jack stepped up out of the water and onto the bank.

Jack looked up at the tree, his own way of looking someone in the eyes to show he wasn't scared and he sure as hell wasn't backing down. Except he wasn't sure where its eyes should be. He figured they must be up high somewhere, so he stared up, and that's when he saw the eagles. Least he thought they were eagles, flying right toward him in a flock. Which made zero sense, since eagles don't fly in flocks.

"I will ask you one more time, where is Garrett? Answer or suffer."

Those sure as shit were not eagles. Jack's eyes went wide as the definitely not eagles drew close and took notice of him on the sand bar.

The tree, which hadn't stopped moving its branches to and fro, suddenly froze still as a rock.

These were huge beasts, way bigger than any eagle, and as they slowed and began their descent, Jack felt a strong sensation to run. He knew what these were, what they had to be. These were pterodactyls. There were half a dozen, plus one really big one.

Sand stirred all around him as the beasts descended, their wings flapping. The big one was red and scaly, and now he realized it wasn't a pterodactyl. Its long talons sank into the sandbar as it stepped past the tree. The others looked like children compared to this one. They stood in a row, watching.

"What is your name, human?" the red dragon asked.

"Jack."

"Why are you screaming Garrett Turek's name?"

"You could hear that?"

"Answer me," the dragon said, huffing two bursts of smoke through his nostrils.

The air around Jack filled with the putrid smell of rotten eggs. Jack swallowed. "I want to kill him!"

The dragon stared down from over thirty feet high. "Where is Turek?"

"Probably back in Petersburg," Jack said, pointing upstream.

"Why then are you yelling for him here?"

"I'm not yelling for him! I'm… I'm angry and I want to kill him. Don't you ever yell when you're angry?"

"No. I burn everything when I am angry," the red dragon said.

"Kill the human," said one of the smaller dragons.

"Yes," hissed another. "Can I eat this one?"

The red dragon twisted his long neck back toward the younger ones. "Silence!" he bellowed. "Yes, the dökkálfar said he would be in Petersburg." He lowered his head. "I desire this human, Garrett Turek. Tell me precisely where he is and, perhaps, I will spare your life."

Jack swallowed again. "Are you going to kill him?"

"None of your concern. Now, answer me."

"Because I can help. I know stuff. I can find him. If you let me help, I can show you!"

"Enough!" the red dragon said.

Jack frowned.

"Kill him, Goch!" a brown dragon said.

"Oh, yes. Let me! Please, Goch, let me burn him!"

"No. The dökkálfar Apep said if Turek is alive he will be in Petersburg. You will tell us, or I will burn it from you – starting with your toes."

Apep? Did he just hear the word 'Apep'? Jack thought back to the night he met the man in the cloak. The night something in his head fractured. He asked the hooded man in the alley that night how he could find him, and the man had said he would know when the time was right and all he needed to do was—

"I tire of this." The red dragon opened his mouth and began to roar.

"Wait – Apep!" Jack shouted.

The dragon roar stopped, and all the other dragons fell silent.

"I... I know Apep... I mean I serve him."

Goch leaned all the way down, bringing his nose close to Jack's. "You serve the dökkálfar!?"

"He lies!" said the grey dragon.

"No! I'm not lying," Jack pleaded. "And I know something else too! You're not the only ones looking for Garrett."

"Who else seeks the descendant of Turek?" Goch demanded.

Jack looked over at the oak tree and pointed.

All the dragons turned to look.

The oak tree stood still as a statue.

"That big-ass tree was threatening me right before you guys showed—"

The oak tree spun, its roots ripping the earth out from under the row of young dragons like a rug being yanked from under a row of elephants. The sound of creaking and twisting wood screeched across the river as the tree thrust a sharp branch thicker than a baseball bat downward, through the chest of the closest dragon, killing it instantly.

Goch spun and leapt forward, wrapping talons around the offending branch, snapping it like bone. The tree shouted in rage as the young dragons got to their feet. The woods beyond the sandbar began to rustle and move as more trees began to make their way onto the sandbar.

Goch roared and let out a belt of fire. The mighty oak tree burst into flames.

All the young dragons began to flap their wings, lifting off the ground, but the grey one wasn't quick enough and in a final war cry the oak tree fell forward, pinning the young dragon beneath it. In the tree's final throes of death, it stabbed branch after branch into the smaller dragon.

Goch spread his wings.

"Wait, you can't leave me!" Jack shouted as the trees closed in.

Goch leapt from the ground, flew over Jack, and wrapped him around the waist in his long talons.

The young dragons circled, burning the woods around the stretch of river as they went.

"Tell me, human. How do we find Garrett Turek?"

"I'll do better than that. I'll show you."

Glossary

Ancient Language of the Gods

Ray doeeshozmue, rah ak ff esh!: All substance, bend to my will!

Flah oz zaeshi ff mue, flah oz zaeshi! flah oz zaeshi!: Feed and grow my pets, feed and grow!

Rah ak ff esh oz eshmue eshoz eshflah!: Bend to my will and ignite with fire!

Shirayshi, akdoe!: Shadows obey!

Akozak ak ff esh!: Transform to my will!

Flahoz—: Relea—

Eshakmue ff esh!: Impose my will!

Rayzae!: Back!

Akdoemue oz doe!: Consume and burn!

Mue—: Def—

Akdoe mue flah ak zae ozoz. Zaeshi ak ff esh!: Obey me roots of the earth. Grow to my will!

Mueeshshi esh ak akdoemue: Bestow gift of tongues

Shirayshi, Esh akoz, oz akdoe!: Shadows I command, you obey!

Eshesh esh zaeray!: Still his heart!

Rayesh ak eshmue, Esh akoz oz flahmue!: Water to ice, I command you freeze!

Spanish

¡Perfecta!: Perfect!

Sí, compañera: Yes, friend

¡Dios mío!: My god!

Me estás tomando el pelo: Are you kidding me

muy obstinada: very stubborn

¡Culpa mía! ¡Lo siento!: My fault! Sorry!

gigantes: giants

¡¿Qué diablos?!: What the hell?!

¡Mierda!: Shit!

¡Eres el amor de mi vida!: You are the love of my life

María Purísima: Holy Mary

Nahuatl

noconetzin: my little child

Acknowledgments

First and foremost, as always, I want to thank my wife for her patience and honesty. I want to thank her for asking questions and for helping me find the answers to mine. Mostly I want to thank her for allowing me to read her the same chapter over, and over, and over. And every time you truly listened. Thank you, my love.

I want to thank my editing team, specifically Kristen Tate at the Blue Garret. Once again, she made editing fun and I learned even more through the process. Turning my ideas into something tangible is like raising a small child. And you know what they say about raising a child – it takes a village. Kristen, you *are* my village. Without you and your team there is no book… at least not a very good one.

A special thanks to the readers who took the time to not only read my work but also review it. Reviews are incredibly important to authors and I appreciate each and every one. It's is like getting a long hug when you need it most… only better.

Finally, I want to thank my friends and colleagues who read the early drafts, for the conversations on the long Saturday trail runs and over lunch at work. Thank you for getting excited with me.

Otto Schafer, September 2020

About the Author

Otto Schafer grew up exploring the small historic town in central Illinois featured in *The God Stones* series. If you visit Petersburg, Illinois you may find locations familiar from the books. You may even discover, as Otto did, that history has left behind cleverly hidden traces of magic, whispered secrets, and untold treasures.

Like many of you, Otto Schafer always wanted to write though, occupied with raising a family and building a successful career, he struggled to find the time. But the stories refused to rest, springing into his mind as he ran the forested trails of Illinois and invading his dreams at night, until finally he began writing them down.

Otto is currently working on the third book in the *God Stones* series. He and his loving wife reside in a quiet log cabin tucked away in the woods. When Otto isn't writing you can often find him running the forest trails near his home, deep in a tangle of thoughts he'll need to rush home to put on paper.

Also by Otto Schafer

Garrett and Breanne's adventure is well underway, but they've got a long journey ahead. If you want to see what happens next please sign up here and I will be sure and keep you abreast on how the next book is progressing as well as other projects I am working on. Just click here to sign up or go to my website: www.ottoschafer.com.

If you enjoyed this book, I'd love to hear from you and hope that you could take some time to post a review on Amazon. Your feedback and support will help this author continue to create future works for your enjoyment. I want you, the reader, to know that your review is very important and so, if you'd like to leave a review, just go to my author page on Amazon. I wish you all the best and thanks again.

Check out my website and blog here: www.ottoschafer.com

Connect with me on social:

Instagram – www.instagram.com/ottoschaferwriter

Facebook – www.facebook.com/ottoschaferauthor

www.ingramcontent.com/pod-product-compliance
Lightning Source LLC
Chambersburg PA
CBHW030419310726
48979CB00009B/1531/J